The King's Exile

www.**transworldbooks**.co.uk

Also by Andrew Swanston

The King's Spy

The King's Exile

Andrew Swanston

BANTAM PRESS

LONDON • TORONTO • SYDNEY • AUCKLAND • JOHANNESBURG

TRANSWORLD PUBLISHERS
61–63 Uxbridge Road, London W5 5SA
A Random House Group Company
www.transworldbooks.co.uk

First published in Great Britain
in 2013 by Bantam Press
an imprint of Transworld Publishers

A CIP catalogue record for this book
is available from the British Library.

ISBNs 9780593068885 (hb)
9780593068892 (tpb)

Addresses for Random House Group Ltd companies outside the UK
can be found at: www.randomhouse.co.uk
The Random House Group Ltd Reg. No. 954009

The Random House Group Limited supports the Forest Stewardship Council® (FSC®), the
leading international forest-certification organisation. Our books carrying the FSC label are printed
on FSC®-certified paper. FSC is the only forest-certification scheme supported by the leading
environmental organisations, including Greenpeace. Our paper procurement policy can be found
at www.randomhouse.co.uk/environment

Typeset in 12/16.5pt Caslon Classico by Falcon Oast Graphic Art Ltd.
Printed and bound in Great Britain by
CPI Group (UK) Ltd, Croydon, CR0 4YY

2 4 6 8 10 9 7 5 3 1

For Mel, Laura and Tom

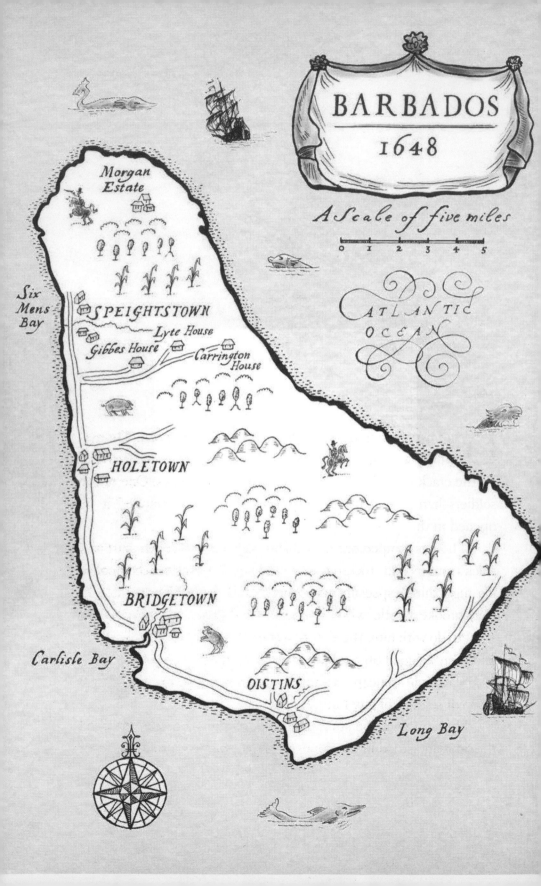

CHAPTER 1

1648

On a frosty March morning the soldiers came at dawn. Thomas
Hill, asleep above his bookshop in Love Lane, was woken
by the crack of their boots on the frozen cobblestones. One of the
soldiers hammered on the bookshop door and demanded it be
opened in the name of Parliament.

Thomas jumped out of bed and pulled on a woollen shirt and
thick trousers and stockings. It would not do to answer the door in
his nightshirt, especially to soldiers. With King Charles held in
Carisbrooke Castle while politicians and generals argued about
what to do with him, there were stories of houses being broken into
and men dragged off for no more reason than a word out of place
or a feather in the cap. No sensible man welcomed a visit from a
troop of soldiers of any kind.

He ran down the stairs and through the shop. He unlocked
the door and stood in the doorway. There were four soldiers, three

7

of them wearing the woollen caps, red coats and grey breeches of Parliamentary infantrymen and the fourth, their captain, a jacket of buff leather. All four were armed with pistols and swords.

'Are you Thomas Hill?' demanded the captain.

'I am.'

The captain took several sheets of paper from inside his jacket. 'Thomas Hill, are you the author of this?'

Thomas took the papers from the captain and glanced at them. There were any number of political pamphlets circulating but he could guess which one this was — the only one to which he had ever put his name. A few on mathematics and philosophy but only one which touched on politics, and even that was more philosophical than political. 'I am. What of it?'

'Thomas Hill, in the name of the people I arrest you for inciting actions against Parliament.'

'Can you read, captain?'

'I am obeying orders.'

'I thought not. If you could you would be aware that this pamphlet, written by me some months ago, argues for a strong Parliament to represent the people and for that Parliament to work in conjunction with the king for the common good. Am I to be arrested for that?'

The three soldiers, who had been standing to attention behind their captain and staring straight ahead, shuffled their feet and looked sheepish.

'My orders are to arrest you and take you to Winchester gaol to await trial,' replied the captain.

'This is absurd.'

'Those are my orders. You are to come with us.'

'And if I refuse?'

'Then you will be taken by force. My orders are clear.'

Orders, orders — the soldier's conscience. Thomas studied the captain's weather-beaten face. It was impassive. There was to be no argument and resistance would be foolish — merely an invitation to violence. Better to do as he was told and get this nonsense over with. 'My sister and nieces are upstairs. Am I permitted to say goodbye?'

The captain hesitated. 'Very well. Two minutes, no more.'

Thomas ran back upstairs. The girls were crying and Margaret was ashen. They too had been woken and had heard everything. He hugged each of them. 'Now don't fret. This is nothing. Just a mistake. I'll be home again in no time. I'll send word. Pass me that shirt, my dear. I may need a spare.' He put it on over the other. 'There. That should keep me warm. Now kiss your uncle, girls, and look after your mother while I'm gone. I'll see you again very soon.' He turned to Margaret. She too was weeping. 'It's really a harmless pamphlet, my dear. They can't keep me locked up for long.' Since her husband had been killed six years earlier at the start of the war, Margaret and her daughters had lived in Romsey with Thomas.

'I wish you hadn't written it, Thomas. I knew it would bring trouble.'

Thomas kissed her cheek. 'Indeed, you said as much. But it's really nothing. Best if I go with them for now. I'll be home tomorrow, just you see if I'm not.' He put on his boots and his thickest coat and hurried back down the stairs. He stuffed a hunk of bread and a piece of cheese from the kitchen into a pocket and went back through the shop. The soldiers were waiting outside.

'Right. Bind his hands, Jethro — tightly, mind, we don't want

9

him escaping — and we'll be on our way.' The captain was impatient to be gone.

The rope was bad enough, the indignity worse. More embarrassed than frightened, Thomas was marched down Love Lane and across Market Square, with only the clothes and boots he was wearing. Although it was early, the soldiers had been heard and as they clattered over the cobbles, he was aware of shutters being opened and faces peeking out. Thomas Hill, bookseller, philosopher and once adviser to the king, was well known in Romsey. News of his arrest would be around the town by noon.

Thomas squared his shoulders and fixed his eyes on the back of the soldier's head in front of him so that if a tear did come to his eye, it would not be seen by a watching friend. He told himself that he would be home again soon, the whole thing forgotten.

The four soldiers, with Thomas between them, marched out of the town on the Winchester road. The hedgerows were white with frost and the ground frozen hard. After another icy winter, the oaks and elms of the New Forest stood tall and stark against a pale sky, their bare branches showing no promise of spring. Thomas stamped his feet and blew on his bound hands. It was a good ten miles to Winchester. God's wounds, how unspeakably grim. The cold was bad enough, but arrested and marched off to gaol to await trial? He shivered at the thought.

And for what? Even in these uncertain times, surely no magistrate would pay much heed to an innocuous pamphlet written by a Romsey bookseller, albeit one who four years earlier had served the king at his court in Oxford. True, he was now an imprisoned king, increasingly short of friends. True, there had been news of renewed fighting in Wales and the north. True, England was a country divided — by faith, by political opinion, by ideas of morality — but to be sent for trial for expressing a balanced, neutral view? A view, what was more, shared by many of the men who had fought most fiercely against the king. Had men been killed in their thousands and families destroyed for such an injustice? What would John Pym, the fiercest of all critics of the king's intolerance, have made of it if he had been alive?

At the village of Ampfield they stopped for a brief rest. A milky sun had melted the ice on the village pond and blunted the sharpness of the early morning chill. Three of the soldiers disappeared into an inn leaving one outside to guard Thomas. 'How long will I be held?' he asked the guard.

The man shrugged and wiped his nose on his sleeve. 'We just take you to the gaol. After that, you're someone else's problem.' Not very reassuring, Thomas thought, and tried no more questions.

They were soon on their way again, marching through Hursley and on towards Winchester. As they neared the town, the road became busier and Thomas had to endure the stares of tradesmen, farmers and travellers, doubtless wondering what terrible crime the prisoner had committed to be in the charge of four armed soldiers.

They went straight to Winchester prison, where Thomas was handed over to a gaoler and shoved roughly into a cell that already held five others. Six men in one small cell was bad enough; filthy straw on the floor and a bucket in the corner made it worse. Compared to Oxford Castle, however, the memory of which still made Thomas shudder, it was almost comfortable.

Aching and exhausted, he backed into a corner and forced down what was left of his food. Without water it was not easy to swallow but he had to keep up what little strength he had left. He listened and answered questions when he had to, but volunteered nothing and took no part in the general banter, which was in any case more bravado than bravery.

Happily, one of the prisoners, an innkeeper from Hursley, was a natural jester. He was a large man, red of face and loud of voice, who stood accused of saying that he would rather serve Oliver Cromwell for dinner than serve him with it. Unfortunately for him, he had been overheard by an informer and reported. He claimed that he was looking forward to his trial when he would offer the defence that he had said no such thing and, if he had, he must have been speaking in jest because he made a point of serving only the very best meat and no customer of his would want anything as mean as Cromwell. Listening to him, Thomas thought that the innkeeper was just the kind of man he'd want beside him in times of trouble but that his chances of avoiding a spell in prison were remote.

Thomas tried to keep his spirits up by examining the crime of which he stood accused. A simple pamphlet, criticizing no one and inciting no one to violence, just proposing a rational, workable system of government. He would have no difficulty in persuading a magistrate to release him, and would be home in a day or two. He would keep quiet and rely upon justice being done. Tomorrow would bring better news.

CHAPTER 2

The night-time noises of five fellow prisoners and no breakfast did nothing to strengthen Thomas's resolve. And by noon the next day there had been no news. Margaret would be expecting him home soon, and anyway, what could she do to help? The first of his doubts were starting to creep in.

Overnight the spirits of all the men had dropped – even the Hursley innkeeper had run out of stories – and they were not revived by the arrival of dinner. A bucket of brown water, crusts of stale bread and lumps of maggoty cheese were dumped on the floor by a silent gaoler, leaving each of them to help himself to what he could stomach. For Thomas that was a small crust and a mouthful of water.

None of the prisoners knew how long they could expect to be kept there. The Winchester petty sessions would be held regularly, but when? When asked, the silent gaoler just grunted. Nor did they have much idea of how a magistrate would view the crimes of which they were accused. What were the penalties for a jest about Cromwell, falling down drunk in church, selling rotten meat, writing a political pamphlet? The stocks, a fine? Surely not prison. No one knew.

Thomas's doubts became more serious. Four soldiers had been sent to Romsey to escort him to Winchester. Four armed men — for just one unarmed, peaceful prisoner. Why? Since then, there had been no information and no contact from outside. What if there was some sort of conspiracy? Someone holding a grudge against him? A more serious charge might be concocted. He was cold and hungry and by the evening he was frightened. Separation from his family and ignorance of what was happening or still to come were punishment enough, never mind the noisome cell and gruesome scraps of food.

After another foul, sleepless night Thomas's mind was wandering. Some malicious ne'er-do-well with an axe to grind had shown the pamphlet to a magistrate and demanded that its author be arrested and brought to justice. And the magistrate had obliged. If so, Thomas was in trouble. He would be lucky to avoid a few days in the stocks or even a spell in gaol.

At dawn, Thomas heard orders being given, doors being opened and men being taken out. Soon his own cell was unlocked and the gaoler, accompanied by two armed guards, stood at the door. 'These men come with me,' he ordered and called out four names, of which Thomas's was the third. Thank God, action at last and his ordeal would soon be over. Face the magistrate, explain himself, take his punishment if he must, and go home.

The four men were led to a small courtyard where a larger group of prisoners was waiting. Gaunt and filthy, and trying to shield their eyes from the light, these were not new prisoners. The magistrate would be having a busy day.

A short, fat man, in a grey woollen coat and a broad-brimmed hat, entered the yard and stood before them. In his hand, he held a sheet of paper. 'I am Captain Fortescue,' he announced. 'I have a licence to remove you from this place and to transport you to the island of Barbados in the Caribbean, where you will be sold as indentured men. We will travel immediately to Southampton where my ship is anchored, and proceed from there to the Irish port of Cork where we will take on board more prisoners to be indentured. Your indenture terms will be seven years.' Two of the prisoners charged at the guards. They were instantly felled by blows to the head with the butt of a musket and dragged back into line. One screamed that he was an honest man, unjustly accused, and another fell to his knees and prayed for death.

Thomas's legs gave way and he collapsed to the ground. Arrested for nothing, thrown into gaol and deported without trial? It was the stuff of nightmares. It could not be. He struggled to his feet and spoke with as much authority as he could muster. 'Captain, my name is Thomas Hill. I stand accused of who knows what and I demand to be heard.'

'Hill?' replied Fortescue, consulting his list. 'Ah yes, Thomas Hill. Hold your tongue, Hill, or it'll be the worse for you. Your indenture has been arranged and you'd best get used to the idea.'

Indenture arranged? How and by whom and for what? It was impossible. 'And I demand justice.'

'Enough, Hill. One more word and you'll pay.'

'This is absurd. Of what am I charged? By whom am I accused?'

'Stop his mouth, Jethro. This one could be trouble.'

A filthy rag stuffed into his mouth, Thomas was led away with the others to a large cart drawn by two shire horses and on to which they were loaded like sheep. Their hands and feet were tied with ropes looped through iron rings set into the sides of the cart. Two guards sat at the front, one holding the reins, the other a loaded musket, while Captain Fortescue rode behind them.

Unable to speak, Thomas sat in misery, ready to explode with frustration and anger. As none of his fellow prisoners spoke to him he had only his own thoughts for company. He thought of escape, of Margaret, of an England that had come to this, of the monstrous injustice. Seven years of indenture. Impossible. Treated like a common criminal. Ridiculous. The mistake would be discovered at Southampton and he would be released. That would be the way of it.

When they arrived that evening in Southampton, Thomas's head throbbed and his backside was bruised from the constant juddering of the cart on the rutted road. The ropes around their feet were untied and each man was hauled upright and made to stumble to the quay where Captain Fortescue's ship, the *Dolphin*, was anchored in the harbour. Although its keel could not have been very deep, it looked a stout vessel, almost pear-shaped, with three masts and a narrow deck, and about eighty feet long from bow to stern. Even though he was in such a miserable state, Thomas's mathematical mind was at work. He counted places for only six cannon, which he assumed meant a mere twelve in total. The *Dolphin* was a ship designed for trade rather than warfare. And he and his companions were part of the trade.

The two guards marched them to the ship. Thomas looked about, expecting to see a friendly face with papers for his release. There was none. Bare-chested labourers were unloading barrels and crates from carts and carrying them on board, sailors were hauling on ropes and shouting instructions and a small group of well-dressed men, merchants probably, had gathered at one end of the quay to see that their goods were safely loaded. Not one of them took any notice of the prisoners being herded on to the ship.

Thomas's hands were still bound and the rag was still in his mouth. He could not cry out for help nor could he hope to escape by making a run for it. Still disbelieving, he was forced to clamber on board with the others and led to a hatch in the deck towards the bow. With difficulty they climbed down a short ladder to the hold. There was just enough light to see that they were in a section partitioned off from the cargo bay and fitted with rows of narrow canvas hammocks fixed to the beams which supported the deck above them and no more than a foot apart.

It was the first time Thomas had been on board a ship. He could only just stand upright, the air was fetid and it stank. It was a dire place, reeking of rats and human waste, cold, dark and threatening. With a terrible clunk the hatch was shut behind them and twelve miserable, frightened men had no choice but to find a hammock and await events. At that moment, Thomas knew he was trapped. Someone, God alone knew who, had used the pamphlet, innocuous though it was, to have him arrested and deported. Someone who hated him enough to do such a thing, someone with enough influence to make it happen. Who?

The one prisoner whose hands had been untied on deck pulled the rag from Thomas's mouth and released his hands. Then the two of them did the same for the other men. Not a word was exchanged between any of them. It was as if they had abandoned hope and resigned themselves to their fate. Even the man who had prayed for death was silent. Thomas longed to shout, to demand a fair trial, to rail against the injustice, to force someone to listen. But it was too late. He was trapped in the hold of a dank, stinking ship and no one was going to listen to him now. He found a hammock in which he could lie with his back to the side of the ship, and, shaking with shock, hoisted himself into it, closed his eyes and tried to calm himself by lying still and breathing deeply.

During the night the hatch was opened three times and more prisoners were pushed down into the hold. Thomas lay quietly, listening to their oaths, sensing their fear and wondering what the morning would bring.

When at last it came, morning brought a clanking of chains as the *Dolphin*'s anchor was weighed, the thump of sailors' feet on the deck, voices raised and a lurch of the ship away from the quay, followed by a slow turn out of the harbour. When Thomas heard sails being raised and the ship started to rise and dip on the waves, he knew they were on the open sea.

Some time later, the hatch was opened again and a sailor shouted at the prisoners to come on deck. One by one they climbed the ladder and emerged into daylight. Thomas was the last of them. Two armed guards stood at the top of the hatch, counting. 'Twenty-three. That's the lot,' said one, a mean-looking rat of a man in a filthy shirt and threadbare trousers cut off at the knee.

'Won't be twenty-three when we get there,' replied the other. 'More like twelve, I reckon.'

Thomas ignored them and stumbled out on to the deck. It was early in the season for an Atlantic crossing or even a short voyage to Ireland, and, despite his two shirts and thick coat, he shivered and wrapped his arms around his chest. He had taken two unsteady steps when the ship rolled, he lost his footing and only just grabbed a thick coil of rope in time to stop himself being thrown against a mast. Around him, all the other prisoners were slipping and sliding about the deck, hanging on to whatever or whoever they could find and cursing loudly while their guards stood and laughed. Thomas peered around. Behind them, the coastline was just visible; in front he could see nothing but an endless expanse of grey water.

Gradually, the prisoners became more accustomed to the movement of the ship and were able to make their way to the middle of the deck, where buckets of fresh water and a few loaves of bread and scraps of meat in old boxes set out beside the mainmast were being guarded by two more sailors armed with short swords and pistols tucked into their belts. They looked for all the world like pirates. Using his hands as a cup, Thomas took his turn to scoop water into his mouth, then tore off a lump of bread and a piece of meat and found a place on the deck to sit. The bread was stale and the meat rotten and he could only swallow them in tiny mouthfuls. But taking his time and returning frequently to the water, he made himself eat it all. No point in dying of hunger while waiting for justice to be done.

Quite suddenly the wind strengthened. The square sails on each of the three masts responded and the ship picked up speed. It bucked and rolled, once again hurling men to the deck. Timbers creaked and waves splashed over the sides. Thomas, still sitting on the deck, looped his arm through a length of rope tied to the ship's side and hoped that the *Dolphin* was as sturdy as she looked. Around him, prisoners were flailing about, swearing lustily and demanding God's assistance in keeping them safe, while the ship's crew, showing no sign of discomfort or surprise, pointed at them and laughed. Suddenly an elderly man came careening down the deck on his backside. With his free hand, Thomas grabbed a leg and held on until the fellow could right himself and find a handhold. He nodded his thanks to Thomas and promptly threw up over his arm. Not wanting to risk losing his grip on the rope, Thomas made no effort to wipe the stuff off.

Gradually most of the prisoners were able to regain their footing and stumble to the hatch. Thomas helped the old man to the ladder and then lay on his stomach to lower him down. He was about to stand up and climb down himself when his ankles were seized and he was tipped headfirst into the hold. He managed to break the worst of the fall with his forearms and found himself in a heap at the bottom. He looked up to see a sailor's face grinning down at him.

'There you are,' shouted the sailor over the roar of the waves, 'safely back in your hole. No need to thank me. Always happy to help.'

Thomas picked himself up and stumbled to his hammock, scraping the vomit off his arm. He shut his eyes. How in the name of heaven was he going to survive this?

He tried in vain to wipe the sweat from his eyes and the image of Margaret and the girls from his mind, and lay listening to the wind turn from a stiff breeze to a howling storm. He could only imagine the scene on deck — sailors scrambling up the rigging to reduce sail and frantically tying down whatever could be tied down, while officers yelled at them to make haste. He hung on to his hammock and waited for the storm to die down or the ship to sink. If it did, would he find wood for a raft and be blown to land by the wind? Or would he be trapped in the hold and drown?

More than once the *Dolphin* listed so sharply that he was sure it would tip on to its side, but each time it somehow righted itself. While they lay helpless in the hold the storm went on and on through the rest of the day and the night until, as dawn shed a little light through the cracks in the timbers of the deck above them, its power waned enough for the hardiest of the prisoners to tumble out of their hammocks and get to a bucket. To Thomas's sensitive nose, the stench was unspeakable. He pressed his face to the side of the ship and tried to smell timber. When that did not work, he buried his face in his coat and thought of lavender.

It was still breezy when at last the hatch was opened and a sailor peered in. 'Any fish food down there?' he shouted cheerfully. There was none. All the prisoners had survived the night. They filed unsteadily up the ladder and into the sea air, clinging on to whatever they could for safety. The buckets were taken up and emptied over the side. The masts were still bare of sails and the deck was a jumble of rope, canvas and crates. The sailor divided them into two groups, each overseen by three guards. Thomas's group was put to sorting out the tangled ropes, then washing down the hold with buckets of seawater. All the time the wind still blew strongly enough to make the work dangerous and each man took at least one tumble.

The nimbleness that had made Thomas a much sought-after dancing partner while a student at Oxford stood him in good stead. He fell only once and was quickly back on his feet. After an hour of unravelling ropes and climbing up and down the steps with buckets, they were herded back into the hold. Having slept not at all during the night, most of them were snoring within minutes. Thomas lay awake and urged the wind to blow harder. The harder it blew, the sooner they would arrive in Barbados and the sooner he would get home.

CHAPTER 3

For two more days and nights the *Dolphin* battled her way westwards along the south coast of England towards the Lizard. Twice each day the hatch was opened and the prisoners climbed the ladder to the deck, where they were given hard bread and biscuits, scraps of meat and bits of maggoty cheese, and allowed to stretch their legs. They were guarded by sailors with short swords and pistols. There were about twenty sailors in the crew, each as rough as the next. Thomas assumed that their quarters were in the other half of the hold. As he did with his fellow prisoners, Thomas spoke to them only when he had to.

In between the hours on deck and bouts of vomiting, he lay in his hammock and seethed. Like an African slave, he had been torn from his home on another man's whim, leaving his family to fend for themselves, and thrown on to this stinking ship on the way to a distant island where he would doubtless be worked to death in a matter of weeks. He had heard accounts of the Caribbean islands, of the heat and sickness and of the landowners' treatment of their slaves and indentured servants, and he knew he would not last long. He must find a way to get home and he must find out who had done this to him and why.

Once they had rounded the Lizard, the wind picked up again and they flew across the Irish Sea to Cork, where they picked up another twenty men — Catholics imprisoned by the army of Parliament and by all accounts savagely treated. Several carried the scars of torture, one had lost an eye, another wore the black habit of a Dominican. The youngest was a boy of no more than fourteen. The priest took the empty hammock beside Thomas's, and spent his time mouthing silent prayers and crossing himself. Fortunately he was as disinclined to talk as Thomas was.

At first, the Irishmen kept to themselves. Then they started to mix with the other prisoners and a hierarchy of sorts emerged. Its currencies were food and knowledge. Despite the meagre food, the weakest were willing to trade some of their ration in return for protection. Two squat Irishmen set themselves up as protectors and offered, for payment in food, to keep predators at bay. Among forty-three men, all taken from some foul gaol, there were a good number of rogues and scoundrels and one or two who would, if they had the chance, use a younger man like a woman. Thomas saw all this, said nothing and kept out of trouble. The two Irishmen, for some reason, did not bother him. Perhaps they haven't noticed me, he thought, or perhaps they think a little fellow with receding hair has no hope of lasting more than a week. And they might be right.

From his position at the side of the ship, Thomas noticed that barriers were breaking down and the prisoners were beginning to make friends. It occurred to him that in such an environment man's instinct to survive takes over. Some, like him, withdrew into their private worlds, others formed alliances. Much like the solitary cat on one hand and the pack-loving hound on the other. Thomas Hill, philosopher, devoted uncle and erstwhile cryptographer at the king's court in Oxford, was very much the cat.

He forced himself to use the hours on deck to walk and stretch. This not only helped to keep his legs from stiffening up but also cleared his head of the sounds and smells of men forced to live cheek by jowl for twenty-two hours a day. He did his best to keep clean, although with only seawater to wash in it was a losing battle. His scalp and beard itched and his clothes were filthy. He picked lice from his hair and nits from his skin. Sometimes he had the feeling that he was being watched by the guards but he put it out of his mind. Of course he was being watched; they all were.

He saw no captain, although there must have been one. Perhaps the man never left his cabin. Perhaps he passed the time in a drunken stupor. Perhaps he was an unearthly creature of the night who emerged only during darkness. Perhaps he was a pirate. Perhaps . . . Your wits are addled, Thomas. Pull yourself together and concentrate on staying alive.

Despite himself, on a good day when the sun was shining and the wind was fair, Thomas could almost enjoy the thrill of the ship skipping over the waves. On such a day, his spirits rose and he could persuade himself that, once in Barbados, he would be able to appeal to the authorities and have his absurd indenture overturned immediately. On such a day he willed the wind to blow and the *Dolphin* to pick up speed. The sooner they reached their destination, the sooner he would be on his way home. But the moment he was back in the hold his spirits sank again and he could see before him only seven intolerable years of separation from his family and raging frustration at what had been done to him.

One calm day a group had gathered by the mainmast. As Thomas approached, he heard them discussing how long they would be on the ship. Having already given this some thought, he reckoned that with a fair wind it would take them five or six weeks to reach Barbados. So far, the wind had been fair and they had been at sea for three. For the first time, he felt the need to talk.

'Barbados is the most easterly of the Caribbean islands,' he ventured. 'I think we have another two or three weeks to look forward to, just as long as we're not detained by a privateer. That would do none of us any good, so if you happen to see a suspicious-looking sail on the horizon be sure to shout as loudly as you can.'

'How do we know if it's suspicious?' demanded a huge red-haired Irishman. The question was sharp and Thomas immediately regretted speaking. The man looked dangerous and might resent Thomas's interference. He tried to laugh it off.

'Best treat them all as the enemy. There may be Spaniards about, too.'

The giant eyed him suspiciously, as if looking for pretence. 'Who are you, Englishman?'

'My name is Thomas Hill.'

'And what do you know of Barbados, Hill? Are there savages?' asked another man.

'I think not, although perhaps there once were. There'll be black men, though. Slaves from Africa to work in the plantations. Many of them.'

'I saw a black man once,' said a dwarfish Irishman. 'A servant he was, in the manor house. Eight feet tall and never said a word.'

'What about snakes? I heard that some of them can swallow a man whole.'

Thomas smiled. 'Don't worry, my friend. One thing I do know is that Barbados is like Ireland. There are no snakes at all.'

'Thank the blessed virgin for that. She must have sent Saint Patrick there too. I wouldn't mind savages or wild beasts — you'd see them coming — but not snakes. Snakes are the devil's creatures.'

'No wild beasts either. Just hogs and monkeys, I believe.'

'How do you know this, Hill?' growled the giant. 'Seems to me you know more than an honest man should.' He advanced on Thomas, his fists bunched and his huge head thrust forward. 'One of Cromwell's spies, are you?'

Thomas held his ground. 'Certainly not. I was unjustly arrested and will be indentured like everyone else on this ship.' God forbid, he thought, but to say anything else would have been asking for trouble. The Irishman was unconvinced.

'I don't believe you, Hill. You're a dirty spy, put here to tell tales to the guards.'

Before Thomas could move, a huge pair of hands had grasped him by the throat. In vain he tried to reach the giant's face, but it made no difference. The giant held on and the breath was squeezed out of him. His eyes closed and he was on the point of passing out when, without warning, the hands around his neck loosened their grip and he was dropped in a heap on to the deck. When he could see clearly again he looked up and saw two guards with pistols pointing at the giant's head.

'Another trick like that, Irishman,' hissed one of them — the rat-faced man who had counted them on their first morning, 'and you'll feed the sharks.'

The giant scowled and spat. 'Shitten little English worm. He won't last the voyage. Why bother to keep him alive?'

'He will last the voyage, Irishman,' replied the other guard, pushing his pistol into the giant's ear, 'because you're going to make sure he does. And if he doesn't, neither will you. Is that clear enough for your heathen brain to understand?'

The giant spat again, stared at Thomas still sitting on the deck and nodded. For a moment none of the watching group moved, then a hand reached down to help Thomas to his feet. The guard spoke again. 'That goes for all of you. This man has been paid for in advance and if he isn't delivered as ordered, you'll all pay.' He turned to the giant. 'Especially you, Irishman. Guard him carefully.' The two guards lowered their pistols. For a moment the giant looked as if he might hit out at them, then he shrugged and slouched off towards the bow.

The guards returned to their posts and the prisoners were left alone. 'And who's paid for you in advance, Hill?' asked one of them.

'I have no idea. As I said, I was unjustly arrested. Someone must have wanted to get rid of me. God knows who.'

'You sound like a Hampshire man. And you do know a lot. How is that?'

'I am a Hampshire man. I come from Romsey. I have a bookshop. I read a lot.'

That seemed to satisfy them. The questions started up again, so it was just as well that, like many a clever man, Thomas had long ago mastered the art of making a little knowledge go a long way. 'What about the white men, Hill?'

'I know little about them except that the island is small, much smaller than Jamaica, so there won't be many of them. They used to grow tobacco and cotton but I think it's mostly sugar now. Perhaps the climate is more suited to sugar.'

'So we'll be indentured to sugar planters then? Working in the fields, I suppose.'

'Yes, I suppose so.'

'Is it hot?'

'Much hotter than Ireland, but the Caribbean islands are wet too, so it'll be humid.'

The questions continued even after they were sent below. Thomas could answer some of them and guessed at others. In truth, however, he didn't know what to expect any more than the next man. What he did know was that the instant he set foot on dry land, he would find a way to plead his case. He would tell the authorities exactly what he had written in the pamphlet, explain that his arrest had been a mistake and demand to be put straight back on a ship sailing for England. He would go home to Romsey, life would return to normal, on long winter evenings he would tell stories about the voyage and they would all laugh.

When the questions finished he thought about what the guard had said. Must arrive safely. Paid for in advance. By whom and why? If only he knew, he could better prepare his appeal. But he had not the slightest inkling. He would have to wait until they reached Barbados.

For three weeks they saw no other ships, privateers or otherwise, and each day it grew warmer. At first that was a comfort and Thomas discarded his coat and extra shirt and used them as bedding. But as they sailed southwards each night in the hold was hotter and nastier than the last. Men grew sick and lay in their hammocks, some having lost control of their bowels but too feeble to get to a bucket, others thrashing about and cursing the pain of distended stomachs and swollen joints. Four bodies went to feed the fish without so much as a piece of sacking to cover them, the

Dominican priest among them. Thomas carried on answering questions as best he could, being careful to avoid taking sides. Although the Irish giant kept his distance, he knew the man was watching him. It was unnerving. Guarded by a fellow prisoner who would happily throw him over the side if he could, and not an inkling as to why.

Being cooped up on the ship made him think of his time in Oxford with the king, of being thrown into Oxford gaol and narrowly escaping death from gaol fever. And what of Margaret and the girls? Two blonde bundles of energy, forever plying Uncle Thomas with questions, jumping on his back, teasing him for his thinning hair, tickling him, insisting on a story. Since their father's death they had all lived with him. There was a little money tucked away but it would not last forever. If he did not return soon Margaret might have to find work, unless she could run the book-shop on her own. In his mind's eye, he saw her washing and cleaning and scrubbing floors and had to press the balls of his thumbs into his eyes to make the image go away.

For Thomas, time lost its meaning. Each day the same as the last one and the next one. Lie sweating and scratching in his hammock in the fetid heat of the hold, feel the ship rising and falling with the swell of the sea, listen to the curses and prayers of the frightened, suffering men around him, climb the ladder on to the deck, swallow what food and drink what water he could, keep out of trouble, climb back into the hold, stay alive.

Stay alive.

CHAPTER 4

The house at the river end of Seething Lane, outside which the black carriage drew up, had been built by a prosperous merchant in the shadow of the Tower of London eighty years earlier. Like its neighbours, it was half-timbered, with an upper storey overhanging the lane and a roof thatched with straw. The windows were shuttered and the house was dark. The carriage was emblazoned with the monogram TR in gold lettering. It was driven by a liveried coachman and drawn by two fine greys.

The cobbled lane was narrow and foul. A stinking drain ran down one side towards Tower Hill and rats scampered about in search of scraps. Despite a warm late April sun, it was a dank place, nasty and inhospitable.

The man who emerged from the carriage was also dressed in black. He barked an order to the coachman. 'Return in fifteen minutes exactly. I shall be watching for you.' And without waiting for a reply, he rapped on the door with a silver-topped cane and was immediately admitted.

He was shown in by a steward. 'Good evening, sir. May I take your hat and cane? The master is waiting for you in his living room.'

'I'll keep the cane,' snapped the visitor, handing the steward his hat. He knew where the living room was and went in without knocking. The man he had come to see was no less than fifty, grey-haired and thin-faced. He was sitting by the fire with a glass of wine in his hand. He did not rise to greet his visitor, nor did he offer refreshment. This meeting would, like their previous meetings, be brief and businesslike. The visitor seated himself on a high-backed chair on the other side of the fire. For all the filth of the lane, the room was warm and comfortable. The visitor was first to speak. 'Can you do it?' he asked.

'It can be done. At a price.'

'What price?' The old man mentioned a figure. 'Absurd. I could get it done for half that.'

'You know my work to be excellent. And the job carries a high risk.'

'The country is still at war. There is risk in walking down the street. I will pay you half that.'

For ten minutes they argued over the price. When a figure had been agreed, the visitor rose and left. 'I will return in one month. Have everything ready then,' he said as he opened the door to let himself out.

'It will be ready.'

The carriage had returned as instructed. He climbed in and settled back into a padded seat. Black velvet curtains hung over the side openings to protect him from curious eyes. He smiled. He was as he preferred to be — alone, invisible, in control. Let Fairfax and Cromwell and their like worry about their royal prisoner and his misguided Welsh and Scottish allies. Let Parliament carry the burden of governing this enfeebled country. Let Puritans rant and Catholics cower. From the shadows, he would observe and calculate, take his opportunities and accumulate power through wealth. For once, the jarring of the carriage wheels over the cobbles did not discomfort him or affect his mood. Wealth, power, and now revenge. Who could ask for more?

The war, like all wars, had brought the opportunities he sought and in the four and a half years since escaping, just, from Oxford he had been clever enough to see them and bold enough to grasp them. Others had done the same but none had prospered more than he had. When, three years ago, a poor harvest had pushed up the price of grain he had bought as much as he could and been rewarded by a second poor crop which increased the price even more. Soldiers had to eat and he had no difficulty in selling all the grain he had, even the old, rotten stuff, at three times what he paid for it.

After Fairfax and Cromwell routed Prince Rupert and the Royalists at Marston Moor in the summer of 1644, he had secured a contract to supply their pikemen with the thick woollen jackets they wore under their breastplates. Having established a price based on the current price of wool he drove his costs down by making promises to the wool merchants which he did not keep and disposing of those merchants unwise enough to complain. He did the same with the red dye needed for the jackets. Then he bribed his way to a similar contract for the supply of blue coats to the prince's regiments, taking care to add a few extra pence to the price. At Naseby a year later both sides in the battle wore coats supplied by him.

And after Cromwell's crushing victory he had paid his own

army of boys to search the battlefield before any other scavengers arrived and to bring him every musket, pistol and sword they could find. He sold the weapons to the quartermasters of both sides at half the price of new ones. Much of the profit from ventures such as these he had used to buy land in and around London. Now he was wealthy in both money and property and the longer the fighting dragged on, the wealthier he would become.

Happily, there was little sign of it abating. Even without their king, the Royalists of Scotland and Wales were far from giving up. They were even making rash noises about invading England and attacking London. From the comfort of his seat in the carriage he thought that unlikely; there were better possibilities closer to home. Fairfax was preparing to take Maidstone and Colchester, where Royalists were still holding out, and there were rumours of rebellion in the navy. Men would die, new equipment would be needed and there was much money yet to be made.

Despite his subsequent success, the memory of Oxford was as sharp now as ever. Had it not been for that tiresome little book-seller, his plan to abduct the queen and use her as a pawn in negotiations with the king would have succeeded. He would have been lauded by Parliament and richly rewarded for his efforts. As it was, Thomas Hill had thwarted him and he had only just escaped with his life. He had waited patiently for an opportunity to exact his revenge and it had come at last when a copy of Hill's pamphlet landed on his desk. A word here, a bribe there and the matter was settled. Hill was arrested and deported as an indentured servant to Barbados, where his partners the Gibbes would take very good care of him until he could pay them a visit himself. Illiterate they might be, but the brothers Gibbes had an eye for business and had quickly learned how to manage the estate to best advantage. That had been another wise investment. He had bought the land cheaply from a failed cotton grower, had it put to sugar and had reaped the rewards ever since. More satisfactory still was the thought of the misery coming to Hill and the delicious pleasure awaiting him in Romsey. It had been worth the wait. The anticipation sent a tingle down his spine.

With a jolt the carriage came to a sudden halt and he was thrown forward on to the seat opposite. He rapped on the side and shouted at the coachman. 'Why have we stopped, man?'

'There's a line of apprentices blocking the road, sir,' answered the coachman.

He raised a curtain and peered out. There were about twenty of them, two lines deep, shaven-headed and armed with knives and cudgels. Some of them were little more than children. These apprentices were becoming a damnable nuisance in London. At the start of the war they had fought for Parliament, now they were demanding the release of the king. They blocked roads, broke windows and attacked carriages. He had no intention of allowing them to get in his way. 'Drive on, man,' he shouted, 'drive through them.'

'They are armed, sir.' The coachman sounded nervous.

'Do as I say, man, and get on with it.' The coachman flicked his reins and urged the two greys on. They too were nervous and he had to use the whip to get them moving.

Until the very last minute the apprentices held their ground, moving aside only when the carriage was almost upon them. At that moment, spooked by something, one of the horses shied and the carriage slowed. An apprentice saw his chance and grabbed a door handle. He pulled aside a curtain and looked in. It was a mistake. With a piercing scream he fell backwards, holding his hands to an eye. He was dead when he landed on the cobbles. The carriage continued on its way while the boy's fellows gathered around his body.

Inside, Tobias Rush wiped the blade on a silk handkerchief, tossed the handkerchief out of the window and slid the blade back into the cane. Ten minutes later the carriage halted outside his house in Cheapside and he climbed out. 'Good evening, sir,' said the coachman. There was no reply.

CHAPTER 5

Heat, hunger, boredom. As the weather grew warmer, the tempers of the prisoners grew shorter. Arguments became more common and more violent. On deck, where they were never without guards, food was grabbed and threats were made. In the hold, fists flew and heads were cracked. Down there it was the flame-haired Irishman who sparked most fights. Although he left Thomas alone, he found plenty of other victims. He took special delight in finding a man groaning from fever or sickness, tipping him out of his hammock and kicking him until he was quiet. None of the other prisoners made any attempt to stop him. It would have taken half a dozen of them to do so.

The questions had gradually dried up, which was just as well as Thomas had run out of answers. He had plenty of questions of his own, but of course there was no one to ask. He kept to himself as much as he could, keeping out of the way of danger and avoiding all but the most harmless conversation. It was not easy — in such a place a stumble or a clumsy word could easily cause trouble — and he was bound to find trouble some time.

It came one morning when the young Irish boy sat down on the deck beside him. He was a skinny fellow, shorter than Thomas, with protruding teeth and yellow hair. 'I'm Michael,' he said. 'I'm a Cork man. What's your name?'

'Thomas Hill. I come from Romsey.'

Michael looked puzzled. 'Where's that then?'

'Not far from London.'

'Oh, London. Wicked place, Ma says, full of whores and harlots. What did you do?'

'I wrote something I shouldn't have.'

'I stole a pig. We had no food.' Thomas nodded and concentrated on his dinner. Even from this harmless wretch he wanted to keep his distance. He was about to get to his feet when two men came over and stood in front of the boy. From their looks and having heard them speak, Thomas knew they were cousins, a nasty pair who liked to boast about what they had done.

'Now, boy,' said the taller one, 'we want what you owe.'

'Hand it over,' ordered the other, 'and there won't be no trouble.'

Thomas glanced at Michael. The boy was frightened.

'I've none left. I've eaten it.'

The cousins exchanged a look. 'What do we do to a boy who doesn't pay his debts, cousin?' asked the first one.

'We teach him a lesson, cousin.' The shorter one bent down, grabbed Michael's throat and hauled him to his feet.

Thomas stood up. 'What does he owe you for?' he asked quietly.

'None of your concern, little man.'

'It is my concern. Michael is my friend.'

'Your friend, eh? Then you'd better pay his debts for him, hadn't you?' The taller one lunged at Thomas, aiming at his eyes. Thomas had learned how to protect himself when a student at Oxford, where many a bigger man had regretted taking him for an easy opponent. He moved smoothly to avoid the attack, grasped the man's wrist and twisted. There was an astonished yelp followed by a foul oath. 'You little . . .' Thomas twisted harder. The man was forced to the deck, his wrist held firmly in Thomas's grip. Thomas planted a foot on his groin and pushed.

'Let the boy go,' he said to the one holding Michael. There was no response. He leaned a little harder on the groin.

'Let him go, for the love of God,' screamed the man. His cousin spat at Thomas and pushed the boy aside. Thomas kept hold of the wrist and spoke slowly.

'This boy is under my care. If you so much as touch him, you'll answer to me. Is that clear enough?' There was no response. He twisted again. 'I said, is that clear enough?' This time, the stricken man managed a strangled croak.

'Clear.'

Thomas turned to the other one.

'Clear.'

He let go the wrist.

'I shall be watching. Now bugger off.'

The man on the deck got up and rubbed his wrist. His cousin shook his head and they slouched off towards the stern.

Michael touched Thomas's arm. 'Why did you do that, Thomas?'

Thomas shrugged. 'Sometimes one does things without thinking. Were they threatening you?'

'They said they would protect me if I gave them half my food every day.'

'I thought so. Don't give them any more, Michael. They are cowards. Keep away from them. I might not be nearby next time.'

Perhaps sensing that Thomas preferred to be alone, Michael did not trouble him again. And apart from looking as if they would happily tear them limb from limb, the cousins did not trouble either of them.

At midday on the fortieth day after they had left Cork, the *Dolphin*, now with a cargo of just twenty-seven prisoners, entered a wide bay on the south coast of Barbados. As soon as it was at anchor, the men were brought on deck, given a bar of lye soap and told to wash. They were a miserable lot — long-haired, unshaven, half-starved and filthy. Knowing that he looked no better, Thomas wondered if he might be rejected and sent straight home. It was a fleeting thought. Every wretch sent off to the colonies must arrive in much the same state. Unless he could escape or find someone in authority to whom to appeal, he would be treated just like all the others. But he was alive. Sixteen of those who had started the journey were not.

On deck he screwed up his eyes against a sun unlike any he had known. It was the intensity of its light as much as its heat that shocked him. Neither had been as harsh at sea — the clouds and the breeze had made them more bearable. Here, though, they were ferocious. He stripped off and scrubbed the grime out of his hair and off his body with the rough soap. A pile of shirts and breeches was dumped on the deck. He waited while the others rummaged in the pile, shoving each other out of the way and squabbling over who would have what. When the rumpus had died down, he found a thin shirt and breeches that almost fitted him and put them on. They were neither new nor clean but they were an improvement on the rags he had been wearing.

No time was lost in getting the men ashore. A relay of rowing boats ferried them to the quay, each boat supervised by armed guards, until they were all assembled. With his first step on land Thomas's legs betrayed him and he fell on his face. He was kicked by a guard until he managed to stand upright and join the line of prisoners who were led, frightened and unsteady, to a low wooden building at one end of the harbour where a throng of impatient onlookers awaited them. From their rough clothing and broad hats, Thomas guessed them to be planters. There might have been thirty of them. A notice announced that this was the Oistins Auction House.

They were herded by the guards into an enclosure not unlike a sheep pen, where they were inspected by the planters. Thomas's head throbbed in the heat and his face and back were dripping with sweat. A plump man in a huge straw hat stepped briskly forward, climbed on to a wooden crate and announced the start of the auction. He described the newly arrived men as healthy and well fed and informed his audience that he expected a good price for each. Thomas said nothing. His time would come soon.

The first man to be sold was the giant Irishman. He was prodded forward by a guard with a short pike and his name called out by the auctioneer. The bidding was brisk and he was quickly sold for twenty guineas. His hands were bound with rope and he was led away at the point of a pistol by his new owner. The giant fumed and cursed and Thomas wondered how long he would last.

One by one the men were auctioned and sold. The smallest and weakest went for a few guineas, the strongest for twenty or more. The boy Michael barely made five guineas and was led away weeping. Thomas waited impatiently for his turn. When he was called, he stepped forward as instructed and looked around for a uniform or some other mark of authority. There was none. Just planters, prisoners and merchants.

He filled his lungs and shouted as loudly as he could. 'My name is Thomas Hill. I am innocent of any crime and I demand to be heard.' Before he could say another word he was flat on his face, felled by a blow to the back of his head from the guard with the pike. He hauled himself upright and tried again. 'This is a monstrous injustice. I will be heard.'

'No you won't,' growled the auctioneer. 'Shut your mouth or it'll be the worse for you.'

'I will be heard. I am the victim of—' Another blow from the pikeman and Thomas was back on the ground, stunned and help-less. Again he struggled to his feet and tried to focus his eyes. He heard the auctioneer say something about this man having been paid for in advance, and after a certain amount of shouting a big, black-bearded man approached and gave his name as Samuel Gibbes. He tied Thomas's hands with a short rope, put another around his neck and led him away.

Thomas smelt drink on Gibbes's breath, and his stomach heaved. He was trapped. His appeal to be heard had brought only cracks on the head and this man, apparently his new master, looked brutish. There was no possibility of escape. He vomited, steadied himself with several deep breaths, squared his shoulders and followed Gibbes to a nearby inn — the Mermaid Inn, its sign proclaimed it to be — where two threadbare ponies were tethered. Again he took a deep breath and shouted, 'I am Thomas Hill, an innocent man. I demand to see a magistrate at once.'

Not one of the Mermaid's drinkers took the slightest notice, so he tried yet again. 'My name is Thomas—' Gibbes yanked the rope around Thomas's neck. It dug into his throat and cut off his voice. Then he slapped Thomas on the face with the back of his hand and hissed at him. 'Hold your tongue, shit-eater, or I'll cut it out and shove it down your gullet. Now get on the pony.'

Too shocked to resist, Thomas mounted the smaller pony and was led by Gibbes on the other, not knowing where they were going or how long it would take. The ropes were still around his neck and wrists, and his throat was burning. His eyes would not focus. It was a struggle to stay on the pony. They rode around the harbour, passing a line of low timber-built houses, a few others built of a pale-coloured stone and all the paraphernalia of a busy trading port. He vaguely noticed a harbour master's house, timber warehouses and, judging by the number of women sitting outside it, what could only be a brothel. Oistins was a midden of a place, a dung heap where drunkards and whores and thieves washed up in the hope of easy pickings. Its smells, aggravated by the heat, were the smells of the sea, cooking fires and toiling men, mixed with others that Thomas did not recognize. These were heady, thick smells – of strange spices, perhaps, or sugar and rum. They made him retch again.

They soon left the ramshackle town behind and rode slowly along a rutted road with the sea on their left. Except where the land had been roughly cleared for planting, unfamiliar trees and bushes, so dense that Thomas could see no more than a yard into them, lined the route. A mile or two from Oistins the road swung inland and they crossed a narrow stream running down from the hills before dropping down to the coast again. Blue and yellow flowers grew unchecked by the roadside and some of the trees were crowned with crimson blossoms. Apart from an occasional cluster of mean shacks and a few other travellers, there was little sign of life.

The further north they rode, the more the forest had been cut back and the land put to use. Thomas recognized tobacco plants, and cotton, but most of all sugar cane. Sugar — the island's gold. The reason men of every class came here to make their fortune, the reason for ships loaded with miserable human cargo. The reason he was here.

An hour later, as the light was beginning to fade, they turned off the road and rode up a hill to their right. About half a mile on they followed a rough path through tall trees until they finally came to a halt. This, it seemed, was it. Thomas stared in astonishment. Whatever he had been expecting, it was not this hovel. He was wondering whether such a place could possibly be a planter's house when another large, bearded man, this time with red hair and beard, came out to meet them.

'Is this him, then?' The voice was loud and coarse.

'It is, John. Thomas Hill by name. He doesn't look much but he can cook, so we're told, and he can read and figure.'

'How old are you, Hill?' asked John.

'I am thirty-three. And I am innocent of any crime. I demand to be taken immediately to the authorities.'

'Demand, eh? Here's what we think of your demand, Hill,' growled John Gibbes. He cuffed Thomas hard on the head and knocked him to the ground.

'He doesn't look much at all,' said Samuel Gibbes. 'Skin and bone, a feeble-looking thing.'

'I'll put him in the hut and we'll see to him later. There's chicken and bread if you're hungry, brother.'

And with that, John Gibbes hauled Thomas to his feet and led him by the rope to his hut. He untied the rope around Thomas's wrists and left him there. 'The last one who tried to run got as far as the road,' warned Gibbes. 'A month in the boiling house and a taste of the whip did for him.'

Thomas slipped the rope over his head, rubbed his neck and inspected the hut. Not that there was much to inspect — just eight or so feet square of horizontal rough timbers nailed together with uprights on each side, a roof thatched with something that was not straw and one small, shuttered window. The door flapped on its hinges.

Inside, he had a narrow cot, a woollen blanket, a small table and a chair. On the table stood a silver inkwell, quite out of place yet somehow reassuring. He picked it up, rubbed it on his sleeve and squinted at his reflection. The face he saw, distorted by the curve of the well, was wide-eyed, hollow-cheeked and wretched. Its chin and cheeks were covered in a straggly beard and its thin hair was long and matted. He put the inkwell down quickly.

'God alone knows what's coming next,' he said aloud, 'but despite appearances I'm alive and I'd better try to stay that way. I will not allow this place or these revolting animals to break my spirit. I will find a way to get home and I will discover who has done this to me.'

Too exhausted to do anything else, Thomas lay down on the cot and closed his eyes. For the first time in weeks he was alone.

CHAPTER 6

Thomas soon learned, however, that at night in such a place a man was never alone. Outside the hut, dogs barked and unknown creatures whistled and croaked. For company inside he had buzzing insects and tiny lizards which scampered over his chest and legs. At first he leapt up at the feel of their feet on his skin, frantically waving his arms about to frighten the things off, and only abandoning this when he realized that, just like their cousins on the Hampshire heathland, they were harmless.

The insects were another matter. Very soon he was scratching at bites on his ankles and wrists and wondering what God's purpose could possibly have been in putting on the earth creatures whose only function was to inflict torment. And there were armies of them. Squash one and ten more would take its place.

Trapped in an airless hut, biting insects, reptiles, heat, dirt, neither food nor water, far from home, no idea what the next day would bring — Thomas Hill, scholar and philosopher, who had once broken the unbreakable Vigenère cipher and had been presented to both the king and the queen of England, might as well have been a slave dragged from his home in chains and doomed to nothing but pain, misery and death. He turned his face to the wall and howled until eventually, shattered in mind and body, he fell into a fitful sleep.

When dawn broke, Thomas rose shakily from the bed, scratched at the red weals all over his body, decided against examining his face in the inkwell and tentatively opened the door of the hut. It would do no harm to explore his prison. As soon as he set foot outside there were shrill calls of alarm from birds in the trees behind the hut and an ancient dog which had been sleeping nearby sloped off towards the Gibbes's house. A large, round, stone-built structure stood no more than twenty yards away and beside it what looked like a well. Thomas went to inspect it and was relieved to find that it was indeed a well, with a rope attached to a ring set into the stone surround. He pulled on the rope and raised a bucket of water. Not knowing what to expect, he peered into the bucket. To his surprise, the water was clear and clean. He took a sip and, finding it pure, gulped down half the bucket. The other half he tipped over his head. It was cool and refreshing and eased the bites on his skin. He lowered the bucket and did it again. That was something. A well full of good water close to his hut.

From the opposite direction to the house, he could see smoke and hear voices and set off towards them. Down a narrow path which opened into fields of what Thomas thought must be sugar cane, he came to a cluster of wooden shacks, with fires set outside and the smells of cooking in the air. A pang of hunger gripped his stomach and saliva filled his mouth. He called out a greeting and the shacks immediately emptied of their occupants. Men, women and children, all with black skins, emerged from the doorways in ones and twos and stared at him. Slaves from Africa. Might they share their breakfast with him?

Before he could find out, from behind him came bellows of fury, followed by Samuel and John Gibbes. Thomas turned in alarm. The bearded brothers were striding towards him, both brandishing whips.

'What the devil are you doing here, Hill?' shouted Samuel. 'Get back to your hut or you'll feel my whip on your back.' His whip was a vicious-looking thing with a leather strap and a tongue like a viper's.

'I was finding my way around,' replied Thomas unsteadily.

The other one, John, stuck his face into Thomas's and spat. 'We'll tell you when to find your way around, you little turd. Get back to the hut now.'

'I have no business being here. I was wrongly arrested and I demand to see a magistrate.'

John Gibbes roared. 'Demand to see a magistrate, eh? What do you think of that, brother?'

'I think Master Hill needs a lesson,' snarled Samuel, raising his whip. Its tongue flicked across Thomas's cheek, slicing the skin, and Thomas cried out in pain. He put his hand to his face and felt blood. 'Now get back to your hut, Hill, or you'll be sorry.'

There was nothing to be gained by arguing. Thomas walked slowly back to the hut, gingerly feeling his cheek and trying not to stumble. God have pity, he thought, what a pair. Vicious, repulsive, barely human. The red one is the ugliest man I've ever seen. More warts and carbuncles than Cromwell. The black one's no better. A pair of brutes. Red brute and black brute. How in the name of heaven did they come to buy me? And how do I escape from them?

The Gibbes soon followed him back up the path. 'Next time we find you sniffing about the slaves, you'll get what they get. A proper taste of the whip and a day on the boiling house ring,' growled Samuel, pointing with his whip to a rusty iron ring set at head height into the wall of the round building. 'Understand?' Thomas understood. These men were dangerous. 'Now get down to the kitchen and get us our breakfast. There's work to be done.' Without waiting for him, they strode off to the house. Thomas followed them.

Outside the hovel, where they evidently did their eating and drinking, there were four rickety chairs and a battered table. Samuel kicked aside another mangy dog asleep in the morning sun and climbed two steps to a patched-up door. John told Thomas to follow his brother and sat down.

Thomas climbed the steps and went inside. There were two rooms. One with a wooden bed on either side, a heap of sacking, a stack of tools and a barrel in the middle of the floor. The other, reached by a door between the beds, was a kitchen. A roasting spit stood over a smoking hearth, there was another barrel in one corner and a heap of filthy platters, knives, spoons, glasses and wooden cups, all piled up on a small table. On a shelf were hunks of meat, loaves of bread and huge jars of sugar. Joints of mutton and pork hung on hooks attached to a roof beam. Around and under the table and on either side of the fire were dozens and dozens of bottles. The dog wandered in through a back door and began licking the earth floor.

'Meat and bread,' ordered Samuel, 'and wine. Enough for two.' And went to join his brother.

He would not get home any sooner by refusing so Thomas inspected the bottles and found one that contained a thin red liquid that might once have been claret. He took it out to the brutes with two glasses and returned to fetch meat and bread. From the shelf he took a dusty loaf and a slab of half-eaten mutton and took them out on wooden platters. The brutes appeared content and were soon tearing at the meat and bread with their hands and drinking the wine from the bottle. The glasses had been tossed aside. Revolting as the food looked and smelt, Thomas was starving and needed to eat. He found a piece of cooked chicken, sniffed it, wiped it on his breeches and took a tentative bite. It was old and tough but it was food. Water from the well would wash it down. He stuffed the chicken under his shirt and awaited further instructions.

They came almost immediately. 'More wine, damn you, and be quick about it,' shouted one of the brothers. Astonished, Thomas took out another bottle. Two bottles of claret for breakfast. How many might there be for dinner?

'Put it there and get back to the hut. We'll be up there when we're done.' Clutching the chicken under his shirt, Thomas did as he was told. The lines of battle had been drawn. The brutes would shout and curse and he would hold his tongue and do their bidding. But only until he could escape and get home.

When the brutes appeared at the hut they were carrying two large ledgers, quills and a pot of ink. 'There you are, Hill,' said Samuel, 'books of account. We need records of what we buy and sell and a tally of the slaves.' He jabbed a filthy finger at Thomas. 'You can write and figure, can't you?'

Thomas nodded. 'I can.'

'Just as well. When our partner visits, he'll want to see the books. Make sure they're right.' So the brutes had a partner. A man who did not care much what company he kept. John produced scraps of paper from a pocket. 'Start on those.' Thomas put the papers, the ledgers, the ink and the quills on his table. It would be better than working in that hellish kitchen. 'When you're done go to the kitchen and get our dinner ready.'

Dear God, the kitchen again. 'What do you wish to eat?'

'Meat.' And with that, the brutes departed, leaving Thomas to the ledgers.

Might as well get started, he thought, testing the point of a quill on his finger. It was sharp enough but too flexible — certainly not from a duck or a swan. He tipped a little of the ink into the silver inkwell. It was thin stuff, nothing like his own writing ink made from good English oak apples. The ledgers, however, were surprisingly good. The paper was thick and they were well bound in red leather. The scraps of paper turned out to be bills of sale from suppliers of tools, barrels, wheels, pots and the many other things needed for the production and sale of sugar, and barely intelligible scribbles recording monies received for the sugar sold.

Indifferent quills, watery ink, but it was the sort of work to which Thomas was accustomed and there was some pleasure in writing in the ledgers and creating an orderly set of accounts. Two hours later when he had completed the work, he closed the ledgers, made a neat pile of the bills, got up and stretched his back. He was astonished by the figures he had entered. The brothers Gibbes, brutish, evil, probably illiterate, were amassing a huge fortune. Where had they got the capital to buy the land and the equipment? Had they stolen it? And how had they learned about sugar? Where had they come from and when? If they were typical of planters on the island, it was a strange place indeed, where ignorant brutes could master a complicated process and rapidly become exceedingly wealthy.

If they were out in the fields somewhere there would be another chance to explore his prison before having to go back to the kitchen. The more he knew about the place, the better. If he was going to run, he had best know where to run to. The well yielded another bucket of good water — he made a mental note to find out why it was altogether better than the brown stuff produced by the Romsey wells — and then he ducked through a narrow entrance into the circular building beside it. In the middle was a large stone furnace over which had been erected a steel frame, with broken pots strewn around it on the earth floor. John Gibbes had called it the boiling house although it was obvious that nothing had been boiled in it for years. Even empty, it was an unpleasant place, dark and threatening, and Thomas quickly retreated back through the entrance.

Keeping an ear open for the sound of the returning Gibbes, he walked cautiously down the narrow path towards the fields. The ground was free of stones but, here and there, heavily rutted. On either side grew the same tall trees which he had noticed on the way from the harbour. High in their branches, a family of monkeys screeched a warning at his approach.

When he reached the place where the path opened up, he stood quietly behind a tree and listened. Far off, he could hear voices singing to a steady rhythm and he knew without looking that they were the voices of slaves cutting sugar cane and loading it on to carts. He peered round the tree. No sign of the Gibbes.

About fifty yards away to his left he saw another, larger circular building, which he took to be a new boiling house, and beside it a windmill, its sails turning smoothly in the breeze, and a third building whose purpose he did not know. The stone base of the mill was much larger than any mill he had seen in England.

The three buildings stood on a rise in the ground where the mill would catch whatever wind there was, and were partially hidden by a stand of thick trees with creepers hanging from their branches. That was why he had not noticed them that morning. Four ragged ponies were grazing in a field beyond the mill. With another look around to be sure he had not been seen, he climbed the slope to the mill.

He made his way past a line of flat-bedded carts and around a mountain of barrels. The third building was empty but for hundreds of earthenware pots, from which a thick brown liquid was draining on to pans set below them. It must be where the sugar dried out until it was cured.

It was too hot to stay there for more than a minute or two, so he went over to the mill and peered through a hole in its stone wall. Inside he saw two naked black slaves, their backs gleaming with sweat, feeding cane through three rollers driven by the windmill, and three more stirring copper cisterns into which the cane juice was being squeezed. The work looked back-breaking and dangerous.

He walked over to the boiling house. The moment he reached it, a blast hit him and he had to turn his head away. When he could open his eyes again, he peered through the door of the building. If anything, the boiling house was worse than the mill. Half a dozen black bodies, all naked, were filling copper kettles of various sizes with cane juice. Two more were stoking a furnace over which the kettles hung and three more were tending huge vats into which the liquid sugar was being poured. Row upon row of earthenware pots lined the walls and a huge heap of broken shards had been dumped in one corner. The whole operation was being overseen by a large man with a whip. With a start, Thomas realized it was John

Gibbes, luckily with his back to the door. He stepped away hastily and trotted back to the trees.

When he was safely inside the tree line, he stopped and turned. God's wounds, what suffering went into a cupful of sugar. If people knew, would they still buy it? Alas, he thought, they would.

He walked back up the path, past his hut and on to the house. The dog was asleep under the table and a fat rat scurried away at his approach. He went through the single room and into the kitchen. Like it or not, he would have to clean it up, especially if his own food was going to come from there. The Gibbes's stomachs might be able to withstand the filth but his could not.

Outside the kitchen door was an area cleared of trees and scrub and used for storage and rubbish. Yet more barrels and pots stood on one side and on the other was a mound of broken bottles, bones, rotting food and discarded tools. A privy had been built beside the rubbish heap with an open channel running from it down a slope into the trees behind. It stank. Thomas held his hand to his face and retreated hastily back into the kitchen. The kitchen he could cope with, this he would do his best to avoid.

From the kitchen Thomas took a loaf of bread, two knives, a spoon and a cooking pot. One knife he would sharpen on a stone and use to trim his hair, beard and quills, the other, and the spoon, he would use for cooking and eating. He would cook his meals on an open fire outside the hut — the brutes could hardly object if it kept him out of their sight — and he would dig his own privy in the trees nearby.

Feeling a little better for having done something positive, he hurried back to the hut. Having soaked the loaf in water from the well, he was able to swallow it in small chunks. Then he lay on the bed and hoped that the biting insects of Barbados did not hunt their prey during the day and that the brutes would not return until sunset. He needed time to plan.

The Gibbes never did anything quietly and Thomas was jolted from his thoughts by the sound of them thundering up the path. He jumped off the bed and pretended to be working on the ledgers, just before John threw open the door of the hut and bellowed at him. 'Get off your arse, Hill. We're hungry and thirsty.' Thomas left them tipping buckets of water over themselves and went down to the kitchen.

When they arrived at the house, dripping wet and smeared with dirt, he had put out a cold leg of mutton and two bottles of wine. It must have satisfied them because they sat down without complaint and set to. They tore the mutton off the bone with their hands and washed it down with gulps from the bottles. It was not long before they demanded more wine. This time he took out four bottles, hoping that would be enough even for these two.

'Now get back to your hut, Hill,' spat Samuel through a mouthful of meat, 'and don't show your prissy face until morning.' Delighted to do as he was told, Thomas returned to his hut with a leg of pork under his shirt.

Having eaten a slice of pork, drunk and washed at the well and found a stone on which to whet his knife, Thomas realized that he had survived his first day at the hands of these animals and that he should do something to record the feat. With the knife he made a tiny notch in the table. Day one of his indenture was over and he would make a notch for each day survived, so when he got home he would be able to tell the girls exactly how many days he had been there.

*

Despite having drunk six bottles of wine, the brutes were up at dawn the next morning and shouting for Thomas. He struggled awake and staggered down to the house. 'We're going to town, Hill, and you're coming with us,' grunted Samuel, scratching at his beard. 'Fetch the ponies.'

'Where are they?' asked Thomas innocently. With a pony, there might be a chance.

'Where they always are,' replied black brute. 'In the field by the windmill.'

'Windmill?'

The brothers looked at each other and shrugged. 'Down the path. Look left. Bring two. You'll walk.' So much for a pony on which to gallop away. Unless they drank themselves insensible, the thought of being pursued by mounted Gibbes was not a happy one.

Thomas collected the ponies. They made him think of riding with his father over the fields and through the woods around Romsey. From somewhere the Gibbes had produced saddles and bridles and within two minutes they were off. With the rope again around his neck, Thomas followed behind.

They walked down the hill and then northwards with the shore on their left. Thomas could not help gazing at the sea. Close in it was almost transparent, moving through deeper shades of blue as far as the horizon. The Caribbean's reputation was well deserved. Beautiful and deadly. He had to tear his eyes from it to examine his surroundings. The road was narrow and rough, barely more than a path scraped out of the forest, and the trees on their right loomed high over them. It would be easy for a man to disappear. And just as easy to stay disappeared. The forest was thick and frightening.

The village of Speightstown was about a mile from the bottom of the hill. It was not much, just two rows of timber- and stone-built shacks and cottages, through which ran the only street, a small jetty to which fishing boats had been tied, an inn and an open square opposite the jetty. The square was full of stalls and, having tethered their ponies outside the inn, that was where they went.

It was not so different from the Romsey market. Traders hawked their wares and clamoured for attention, planters and their women examined each item carefully before parting with their money and, despite the early hour, the inn was overflowing with drinkers. It was crowded and noisy. As at Oistins, though, the smells were different. In Romsey, the smells of the market were those of fresh food and cooking fat. Here they were more of sweat, drains and rotting vegetables. And the heat was fierce. Thomas felt his head burning and tried to stay in the shade. Everyone else wore a hat.

Still led by the rope, Thomas followed the Gibbes around the stalls, while they filled two sacks with meat, poultry and bread, but showed no interest in the fish, fruit or vegetables. None of the other planters spoke to the Gibbes, nor did they actually pay for anything. At each stall, having taken what they wanted, one of them muttered 'end of the month', and they moved on. There was no argument. As they made their way around the square, Thomas was aware of being inspected. Another wretch at the mercy of the Gibbes was what the traders would be thinking and, if so, they were right.

Having heaved the heavy sacks on to the backs of the ponies and secured them carefully, Thomas wondered what was coming next. He should have known. Leaving him tied to a stunted tree with orders to stay put and watch the ponies or feel the whip, the Gibbes marched into the inn.

Thomas sat on a low wall in the meagre shade of the tree, wiped the sweat from his brow with his sleeve and wondered if there was a well in the village. He was about to ask when a voice behind him said, 'Good day, sir. I saw you with the Gibbes brothers and wondered if you would care for a drink?' Thomas turned in surprise. A slim young man of no more than twenty was holding out a leather flask. 'It's coconut water. Good for the stomach.' It was an unusual voice with a slight lilt to it — both educated and musical.

Thomas took the flask and swallowed a mouthful of coconut water. It was cool and sweet and he took a second gulp. 'Thank you,' he said, handing back the flask.

'My name is Patrick,' said the young man with a grin that showed off his gleaming teeth. 'I'm employed by Mr Lyte and his sister Mary. Their estate borders on the Gibbes's, so we're neighbours.'

Thomas stood and offered his hand. 'I am Thomas Hill, indentured to the brutes, I mean the Gibbes.'

Patrick chuckled. 'How long have you been with the brutes, Thomas?'

'This is my second day.'

'It didn't take you long to discover what they're like.'

'Are your owners any better?'

Another huge smile. 'I'm a lucky man. I was born here to a white father and a black mother. I have lived on the Lytes' estate all my life. When they came here the Lytes bought the plantation with all its slaves. I was one of them. They are good people, as different from the Gibbes as you could imagine.'

'So you're a slave.'

'I am because my skin is black or at least it is not white, but I'm treated as a trusted servant. I count myself fortunate. How long is your indenture?'

'Seven years. It's beyond imagining.'

'Then don't imagine, Thomas. Take each day as it comes. The time will pass. Why were you indentured?'

Patrick listened while Thomas told the story of his arrest and deportation and of being forced to leave his sister and nieces to fend for themselves. 'And you really have no idea who arranged it?' he asked when Thomas had finished.

'I have tried and tried to work out who might have done this to me. It must have been someone who bears me a grudge, but who? I can think of no one.'

The Gibbes emerged from the inn, each with a bottle in his hand. John untied the rope from the tree and bellowed at Thomas to get moving. 'There's work to be done, Hill. Leave that blackamoor to his thieving and hurry up.'

Thomas shrugged. 'Goodbye, Patrick. Thank you for the coconut water.'

'Goodbye, Thomas. Go well.'

The walk back up the hill was a good deal harder than the walk down and by the time they reached the house Thomas was in urgent need of water. First, however, he had to carry the sacks into the kitchen and unload them while the brutes unsaddled the ponies and kicked the saddles and bridles under their beds.

'Take the ponies back to the field, Hill,' ordered Samuel, 'then cook dinner. Roast that piglet. We won't be far away, so don't try anything.'

Try what? Thomas asked himself, as he walked the ponies up the path. Even if I run, how do I escape from an island prison if I can neither swim nor fly? Daedalus's wings? Noah's Ark? Realizing that the heat and thirst were already sapping his spirit, he shook his head, breathed deeply and ordered himself not to despair. He would find a way.

After a sweltering afternoon in the kitchen turning the piglet on the spit over the fire, Thomas sat outside the house and waited for the Gibbes to return from the fields. When they did, he brought out the piglet and four more bottles and left them to it.

Back at his hut he drank from the well, washed, scraped his beard with the little knife, examined his face in the inkwell and lay on his bed. Before he fell asleep, he took the knife and cut another notch in the table. Two notches. Two days. How many more would there be?

CHAPTER 7

Since the war had erupted again Tobias Rush seldom left London. Travelling was dangerous and it would be all too easy to get caught up in a skirmish or attacked by a gang of club-men. It was not that he was afraid, just that such a thing would be a nuisance. He planned carefully and disliked his plans being disrupted. From the safety of his house in Cheapside he kept himself informed by regular reports from his agents, which were much more reliable than London tittle-tattle or the newsbooks.

For this task, however, he had no choice. He had to make this journey himself. Fortunately, his luck held and they encountered no difficulties on the road from London to Winchester and thence to Romsey. When they reached an inn on the outskirts of the town he instructed the coachman to stop and to arrange stabling for the horses and the best room available for himself. The coachman would sleep with the horses. It was always wise to have a means of escape prepared, just in case. Carrying his silver-topped cane and a slim leather case containing the papers, he walked the rest of the way.

He had no difficulty in finding Love Lane or the shop. As much out of habit as for fear of being observed he walked up and down the lane twice before stopping to peer through the shop window. He waited outside until a customer left clutching a book, let himself in and quietly locked the door behind him. The woman sitting at the desk at one side of the shop looked up. 'Good morning, sir,' she greeted him. 'May I assist you?' But for the strain etched into her face and the tiredness in her eyes she would have been good-looking. He could see the resemblance.

'On the contrary. It is I who may assist you. Are you Margaret Taylor?'

She peered at him. 'I am. Are you selling books?'

Rush scoffed. 'Do I look like a seller of books? No, I have come about another matter.'

'What matter would that be?'

'Your brother.'

Margaret was immediately on her feet. 'Thomas? What do you know of Thomas? Where is he? Is he alive?'

'We will come to that. Where are your daughters?' His tone was icy and suddenly Margaret was frightened.

'With a friend. Why?'

'I wish us to be undisturbed. Sit down and you will find out why I am here.' Margaret sat. Rush picked up a book and turned it round to read the title. Then he glanced around the shop. This was a moment he had been looking forward to and he was going to savour it. He took his time until eventually he looked Margaret in the eye and smiled his thin smile. 'My name is Tobias Rush.'

The blood drained from Margaret's face. She knew the name at once. Tobias Rush was the traitor whom Thomas had exposed in Oxford. The murderer of Thomas's old tutor who had very nearly murdered Thomas as well. A fiend from hell was how Thomas had described him, a fiend who took pleasure in inflicting pain. But it could not be Rush. He was dead. The king himself had seen his body. She remembered exactly how Thomas had described it. A traitor's death, his body broken and his face a bloody mess. She stared at the man. Could the king have been mistaken? Or was this man, for some unthinkable reason, an impostor?

'I assure you it is so. The king was easily deceived about my death and your brother accepted his word. Fools, both of them.' It was as if Rush had read her thoughts. He held up the silver-topped cane and slowly withdrew the slim blade. 'Did he tell you about this?' Margaret put her hand to her mouth. Not only had Thomas told her about it, there was another just like it in his bedroom. He had brought it back from Oxford. Rush slid the blade back into place and rested the cane within easy reach against a bookcase.

'You have come to murder us.'

'In fact, I have not. Not yet, anyway. I have come to show you these.' He opened the leather case and withdrew the documents inside. Two of them he handed to Margaret. 'Do not bother to destroy them. I have copies.' Margaret spread both on the desk and read the first. Then she read it again, before turning to the second, much shorter one. Rush's eyes never left her face as she read.

'They are forgeries,' she said calmly, without looking up.

Rush had expected this. 'I deny it. In any case, forgeries or not, there are three reasons why they will be enforced. First, it cannot be proved that the letter and his signature on the contract are not in Thomas Hill's hand, as they are a perfect match for it. Second, any attempt to show otherwise will result in his suffering greatly; and third, you have two lovely daughters.'

'You would threaten my daughters?' Margaret almost shrieked the words. Rush merely raised an eyebrow and stroked the top of the cane. 'If my brother is alive, where is he? Tell me where he is.'

'He is alive and in good hands. You do not need to know his whereabouts.'

'Can you prove that he is alive?'

'Can you take the risk that he is not?'

Margaret put her head in her hands. No wonder all her efforts to discover what had happened to her brother had proved futile. There had been a wall of silence, built by this man. If Thomas was alive but in the hands of this monster, he would be better dead. And so would she. Tobias Rush. It was beyond imagining. Tobias Rush, the man Thomas had proved to be a murderer and traitor, and who had died in Oxford, was standing before her. So it was he who had arranged for Thomas to be arrested. And now he claimed to own the shop and the house. And he was right. The contract transferring the title to the property from Thomas Hill to Tobias Rush was properly sealed, witnessed and signed by both parties. Had she not known better, she would have taken Thomas's signature to be his. It was a perfect forgery. As was the letter in his hand explaining to her that he had agreed the sale of the property to Tobias Rush because he was about to be deported to the colonies and trusted his old friend to take care of both the property and his family. If he did not return, their future at least would be secure. He instructed Margaret to do exactly as Tobias Rush told her. When she could speak, Margaret asked quietly, 'What would you have me do?'

'Fetch the deeds to the property and give them to me. And

remember what I have said about your brother and your daughters.' Despite her shock, Margaret knew she was trapped. Nothing would make her put Polly and Lucy at risk. She climbed the stairs to Thomas's bedroom, reached under the bed and pulled out his strongbox. She used a key on her ring to open it, riffled through the documents inside, found the deeds and took them down to the shop. Without a word, she handed them to Rush. He checked that they were complete and tucked them into his case. 'Excellent.'

'My daughters will be home soon. Must they find you here?'

'That will not be necessary. For now you will stay here and continue as before. Let it be known that your brother is dead. I have men in Romsey and you will be watched at all times. Any attempt to disobey my orders or to run away will be fatal. For all of you. Do you understand?'

Margaret nodded. 'Will you tell Thomas we are well?'

Rush smirked. 'I might.'

It had been as delicious as he had hoped. As he walked back to the inn, Tobias Rush swung his cane and replayed the encounter in his mind. Delicious.

CHAPTER 8

U sing the knife taken from the kitchen, Thomas had scored a horizontal line through each group of nine notches on the table. When he scored through the fourth group, forty days had passed. Forty days in the kitchen, of making entries in the ledgers, of agonizing about Margaret and the girls, of solitude and anguish.

On his trips with the Gibbes to the market he had not met Patrick again and he knew little more about the island than he had when he first stepped ashore. His knowledge of its geography was limited to the road from Oistins to Speightstown. The Gibbes spoke to him only to give orders or make threats and neither the planters nor the traders ever addressed him.

Forty days of watching carts pulled by teams of slaves trundling backwards and forwards up the path towards the mill, empty on their way there, loaded with pots of sugar on their way back. Forty nights of nightmares, demons and biting insects.

Forty days and nights with not even Montaigne for company — his old friend had deserted him again just when he was needed most. Strangely, in the absence of Montaigne, the Franciscan friar Simon de Pointz had often come to mind. That unusual man, who had twice saved Thomas's life in Oxford, had tempered his faith with what he called 'pragmatism and humour' — two most un-friarly qualities. Determined to survive whatever the brutes threw at him, Thomas found pragmatism straightforward; humour, how-ever, well nigh impossible. Oh for Simon's company in this distant, lonely prison.

Thomas had occupied himself with the ledgers and in clean-ing out the kitchen and yard. He had dug a deep hole in the trees behind the hovel in which he had buried hundreds of empty bottles and mounds of rotting waste, and a second hole was already filling up. The yard was still home to legions of ants and cockroaches and used daily by the dogs, but he shovelled up the muck and kept it as clean as he could. He swept the kitchen floor whenever he was in there and protected the meat from the worst of the flies by covering it with linen cloths he had found stuffed in a barrel and had washed in rainwater. Bookkeeper to the brutes was bad enough; cook, cleaner and housekeeper, much worse.

In the forty days the weather had become hotter and wetter. Storm clouds now swept in from the Atlantic, bringing rain that turned hard earth into mud within minutes and filled the holes and ruts on the path with brown water; the winds that blew in the rain could fell a tree or lift a roof. Thomas struggled to plug the leaks in the roof of his hut, using whatever he could find to do the job. Palm fronds, branches, planks from old carts — all were pressed into service.

He had dug himself a privy behind the hut — at least the rain washed the muck away down the hill — and unless it was raining he cooked his meals on an open fire outside his door. He helped himself from the brutes' kitchen and drank water from the well.

He had also experimented with the fruits that grew abundantly around the estate. Not knowing their local names, he had christened them himself. There were a greenish-yellow fruit in the shape of a hand — *the finger fruit*; a yellow-skinned fruit in the shape of a crescent moon, which hung in big clumps from the branches of its tree — *the crescent fruit*, and small green fruits which grew on bushes protected by spikes sharp enough to draw blood at the slightest touch, which he knew were limes. All of these, taken with a little sugar, were delicious. And there were cassava and sweet potatoes. If he made a hole in the shell of a coconut with his knife he could drink the water inside and then break the shell open with a stone to get at the white flesh. The first settlers on the island would have discovered all these things and many more twenty years earlier, but for Thomas each new discovery was a small triumph. He was not going to ask the brutes for advice and there was no one else. He dare not go down to the slaves' huts — anyway, they would probably ignore him — and there had been no opportunity to talk to anyone in the market.

Having abandoned the idea of keeping a journal on the grounds that every entry would be the same, Thomas had instead carefully cut a page from one of the ledgers and on each tenth day had written on it a new adjective to describe the brutes. On his fortieth day, he had: brutish, coarse, filthy and carnivorous.

On the forty-first day, the Gibbes strode up to the hut and threw two sacks at him. 'We're needed in the windmill,' bellowed Samuel. 'Go to the market and buy a turkey and a shoat. And buy milk. Make sure it's today's. Tell them it's for the Gibbes.'

'And don't think you can use our credit for anything else, Hill,' added John, pointing his whip at Thomas's eyes. 'We'll know if you do. Get straight back here when you're done.' After forty days, his chance might have come. Find a friendly trader to help or simply make his way to Oistins harbour and hide on a ship bound for England. 'And if you so much as think of running you'll be roasting your own balls for our dinner.'

Speightstown market was busy that morning. With the sacks over his shoulder, Thomas walked around the traders' stalls, pretending to inspect the goods on offer while deciding what to do next. If he picked the wrong trader that might be the end of him and none of them had ever been friendly. They all knew Thomas was indentured to the Gibbes and the Gibbes owed them money. Why would they help him?

He felt a tap on his shoulder. 'Good morning, Thomas. I'm glad to see you still alive. On your own today?'

'Patrick, good morning. Yes, no brutes today. I think they want me to run so that they can hunt me down and do their worst. They sent me to buy a turkey, a shoat and milk.'

Patrick grinned. 'A turkey and shoat dinner. And I know who'll be coming to dine. Adam Lyte and our neighbour Charles Carrington. A good man and more than close to Mary Lyte, although I shall beat you to death if you repeat that.'

'Adam Lyte's sister. You mentioned her name.'

'A beautiful lady, unfortunately for Mr Carrington engaged to a young man in England, Perkins by name. I have often heard her arguing with Mr Lyte about him.'

'So they're dining with the brutes. When is it?'

'Tomorrow. Do you know about the turkey and the shoat?'

'I know that I shall have to cook them. What else is there to know?'

'Ah, allow me to instruct you. When the war broke out in England the island desperately wanted to keep out of it, although the majority of landowners are for the king. So the Assembly in Bridgetown passed a law forbidding the use of the words "Cavalier" and "Roundhead". Anyone using the words is obliged to buy dinner — a turkey and a shoat — for everyone who heard him.'

'So the brutes were heard saying Cavalier and Roundhead.'

'Yes, but the law is often used as an excuse for a good dinner. They would have done it on purpose. Mr Lyte thinks they want to propose some business venture. The three estates are close to each other. He's not looking forward to it and neither is Mr Carrington. They loathe the Gibbes, but in the interests of peace and prosperity they feel bound to go.'

'You're very well informed, Patrick.'

'It comes from living with the Lytes and being treated as one of the family. Now make your purchases, Thomas, then come down to the beach by the jetty. I sometimes take a bath there. Then I'll help you up the hill with your sacks.'

Thomas decided to take a risk. 'Let's go down to the beach first, Patrick. There is something I want to discuss with you.'

Patrick looked surprised. 'Very well. Then we'll find a turkey and a shoat worthy of your talents in the kitchen.'

On the beach, they stripped off their shirts and waded into the sea. Patrick handed Thomas a small earthenware pot. 'There, try that. It's aloe, very good for washing. It grows everywhere.'

The aloe was indeed good for washing and Thomas, for the first time since leaving England, felt clean. 'Now what is it you want to discuss, Thomas?' asked Patrick, when they were back on the beach. 'Remember that I'm only a slave and may not have much to offer.'

Thomas saw the twinkle in his eye and smiled. 'I doubt that.' He paused. 'Patrick, I've been here for forty days and I can stand no more. I must escape.'

'Escape from the brutes or from the island?'

'Both. I must get home to my family before the brutes finish me off. I need a magistrate who will listen.' Before Patrick could reply, there was an agonizing scream from the market. 'Good God, what was that?'

'That, Thomas, was the result of a magistrate listening to the complaint of an indentured man. The misguided wretch was sentenced to a public flogging for his trouble.'

'For complaining?'

'The magistrates are landowners themselves. They discourage complaints from indentured servants.'

'But I have committed no crime and I am not a prisoner of war. It's monstrous.'

Patrick sighed. 'Thomas, you are hardly the only indentured man on the island who claims that he was wrongly arrested and deported and that he is badly treated. It would do you no good.'

'Then I must find a ship and work my passage home. Will you help me?'

'Alas, my friend, even if you found a ship you would almost certainly be locked in the hold, taken to another island and sold there as a slave. It happens often.' There was another scream from the market. Thomas put his head in his hands and tried not to scream himself. How in the name of God was he to get off this island?

He felt Patrick's hand on his arm. 'Thomas, let me speak to the Lytes about you. Perhaps they can help.'

'Would they? What could they do?'

'Adam Lyte is a member of the Assembly. He's a decent man and a strict upholder of the law. He might be willing to do something. At least do nothing rash until I've spoken to him.'

Thomas sighed. What choice did he have? 'Very well, I'll try to survive until then.'

'Good. Now let's go and find your dinner.'

Having chosen a turkey and a piglet, they loaded them with Patrick's sacks on to his pony and set off. Much relieved at not having to carry the sacks, refreshed by his bath and allowing himself to hope that Adam Lyte would be willing to help him, Thomas took the opportunity to put to Patrick all the questions he had been wanting to ask.

By the time they reached the turning to the Gibbes's estate he could recognize an aloe plant, he knew that limes rubbed on the skin kept mosquitoes away, that the fruit shaped like a hand was a carambola, that the yellow fruit growing in bunches was a plantain and that the creepers hanging off the tree under which he often sat when the Gibbes were in the fields were actually its roots and that it was called the bearded fig, from which had come the name of the island. And he knew that the creatures which made such loud whistling noises at night were tiny frogs.

He also knew that Bridgetown was the largest town in Barbados, the Assembly consisted of thirty elected members and the name of the governor was Sir Philip Bell. He felt foolish not knowing these things but, as he explained to Patrick, he had spent forty days in a state of ignorance and isolation.

'The brutes do not much care for conversation,' he said, 'and neither of them can read, so we have neither books nor news sheets.'

'That at least I can help with,' replied Patrick, reaching into his sack. 'I carry a book to read on the beach. You have it.' He pulled out a slim book and handed it to Thomas.

'Henry More's *Philosophical Poems*. Thank you, Patrick. He'll keep me company until you have spoken to Mr Lyte.'

So intent had he been upon extracting information about the island that he had asked Patrick nothing about himself. Angry with himself for his ill manners, Thomas apologized and promised to repair the omission next time they met.

Patrick laughed. 'It's of no account, Thomas. I'm pleased to have been able to help. We all know what the Gibbes are like. I hope the dinner goes well. Or at least the cooking. I will tell Mr Lyte to expect a banquet.'

'Thank you, Patrick. I will try not to disappoint him or Mr Carrington.'

Could it possibly get any worse? Despite Patrick's offer to speak to Adam Lyte, after three hours in the sweltering kitchen turning the spits on which the turkey and the piglet had been roasting since midday, Thomas was ready to lie down and wait for the end. Sweat poured off his forehead, his head and arms ached abominably and his mouth and throat were on fire.

When at last both creatures were cooked he wrapped his hands in wet cloths, heaved the first spit from its supports, slid off the turkey and lifted it on to one of two huge platters produced from under the brutes' beds and polished that morning with sand and grease. The brutes kept everything of value under their beds. Thomas had seen saddles, plate and good leather boots dragged out when needed. For all he knew, there were caskets of gold coins under there.

The turkey was followed by the piglet. The fowl went quietly but the pig hissed and spat in protest, its skin bubbling and blistering in its own fat. A dollop of fat landed on his bare arm, making him yelp and drop the wretched thing on to the earth floor. He rescued it hastily, hoping the yelp had not been heard, and managed to wipe off at least some of the dirt. But in spite of his efforts at cleaning and sweeping, the floor would be hiding all manner of unpleasantness. The plantation dogs wandered in and out, millipedes and cockroaches lurked in dark corners, ants devoured scraps and crumbs and his masters were not above spitting on it. When he had the chance to eat he would give the pig a miss and content himself with a little turkey.

Ye gods, he thought, this place is hot enough without having to spend the afternoon beside an open fire, being attacked by boiling fat. With another oath he picked up the first platter and carried it through to the four diners.

'Come on, Hill, put it here and be quick about it. Our bellies are empty and we need feeding,' bellowed Samuel Gibbes at the head of the table, sweeping away empty bottles to clear a space for the food. He belched loudly. 'And bring more wine. We'll need it in this heat.' The four diners had already drunk five bottles that afternoon although neither of the guests had taken much. Compared to the Gibbes, Charles Carrington and Adam Lyte were practically abstainers. Thomas wondered how they could bear to dine with the Gibbes, even for the common good. Adam Lyte, a little overweight, fair-haired and red-faced, was, as Patrick had said, a decent man and a proud member of the Assembly. The athletic-looking Carrington, clean-shaven, long black hair tied neatly back, dark-eyed and skin weathered by the Caribbean sun, was more of a free spirit.

'Devilish fine law in my opinion,' said Samuel, as he hacked at the turkey with a heavy knife. 'We only have to say "Cavalier and Roundhead" and it's turkey and pork for all.' Laughing at this excellent joke, he shovelled chunks of leg and breast on to four wooden trenchers.

'Indeed, Samuel,' replied Lyte, 'although we in the Assembly did not reckon on anyone using the words just as an excuse for a good dinner. We meant to promote peace and prosperity on the island by banning them, not the wholesale slaughter of turkeys and pigs. Still, I thank you for inviting me. The favour shall be returned within the month.'

'I thank you too, Samuel,' added Carrington. 'This much meat will keep me alive for a week.'

'Assembly, my liver,' muttered John gruffly, scratching at his scarred face, 'damned fools know nothing. We don't need laws to tell us what we can and can't say, any more than we need them to tell us how to grow sugar. We're the ones who've made Barbados rich and we'll do as we choose. Bell and Walrond, Drax and Middleton, they're interfering old women. To hell with the lot of them and their meddling laws.' If this was meant to rile Adam Lyte, it failed. He tactfully said nothing. 'Where's that damned shoat, Hill? Bring it here, for the devil's sake.'

Only the name of Bell meant anything to Thomas, although if the brutes hated them all, they would have his support. As he came through with the pig, he managed to catch Carrington's eye and shook his head just enough to signal a warning. Carrington raised an eyebrow but said nothing.

'Now, gentlemen, some pork with your turkey?' Holding his

knife like a dagger, Samuel thrust it into the pig. Juices spurted out on to his grubby fingers, which he licked with relish.

'In truth, Samuel, pork has never really agreed with me. I think I'll settle for this excellent turkey, thank you.' Carrington had taken Thomas's hint and with a gentle nudge had passed it on to his friend.

'I fear I am much the same,' said Lyte, 'but if I may, I will take a drop more of your excellent wine with the fowl.'

'Ah well, all the more for us, eh, John?' Samuel, not a bit put out, shovelled a huge heap of pork on to his plate and another on to his brother's.

With the diners provided with more meat and wine than five times their number could possibly consume, Thomas slipped out-side with a small plate of turkey and sat on a wooden box he had placed under the bearded fig tree. He called it his listening tree. From there he could not see the diners but he could hear them. It was cooler under the tree and he sipped a cup of plantain juice.

Stretching his aching back, he looked again at the Gibbes's house, shook his head sadly and thought yet again how utterly revolting it was. How anyone, even these brutes, could live in it was beyond understanding. Not a drop of paint had been employed on the rough timber, the roof leaked and armies of termites had been feasting on the corner posts. Revolting was the word for it. Ramshackle and revolting.

'Hill, Hill, where are you, man?' It was John this time, full of meat and claret, and rapidly reaching the point at which he might become dangerous. Thomas roused himself smartly and went back to the house. 'Ah, there you are, queenie. You are a queenie, aren't you? I hear all the king's men are.' Either he had forgotten that his guests were supporters of the king or he did not care. Probably the latter. He was always more vicious to Thomas in company. It was his way of showing off.

'I don't think so, sir. But is there anything else I can do for you?' The 'sir' stuck in his throat, as it always did, and it was a risky reply. For a horrid moment both Gibbes stared at him and he thought there was going to be trouble until Charles Carrington came to the rescue.

'Excellent turkey, Thomas,' he said, adding with a grin, 'and I daresay the piglet was good too. Eh, Samuel?'

'What? Yes, yes. A decent pig. Better than your last effort, Hill. More flavour. Now bring us the milk pudding. And we'll need more wine.'

He fetched the wine and then returned with a large pudding from the kitchen. He had made it with the milk bought at the market, the juice of ten limes and a good deal of stirring. 'Will the pudding be good, Thomas?' asked Carrington with a wink.

'Oh yes, sir. Very good, I should think.'

'Excellent. Better have some then, eh, Adam?'

While they were tucking into the pudding, Thomas sat outside and listened to the four of them talking about the sugar that had already made them rich, and about the soaring value of land which was making them richer still. When two or more planters were gathered together, even bedfellows as strange as these, he supposed that the conversation would invariably turn to the price of land and the production of sugar. Planters would speak of sugar as churchmen speak of faith — as if there were nothing else.

For all the squalor and debauchery, the Gibbes knew about making money from sugar and could hold their own on anything to do with the intricate processes of planting, harvesting, milling, boiling and curing. Oddly, they became rational and coherent when discussing business. Before dinner, they had taken their guests to inspect the windmill and had tried to persuade them to form a partnership to build another for their shared use. Lyte and Carrington had wisely asked for time to consider the matter, although Thomas had the impression that had the proposal been made by anyone else they would have jumped at it. Windmills must be expensive to build and would need to be kept busy. A shared one made sense.

The vexed issue of labour got the Gibbes really heated. Thomas had heard it all before. 'We have fifty acres planted and we need at least thirty men to work them and more to man the mill and the boiling house. We need slaves, and lots of them. A black slave is better suited to the work than an indentured man and he's a better investment. He's here for life and if we want him to, he breeds more workers.'

Adam Lyte spoke mildly. 'You may well be right, Samuel, and of course you know your business best, but Mary and I have mixed views on slavery and we've been fortunate with our indentured men. Most of them chose to come here as indentured servants, none of them has been involved in an uprising and, as far as we can tell, none of the convicts was guilty of anything more serious than petty theft or poaching. They know they're better off here than starving in some prison at home and they're good workers.'

'That's as may be, but indentured men cost a good twelve pounds each and they're only here for a few years. We'd rather do without them.'

'What about your man Hill?' asked Lyte. 'Where did he come from?'

'Hill's our only indentured man. We bought him because he can write and figure and he can cook. He keeps the books and cooks when we tell him to. We bought him from an agent who got him from Winchester gaol. Can't stand the prissy little scab myself but he's useful enough.'

'I daresay he's better than the Irish they send us, although that isn't difficult.' John Gibbes, half comatose from the drink, stirred himself to join in. 'They're coming over in shiploads now, men and women, the women no better than whores, and they're troublesome pigs. They hate honest Englishmen and don't mind saying so. Land of papists, Ireland is. Papist pricks and poxed whores. They have a word for being sent here. Barbadosed. Barbadosed, my liver. It's Hellosed they deserve.'

'Hellosed. Ha. That's a good one, brother. Hellosing for the Irish. Fine idea.' Samuel paused in drunken thought for a moment, then let out another bellow. 'Hill, Hill, get off your arse and bring us a bottle of that excellent rum we made from the molasses last year. A glass of rum, gentlemen, before you go? Fetch the rum, Hill. Or is it Hell? Ha, fetch the rum, Hell, or to hill with you.' Now completely drunk, Samuel was delighted at his own wit.

Thomas fetched the rum and four glasses. If that doesn't finish them off, nothing will, he thought. Sweet Barbados rum was fierce stuff and on top of all that claret must surely bring the dinner to an end within the hour. God willing, it might even bring the brutes to an end.

'Your sister's much admired, I do hear, Adam.' John was slurring his words but could still just about string them together intelligibly. 'A lovely girl by all accounts. It's a wonder she's not married. Queues of young men at the door, eh? There's taverns-full of them to choose from. What is she, nineteen, twenty? Perfect age for a woman. Fully grown in every department but still fair and

supple. Just the thing to keep a man happy on a hot night.'
Thomas, cringing behind the tree, reckoned that this would break
up the party even sooner.

'Mary will be nineteen in June.' Adam's voice was icy. The
thought of either uncouth Gibbes so much as thinking of touching
his sister must be abhorrent.

'Expect you'll be wanting a young wife to warm your bed
soon, Charles. Could do worse than Adam's sister, eh? The Lyte
family after all, no paupers, good breeding stock and a fine-looking
woman, they say. Might be willing to take her on myself.'

That should do it, thought Thomas, and about time. He
risked a look around the tree.

'I do not have the honour of knowing Miss Lyte at all well,'
replied Charles with quiet force, 'but on the few occasions that I've
had the pleasure of her company, I have found her to be a lady of
charm and virtue. I believe she merits the respect of all, not lewd
suggestions.'

'Indeed not,' agreed Adam, 'but she needs little guidance
from me. Mary is an honourable and spirited lady. She would deal
swiftly with any unwanted attentions.'

John Gibbes was unabashed. Incapable of embarrassment, he
leered suggestively and took another swig of rum.

Charles rose to go. 'Time for us to take our leave, Adam. I
thank you, gentlemen, for your hospitality if not your
conversation.'

'As do I.' Adam managed, just, to remain civil but he was
already on his feet. 'My thanks for dinner. And kindly thank Hill
for his excellent pudding.' Thomas knew that thanking Hill was
not something that either brute would be doing.

The two guests walked briskly to a stand of trees where their horses were tethered in the shade. Darkness was falling and the tiny frogs had begun their chorus. They stood there for a moment and spoke loudly enough for Thomas to hear. 'God in heaven, Charles, never again. It may be our duty to do what we can to keep the peace and protect our trade but I for one am not willing to sacrifice myself like that again. If our prosperity breeds animals like those two, better that we are poor.'

'Fortunately, my friend, there are few in Barbados as evil as the Gibbes but, of course, you're right. They are gross and despicable. I pity poor Hill; he's plainly a decent man and well educated. I hope he's stronger than he looks or the climate and the work may get the better of him. Now enough of them. How's Mary?'

'Well, thank you. She sends her compliments.'

'Please return them,' said Charles, 'and if either Gibbes so much as looks at her you will have to be quick to run him through before I do.'

Adam laughed. 'I know. Let us pray it does not come to that.'

'Goodbye, Adam,' said Charles, mounting his horse. 'Let us meet again soon.'

'Indeed. Go safely, Charles.' Behind his listening tree, Thomas kept quiet. There had been no mention of helping him. Perhaps Patrick had not yet had a chance to speak to Adam Lyte.

As soon as his guests were out of earshot, Samuel spat on the floor and swore loudly. 'What a pair of pomposetting pricks. Royalist piss-pots think they're too good for us. I'll wager the girl's been bedded by half the young men in Holetown. And a few filthy slaves too, I shouldn't wonder. What was it? Mixed views about slavery? My eye. That's the last time we give them turkey and pork, by God. And we'll see about "unwanted attentions", eh, brother?'

But his brother was past caring. Snoring loudly, his big, red, louse-infested head resting on his arms, he had passed out. Samuel shrugged, left him there and staggered off to his bed.

Thomas slipped off to his hut, expecting to be asleep within seconds. But exhausted though he was after an afternoon in the sweltering kitchen, he found, when he lay on the bed, that his thoughts skipped from one thing to another, as a restless man's do, and images of people and places flittered in and out of his mind's eye, returning repeatedly to his home and the horrors of a war as bloody and pointless as any war could be. He tried not to dwell for the hundredth time on his arrest and imprisonment, the sudden separation from his family or on the miserable voyage that had brought him here. It had happened. Now survival was everything. He must hope Patrick could persuade Adam Lyte to help. He must hope.

CHAPTER 9

1649

It had started well enough. The king, having been ferried by
barge from St James's Palace to Whitehall Steps, was marched
into Westminster Hall by a troop of halberdiers. Two hundred men
stood guard inside the hall, and two hundred more outside. There
was barely an inch of space.

For the king's trial it had been stripped of the low partitions
that usually separated one court from another, and of the booksellers' stalls and coffee shops among them. In their place a stage
had been erected at the north end of the hall, on which sat the
Lord President of the Court and the rows of commissioners who
would decide whether or not the prisoner should be allowed to live.
Rush had bought a seat in one of the stands set up around the hall
rather than be forced to stand with the rest of the audience behind
a screen high enough to obscure all but the king's head. No one
knew how long the trial would last and he did not relish the

prospect of having to mingle with the common herd for any length of time. He really should have been about his business but the prospect of the entertainment on offer had been too much of a temptation.

While the Lord President opened the proceedings by describing the king as 'the principal author' of 'the evils and calamities' brought upon the country, and the Solicitor General read out the lengthy charges, accusing him of 'high treason and high misdemeanours', the king sat impassively in a red velvet chair facing the stage, feigning lack of interest and tapping his cane on the floor. Just like Rush's, the king's cane was embellished with a silver top, although Rush doubted if it hid a sword of the finest Toledo steel. He smiled in anticipation of the humiliation to come for the fool who had ordered him to be interrogated and tortured and thought him dead.

But the day dragged on wearily. First the king refused to recognize the authority of the court to try him, then he refused to plead. After more exchanges, he refused to plead again. It was tiresome and repetitive and the pleasure of anticipation soon turned to frustration. It had taken Parliament far too long to bring the man to trial and now that it had, a day of verbal jousting had achieved next to nothing. Apart from some interventions from the spectators, there had been precious little entertainment and the obstinate little man on trial had shown not a sign of remorse or fear. It was most disappointing. If he would not defend himself, of course he would lose his head. For all the deference of the court, the solemn legal argument and the insistence on proper procedure, that was what would happen. The disappointment was that he did not seem to care.

When the court was adjourned Rush left his seat, made his

way past the halberdiers and through the enormous crowds outside the hall, and walked briskly to the carriage waiting for him nearby in Axe Yard. All London was in a fever about the most dramatic event in its history and he had been bored. There had been no fear, no pain, no humiliation. He ordered the coachman to take him straight home. He would not come again the next day. The judges' decision would be announced soon enough.

He had to wait just two days to learn the inevitable verdict and another two to hear that the king's execution would take place in Whitehall on the thirtieth day of January. He laughed out loud when he read that the king's request to justify his actions to the court had come too late and had been dismissed by the judges. Sentence had been passed and the prisoner was no longer permitted to speak. It was typical of the man. He would not speak when asked to do so and would speak when told he could not. A foolish, arrogant man who deserved what was coming to him.

On the appointed day, Rush arrived early in Whitehall in order to secure a place at the front of what was bound to be a large crowd. The trial had been dull but the punishment would surely make up for it. Tobias Rush had cheated death, and now the man who had ordered it, the King of England, was on the way to his own.

During the morning the crowd grew until it entirely filled the space on three sides of the scaffold which had been erected outside the Banqueting Hall. The scaffold was draped in black and guarded by a row of pikemen who kept the crowd well back from it. Some who had come to watch stood on boxes for a better view; a few had actually arrived on horseback. The windows of the hall and the parapet on its roof were crammed with onlookers, as were the windows of every house with a view of the scaffold. While they waited, men and women hopped up and down and blew on their hands against the cold. 'A bitter day in more ways than one, sir,' said a round little man standing beside Rush. When there was no reply, he tried again. 'A bitter day for England, don't you agree, sir?'

Rush turned his head towards his neighbour and peered down at him. 'I think not, sir. A man found guilty in a court of law must pay the penalty for his crimes.'

'Surely, sir, he should not have been tried in such a court. He is the king.'

'That, sir, is exactly the opinion that has brought him to this end,' replied Rush, turning his back on the little man. He was spared further irritation by the arrival on the scaffold of the executioner and his assistant, both hooded and heavily disguised.

When the king, in cloak, doublet and white cap, stepped through one of the tall windows of the Banqueting Hall on to the scaffold, the crowd came to life. There were cheers and groans and cries of 'Long Live the King'. The little man beside Rush jumped up and down, holding out his hands as if trying to reach the king. 'Do not permit this, sire,' he cried. 'It must not happen.'

The king stood and faced the crowd, scanning the faces he could make out at the front. At the moment the king's gaze alighted on him, Rush doffed his hat and inclined his head. The king's change of expression was so fleeting that not another man in the crowd would have noticed it. Rush did. It might have been recognition, it might have been disbelief, it might have been horror. But it was there.

After trying in vain to address the crowd, the king spoke for a few minutes to his attendants on the scaffold. When he removed his cloak and doublet before putting the cloak back on, the crowd went silent. He handed the badge he wore to an attendant and knelt down with his neck on the block. For a few moments his lips moved in prayer and he looked up to the sky. Then he extended his arms and the axe fell. The crowd groaned. The executioner held up the severed head and the crowd groaned again. Men wept openly. Women and children screamed. Tobias Rush suppressed a smile. He made his way through the crowd, out of Whitehall and walked home.

That evening, having enjoyed a bottle of his very best Spanish wine, Rush sat in front of the fire in his living room. The year had begun well. The king was dead. Hill was enjoying the hospitality of the Gibbes brothers, while his sister was living in fear for her daughters and her brother. And his wealth grew by the day. In the spring he would pay another visit to Romsey. Then he would travel to Barbados. It was time he inspected his investments in both places.

CHAPTER 10

The notches were mounting up and still there had been no news. Every morning Thomas woke hoping that he would hear something and by every evening he was disappointed. He had not even seen Patrick again.

He was at the ledgers when John Gibbes arrived at the hut and growled at him. 'We need a new place to shit, Hill. Get a shovel and follow me.'

Thomas followed him to a place a few yards from the stinking hole that served as their privy. A shallow trench running from the hole down to a gully in the woods allowed the rain to wash away the contents. In the dry season buckets of water were occasionally tipped in to help the stuff on its way.

'Dig it there and run a new trench to meet the other one over there.' Gibbes pointed to the spot. 'Make it run downhill or we'll be covered in shit. And so will you. Now get on with it.'

Thomas set about digging. He doubted if the brutes would notice if they were covered in shit but he would make the hole about three feet deep, with the trench dropping by another foot. He reckoned it would take him all morning. He had no idea why they had suddenly decided a new privy was needed. The old one still served. It was probably just another bit of spite at his expense.

At midday he stood back and examined his work. It looked serviceable but to be sure, he threw a bucket of water into the hole and watched it wiggle its way down the new trench. Satisfied, he returned wearily to his hut to wash and eat. Heavy digging on an empty stomach had made him ravenous.

He had barely finished a bowl of broth made from chicken bones when both Gibbes came thundering up the path. 'Hill, get off your arse and go down to the market. We need meat and bread. Tell them we'll pay next week.' There was ample meat and bread in the kitchen store but there was no point in arguing. Down the hill he would go and back he would trudge with bread and meat. Privies, pork, perspiration and pain today, Thomas, and not a scrap of pleasure. Another day in hell but no complaining. Off you go and get it done. Survive and hope.

An hour later, two bulging sacks slung over his shoulders, Thomas started for home. His eyes stinging from the sweat of his brow, his hands blistered from digging and his feet aching, he decided first to sit on the little beach for a while. It was deserted but, to his surprise, the water was not. 'Patrick,' he called, 'is that you?'

'Good day, Thomas. I thought I'd have a quick bath before the market.' Patrick emerged from the water, shook himself like a dog, and strode up the beach. He wore only a torn pair of old breeches which barely reached his knees. 'Are you bathing today?' he asked. Thomas did not reply. He was lost in thought, trying to remember who Patrick reminded him of. It must have been a figure in a painting or an illustration in a book but he could not place it. Patrick tried again. 'Thomas, are you well?'

'What? Oh, quite well, thank you. What did you say?'

'I asked if you were going to bathe today.'

'No, Patrick, I think not. It's been a tiring day.'

'Then let's sit a while.' When they had settled under the palm tree, Patrick said, 'I have spoken to Adam Lyte about you and he has promised to give the matter thought. He would like to help but he is conscious of his position in the Assembly. He is not a man to rush into decisions.'

'I shall keep hoping.'

'Good. Never lose hope. And how are the lovely brutes? I hear that the turkey and shoat dinner was not a complete success.'

Thomas shrugged. 'They're repulsive, Patrick. Repulsive, filthy, brutal and many other things. The dinner was excellent but the conversation less so.'

'If you say so,' laughed Patrick. 'How did a country as civilized as England manage to turn out those two brutes?'

'England civilized? With the king imprisoned, cousin killing cousin and innocent booksellers sent here on trumped-up charges and without trial? While England burns, I daresay there are parts of Africa more civilized.'

'Perhaps there are. Perhaps there are places where all laws are just, no one breaks them, everyone is equal, healthy and prosperous and there are no arguments ever. Not here, though.'

They were silent for a while, until Thomas asked suddenly, 'Did you know that in England Parliament was so frightened of witchcraft that it appointed a man named Hopkins to search out witches? A man to find witches, for the love of God. Sixteen and a half centuries after the birth of Christ and we're looking for witches. They find an old widow who lives on charity and can't defend herself and do you know how they prove she's a witch? If she makes a mistake reciting the Lord's Prayer or if she has some kind of mark on her — the Devil's Mark, they call it — or if she doesn't drown when they tie her up and throw her in the river, she must be a witch. So they hang her or burn her. It defies belief.'

'And if she does drown? Are they murderers?'

'I think they are but the law says otherwise. It's hardly the justice of a civilized society. Based on superstition and benefiting no one.'

'And yet you want to return there.'

'Only because my family are there. I'd want to go anywhere they were, however uncivilized.'

'How old are your nieces now?'

'Polly is ten and Lucy eight. I miss them beyond words and I think of them every day. It's summer in England. They should be playing in the meadow, paddling in the stream, collecting flowers, but they could be anywhere. They have only a little money and Margaret might have been forced to leave the house and move away.'

'You'll see them again, my friend, civilized society or not. Never doubt it. Now, I've got another book for you and a pair of tallow candles. They're not very big but you'll get some light from them.'

'Thank you, Patrick. What's the book?'

'It's a book of poems by a Lady Mary Wroth. Do you know her?'

'I do. I once suggested to a dear friend that she follow Lady

Wroth's example and write poetry.' Thomas took the small leather-bound volume from Patrick and examined it. 'Thank you, I'll return it next week if I survive.'

'You'll survive, Thomas. You have a survivor's look about you.'

'How does a survivor look?'

'He has something to go home to. Most haven't. It shows in the eyes.'

'I hope you're right. Thank you for Lady Wroth. She'll make a change from Henry More.'

'Thomas, your sacks look heavy. Can I help you up the hill with them?'

'Thank you.'

The climb was easier as much for Patrick's company as for his pony carrying Thomas's sacks. 'I envy your knowledge, Thomas,' remarked Patrick as they walked.

Thomas laughed. 'I fear it is very slight.'

'My mother speaks of an elder of her village who was never short of wise advice for anyone who cared to listen. He liked to explain the importance of knowledge. In the forest it was everything. What to eat and what to leave alone, how to tell where you were, what were the signs of danger. The means of survival. Opinions were dangerous unless they were based on knowledge.'

'He sounds very like an ancient Greek philosopher named Socrates. Have you heard of him?'

'I don't think so.'

'He was a strange man but he prized knowledge above all else. He said it came from rational thought and could be supported in argument. Mere opinion could not. Could your village elder have read his works, do you think?'

'An interesting idea,' laughed Patrick, 'though unlikely.'

When they reached the path to the brutes' house Patrick asked if they should take the sacks in. 'Better not,' replied Thomas. 'If the brutes see you they might kill both of us and eat your pony.'

'Very well. Keep hoping, Thomas. I will speak to Mr Lyte again.'

'Thank you. Go well, Patrick.'

Thomas took the sacks straight to the kitchen. The chance meeting with Patrick had cheered him but he was weary and sat down to catch his breath. Before long, however, and unable still to remember the subject of the painting, he thought he would give the new privy a quick try before the brutes appeared.

He was about to do so when they did. 'Go and fill in the old privy before we shove you down it,' snarled John Gibbes. Thomas picked up the shovel. And then he remembered. It was Odysseus, after yet another narrow escape. The illustration was in a children's edition of Homer's *Odyssey*. It used to make him laugh. Shipwrecked, starving, naked, far from home, yet managing against everything the capricious gods could throw at him to look happy and heroic. He'd better not tell Patrick; he might think the heat had boiled what was left of Thomas's brain.

Thomas carried on doing as he was bidden, cooking when required, keeping the ledgers neatly and accurately, taking the abuse, giving them no excuse for the whip. Not that they needed an excuse; the terrible thing might appear at any moment. And the evening he saw them coming up the path towards the hut, he thought that moment had come. A bottle in one hand and his whip in the other, Samuel looked murderous.

John, close behind and also carrying a bottle, pushed past his brother, grabbed Thomas by his neck and hissed at him through black fangs. 'We're going out, Hill, and we don't want to see you when we get back. If we do, you'll taste this again. Stay here and keep out of our way. Is that clear?'

Again, Thomas nodded. Gibbes reached out and smashed the bottle he was holding against the hut. He held it a few inches from Thomas's eyes. 'And you'll get this if we so much as hear you fart.'

Relieved at having escaped the whip or worse, Thomas watched them swagger back to the house. He had no idea what they were planning to do but being seen or heard when they returned would probably not be a good idea. He would stay in his hut and use his last stump of candle to read Lady Wroth until he fell asleep.

When he woke, it was pitch dark. At first he thought the rain beating on the roof had woken him. The Atlantic winds often brought rain at night. He lay still, listening to the storm and hoping not too much of it would find its way inside the hut. When the storm passed, the air had cleared and the tiny frogs resumed their singing. They were always noisier after rain.

He was on the edge of sleep again when he heard a scream. There was no mistaking it. It was a scream of terror and it had come from the house. It must have been a scream that had penetrated the storm and first woken him. Reminding himself that the brutes would be less than pleased to see him, he lay on the narrow cot and tried not to listen.

He wondered hopefully if they might be killing each other — delicious thought — but the scream had been that of a woman, high-pitched and agonized. No matter, he would ignore it. And then it came again. Louder this time, even more anguished and full of rage. But it was a different scream. There were two women.

Taking care to be completely silent, Thomas pulled open his door and slipped, barefoot, out into the darkness. He was in very little danger of being heard as he approached the house. The brutes would be too drunk to notice anything. But in case one of them came outside, he stayed well away from the door and worked his way round to the other side where he knew there was a hole in the wall big enough to look through without fear of being seen.

He peered through the hole. Inside, a naked woman lay on the floor on her stomach, her arms outstretched above her head and her hands tied at the wrists. Her back and buttocks were lashed and bleeding and she was motionless. Bent over the barrel was another woman. Her hands were also tied at the wrist and while John Gibbes held her down by the neck, his brother was thrusting at her from behind. With each thrust Samuel grunted and the woman screamed but her screams were becoming whimpers. Thomas could not see her face but he could see blood on the floor and he could see the evil in Gibbes's eyes. He stepped back quickly. So this was why they wanted him out of the way. They had gone down to one of the Speightstown inns, offered these women enough money to lure them back to the house, tied them up, worked themselves up into a drunken frenzy and then viciously whipped and raped them.

Thomas retreated quietly to the edge of the trees and tried to think clearly. There was no point in attempting to intervene. He had no weapon — he would have to risk going into the kitchen to reach the kitchen knives, and the brutes' pistols, even if he could get to them, might be unloaded. Half-crazed with lust and drink, they would swat him aside like a fly. And it might go all the worse for the wretched women. The brutes might even kill them. And him. The sensible thing would be to creep back to his cell and pretend nothing had happened. In fact, that was the only thing to do. The women were tavern whores and would have to fend for themselves.

But when at last the whimpering and grunting stopped, Thomas was still in the trees. And when he heard snoring, he crept forward and peered through the hole. There were four bodies on the floor. The two women lay face down, naked and bleeding, their hands still tied at the wrists, the ropes looped round the legs of one of the beds. They did not move and they made no sound. The brothers lay on their backs, naked from the waist down, mouths open, snoring loudly. Empty bottles were scattered about and John Gibbes still held the whip in his hand, as if he might be about to jump up and use it.

Thomas sneaked round to the front of the house and stood silently at the open door. Neither of the women had moved. He waited a while to make sure the Gibbes were beyond hearing, then went quietly in.

The first woman lay with her feet towards the door. She had passed out but was breathing. He knelt at her head and gently stroked her cheek. It was what his mother used to do to wake him when he was a child. When the woman opened her eyes he thought she was going to scream again, but the stroking had worked, she understood his signal to be quiet and lay still while he untied the rope around her wrists. Then, satisfied that she was calm, he woke the second woman in the same way. He collected their clothes from where they lay on the floor and motioned to them to follow him outside. One stumbled and nearly fell, the other held her and, still naked, they managed to get to the trees where Thomas had hidden earlier. He whispered to them to stay there and slipped off to fetch water from the well.

He returned to find them recovering. Tough women these tavern whores, he thought. I suppose they have to be. They drank a little from the bucket and used the rest to wash the blood off each other's backs. When they were dressed, they stood up and for the first time he could see their faces. With their auburn hair, green eyes and snub noses, they were very alike although one was a good deal older than the other. With a shock, he realized that they were mother and daughter.

There was nothing more he could do for them. They would have to find their own way back to their tavern. When he pointed to the path, they nodded and the younger one touched his face and smiled. Then they turned and left. Neither had spoken but they were alive. Had the Gibbes woken in the morning to find them there, they might not have been. Tavern whores or not, they were human — certainly more human than the brutes — and they had been beaten and raped. Thank God he'd been able to help. At least now they had a chance.

Thomas sat in his hut, able to think only of the woman lying bleeding on the floor while her daughter was being raped. Sometimes, to his horror, their faces turned into the faces of Polly and Lucy and twice he had to go outside to vomit. He knew the women would not even think of reporting the Gibbes to a magistrate. They were whores, and whores could expect nothing. In the morning, though, the brutes would find them gone and he would have to face their fury. There was no more sleep for Thomas that night.

*

The next morning, he kept out of sight and hoped that the brutes had been so drunk that they remembered nothing. Around noon, however, he was working on the ledgers when he heard them lumbering up the path, arguing loudly about who did or did not tie the women up properly. Fingers firmly crossed, he went outside to meet them.

Samuel, even more brutal, revolting and evil-looking than ever, glared at him. His voice rasped in his throat. 'Well, Hill. Did you do as you were told? Or did you go poking your snotty nose into our business?'

'I slept well, thank you, sir, despite the rain. It's extraordinary how much noise the frogs make after a storm, isn't it? And they're very small, you know.'

John's mind was barely functioning, even by his own miserable standards. 'Frogs? Storm? What the devil are you talking about, you little runt? Did you see or hear anything? That's what I want to know. Intruders running off?'

'Intruders? No, sir, no intruders. Nothing at all in fact. Just the frogs.'

'Fuck the frogs, Hill, and fuck you. If I find you're lying, you'll wish you were dead.' John shoved Thomas aside and went into the hut. 'What the devil's this?' he bellowed, holding up the precious copy of Lady Wroth's poems, which Thomas had carelessly left on the bed.

'It's a book of poetry.'

John's eyes narrowed suspiciously. 'And where did you get it, Hill? Stole it, did you?'

'No. It was lent to me by someone at the market. I shall return it when I next go.'

'No you won't. It's going to the privy. It'll be more use there.

And get a bigger book next time. This one won't last long.' And off they lumbered. No more Lady Wroth, and he'd have to explain why to Patrick, who might not care to lend him any more books if they were to end their days wiping the brutes' backsides.

CHAPTER 11

On the day that news of the king's execution arrived in Barbados, there were nearly thirty rows of notches on the table and Thomas had added more adjectives to his list, including lewd, inhuman and grotesque. He had been in his island prison for the best part of a year. So far he had resisted the urge to run. Runaways lived their lives out in the forest. They did not get home. For that, he needed help.

He had not seen Patrick in the market for weeks and he had given up hope of Adam Lyte offering to help. Each time he looked at himself in the inkwell, he saw a hollower, rougher, more haggard face. His thin hair and straggly beard were streaked with grey and his eyes were red and sore. The manual work and meagre diet had removed every ounce of fat from his body so that his ribs stuck out. If Polly and Lucy could see him, he doubted they would recognize him.

He had woken, as always, at dawn, splashed his face with water from the well, pulled on his only shirt and prepared to brave another day in hell. To his surprise a messenger had arrived and was tethering his horse. The messenger strode up to the house, knocked on the door and waited. He knocked again, this time more loudly. Knowing better than to interfere, Thomas stood in the shadows and watched. Eventually, the door was opened by a bleary-eyed Samuel Gibbes.

'Good morning, Mr Gibbes,' said the messenger politely. 'I come from Colonel Drax.'

'And what does Drax want at this hour?' grunted Samuel, rubbing his eyes.

'A boat from Plymouth arrived yesterday evening, sir. It carried copies of an announcement made by Parliament. The king has been executed. Colonel Drax has called a meeting of land-owners in the Mermaid Inn at midday today.'

'What for? If the fairy's dead, a meeting won't bring him back.'

'I know,' said John, who had joined his brother at the door, 'it's a banquet. A banquet to drink to the fairy's death. Excellent. Tell Drax we'll be there and we'll be thirsty.' Duty done, the messenger left.

'Best give Hill the news, eh, brother?' asked John, with a foul leer. 'It'd be cruel not to.'

'Come on, then.' And off they lumbered up the path. Thomas made a quick retreat through the woods to his hut and came out to meet them.

'Hill, we've got news for you,' shouted John as they approached. 'We're going out and you're coming with us.'

'Don't you want to know where we're going, Hill?' demanded Samuel. Thomas held his tongue. 'Well, I'll tell you. We're going to Oistins. There's to be a meeting. Your precious king is dead.' The Gibbes laughed. 'We thought you'd like to be there.'

Thomas found himself oddly unmoved by the news. The regicide was an act of barbarism, to be sure, but in Oxford he had found the king an odd little man with his pointed beard, stammer and limp; not a man one could warm to. The king he might have been, but it was difficult to mourn for him and change brings opportunity. Clutching at straws, Thomas? he asked himself. Well, why not? There's little else to clutch at.

The Mermaid Inn, which Thomas had passed when he was led away by Samuel Gibbes on the day he arrived, had just a single storey built of stone and timber, and stood beside a popular brothel. After six weeks at sea, Thomas had taken in very little. Led by the black brute, he had ridden past the brothel, past the Mermaid, past a row of mean hovels and could barely remember any of them.

Today, he noticed everything. The inn was overflowing with customers and some had spilled outside on to the road. A continuous supply of strong drink was being sloshed into jugs and mugs by the innkeeper and carried precariously by his serving girls, who flounced about promising themselves to anyone with a guinea to spend.

It's an ill wind, thought Thomas, as they approached. The innkeeper was doing well. He tethered their ponies and followed the Gibbes to the inn. When they disappeared inside, he waited at the edge of the crowd and gazed at the harbour. Was the place where he had first set foot on the island the very setting for a daring dash to freedom? Dash to where? To the forest, where he would be hunted down and returned to the brutes for punishment? To a ship whose captain would like as not hand him straight back to the brutes? No, Thomas, no. There must be another way.

He noticed Charles Carrington and Adam Lyte and worked his way around the crowd in the hope of overhearing what they had to say. These two were as likely as any to talk sense at such a time. Neither of them noticed him among the drinkers.

'What do you make of this dreadful news?' asked Adam.

'No more than you, I daresay. Perhaps we shall learn more from Drax.'

'Let's hope so. And that this isn't the match that lights the powder. Hotheads and extremists will shout and scream and we shall sorely need wise heads in the Assembly.'

'That we shall,' agreed Charles, and, looking around, 'Modyford and Middleton are here. Ah, here's Drax.'

Colonel James Drax marched purposefully towards the inn. Over six feet tall, slim, dark of hair and eye, clean-shaven but for a small pointed beard and elegantly turned out in blue cloak and broad-brimmed hat, Drax was a man of notable presence. The crowd grew silent as he approached and made way for him to enter the inn. But he preferred to remain outside, declined the offer of drink and spoke loudly enough for all to hear. Most of those inside came out, including four disgruntled dice players, not at all happy at having their game interrupted; all talk ceased and every head turned towards him. Thomas stayed where he was and listened.

'Gentlemen,' began Drax, 'I thank you all for coming. I know you would rather be about your business but the news from England is so grave that the members of the Assembly have asked me to call a meeting of our leading landowners to prevent rumour and falsehood growing and festering among us.'

There were murmurs of assent. When he was sure that he had the full attention of his audience, Drax continued. As accomplished speakers and actors do, he spoke without undue emphasis and at a level that forced his audience to remain quiet and listen carefully.

'Let me begin with the facts. On the twenty-first day of January, King Charles was brought to trial in Westminster Hall before sixty-seven judges, on charges of high treason and high misdemeanours. The king declined to recognize the authority of the court to try him but on the twenty-seventh of January he was unanimously found guilty of the charges and at just after two o'clock on the thirtieth of January, outside the Banqueting Hall at Whitehall, he was executed by a single stroke of the axe.' Drax paused to let the facts sink in.

'As you know, I have supported the cause of Parliament during the war in England but have put the peace and prosperity of Barbados before my political views.' At this, there were a few 'Hear, hear's. He went on, 'Nor do I choose to comment today on the legality or otherwise of the king's execution. What I want to say is this. Now is not the time for hasty words or actions. Let us continue to observe the agreement to remain neutral which we all made four years ago. Let us put our families and our fortunes first and await developments in England.' That's all very fine if you have a family and fortune on this island, thought Thomas, but what if you're an unjustly indentured wretch who has nothing?

Charles and Adam joined in the applause with relief. 'Well,' said Adam quietly, 'that's a blessing. I thought he might come out in favour of Parliament and advise us to do the same. Can we trust him?'

'I think so. Perhaps he thinks Parliament would stop us trading with the Dutch. With seven hundred acres and two hundred slaves, he stands to lose more than any of us. He's taking a commercial view.'

'He might also fear a Royalist backlash. The Walrond brothers are forever threatening to raise a militia. This may force their hands. That would be dangerous for him.'

'For us all, I daresay.'

The reaction of the crowd was mixed. 'God save the king.'

'Has England a king any more?'

'Of course she has. Charles Stuart is his father's heir so now he's our king.'

'The king is dead. Long live the king.'

'Where is he then? In London or skulking in France with his mother?'

'The army's running the country now. The army and Parliament.'

'Where's our governor? What does he think?'

'Yes, where's Bell?'

'We need slaves and we need servants. Who's going to get them for us?'

'And we need the Dutch. Will Parliament stop us trading with them?'

Just as it looked as if the meeting was about to break up in disorder, Charles Carrington stepped forward. Like Drax, he commanded the attention of the crowd with ease. He raised his arms for silence and spoke slowly. 'Gentlemen, unlike my friend Colonel Drax, I have supported the king throughout the war in England. But I agree entirely with what Colonel Drax has said. Are we now to jeopardize our trade by reacting to today's news without proper thought? It may be that Barbados will, at some future time, have to face the prospect of declaring for one side or the other, but let us not take that awful step until we have to. Today we do not have to. Let there be no talk of militias. Let our heads rule our hearts and let us return to our estates in peace.'

Carrington had barely finished when the door of the inn was flung open and a shrill voice, a voice filled with righteous passion and indignation, called for silence. All conversation ceased and all heads turned to the door. A diminutive figure emerged and pushed his way through the crowd, brandishing a Bible and calling for silence in God's name. He wore the black of an Anglican church-man, stood little more than five feet tall and sported on his bare head only a very few strands of wispy hair. His face was not one that had spent much time in the Caribbean sun and he squinted at the crowd through watery blue eyes.

'I am the Reverend Simeon Strange,' he began, 'and I am here on the Lord's work.' This did not go down well with a congregation of tough sugar planters who had heard enough speeches and were suffering from heat and thirst. Thomas was astonished. The little reverend was either a brave man or a very foolish one.

'Put him on a table where we can see him.'

'Not now, parson, we're thirsty.'

'Strange by name, strange by nature.'

'No sermons, Reverend. It's only Wednesday.'

'Don't go on about church on the sabbath again, Strange. Cane grows on the sabbath and it needs cutting.'

But Strange would not be silenced. 'It is not politics we should be discussing, brothers, not trade, not sugar, not money. IT IS THE WILL OF GOD.' He bellowed this so loudly that even those who were drifting away stopped and took notice. 'The will of God, I say. Each day I observe drunkenness, debauchery, blasphemy and ungodly acts of every description. Almighty God looks down upon you in his wisdom and despairs. When the day of reckoning comes, his punishment will be severe. Two years ago, in his mercy, he sent the yellow fever to you as a warning but his warning went unheeded. And now to this depraved island have come representatives of the most heinous and bestial men and women in Christendom – PAGANS, ADULTERERS AND FORNICATORS. I speak not of the Irish Catholics and their whores nor of the Quakers, though they are accursed enough. No, brothers, I speak of a new pestilence that has now inflicted itself upon us – that vile, base disease that calls itself THE RANTERS.' Again, Simeon Strange delivered the words with a force that belied his meagre stature. 'The Ranters, I say. Libertines and heretics every one of them, and now come among us with their profane and immoral habits. These animals CAVORT NAKED IN THE FIELDS.'

Strange had been straining so hard for volume and effect that the veins in his neck and face looked as if they might burst. He had to pause for breath or run the risk of a seizure. Those of his audience who were still listening took the opportunity to ask if anyone had any idea what he was talking about. Ranters? What were they? After a few deep breaths, Strange was off again.

'Listen carefully to me, brothers. If we do not act at once to rid Barbados of this dangerous depravity, we shall all be doomed to everlasting purgatory and neither sugar nor slaves will save us. Let us banish these abominable Ranters from our shores for ever.'

And with that, the Reverend Simeon Strange, having given his all, collapsed, eyes bulging and breath labouring, on to his scrawny backside. Thomas feared that the little man might have suffered a fit and was about to offer his help when the reverend appeared to recover his composure.

'Where might one find these Ranters, Mr Strange?' came a voice from the back.

'They are given to practising their foul rituals on the ridge above Oistins. There you will find them and I urge you to do so without delay.' Fortunately, perhaps, Strange was so full of the Holy Spirit and so short-sighted that he did not notice the winks and grins exchanged at this information and appeared heartened by the reply.

'You may be sure that we shall, Reverend, and we thank you warmly for alerting us to this matter.'

While the little reverend had been giving his all, Charles Carrington had been talking quietly with Adam Lyte and James Drax. When the Gibbes emerged from the inn, Adam was shoved roughly aside by Samuel, who planted his face inches from Charles's. 'It doesn't matter a barrel of shit how many Royalists come here,' he spat, poking a filth-encrusted finger into Charles's face. 'You can stuff the Assembly full of them, but we're the ones who've grown the sugar and made the money and we'll say who's to govern us. And it won't be any Royalist fairies.'

Charles peered down his aristocratic nose. His voice was icy. 'In that case, it's as well that Colonel Walrond is talking of raising a militia. We may well need it to keep the peace.'

'That isn't what you said earlier, Carrington. You said we didn't want militias. Didn't you, Carrington?'

'I did, sir. And what of it?'

'What of it? What of it?' Yellow spittle flew from Gibbes's mouth and his eyes bulged in fury. 'You're a liar, Carrington, a fairy, a coward and a liar. That's what of it.'

Charles was unmoved. 'I was provoked, sir. When confronted by a rabid dog I find it best to take action to avoid its teeth and claws. That does not, I think, make me a coward.' Thomas, keeping well out of the way, swallowed a laugh.

It took a moment for the insult to sink into Samuel's addled brain but when it did, he lurched at Carrington as if to throttle him. Carrington stepped nimbly aside, stuck out a leg, helped Gibbes on his way with a shove in the small of his back and watched him crash into a table before collapsing, winded, in a heap on the ground.

John Gibbes, too drunk to have joined in their exchange, now seemed to sense that he ought to do something. He pulled a knife from inside his shirt and lunged at Samuel's tormentor, aiming at his stomach. This time, Charles took just half a step aside, extended his arm and thrust his knuckles into Gibbes's throat. With no more than a strangled gurgle, Gibbes joined his brother in the dust. 'My apologies, gentlemen. I deplore unnecessary violence but there seemed no better way.' Quite unruffled, Charles turned back to Drax. 'The cause of Parliament is not helped by such people, James. Would you be kind enough to have them removed and sent on their way?'

Drax laughed. 'It will be my pleasure. And remind me not to face you if it comes to a battle.' And with the help of two large planters, Drax marched the Gibbes away. Thomas, still trying not to laugh, followed at a sensible distance. He had much enjoyed the exchange and the sight of both brutes so easily dealt with by Charles Carrington, but it would be wiser not to show it.

Drax spoke quietly but the menace was unmistakable. 'Take my advice, you two. Keep your foul mouths shut and don't come back here again. Neither Barbados nor Parliament needs your kind.' One doubled up in agony and the other clutching his throat, neither Gibbes managed a reply. Enraged and humiliated, they staggered off to find their ponies.

Neither of them spoke on the journey back to the estate. When they arrived, John stuck his face into Thomas's and hissed, 'Not a word, Hill, or you'll be sorry.'

Samuel fished into a pocket and brought out a wad of pamphlets. 'Take the ponies to the field, Hill, then put those in the privy.' Thomas took the pamphlets and did as he was told but not before slipping one under his shirt.

In the safety of his hut, Thomas retrieved the pamphlet and brushed the dust off it. It was headed 'Vivat Rex' and had been written by none other than Colonel Humphrey Walrond. It consisted of a diatribe against Parliament and all who supported its cause, demanded that the Assembly make a formal declaration in favour of the king and urged loyal Royalists to raise militias to defend their property against the likes of James Drax and Thomas Middleton, two well-known Parliamentarians. Now that he has learned that the king has been executed, thought Thomas, God knows what Walrond will have to say. Barbados could become a very dangerous place and not just for me. He stuffed the pamphlet under his mattress with the list of adjectives.

When a visitor arrived at the house a week later, Thomas, labouring in the kitchen, heard him shout a greeting and went out to see who it was. The Gibbes did not receive many visitors and he was surprised to find that this one was Adam Lyte. He wondered what could be important enough to bring him to the brutes' house so soon after their humiliation at the Mermaid Inn.

'Good morning, Mr Lyte. An unexpected pleasure.'

'Good morning, Thomas. Is Samuel Gibbes here?'

'He and his brother are at the boiling house. There's been an accident. Mr Sprot is there.' Thomas assumed that Adam would prefer not to encounter Robert Sprot at work. Sprot's dubious skills were much in demand and he charged more or less what he liked for them. On one of his frequent visits he had proudly explained that he had worked out his tariff on sound business principles — the price for removal of an arm or leg doubled during the cane-cutting season and mangled fingers caught in a mill could be detached at a shilling each or four for three shillings; thumbs carried a surcharge of two shillings.

His speciality, however, and one of which he was mightily proud, was the removal of impediments from within the body. The Sprot Saviour, designed by himself, was a very long, very thin pair of forceps which could, with a little manipulation, be inserted into the bladder, gall bladder or incised scrotum. He claimed it at least doubled the chances of success. Whether success was measured by the number of stones removed or the number of patients who survived the treatment, he did not say, but in the market Thomas had heard it said that a wise man would endure any pain, however vicious, rather than seek relief from Mr Sprot. Luckily for Mr Sprot there were many unwise men in Barbados and he had built a busy and lucrative practice, being careful always to request payment in advance.

Screams of agony were coming from the direction of the boiling house. 'Perhaps I'll sit here until he's finished,' Adam said thoughtfully.

'Very well, sir,' replied Thomas. 'I can offer you some plantain juice. Or a glass of wine?'

'Thank you, Thomas. A cup of plantain juice would be welcome.'

With the drink Thomas brought a copy of the pamphlet which the brutes had brought back from Oistins. 'I thought you might not have seen it, Mr Lyte. I would much appreciate your opinion.'

Adam read the pamphlet carefully and then read it again. 'Oddly, I have not seen this before. I take it you've read it, Thomas?'

'I have, sir. It's serious, is it not?'

'It is. With the king dead, the last thing we need is Humphrey Walrond stirring up trouble. It's exactly what Charles Carrington warned against and I agree with him.'

'The Walronds are a Devon family, aren't they?'

'They are. Colonel Walrond retired here to his estate at Fontabelle two years ago. He and his brother Edward are power-ful men with powerful connections. When did this appear?'

'I saw it on the day of the meeting in the Mermaid.'

'Well, Thomas, in my opinion this is a dangerous thing. It will inflame feelings and revive old enmities. And what is your opinion?'

'I have learned to my cost that all such pamphlets cause trouble, sir, and if I were governor I would not permit them to be published. I was foolish enough to put my name to one a great deal less threatening and this is where it got me. I thought my views were harmless but I was wrong. They were used to cause me great harm. And this pamphlet is something quite different. It's deliberately inflammatory. Colonel Walrond wants confrontation. But why? Is it really his beliefs driving him or an eye to profit? Is it loyalty he wants or land?'

'Thomas, wouldn't banning free expression of opinion be a restriction on a man's liberty? Isn't that why Cromwell and his like are so hated?'

'Is society itself not a restriction on a man's liberty, sir? Is it any more than a set of laws restricting individual freedom in the interests of the community? Different societies may have different laws and a man may have different rights and duties conferred by them, but aren't they all restrictions on individual liberty? What restrictions are justified and what are not must be a matter of opinion. And, in my opinion, a man should be restricted from expressing a view of a nature or in a manner likely to cause confrontation and perhaps bloodshed. That is why I would ban it.'

'What do you mean by "in a manner", Thomas?'

'I mean, for example, by means of a pamphlet like this — circulated widely and likely to be read by or to men disposed to take one extreme position or another. The same view expressed privately, mind you, may be quite acceptable.'

'So it's the manner of its expressing rather than the view itself that you would restrict?'

'In this case, it is both.'

Adam changed the subject. 'Thomas, Patrick has told me how you came to be indentured. He asked me to help, but in these delicate times and as a member of the Assembly I did not feel that I could. The laws of indenture are clear. Whatever the reason for a man's indenture, voluntary or forced, once here he must serve his term. It would be wrong of me to argue otherwise.' He paused. 'However, the behaviour of the Gibbes at the meeting made me think again and Patrick has suggested another approach, which is why I am here.' The screaming had stopped. 'Perhaps I'll walk up to the boiling house. You might care to accompany me.'

At the boiling house, a smiling Sprot, his bald head protected as ever from the Caribbean sun by a large straw hat, was packing away the tools of his trade in a battered leather bag. He saw the two men approaching.

'Mr Lyte, good morning,' he greeted Adam warmly, ignoring Thomas altogether.

'Good morning, Sprot. I see you've been busy.' The brown stains on Sprot's jacket were mixed with bright red ones — a sure sign of recent custom.

'Just a routine affair, Mr Lyte. The man got his arm caught in the mill. I thought I might save it and just took the hand off first, but then I observed that the forearm would have to go sooner or later, so off it came. I have only charged for one cut, mind you; I don't care to profit unduly from another's misfortune, as you gentlemen will vouch. I'm quick with the saw though I say so myself and the man is alive. They have taken him to the slave quarters. He'll have a sore head when he wakes up with all the rum he swallowed but he should survive. I don't know what they'll do with him, though. One-armed slaves aren't worth much.' Thomas dreaded to think what the brutes would do with the poor wretch.

Sprot went on cheerily, 'Good day, Mr Lyte. You know where I am if you need me. Free men, indentured or slaves, and I'll make you a good price. And between ourselves, I have just received a consignment of a most efficacious new medicine from London, should you have need of it. It comes highly recommended by the distinguished apothecary Nathaniel Foot, as a sovereign cure for various ills including headaches, vomiting, gout and fatigue. And I am able to offer it to my best customers at only a guinea a bottle. Be sure to look lively, though, my stock won't last long.' Sprot lowered his voice. 'And, if I may, a word of warning. There are charlatans about. I have come across one who claims that a cup of the late king's blood, taken with seawater, will cure the scrofula.

And so it may, but the late king's body must have held a deal of blood and been shipped here with great speed. The man has sold gallons of it.'

Sprot had just left when the Gibbes returned from the slave quarters. 'Well, well. Look who it is, brother. Good day, Mr Lyte. Come to tell us the king has come back to life or for another turkey and shoat? I thought it was your turn.'

'Good day, gentlemen,' replied Lyte politely. 'No, not looking for dinner today and my apologies for not giving you notice of my visit. There's something I want to ask you both.'

'How to make his slaves work harder, eh, Samuel? The whip, Lyte, the whip, and as often as you please. Or where to find the choicest women? No, no, he must know that by now. I have it. Where to find a good husband for his sister? That'll be it. Well, look no further, sir. John Gibbes is your man.'

Thomas saw the disgust in Adam Lyte's face and the effort it took him to ignore the remark. 'No, gentlemen, nothing like that. As a matter of fact, I wanted a word about Thomas here.'

'Hill? What have you done, you puffed-up little prick? Something serious, I hope. It's time you had a thrashing.'

'No, no. He's done nothing wrong, as far as I know,' said Lyte quickly. 'I just wanted to make you a business proposition.'

At this all four bloodshot Gibbes eyes narrowed in suspicion. 'About the windmill?'

'No, something else.'

'Best go down to the house then. Back to your hut, Hill, while we listen to what Mr Lyte has to say.'

Thomas waited until they had rounded the bend in the path down to the house, and then quietly followed them. Whatever Patrick had suggested, he wanted to know. He crept through the woods and round to his listening tree in time to see them sit down at the battered oak table on which the turkey and shoat had been served. 'Right then, Lyte. What is it?' Samuel asked impatiently. 'We've wasted too much time already today.'

'Mary and I would like to buy Hill from you. We'll use him to keep our records and accounts.'

Again the Gibbes's eyes narrowed. 'And how much had you thought of paying?' asked John Gibbes.

'Thirty guineas we thought would be a fair price.'

It was a huge price. Two or three new men could be bought for that. The Gibbes hesitated, but not for long. 'Thirty guineas? I don't think we'd sell him for that, would we, brother? He's a good cook as you know yourself, and well trained. Stronger than he looks, too. Works hard with a little persuasion. He'd not be easy to replace. Thirty guineas wouldn't do it, sir, not by a distance.'

'I could go to thirty-five.'

'Nor thirty-five.'

'Forty is my final offer.'

The brothers exchanged glances as if they suspected a trick. 'We'll discuss the matter and send word. Good day.'

Adam rose and left. Thomas, behind his tree, kept listening. So that was Patrick's idea. A perfectly legal transaction. Simple. And forty guineas. Surely the brutes would be tempted.

The brutes were smug. 'That'll teach the devious scab not to come here and try lording it over us. Forty guineas? It's a good price.'

'Let's go and find Hill and tell him the news.'

'Ha. Excellent idea, brother. We'll take a drink first.'

By the time they came thundering up the path Thomas was back in his hut. 'Hill, come here,' shouted Samuel. 'Lyte has an offer for us. We thought you'd like to know what it is.' I do know, thought Thomas. What I want to know is whether you're going to accept it. 'The pompous toad wants to buy you. Any idea why?'

'None.'

'Want to know how much he was willing to pay for you? Forty guineas, that's how much.' Thomas pretended to be astonished, which at the price he was. 'We thought you'd be pleased to know how much he thinks you're worth. We're pleased too.' John had a sly look about him. Thomas held his breath and waited. John jabbed a finger into Thomas's chest. 'But we're not going to sell you. The Lytes can go and hang themselves. You're not up to much but we're not letting you go to be pampered by a pair of prissy king-lovers.' The Gibbes laughed. 'Now get back to the books. The magistrate would be only too pleased to order a public flogging if we asked for one. And don't even think of running off. We'll make sure you can't run anywhere again if you do. Even Lyte won't want a gelded cripple.'

CHAPTER 12

On a bright spring morning the black coach emblazoned with the monogram TR drew up at the coaching inn outside Romsey. The brutal winter was at last over and the roads were passable again. As before, Rush left his coachman to take care of stabling for the horses and accommodation for himself and walked into the town. The market square, bustling and busy when he had last been there, was deserted. There were no drinkers outside the Romsey Arms and no children in the streets. It was as if the whole miserable place was still in mourning for the late king.

Business and the weather had detained Rush in London longer than he would have liked and he was impatient to see the woman again. Reports from his agent had been satisfactory enough but he wanted to check for himself that all was well. He strode up Love Lane to the bookshop.

There were no customers inside so Rush went straight in. Margaret Taylor was sitting behind her desk, writing in a ledger.

From upstairs he could hear children's voices. She looked up from her writing and stared at him. 'I know where my brother is and I want proof that he is alive.'

Rush hid his surprise. 'I am aware that you have disobeyed me and made certain enquiries.' The lie came easily.

'You are not the only one with contacts, Master Rush. I know that a ship named the *Dolphin* left Southampton for Barbados in March last year and I know that my brother was among the prisoners on board. I want proof that he arrived safely and is alive.'

'And if you don't get it?'

'My daughters and I will disappear.'

'You will be found.'

'That is a chance we will take. I want to know that my brother is alive.'

Rush thought for a moment. 'I can tell you that he arrived safely at his destination and that I have received no message to suggest that he is not perfectly well.'

'I want proof.'

'How do you suggest that I provide such proof?'

'You will send him a message asking him to write a single word on a sheet of paper to be delivered to me. He will know what the word is and I will know if you attempt another forgery.'

'Why should I agree to this?'

'I have explained the consequences if you do not. We will no longer be pawns in your vicious game.'

'Your brother will suffer if you try to escape me.'

'If he is alive, he is already suffering. If not . . .' Margaret let the thought hang in the air.

'It has taken you some time to arrive at this.'

'But now I have.'

Again Rush thought before replying. The woman had surprised him. 'It will take time.'

'It is a six-week voyage to Barbados. I will wait until the first day of August. If I do not have the letter by then, I shall assume that my brother is dead.'

'I could kill you and your daughters now and tell him you are alive and well.'

'You could, but then your pleasure would be the less. Only he would be under your control and then only by virtue of a lie. If he knew we were dead he would have no care for himself. Equally, I could kill you with the loaded pistol on my lap but then I would not know that my brother is alive.' Margaret raised the pistol just enough for Rush to see the barrel. 'Since you first came here it has never left my side. You might wish to tell your incompetent spy that.'

'It will be done.'

Rush did not return directly to the coaching inn but made his way around the old abbey to Church Lane. He turned into a narrow alley running off the lane and stopped outside a rough cottage. He tried the handle, found the door unlocked, and went in. It was a mean hovel, with just a few sticks of furniture. In one corner blankets had been thrown down to make a bed. On the bed lay the man he had come to see and astride him a fat woman with lank red hair. He slid the blade from his cane and thrust it into the woman's neck. Blood spurted from the wound and she fell sideways. A second thrust into her eye and she was dead. Rush glared at the naked man. 'I do not pay you to spend your time whoring. The woman has been asking questions.' The terrified man tried to rise. Rush kicked him back. 'I have no use for incompetent fools.' He whipped the blade across the man's throat, watched him die and left.

CHAPTER 13

Weeks of nothing, then, suddenly, a torrent of newsbooks, pamphlets and reports from the Assembly. Despite James Drax's plea for calm, the king's execution had given the Walrond brothers the opportunity they had been waiting for and they were not going to miss it.

On the little Speightstown beach, Patrick was bursting with news. 'While the Assembly was sitting Walrond led a troop of his militia to the Assembly House and demanded to be heard. Bell went out to meet him and found him mounted, dressed as a Royalist officer and backed by a hundred infantrymen armed with muskets and pikes. When Bell demanded to know why he was at the head of an armed force, Walrond replied that he had a thousand men at his disposal and would not hesitate to use them. He insisted that Bell immediately step down as governor and that he be appointed as his successor.'

'Then what happened?'

'Bell asked for time to consult the Assembly. When he

appeared again word had spread and a large crowd had gathered. Bell announced that he had resigned and that Humphrey Walrond had been appointed as his successor. And that was that.'

'And what did Adam Lyte make of it?'

'He is furious. He does not trust Walrond.'

'So Barbados has a new governor,' said Thomas. 'What will that mean, I wonder?'

'For you it might mean a way home,' replied Patrick. 'Walrond has hinted at an early release for men indentured to any landowner who refuses to swear an oath of loyalty to the king.'

'Has he now? Awkward for the brutes.'

'Let's hope the brutes refuse to swear. Then you can go home and they can go to hell.'

'An excellent outcome.'

'However, Mr Lyte thinks that we'll soon see Cromwell's ships in Carlisle Bay. And there's another thing. Word has come that Lord Willoughby has Charles Stuart's commission to take over as governor and plans to sail soon.'

'Lord Willoughby of Parham?' asked Thomas in surprise. 'Once Parliamentarian admiral, now loyal servant of the man who would be king?'

'The same. Mr Carrington and he have known each other since they were boys.'

'So we shall be visited by both sides.'

'Probably, and one way or another there's going to be trouble. On some estates there's been singing in the fields. The news of master fighting master has spread fast. There is unrest among the slaves and some are waiting for the right time to strike. I have warned the Lytes.'

Thomas sighed. 'Bell and Walrond, Cromwell and Willoughby, master and slave, king and Parliament. I fear you're right, my friend.'

'The Lytes are talking of building defences around the estate and laying in stocks of food and weapons.'

'I don't suppose they'd like me to come and help?' asked Thomas. 'I'm sure the brutes wouldn't mind.'

'And how are the brutes, Thomas? Charming as ever?'

'Bestial. One night they had two whores at the house — mother and daughter. They nearly killed them.'

'For the love of God, Thomas, don't provoke them. They could easily kill you.'

'Adam Lyte told me it was your idea for him to offer to buy me.'

'It was, and I'm sorry it took so long. He was not willing to speak to a magistrate about you, and that seemed to be the end of the matter. I only thought of buying you later. How much did he offer?'

'Forty guineas.'

Patrick whistled. 'A lot. Will they take it?'

'You haven't heard?'

'No.'

'They won't sell me.'

'Damnation. Why not?'

'They should have been tempted. There must be a reason why they refused. They treat me like an animal but they haven't whipped me to death and they won't take forty guineas for me. They could get three more animals for that.'

'It is odd, I agree. And what now? For the love of God, please do nothing foolish.'

'For the love of my family, I shall try to survive. What else is there?'

The following week Thomas was in his hut, working diligently at his ledger ,when he heard what sounded like a troop of horses arriving at the house. Knowing the Gibbes were out in the fields, he put down his quill and went to attend to the visitors. There were six of them, all mounted and armed. Their leader was a young man, once handsome perhaps, but now raddled by rum and debauchery. He spoke with authority. 'I am here on the command of the governor, Colonel Humphrey Walrond, to speak to Samuel and John Gibbes. They are, I believe, the owners of this estate?'

'They are, sir. And I am Thomas Hill, an unjustly indentured man, their bookkeeper and sometime cook.'

'So, Hill, where are the gentlemen in question?'

'In the fields, sir, as is their custom. Shall you wait for their return?'

'I will send word for them. Corporal, Hill will show you where they are. Bring them back at once. We shall wait here.'

The corporal dismounted and followed Thomas back up the path, past his hut and down to the fields. They crossed one field of newly cut cane. Thomas thought the brutes would be in the next field, where he could hear the slaves singing. As they approached, he saw them, whips in hand, overseeing the cutting. It occurred to him how easily one can tell from the set of a man's head and shoulders what sort of a man he is. Aggression, diffidence, stupidity, intelligence — all are evident without sight of a face. Samuel saw them first. He summoned his brother and they strode towards Thomas and the corporal.

'What are you doing here, Hill? Why aren't you at the books? Or have you come to do some real work for a change?'

'I have brought this gentleman with a message. His captain was most insistent.'

'Captain, what captain?'

The corporal looked nervous but held his ground. 'Our captain, representing the governor, is here to speak to you on an urgent matter. He asks you to return with me immediately.'

'Does he now? And what might he want to speak about?'

'That I am not at liberty to disclose but the captain has the authority of the governor to insist on your presence.'

'The governor, eh? Do you hear that, brother, Walrond himself commands us. Then we'd best oblige the man, eh? We can tell him what we think of Royalist fairies.'

The captain and his mounted troop were waiting for them. 'Are you Samuel and John Gibbes?'

'We are. And what of it? Who are you and why are you on our land?'

'I am here with the authority of Colonel Humphrey Walrond, governor of Barbados, to instruct you to present yourselves at the Assembly House at midday tomorrow.'

'You look familiar. Where have we seen your ugly face before?'

'That I cannot say. The Assembly House tomorrow at midday, if you please.'

'And why would we want to do that?'

'The Assembly has passed a law requiring all landowners to swear an oath of allegiance to Charles Stuart, our rightful king. Your oaths must be sworn and witnessed tomorrow.'

The brothers looked at each other and grinned. Oaths of loyalty? To a Stuart? Who did they think they were dealing with?

The Gibbes did not swear loyalty to anyone unless they were very well paid for it. 'All landowners, you say?' asked John shrewdly.

'That is correct. All landowners.'

'So has Drax sworn? Or Middleton?'

'I cannot say.'

'And what if we refuse?'

'If you do not attend tomorrow I shall return with a troop to remove you from this property and sequestrate it and all your possessions in the name of the Assembly.'

'You'd have to fight us first.'

'So be it.'

Again the brothers exchanged glances. 'We'll think about it. Now get off our land before we throw you off.'

Having delivered his message, the captain left.

Thomas returned to his hut to continue working on the books. After the excitement, he found that columns of figures did not hold his attention and after his fifth mistake he closed the ledger and lay down on the narrow bed. Walrond had tried to force the Assembly to agree to an oath of loyalty before, only to find himself thrown out on his ear. Now he had resorted to force and was the governor. That would certainly divide the island and might well lead to war. Royalist sympathizers far outnumbered them but would the Parliamentarians allow themselves to be trampled on? Surely they would fight back. And what would the brutes do? They hated Royalists but they were not fond of Parliamentarians either. Perhaps his time had come. Perhaps he would soon be on a ship headed for England. Perhaps he would see Margaret and the girls before summer in England was over. Perhaps he would find out tomorrow.

Before the Gibbes set off the next morning they told him to

prepare dinner. He knew what they wanted and he knew how to cook it. Meat and plenty of it, bread and wine, with a handful of squashed cockroaches to flavour the meat. And this time, far from dreading their return, he would be waiting impatiently. He would not allow his hopes to get too high but there was a glimmer.

He was in the kitchen when he heard them return and knew at once that the glimmer had died. They were laughing. Condemned men do not laugh. Merciful heaven, what trick had fate played now? He went to find out.

'There you are, Hill. We're hungry and thirsty. Bring our food and bring wine. We're celebrating.'

Celebrating? God's wounds, celebrating what? He soon found out. When he brought the wine through, they were bellowing with laughter and congratulating themselves on their success.

'Ha. So much for that, eh, brother? Nothing more than a piss in the wind.'

'Swear a poxy oath or give up our estate and be shipped back to England? What did they think we'd do? Who gives a whore's arse for an oath? I'll swear all they want if it suits me. And today it does. To hell with them all.'

'And there'll be chances for us, Samuel. We'll get more land if we keep an eye open. There's bound to be some for sale to honest Royalists like us.'

'Bound to be, brother. A toast to Charles Stuart. He has our loyal allegiance.'

'And another to Cromwell. So does he.'

Thomas came back with a loaf of bread and a plate of mutton. 'What about you, Hill? Would you like to drink a loyal toast to anyone? How about the king of France? Or the Pope?'

Thomas was crushed. Of course the brutes would swear an

oath if it saved their own skins. And it wouldn't matter a farthing who or what they swore it to. He should have known. If everyone else either swore or was banished, Walrond would have succeeded and there would be little hope of an early escape. He trudged miserably back to his hut.

CHAPTER 14

There was another row of notches on the table. No word from Adam Lyte, no banishment for the Gibbes, no prospect of escape. The Gibbes had left for Holetown, telling Thomas they would want dinner when they returned. God forbid that they had gone looking for women again.

Thomas sat under the listening tree and thought of home. But no sooner had he conjured a picture of Polly and Lucy chasing butterflies in the meadow than the picture turned into a poor-house, the girls in rags and Margaret begging on the street. Again and again he tried, summoning to mind every happy image he could think of. The shop, his books, the trout stream just outside the village, the girls again.

But the images swiftly melted away, to be replaced by something foul. He thought of trying to sleep but the punishment if he failed to wake before the brutes returned would be painful. He thought of walking but it was the hottest time of the day. And he thought, as he did every day, of escape. Escape, a voyage home, justice. Patrick had urged him to be patient but there had still been no word. He must do something.

Alone at night, Thomas had even wondered if he could find it in himself to kill the brutes. Now he wondered again. There were opportunities enough when they lay snoring on the floor; the heaviest kitchen knife would do the deed. But having never wielded a knife, nor for that matter any weapon, in anger, he had not resolved the important question of how to use it to best effect and he doubted he ever would. A stab to the heart might require more strength than he had at his disposal, he was unsure of the correct technique for throat cutting and a thrust into the eye or the mouth would surely be beyond him. To test this, he picked up a stick, closed his eyes and imagined pushing it into a sleeping brute's face. No, he could not do it. A strike with a shovel or an axe might work. But what if he made a mistake? What if the first victim's shriek woke the second? What then for Thomas Hill? An unimaginable end, that was what. He knew, deep down wherever his soul was — didn't Aristotle say it was the stomach? Or was it the heart? Or the bowel? — that he would never do it.

He sat despondently for a while and was about to abandon his musing to inspect the dinner, when a new thought occurred. The knife and the axe might not be the only ways to achieve the desired result. What about something more subtle, something not involving brute force and bloodshed? What about poison? Could he possibly poison them? If he could, the chances of detection would be far less. Poison — the weapon of the Medicis. Why not the weapon of indentured booksellers? Now what could he put in their food that they would not notice but would be sure to kill them? Rotten meat? Urine? No, they might not work, and, however drunk, they would notice. What then? Unfortunately,

Barbados was remarkably free of poisonous insects and plants. Only the ugly centipede could inflict a really nasty sting and he was not going to go looking for one of those.

And then it came to him. The manchineel tree. On the way back from a trip to the market, they had sheltered from a rainstorm under a stand of trees by the beach at the bottom of the hill. When he had moved a little away from the Gibbes he had noticed their evil grins. He had stood under a pretty tree with green fruit dangling from its low branches and waited for the rain to stop. A few drops fell through the branches, touched the fruit and landed on his arm. To the Gibbes's delight, the arm immediately blistered painfully and they gleefully suggested he might eat the manchineel fruit as a way of ending his indenture.

The more he thought about it, the more promising the little manchineel tree seemed. He considered the problems of how to collect the apples and how to administer them. He assessed his chances of success and the consequences of failure. Poisoning was, after all, poisoning; it would be murder. Murder of two thoroughly deserving brutes but murder nevertheless. If found guilty of murder or attempted murder, he would surely hang. Whatever the provocation, taking a life in cold blood could not be condoned.

And how could Thomas Hill, hater of violence, justify an act of killing? Could he call it self-defence — if he did not kill them, sooner or later they would kill him? A little contrived but it would have to do. It might take some time, but he could just about persuade himself that eventually the brutes would kill him.

He examined his resolve. It seemed, at that moment, firm. He jumped up and went back into the kitchen to find a sack and some linen cloths.

It was about half a mile to the coast. If Thomas was going to fetch poisonous apples and prepare them in good time for the return of the brutes, he had better leave at once. Fortified by a small tot of dark rum, he set off down the hill to the beach where manchineels grew. He took with him the cloths to protect his hands from the fruit and the sack to put them in. He reckoned on collecting twenty apples. Thomas took this route when he went to the market. Keeping an eye out as he went, he walked as quickly as he dared without running the risk of drawing attention to himself. He met no one on the way down the hill and, much relieved, was soon on the beach. A narrow crescent of white sand running into the clear waters of the Caribbean Sea, it might well have been an inspiration to a passing artist or poet but Thomas had eyes only for the line of trees that separated sand from soil all along its length.

He checked that there was no one about and then, using the cloths as gloves, carefully picked apples from the lower branches, some of which almost touched the ground, and put them in his sack. Twenty apples became thirty, just in case of accidents. He might lose some in the preparation and there was no point in risking the poison being too weak. '*Fortuna fortes fovet*,' he said out loud to himself. Fortune favours the brave.

With a sackful of poisonous manchineel apples over his shoulder, the return journey was the riskiest part of the operation. Again he walked quickly but the sack and the hill made for hard going and he did not keep as careful a lookout as he had on the way down.

Not far from the turning to the Gibbes's house, a rider appeared from around a bend in the path a little higher up the hill. His pony was picking its way down slowly and had Thomas seen him a few seconds earlier, he might have been able to slip off the path into the trees. But it was too late. The figure had waved a greeting. It was Patrick.

'Good day, Thomas. Been to the market? That sack looks heavy.'

Thomas was flustered. So near home, he had let his guard drop and he could be in trouble. He did not want to have to explain a sack of manchineel apples. Knowing he was a hopeless liar, he almost panicked. He would have liked to ask Patrick if Adam Lyte had said anything about him yet, but he did not want to be drawn into a discussion. 'Yes, yes, Patrick. The brutes have gone off and left me to cook their dinner. I had to walk down to the market and buy meat. Hot work, and I'm thirsty. Kitchen'll be hot too, I shouldn't wonder.' The words tumbled out and Patrick looked quizzical.

'Not like them to run out of meat. I'm on my way to the market now. Busy down there, is it?'

'Er, no. Not too busy. But not quiet. Middling, really.'

'Ah, well. I must be on my way. Take care, Thomas.' Patrick lightly flicked his reins and rode on.

'Thank you, Patrick. Go well.' Thomas watched him ride cautiously on until he was out of sight. He knew that he would not be able to carry off another deception. He turned and ran.

There was a chance that the brutes had returned earlier than expected but when he arrived, thank the Lord, all was well. He went straight into the kitchen, where the mutton and chickens were gently roasting, and put the sack in the corner. He would catch his breath before tackling the manchineel pudding. He sat down.

It was a mistake. Up to that point, the need for action had

driven him on but having thought of the plan and carried out half of it, it suddenly seemed absurd. All manner of things could go wrong. The apples might not be poisonous enough at this time of year, the brutes might not eat the pudding, they might notice the guilt on his face and force a confession from him or they might be feeling charitable and invite him to share their dinner. The last was unlikely but, at such times, the mind can play odd tricks. And he had no idea what to do when they were dead. What would he do with the bodies? Bury them? Burn them? Leave them to be found and hope no one guessed the truth? Two dead Gibbes would be something the magistrate could not overlook and he would never stand up to examination.

There was also the matter of conscience. Was Thomas Hill, law-abiding, peace-loving Thomas Hill, doting brother and uncle, educated bookseller and philosopher, really capable of committing murder? Not one of his friends or family would have said so. There was provocation enough, to be sure, but provocation did not alter the fact that it would be murder. Thomas Hill would be a murderer. Hopefully, only he would know that but he would nevertheless be a different Thomas Hill. He would be obliged to spend whatever remained of his life knowing he had killed two human beings in cold blood. Could he live in peace with himself if he carried out the rest of the plan? Had he the courage to do it? Would he take the risk? He rose from his chair, walked over to the corner and picked up the sack of apples. The Gibbes were brutes, not human beings. The answer was a ringing yes.

He placed ten apples on one of the cloths, folded the corners over and started mashing them up with a heavy stone, tentatively at first but soon more forcefully. It was not long before the apples were pulp and their juice was leaking through the cloth. Taking care, he squeezed the juice into a bowl and threw the pulp away. When he had repeated this process three times he had a bowl full of greenish manchineel juice, which he put to one side.

Then he prepared the sweet pudding, mixing up cream, sugar and almonds, and set it beside the bowl of juice. Reckoning that the potency of the juice would be greater if left to itself for as long as possible, he would mix them together just before serving. Having covered both bowls with the cloths, he dealt with the roasting meat and sat down again to wait for the return of his victims. His mind and conscience were clear and his determination unwavering. He would poison the brutes, find their money and buy a passage home. He might never discover who had arranged his arrest and indenture but Margaret and the girls were waiting for him, they would be overjoyed to see him and they would all go back to their peaceful life in Romsey.

When the brutes returned, they were in an evil mood. 'Get off your arse and bring the dinner, Hill, and be quick about it. And bring wine. We're parched.'

Thomas had been watching for their return and was ready. He brought the mutton and chickens out immediately and went back for bread and wine. By the time he had fetched these, the brutes were tearing at the meat with their hands and stuffing lumps into their mouths. He left the wine and bread on the table and returned to the kitchen. The moment was approaching.

After a few minutes, he took a quick look to check that the brutes were fully occupied. Happy that they were, he picked up the bowl of juice and poured it into the pudding. He mixed it in thoroughly with a long wooden spoon and stood back to await their summons. Light-headed at the prospect of being rid of the brutes and astonished that anticipation of an act for which he might hang should afford such pleasure, he barely resisted the temptation to take the pudding through straight away. But that might be fatal. So unpredictable were they that the brutes were quite capable of throwing it out of the door and demanding that he bring another one when they called for it but not before. So he waited quietly and hoped that the little green apples of the manchineel tree would live up to their reputation.

How long he waited he was not sure, but when he heard the first rumbling snore he shot out of the kitchen to where the brutes were eating. Or rather, where they had been eating. Samuel and John Gibbes, stuffed with meat and wine, their mouths open and their heads resting on the table, had passed out. There was nothing new in this but, at the instant of taking in the scene, Thomas went cold. Even if he woke them, they would only take out their fury on him and then go back to sleep.

His daring plan, his careful execution — both come to nothing. His hopes for escape dashed. He cursed himself for not bringing the pudding in sooner, he cursed the brutes for passing out and he cursed his cruel luck. He stopped short of cursing the Almighty but, after months in purgatory, only just short. For a minute or two he stood unthinking outside the hovel; then, seeking the meagre comfort of his hut, he left them to snore.

The hut was as hot and airless as ever. He lay on his cot and stared at the ceiling. He saw Margaret and the girls in a foul hovel, dressed in rags, pleading for him to come home. He saw the brutes lying dead in a field, their bloated corpses being eaten by dogs. And he saw himself, emaciated, starving, a beggar on the streets of Bridgetown. He had missed his chance and might never have another. He was a clod.

When at last coherent thought returned, he began to consider his options. Spooning the pudding into the brutes' mouths and hoping they swallowed enough to kill them was tempting but unlikely to work. He would have to move their heads to get at their mouths and they might wake up. Keeping it for another day might be more sensible. He could hide it in his hut and produce it the next time they demanded sweet almond pudding. But they might find it, or the manchineel juice might have lost its poison by then. Perhaps he should acknowledge defeat and throw it away; another plan might occur. Or perhaps he should give up the struggle and eat the pudding himself. That would solve all his problems. He had never been quite sure whether men who took their own lives were brave or cowardly and now, alone and desperate, he did not care. He lay there and pondered.

The decision, when he made it, seemed obvious. He got up, left the hut and ran back to the house. A dead dog lying by the side of the path barely registered. Dead dogs were common enough. Thomas passed by without a glance. The brutes were still snoring. He walked briskly round them and into the kitchen.

On the upturned barrel where he had left it was the empty bowl which had contained the juice. But it was alone. There was no pudding bowl. Hadn't he put it on the barrel after mixing in the juice? Or had he taken it through when he heard the snoring? Irritated at not remembering, he went and looked, but there was no sign of it. What had he done with it? Surely he hadn't taken it outside?

Retracing his steps, he walked back towards the hut. He looked about as he went, as if hoping that the bowl would suddenly and miraculously appear. He simply could not remember what he had done with it. The dead dog was there, although the scavengers would be at work on it soon, and there in the grass beside it – though he had to look closely to be sure – was the upturned pudding bowl. He kicked it over and saw that not a spoonful of pudding remained. He stood and stared at the bowl and the dog. Then it hit him and he laughed. A dog which could take a bowl from the barrel, carry it away and eat its contents must have been a clever dog. Clever but dead.

Well, now I know the poison works, he thought, at least on dogs. I may not be clever but I am alive. I am not a murderer and I have not done away with myself. Just as well. If I had poisoned them, I'd probably have run straight down to the magistrate and confessed.

Now he would have justice and he would see his family again. He heard Montaigne laughing quietly. 'There are some defeats, Thomas, more triumphant than victories.' His old friend was back. He would survive.

CHAPTER 15

The number of rows of notches had grown to seventy-five when the Gibbes again announced that they would both be out all morning. At least one of them normally stayed at home to ensure a full day's labour from the slaves. Either they had important business or they would return drunk and arguing, as usual.

'Stay here and do the ledgers,' ordered Samuel before they left. 'Don't waste time sweeping the kitchen, and don't go to sleep. We'll want to see them later.'

As Thomas was sure neither could read or write, this was a surprise, unless it was merely a question of seeing whether or not the pages were covered in words and figures and whether the ink was dry. They had never done such a thing before.

When the brutes had gone Thomas set to work. He could write down almost anything he liked in the ledgers and they would not know the difference, but partly from his sense of order and partly for the sake of knowledge he had always tried to be accurate.

In one ledger he kept a record of all purchases on the left-hand page and of all sales on the right-hand page. As the sugar cane was continually sewn and harvested there were always entries on both sides of the ledger. At the end of the month he added up both columns and arrived at a balance. It was like keeping the bookshop accounts except that the figures were larger. Very much larger.

Even allowing for their being only as accurate as the inform-ation he was given, which was probably not very accurate, the surpluses were growing each month. Labour as good as free, other costs minimal, prices rising, and demand for sugar insatiable. Most planters would be doing just as well and as long as they continued to have access to European markets through the Dutch merchants he could see no reason why things should change. Brutes or not, they knew about sugar.

In the other ledger he wrote down all slave births, deaths and purchases. These were given to him, like the accounts, on grubby scraps of paper which he deciphered as best he could. The ages of purchased slaves were estimated, but other than that the ledger contained a complete record of each man, woman and child. As he never conversed with the slaves, to Thomas they were no more than names on a page. That was a blessing. It would have been much more painful if the names had had faces.

If only the cane would grow as well in good Hampshire soil, he could take some home and spend the rest of his life happily count-ing his fortune and reading his books. Perhaps he'd try it, although he did have to get home first.

The Gibbes returned mid-afternoon. He heard their horses and listened for a summons. When it came it was loud and urgent.

'Hill, Hill, where are you, you idle piss-licker? Come here and bring the books.'

The brutes were nothing if not cunning. 'We've done some figuring,' said John, 'and we know exactly how much money we've got in gold and coin. Now you're going to tell us how much the book says we should have. Then we'll know if you've been doing your job right, won't we?'

Thomas wondered why they had never done this before; he guessed it was because they had to find someone else to count the stuff for them and they did not like moving it. He did not know where they kept it — much safer not to — but he doubted they would have entrusted it to anyone else. They must have taken it into town and stood by while a merchant or a magistrate counted it. He opened the ledger to check the last entry and read out the figure to them.

'Close enough, Hill, and lucky for you it is. Our partner has arrived from England and he'll be paying us a visit tomorrow. He won't be happy if there's so much as a shilling missing.' The partner. So Thomas was about to find out what manner of man had taken the brutes as partners. That should be interesting.

The Gibbes did not go out to the fields the next morning as they normally did but stayed in their hovel, awaiting the arrival of their partner. This partner must be important, thought Thomas, to keep them away from their cane and their slaves. No food had been ordered so the partner could not be staying long. Just a quick look at his investment, no doubt.

He was at work on the slave records when he heard the carriage arrive. He slipped out of the hut and down the path towards the hovel. Thinking it wiser not to be seen, he hid in the trees and watched.

The moment the partner stepped out of the carriage the blood drained from his brain and he went cold. It had never occurred to him. It was impossible. He looked again. Quite impossible. Died under examination, the king had said; he had inspected the body himself and ordered it burned. Over six years ago. But this was no ghost. Even in the heat of Barbados, black shirt, black hat, black cloak. And a silver-topped cane in his hand.

God in heaven, how? How did he escape? How was he still alive? Where had he been hiding? How did Thomas not know?

Impossible, yet there he was. Rush the murderer and traitor had somehow cheated death and survived. And it was he who had arranged it all. Not just Thomas's arrest and deportation but his indenture to the Gibbes with instructions on what to do with him. They had given not a hint of it, even when drunk not the tiniest hint – Rush must have ordered them not to. Doubtless wanted the pleasure himself.

When the Gibbes came out to greet their visitor Thomas waited until they were all seated at the table before returning unsteadily to the hut. He sat on his cot, head in hands. Now it was clear. Just as his arrest for writing an innocuous paper and his deportation without trial had the filthy hand of Tobias Rush all over them, so, of course, did the brutes. He'd probably got them out of some stinking gaol and sent them here to manage his estate, knowing that they would do his bidding and make him money by whatever means he wished. That would explain how the estate and equipment was purchased. And they were just the men to treat Thomas as Rush wanted him treated.

He remembered wondering why the guard on the *Dolphin* had saved him from being strangled by the giant Irishman and he remembered the feeling of being watched. He was being watched. Rush had paid the guards to make sure he stayed alive. He wanted Thomas in the hands of the Gibbes and he wanted him to suffer. And he had succeeded. Just as he had somehow succeeded in returning from the grave.

He heard them coming up the path and got to his feet. Steady now, Thomas, he thought, blind fury won't help. Bide your time. He stood at the door and watched the three of them approaching. A murdering monster with a brute on either side. Both Gibbes carried whips. The murderer was taking no chances.

'So, Thomas Hill, we meet again. Here I am, back from the dead.' The same reedy voice and thin smile.

Thomas said nothing. He looked in disgust at the long nose, the narrow black eyes, the sallow face, the thin body and thin arms.

'Have you nothing to say?'

'My family. If they have been harmed you will burn in hell.'

Rush scoffed. 'I recall your saying that once before. For the moment, however, I am alive and well. As is dear Margaret. Rather than face eviction from a house and bookshop I now own, she lives happily with me, as do her lovely daughters. A comely woman, most accommodating. And such pretty children. I look forward to sampling them before long.'

It was too much. Thomas threw himself at Rush and knocked him to the ground. His hands were round the scrawny throat before either Gibbes could react. Rush's eyes bulged as he struggled to throw Thomas off. But, light as he was, Thomas was not to be thrown off. He knew how to fight and even after two years with the Gibbes he was much stronger than he looked. Had Samuel not picked up a stone and cracked Thomas on the head, Rush would never have got up. Stunned, Thomas rolled off and lay on the ground. When he opened his eyes, his arms and legs were pinned down by the Gibbes, and the black eyes were squinting down at him.

'That was a mistake, Hill. A mistake for which you will pay. Just as you have paid for your work in Oxford. Few people cross Tobias Rush without living to regret it. I have waited more than six years for the pleasure and now I have you, your house and your sister. And soon I shall have your nieces. Both of them. I can hardly wait.' Thomas jerked as if to throw himself again at Rush but the Gibbes held him fast. 'It wasn't difficult to arrange matters. A stupid pamphlet, a word in the right ear, a little money in the right hands and the willing help of my partners, Samuel and John Gibbes. Loyal partners and experienced in such matters. An easy enough task for Tobias Rush. Just as bribing my bovine gaoler in Oxford and finding a suitable substitute to deceive our late king were easy. I knew the fool would see what he expected to see. Few men do otherwise. Had I not been so busy in London, and taking care of matters in Romsey of course, I would have visited you sooner. Never mind. Absence, they say, makes the heart grow fonder. Did you really think you'd seen the last of me?'

'Margaret would kill you before you touched the girls, Rush. As the king's executioner should have and as I shall if you have touched her.' Thomas could barely speak. The words came out in a croak.

'No you won't, Hill. You can forget your family or you can think about how much I'm enjoying myself with them. It matters not to me. You should have accepted my generous offer and come to London. You'd be a wealthy man and living in style, as I am. Instead of which, here you are on this foul island without a hope of escape. Never mind, my partners will take good care of you, won't you, gentlemen?'

'We shall, Tobias, you may be sure of it. Shall we start now?'

'Before you do, I have a small task for Hill. Bring him into the hut.' The Gibbes picked him up and dragged him to the doorway. 'Sit him on the chair.' When Thomas was seated, both arms still gripped by the Gibbes, Rush continued, 'Your sister requires proof that you are alive, Hill. If you do not provide it, she will die and so will you.' Thomas said nothing. 'Write a word on a sheet of paper and give it to me. One word only.'

'What word?'

'She claimed you would know.'

John Gibbes put an arm around Thomas's throat, let go his right arm and pushed the inkpot and box of quills across the table. Thomas picked up a quill, dipped it in the inkpot and wrote a word on a page of one of the ledgers. Rush peered over his shoulder, saw the word and carefully tore the page out. Thomas smiled. His sister was a clever lady. Only her brother would know that the word she expected to see was 'Montaigne'.

'Shall we continue now?' asked Samuel.

'Why not? I have waited long enough.'

Thomas was hauled to his feet, dragged to the old boiling house and tied by his hands to the ring on the wall. The first lash ripped his shirt and his skin. When the second bit into his shoulder, he screamed. Ten lashes later, he was barely conscious. They dragged him to the well and threw a bucket of water over him.

'Excellent,' said Rush, 'just about right. Make him suffer but keep him alive. Dead men don't suffer. Now bring the money. I'll take it and be off.'

Despite the agony, Thomas hauled himself to his knees and lunged at Rush's legs. Rush toppled backwards and Thomas was on top of him again. He screwed his thumbs into Rush's eyes and would have blinded him as the monster had blinded others if the brutes had not grabbed his arms and pulled him off. Rush got unsteadily to his feet.

'Another mistake, Hill,' he spat, 'for which you will pay. Hold him tightly.' The Gibbes strengthened their grips on his arms as Rush pulled the thin blade from his stick. 'You know what this can do, Hill. Struggle and I may miss my target. That would be unfortunate.' Thomas ignored him and strained to free himself.

'Very well, have it your own way.' The point of the blade traced a circle of blood around Thomas's left eye, then travelled slowly down his cheek. For a moment the blade was still. Then Thomas felt it cut a shape into his skin.

'I have left you your eyes in order to do your work,' hissed Rush, 'but if you ever lay your hands on me again you will lose them. Is that clear?' Thomas held his gaze. 'Is that clear, Hill?' Thomas blinked.

'I shall assume that means it is. For now, you are marked with the sign of your owner. Me.'

Rush turned to the Gibbes. 'And if he does it again, you two will pay as well. You'll be back in a stinking gaol and next time I won't be there to get you out. Back with your whore of a mother who's probably still spreading her legs for that wall-eyed gaoler. Now get him out of my sight. I have work to do.' They dragged Thomas to his hut and threw him inside. Unable even to wipe the blood from his face, he lay on the earth floor and passed out.

It was dark when he came to and struggled on to the cot. He knew he had been foolish and that Rush might easily have killed him. His face was caked in blood and one eye had closed. His back was on fire and he craved water. He seethed with hatred and frustration. Tobias Rush. Executed, burned and still alive. Tentatively, he put a finger to his face and traced the line cut in his cheek. It was in the shape of the letter 'R'. Rush had branded him with his initial. God in heaven.

CHAPTER 16

The brutes, the whip, and now Tobias Rush and a face scarred by the monster's sword. Yet if Rush was telling the truth, Margaret and the girls were in more pain and more danger than he was. And he was helpless to do anything about it. He went through the motions of cooking and bookkeeping because he had to but his mind was in Romsey. He cursed Rush with every waking hour. The traitor who had murdered and tortured, had tried to kill him and had cheated death by bribing his executioner. The gloating monster who had bided his time and then exacted cruel revenge by having Thomas indentured to two brutes as evil as he and by forcing his sister and nieces to do his bidding. One day Rush would answer for what he had done. One day.

He was in his hut when he heard a scream. It was like no other he had ever heard. It came from the direction of the boiling house and was followed by another and then another, each one exploding with agony. The screams of slaves with their fingers mangled by the rollers were not uncommon, but even at Newbury when he had watched two armies blasting and hacking each other to pieces Thomas had never heard screams like these. They were filled as much with fury and despair as with pain. He put down the bucket and listened. The screams went on and on, each as terrible as the last. He could not ignore them. He ran down the path and up the slope to the boiling house.

Outside the house a handful of naked slaves stood around a man sitting on the ground. By the time Thomas reached them, the injured man's screams had turned to whimpers. He pushed his way through the circle of onlookers. From shoulder to wrist, the man's left arm was covered in scalding brown sugar which had stuck to his skin like glue. Not knowing what else to do, Thomas knelt beside the man and examined his arm. The sugar had burned through the skin of his upper arm and was sticking to raw flesh. Below his elbow, where the heat had been a little less intense, the skin was torn and blistered. His right hand was streaked with sugar and skin from his arm. The man's eyes closed and he lay down. Not one of the other slaves made any attempt to help him. Thomas looked up to see both Gibbes lumbering up from the cane fields.

'Get back to work, you black bastards, or I'll take the skin from your heathen backs,' yelled Samuel, waving his whip at them. They left the man on the ground and went silently back into the boiling house. Thomas stood up and waited for the brutes to reach him.

'What the devil are you doing here, Hill?' demanded John, panting from the climb.

'I heard screams and came to help,' replied Thomas more calmly than he felt.

The Gibbes ignored him. Samuel nudged the injured slave

with a boot. His eyes opened but there was no life in them. 'Finished,' he said. 'Leave him there. He'll be dead by tonight.'

'That makes us one short for the boiling,' said his brother. 'I'll fetch one from the cutting.'

'I have a better idea. Hill came to help. Let him help. Strip off and take his place, Hill. And mind the sugar. Tobias won't be pleased if we have to pay Sprot to take your arm off.'

Thomas stared at him. They were going to put him in the boiling house, the most dangerous place on the whole estate. They were mad. If Rush wanted Thomas kept alive, this was no way to do it. An accident with one of the copper kettles which held the boiling mixture or a nudge into the furnace and he was dead or crippled, just like the poor wretch on the ground in front of them. What indeed would Rush have to say about that?

'Are you sure that's wise?' he asked Samuel.

'To hell and back with wise, Hill. We're harvesting the cane and we need the mill and the boiling house working. Strip off and get inside. You can stoke the furnace. Make sure it stays hot. Get on with it.'

There was no alternative. Thomas took off his shirt and breeches and stepped gingerly into the boiling house. He was barely inside when he felt as if he had run into a stone wall. His hands went to his face and he staggered backwards. The stench was so thick he could almost touch it and the heat from the furnace and the coppers above it was so fierce that it penetrated his skin and his eyes. Had the Gibbes not been standing guard at the open door, Thomas would have turned and run. No punishment could be worse than this. Both of them held their whips ready to strike at bare flesh and both were grinning.

'You'll soon get used to it, Hill,' taunted John. 'If the slaves can do it, so can you. Stoke the furnace and keep stoking. There's sugar to be made and plenty of it.'

Thomas tried again. This time the heat was a little less intense and he managed to get to the furnace. He watched the man stoking it lift a heap of dried-up canes and wood and fork them into the mouth of the furnace. With a nod to Thomas he handed over the fork and joined the team transferring the boiling sugar into smaller and smaller coppers until the crystallized mixture was tipped into a cooling vat.

As the coppers hung over the furnace, Thomas would be working below them. A splash from a copper and he could easily lose a hand or an arm. The Gibbes watched him fork in three or four loads and then left. The cane was being cut and they would want to make sure it was cut properly. Thomas wiped the sweat from his eyes and bent his back to the forking, one white body among the black ones.

After an hour he had to rest. His back ached and his arms were shaking. He threw down the fork and went outside. The slaves ignored him and carried on with their tasks. Cartloads of cane were being trundled up from the fields for their juice to be extracted in the mill and gallons of the syrupy mixture were being carried across for boiling. If the boiling men stopped to rest, a backlog would soon build up and the Gibbes would want to know why. The slaves preferred to keep working.

The injured man still lay outside the boiling house, silent and unmoving. Thomas drank from the well by the mill and tipped a bucket of water over his head. He offered some to the stricken man, who ignored him. He wondered at the slaves' ability to work for long periods in such a place. Could Dante himself have imagined worse?

Keeping an eye out for Gibbes, Thomas sat with his back to the well and breathed deeply. He had quite forgotten his nakedness. In the boiling house it had seemed natural; in there any scrap of clothing would have been unwelcome and would have come out reeking of sugar. The light breeze which was turning the sails of the windmill cooled his skin and eased the tension in his back and neck.

For a moment he closed his eyes and thought of home. In his mind's eye he was walking by the river with Polly and Lucy. It was a spring day, the oaks were coming into leaf and the girls were picking primroses. He slipped into sleep.

'On your feet, you shitten little worm,' roared a voice.

Thomas's eyes opened in shock. John Gibbes was thundering up the slope, whip in hand. He jumped up and made for the boiling house. He was halfway through the entrance when he felt the sting of the whip on his shoulders. His back arched and he yelped in pain. A second lash drew blood and a third sliced across its mark.

Then it happened. It had not happened when he had thrown himself at Rush — that was the product of blind, unthinking fury. It had not happened when the Gibbes taunted him or when they had threatened to kill him. But now, after long months of lonely misery, it happened. The thing he called 'the ice' — an unshakeable calmness and intensity of purpose. The last time had been in the courtyard of Pembroke College, when a cowardly young captain had goaded him once too often. It was as if his mind had left his body and he was watching himself.

Thomas moved so fast that Gibbes had no time to react. In one movement he turned and launched himself. The whip dropped from Gibbes's hand and he fell on to his back with Thomas on top of him. Thomas was on his feet again in a trice. He planted a foot on the man's throat and bent to speak. 'Enough, Gibbes. Take your evil ways back to your pigsty and take your brother with you.' Before Gibbes could get to his feet, Thomas picked up his clothes and strode off up the path to his hut.

The deed was done and the ice departed as quickly as it had come. By the time Thomas reached the hut, he knew that his Rubicon was behind him. Whatever the consequences, this time he must flee and he must not come back. If he were caught again the Gibbes would flay him to death, Rush or no Rush.

He stopped only long enough to pull on his clothes, then continued on past the brutes' hovel to the road. John Gibbes would go and fetch his brother before following him so he might just have time to get away. At the junction with the road down the hill he did something he had never done before and turned left. Instinctively he thought that the Gibbes would look for him in Speightstown or Holetown. If they came looking in the middle of the island, they would soon find themselves on rough paths through dense undergrowth until they reached the hills. He knew this from Patrick and he knew that almost no one lived there. They would not go into the forest. They would head down to the coast.

He would go to the Lytes and throw himself on their mercy. He had a good idea where their estate was. He knew it bordered the Gibbes's on the north-eastern side and that their house was at the northern tip of the land. Where else was there to go?

Thomas could still run. He had always been fast and at Oxford he had outrun all his friends. He found a rhythm and was soon deep in the forest. The road twisted and turned up the hill, wide enough for a cartload of sugar, until he reached a fork where it separated into two narrower paths. He stopped and tried to work out which path to take. This high up, they had both been cut through forest thick enough to obscure any view. He knew that the Atlantic Ocean was in front of him and the Caribbean behind, but that would be so whichever fork he took. The twisting and turning up the hill made it difficult to know exactly where he was. Either path might turn back down the hill or take him deeper into the forest. He might even have already passed the Lytes' estate. Left fork or right?

While he was deliberating, a troop of monkeys dropped out of a tree and walked slowly up the right path. Abandoning any further pretence at navigation, Thomas followed them. At least the monkeys would know where to find food. He had not eaten all day and his strength was fading. The monkeys were in no hurry and Thomas easily kept up with them, staying far enough back not to frighten them.

Quite soon the forest thinned a little and they came to a line of palm trees. The monkeys made for a tree laden with green coconuts. Thomas picked up a fallen nut and weighed it in his hands. It was heavy with water. He looked about for something with which to break the shell, cursing himself for not thinking to bring a knife with him. With a sharp stone he tried to bore a hole in the nut so that he could drink the water. When that did not work he smashed the stone down on the shell, breaking it open and scattering the monkeys in alarm.

Refreshed by the coconut, he continued up the path. It was not long before he knew that the monkeys had deceived him. The path had been getting narrower and narrower until two men could not have walked along it side by side. Not very clever, Thomas, he said to himself. Chief cryptographer to the king, breaker of the Vigenère cipher, philosopher and now follower of monkeys. No wonder you're lost. He turned back and retraced his steps down the hill.

That deep in the forest there was little sunlight and suddenly there was none at all. The storm that swept in from the Atlantic blackened the sky and shook the trees. Within seconds, rain was falling in torrents and Thomas was soaked. Water was pouring down the path, turning it to mud and making each step treacherous. Trying to shelter was futile, so he just stood to one side and waited for it to pass.

When it did, he set off again very cautiously. He was wet, he was tired, he was heading back where he had come from and if the brutes got their hands on him, he was dead. He did not want to make matters worse by slipping and turning an ankle.

But at a place where the path turned sharply, he did slip. His feet went from under him and he slid on his backside across the bend and into the undergrowth. The bushes slowed him and he came to a halt a few yards off the path. He got to his feet but his left ankle immediately gave way. He lost his footing and was on his backside again, slipping down the hill. Without warning, the ground under him disappeared and he was bouncing down a stony slope. He flailed about with his hands to find something to hold on to, found nothing and kept on going down. By this time he was flat on his back. His head hit a rock and when he finally came to a stop he was unconscious.

Had it not been for the arrival of another storm, Thomas might have lain there unconscious for hours. He came to when rain began to fall on his face. Water gushed down the hill, bringing debris and mud with it, and he was struck by branches and stones. He lay curled up on his side, his hands protecting his head, until the storm passed.

When he tried to stand he found that his ankle had swollen to twice its normal size, he was bruised all over and he could not focus his eyes. He seemed to be at the bottom of a deep gully, its walls rising steeply on either side and with a vertical cliff face in front of him, but that was more sensation than sight. Trying to focus on the slope he had tumbled down, he saw vaguely that it was the least steep of the gully sides and would offer some handholds in the form of rocks and shrubs. Ankle or no ankle, it had been his way in and it would have to be his way out.

It would be foolish to attempt the climb before his vision cleared, so he sat on the sodden ground, rubbed the ankle and waited. He felt all the parts of his body that he could reach to make sure that no bones had been broken. There seemed to be only cuts and bruises, although some were painful.

When at last he could focus his eyes the light was beginning to fade. In Barbados there was very little dusk and it would soon be dark. At the bottom of this gully in the middle of the forest, neither stars nor moon would shed much light. Despite a throbbing ankle and an aching head, he must try to climb out.

Using a tree as a support, he stood up and hobbled to the base of the slope. Very cautiously he started to climb. One step up, grab a rock or a bush and heave himself a foot higher. Repeat the process and repeat it again. It was slow and tiring and after five minutes he had climbed no more than ten feet. When he looked up, it was too dark to see the top of the gully and he knew he was not going to make it. One step down, reach for a handhold and lower himself foot by foot until he was back where he had started. Ten feet up and ten feet down, hurting and exhausted. The tiny frogs began to whistle and clouds of insects rose from the ground. It was going to be a long, uncomfortable night in the gully.

And so it was. When dawn at last broke, there had been rain, insects and pain. Of sleep or food there had been none. Using a fallen branch as a crutch, he struggled to his feet and examined himself. His arms and legs were decorated with a patchwork of bites and bruises, he could not say which part of his body hurt the most and he was ravenous.

And there was, of course, the little matter of the brutes. Even then, having searched in vain in Speightstown and Holetown, they might be climbing the hill after him, whips in hand and thirsting for blood. He had knocked red brute down and humiliated him. He had run away. There would be no mercy. They would kill him and make up some story about his catching a fever. His corpse would be thrown to the dogs. They would laugh as they watched it being torn apart and devoured.

Enough, Thomas. They have not found you yet. Get out of this gully alive and you might yet survive. You must survive. If you do not, neither will Margaret, Polly and Lucy. And be quick about it.

He began the climb again. A step at a time, favouring the swollen ankle and carefully testing each rung of his ladder before trusting his weight to it, he made steady progress to a point about halfway up, where he held on to a sapling and paused for a rest.

But for the birds, the forest was silent. Taking a deep breath, he continued to climb and had almost reached the top when he glanced up and saw a face watching him. He missed his footing and slid down a few feet, scrabbling for a hold with his fingers and luckily coming to rest on the stump of a fallen tree. A shaft of pain shot through his ankle and he cursed. Then he looked up again and laughed. The monkey was still watching. Then it ran off. Probably gone to fetch his friends, thought Thomas.

He started to climb again and took care not to look up until he reached the top. When he did, he lay on his stomach, catching his breath and wishing his ankle would stop throbbing. Eventually he picked up another branch and set off slowly down the path. It was still treacherous and he took great care. Another slip and another gully might well finish him off.

When he came to the palm trees, he split another coconut and ate its flesh. Where the path forked, he turned up the left-hand path, offering a silent prayer to any god who might be listening that it would lead him to the Lytes' estate. He had not gone far, however, when his eyes refused to focus. No amount of blinking or rubbing helped and his legs began to feel heavy. He knew something more than a twisted ankle was wrong and sat down with his back to a tree. His eyes closed and he slid to the ground.

When he came to, he was lying on a blanket. He struggled on to his elbows. He was in a clearing in the forest where a circle of men and women were sitting cross-legged on the ground, eating, drinking and laughing. Every one of them was naked. Thomas sat up, rubbed his eyes and looked again. About twenty of them, chatting happily and not a stitch of clothing between them. Something stirred in his memory. The little parson in the Mermaid. Was it Mange? No, Strange. He had been talking about these people. Ranters, that was it, Ranters. His brain was fuddled and he could not recall if Ranters were dangerous or not.

They were not. When one of them noticed that Thomas was awake, he got to his feet, spread his arms in greeting and spoke in a clear, musical voice. 'Good day, brother. I am Jacob, leader of this family. You will share our food. All are welcome to join the Ranters.'

When Thomas did not move, Jacob tried again. 'Do not be afraid, brother, the ways of the Ranters are peaceful. Come and sit with us.'

Still Thomas did not move, so Jacob walked slowly towards him, arms outstretched, until he could take Thomas's hand, help him to his feet and lead him into the group. Favouring his ankle, Thomas limped behind him. Every Ranter stood and held out a hand to touch the newcomer. Jacob helped him to sit in the shade of an old fig tree and a slim young woman with long black hair gave him a piece of bread and a fruit he did not recognize. He asked for water and was handed a leather flask. The Ranters sat around him, watching him eat and drink.

The water did a little to bring Thomas to his senses. He was still befuddled but gradually it dawned on him that he was not where he should be. He had lost his way, passed out and been found by these Ranters. They had given him food and water and they were friendly enough. He looked about. Roughly equal numbers of men and women, not in the least abashed at their nakedness, and perfectly happy to have a stranger amongst them. He wondered if he should take off his clothes, decided they would tell him if he should and sat quietly.

When Jacob spoke again, the fog was clearing and reason was slowly returning. 'What is your name, brother?' the Ranter asked gently.

'Thomas. Thank you for the food.'

'The Ranters believe that nature's bounty should be shared. We found you in the forest. We have treated your injuries. Where were you going, Thomas?'

'I was running away. Where are we?'

'We are in the hills above Speightstown. Did you come from there?'

'Nearby.'

'Do you work there?' asked another voice.

Thomas glanced up. The face and voice were familiar. Someone he had met in the market, perhaps. 'I do. I am indentured.'

'Indenture is slavery,' said Jacob quietly. 'The Ranters do not condone slavery.'

'All men and women are free,' said the young woman who had given Thomas the bread and fruit. There was a chorus of agreement.

'God is in all of us. Submission to the rule of others is wrong.'

Not feeling up to a discussion on faith and morality, Thomas nodded politely. The Ranters must have sensed his mood because after a while Jacob began to play a flute while the others danced naked around him. Among the dancers was the man who had asked him if he worked in Speightstown and when Thomas looked at him, it came back to him. The little man with thin wispy hair and watery eyes was none other than the Reverend Simeon Strange himself. The parson who had declaimed so mightily against the Ranters had become one of them. Thomas wondered if any of the other dancers were parsons or even members of the Assembly. For all he knew, Walrond or Bell could be among them.

He was in trouble. By now the brutes would be searching for him. If they found him they would flay the skin from his back. He knew he should do something but had no strength for it. He looked at the sky. It would soon be dark. Despite his ankle, he should go.

The music and dancing came to an end and the Ranters gathered up the remains of their food. The young woman who had spoken against submission to the rule of others took Thomas's hand and helped him to his feet. 'I am Catherine,' she told him. 'It is too late for you to leave now, Thomas. You must spend the night with us.' She was right. Better a night with the Ranters than another alone in the forest. Thomas allowed himself to be led by Catherine along a path through the trees to another clearing where a circle of neat shelters made of branches and palm fronds had been erected.

'There is a place for you here, Thomas,' said Catherine, indicating one of the shelters. Thomas ducked inside. It was dry and cool and more fronds had been laid down to make a floor. Even if it rained he would be quite comfortable for the night. When he smelt cooking, Thomas emerged from the shelter and found that a fire had been lit in the centre of the ring and the Ranters were preparing to eat. While the men gathered wood for the fire, two women stirred a large pot simmering over the flames. Thomas breathed in the aroma and realized how hungry he was. When the food was ready it was ladled by one of the women into wooden bowls and handed out by Catherine. Each Ranter sat with their bowl and platter around the fire.

When she had served everyone, Catherine came and sat beside Thomas. 'Are you familiar with the Ranters, Thomas?' she asked between mouthfuls.

'I have heard of you but know little of your ways.'

'Would you care to know more?'

'If you would care to tell me.'

'Ranters reject the teaching of the Church. We believe that God exists in every living creature and that man is thus free of sin and of his own laws.'

'Should a man not be punished for robbery or murder?'

'He will be punished by God.'

'Do you not believe in any form of government?'

'We believe in the freedom of the spirit.'

'I see,' said Thomas, although he did not. Ranters sounded very like anarchists, albeit peaceful ones. 'And why are you here?'

Catherine bit off a chunk of bread and chewed it thoroughly before answering. 'There are some in England who fear our ways. When they passed laws against what they call blasphemy and adultery, it was to give them an excuse to prosecute us. Some of us chose to come here to practise our beliefs.'

'Are you free to practise them here?'

'For most of the time, we are. There are always a few who seek to interfere. We turn them away.'

'I notice that Simeon Strange is one of you.'

Catherine giggled. 'Simeon spoke vehemently against us until God persuaded him to join us. Even now, his faith is fragile and from time to time he turns against us once more. We tolerate this because we believe that he will see the truth once and for all when God wishes him to.'

'Does his congregation not object to his being with you?'

'I doubt if Simeon has told them.'

Catherine had finished her dinner and turned to sit facing Thomas. 'And you, Thomas, how did you come to be on this island?'

While Thomas told Catherine the story of his arrest and indenture to the Gibbes, she sat in silence and listened. Not once did she interrupt with a comment or a question. 'What a wonderful listener you are,' he said when he had finished the story. 'Listening is a great skill and much undervalued.'

'We are taught to listen,' she replied. 'Our leaders insist upon it. They teach the art of deep listening.'

'What is deep listening?'

'It is listening beyond the words. Listening to the tone and the manner of the one speaking. That way, we learn the truth.'

'Do they insist upon the removal of your clothing?'

'That is a matter of choice. In this warm climate we choose to hide nothing from each other.'

While Thomas and Catherine had been talking, the other Ranters had gone to their shelters. None of them went alone. When they were the only couple left by the fire, Catherine rose and kicked earth on to it to kill the flames.

'Come now, Thomas,' she said, 'it is time to rest.' Thomas followed her back to their shelter and lay down on the palm fronds. Catherine lay on her side facing him and put her arm around him. As she gently stroked his neck, he realized how much he craved the comfort of another body. It had been a long time. Catherine sensed it and did not hurry, nor did she mention the scar on his cheek. She was slow and skilful and when it was over, she whispered, 'Sleep peacefully, Thomas. Wake me if you need me again.'

The Ranters had chosen their camp site well. The insects and the singing frogs must have preferred lower, wetter places and Thomas slept untroubled by either of them. Some time in the night he woke and felt for Catherine. She moved closer but did not wake. Before he fell asleep again he thought, as he always did in the night, of Polly and Lucy. He thought of England without a king. And he thought of Tobias Rush.

When dawn broke Thomas stirred again. Catherine had gone and for a moment he did not know where he was. He scrambled out of the shelter and stretched his arms. His ankle was much improved but he still felt drowsy. If it were not for his family, he could easily stay here with his new friends. The Ranters had much to recommend them.

Gradually the Ranters emerged from their shelters and began preparing breakfast. Simeon Strange was one of the last to appear, his arm around Catherine's waist. She smiled at Thomas and asked if he had slept well. 'Like a baby, thank you, Catherine,' he replied. 'I am grateful for your kindness but I must soon be on my way. It might be dangerous for you if I were found here.'

'Where will you go?' asked Strange.

'I was trying to find the estate of Adam Lyte when I lost my way.'

'I know where it is,' said Strange. 'I could take you there if you wish.'

'Thank you. But we must be careful. The men to whom I am indentured will be looking for me.'

Strange nodded. 'We will keep to the forest paths.'

They left after they had eaten. For the journey, Strange dressed himself in the clothes of a planter. At first they took a path further up the hill until they were deep within a forest of bearded fig trees, palms and thick undergrowth. After a mile or so, they joined another path to their right which ran down again. 'It's a long way round,' said Strange, 'but safer than using the coast road. Very few people come up here.'

When they stopped for a brief rest, Thomas plucked up the courage to ask his guide how he came to consort with the Ranters. But the little reverend was not to be drawn and replied only that they were all sinners in the eyes of God. Thomas left it at that and they did not speak again until they reached the Lytes' estate.

There Strange pointed out a wide path through the trees on their right. 'This is the way,' he said. 'I will leave you here, Thomas. May God bless you.' Thomas thanked the little man and watched him carry on down the hill until he was out of sight. Strange indeed, by name and by nature. One day a parson, the next a Ranter. His God really did move in mysterious ways.

Thomas walked slowly up the path to the Lytes' house. He was nervous. What would he find there? Would he be welcomed or rejected? He took a deep breath. Only one way to find out, Thomas, so you had better get on with it.

The Lytes' house could hardly have been more different from the Gibbes's hovel. It stood in the centre of a large clearing, immaculately swept and cleared of scrub. A shaded seating area with a simple thatched roof some ten feet deep ran the length of the house. A table and chairs had been set there. The house was built of the pale, pitted stone found on the island, the roof was tiled and the windows shuttered. It was a substantial plantation house, designed for comfort and practicality.

Thomas approached the house. He was a few steps away when the door was flung open and a grinning Patrick appeared. 'There you are, Thomas,' he declared. 'I've been expecting you.'

'Have you?'

'Indeed I have. The Gibbes have been after your blood, and when they could not find you they tore the Serpent to pieces, broke a chair over the landlord's head and hurled bottles at anyone who tried to stop them. It took six men to overpower them and take them to the magistrate. They're in a cell there. I guessed you would come here.'

'I did not know where else to go.'

'The magistrate perhaps, to throw yourself on his mercy?'

Thomas hung his head. 'Must I?'

'You must not. Come inside and tell me what happened.'

An hour later, Patrick had heard the story. He knew about Tobias Rush, about Thomas finally losing control, about the storm and the gully, and about the Ranters. Only Simeon Strange went unmentioned. When he had finished, Patrick showed him where to wash, gave him a salve for his scar, found him some clean clothes, and went to prepare food for them both.

The Lytes' house had been simply designed around a large square living room, from which doors led to four bedrooms and at the back to a kitchen and parlour. The walls of the living room were decorated with paintings of local scenes, the furniture was good, plain English oak and there were rugs on the floor. Best of all, there was a bookshelf with about twenty books on it. When he emerged bathed and shaven, Thomas made straight for it, picked up the first volume that came to hand and read the title. 'Well now, who would have thought it? *The Canterbury Tales* of Geoffrey Chaucer. Have you read them, Patrick?'

'I have not. English chivalry and courtly love are not to my taste. I'm just a black slave.'

'Black and a slave you may be. Just you are not. In any sense. And they're about more than chivalry. Now that I think of it, the brutes could be descended from Chaucer's miller. He was almost as revolting as them.'

They sat outside to eat. 'The Lytes are in Holetown to see a merchant,' Patrick told Thomas. 'I expect them back very soon.'

'What shall I do, Patrick?'

'You will sit here until they arrive and then you will go and inspect the estate while I speak to them.'

'Are you sure?'

'Quite sure. What is there to lose?'

They heard the Lytes riding up the path to the house. 'Off you go, Thomas,' ordered Patrick. 'Twenty minutes should be enough.'

The Lytes' estate was as orderly as their house. Thomas walked past a neat row of timber cottages which must have housed their slaves and indentured men, around their boiling house and mill and beside a cane field where the cane was being cut. He saw no sign of whips and heard no screams of pain. He did see men labouring in the heat of the afternoon, he knew the boiling house would be as hot as any other and he inhaled the sweet smells of raw sugar and molasses. As a prisoner of the Gibbes, he had seen only dirt and squalor. Here, for the first time, he saw beauty, order and colour, trees and flowers, shades of blue and green and, everywhere, lush growth. Barbados was a beautiful island. He realized that he had not appreciated this before because his mind had not allowed him to. Only now could he see clearly. When he returned, Adam and Mary Lyte were waiting for him.

Adam rose and held out his hand. 'Thomas Hill, welcome. When he returned from Speightstown yesterday, Patrick was a little concerned about you.'

'Thank you, sir,' replied Thomas, taking his hand, 'and I am relieved to be here. Has Patrick told you what happened?'

'He has. You're a brave man, Thomas. I for one would not care to throw myself at either Gibbes.'

'Unfortunately, I also threw myself into a gully.'

'So I hear.' Adam turned to his sister. 'This is my sister Mary, whom you have not, I think, met.'

Thomas bowed and took her hand. As Patrick had said, Mary Lyte was a beautiful young woman. Coal-black hair, blue eyes, skin lightly touched by the Caribbean sun and with more than a hint of sensuality to her mouth. Her smile would have lit up any room in London or Paris. 'Thomas, I have so looked forward to meeting you. Adam has told me all about you and the evil man who had you sent here. What was his name?'

'Rush, madam, Tobias Rush. And evil he certainly is.'

'Rush, yes. And your sister and her daughters are forced to do as he wishes.'

'Yes. I can hardly bear to think of it.'

'Indeed. Now, let us sit here and talk.' She spread her arms to indicate where they were sitting. 'This we call our parlour. We prefer to eat and sit here as long as it is not raining. Feel free to use it as you wish. Patrick is preparing something special. My brother will tell you the news from England while he gets it ready.'

'What do you know of events there, Thomas?' asked Adam.

'Since the death of the king, very little. I should be glad of news.'

'At first, it seems, the execution of the king shocked the country into a state of paralysis — quite the opposite of what has happened here. Even those who had fought against him could hardly believe it. Despite having been publicly executed, he was given a state funeral and Cromwell himself visited his body in the chapel at St James's. The country was confused and it still is. And no wonder. How is a man to know who is governing him without a king, with half the members of Parliament excluded from the house or choosing to stay away and with the one man who, more than any other, might restore a form of order away in Ireland?'

'Cromwell is in Ireland?'

'He is. And still drinking Irish blood, by all accounts. God knows what else will befall that sad country.'

The memory of Newbury, where thousands had died for no purpose at all, came back to Thomas. Cannon, musket fire, the screams of the wounded, smoke, bodies, blood, death. The stuff of war. And six years later, still going on in Ireland. 'What will happen next, do you think?'

'I can only guess. When Cromwell returns from killing Irishmen, he'll find someone else to fight. The Scots, perhaps. He's only happy with a sword in one hand and a Bible in the other.'

'And England?'

'Who knows? Anarchy, revolution, war? I thank God that Mary and I left when we did.'

'As do I,' agreed Mary. 'Barbados is our home now. I for one do not wish to return.'

At this, Adam raised his eyebrows and Thomas sensed tension between brother and sister. He remembered Patrick mentioning a suitor in England. Best to change the subject.

'And what now for Barbados, sir?'

'Since Colonel Walrond became governor we are no longer neutral and we have been holding our breath. He is an un-compromising man, fiercely loyal to the crown. Already some landowners who have refused to swear an oath of loyalty to the king have been banished to England or to another island. That is causing serious problems.'

'Have their estates been sequestered?'

'They have and, worse, their slaves and indentured servants have taken the opportunity to escape into the hills. We fear they will start attacking plantations. Militias are being formed and they too are making trouble. Some do not care who they fight. And there's the threat of reprisals. If James Drax and Reynold Alleyne are forced to go, you may be sure they will return and at the head of an army.'

'So there it is, Thomas,' said Mary. 'Slave and master, king and Parliament, wild militiamen. The peace we have so carefully preserved may be about to shatter into bloody pieces.'

'Which brings us back to you, Thomas,' said Adam. 'The question is — what is to be done with you? Naturally, my sister and I would like to help a man who has been so unjustly and harshly treated but we must also be aware of the law. The fact is that we are sheltering you illegally and in my position that is a serious matter.'

'My brother is a member of the Assembly,' said Mary proudly.

'Indeed I am, and expecting to be appointed soon to the governor's council. I'm sure you will understand the delicacy of the situation.' Thomas understood. Adam Lyte's position came first.

'I can hardly offer to buy you again because it would mean telling the Gibbes that I know where you are. Nor can we return you to them and tell them that you have been our guest.'

'The longer I am here,' said Thomas, 'the more difficult your position. I must go back to the Gibbes and concoct some story about being lost in the forest.'

'You must do no such thing,' said Mary. 'You will stay here until you have fully recovered your strength and my brother has decided what to do for the best.'

'I am grateful, madam.'

Adam cleared his throat. 'I must be discreet, Thomas. Your presence here must remain a secret until arrangements can be made. It might take some time. And there is one condition, Thomas. I would like you to attend to our books of account. I have been too busy in the Assembly and they are in a sorry state. Patrick says that you are the very man for the job.'

'I would be only too pleased to assist, sir.'

'Excellent. Only when you feel up to it, of course. Until then, Patrick will take care of you.'

Before Thomas could respond, Patrick appeared from the kitchen, leading a line of boys bearing dinner. On the table they put a huge bowl of fish soup, a heap of freshly baked bread, a lamb pie, a roasted capon with pickled cucumbers and sweet potatoes and an assortment of other fruits and vegetables which Thomas did not recognize. Patrick stood back and let them admire his work.

'Are we expecting an army?' asked Mary sweetly.

'I trust not, madam,' replied Patrick, beaming, 'although I did wonder if Mr Carrington might be joining you.'

'He often does,' said Adam. 'He seems to know when there's food on the table. I can't imagine how.' Thomas thought he detected a blush rising to Mary's cheeks.

Two hours later, his stomach full and his mind somewhat befuddled by more wine than was good for him, Thomas was shown by Patrick to a bedroom. What do you make of that, Monsieur Montaigne? he whispered, before falling asleep. Within the space of three days, naked in a boiling house, whipped, lost in the forest, rescued by naked Ranters and entertained to a splendid dinner. The fates have recanted. If Adam Lyte can just put his scruples aside and find me a passage to England, the nightmare will be over and Tobias Rush will face justice.

Patrick insisted on showing Thomas the estate and describing its workings. One morning while they watched a party of men cutting cane with bills, Patrick told him that they were cutting the ratoon.

'What's that?' he asked.

'Ratoon cane, Thomas. The second crop which sprouts after the first. Have you learned nothing about sugar?'

'I have tried not to. That reminds me, do you know why the water in the wells is so pure?'

'Yes. It's filtered through the coral stone of which the island is made.'

'The same coral stone of which houses are built and into which the rain cuts gullies to trap unsuspecting travellers, I suppose.'

'The same. Most travellers take care to avoid them. Only the most foolish fall into one.'

Unlike the Gibbes's mill, the Lytes' was powered by cattle roped to a huge wheel which drove the rollers into which the cane was being fed. 'It never stops during the cutting season,' said Patrick. 'Cut the cane, squeeze out the juice, boil it, cure it and sell it. Very little waste and an endless process bringing great wealth to the planters and merchants.'

The Lytes' boiling house had been designed to be as safe as possible. It was also larger than the brutes'. Instead of one furnace, there were three with a row of copper kettles over each of them. It was hot, very hot, but openings on all four sides did allow whatever breeze there was to circulate.

The men working there were both black and white. They wore linen breeches, leather boots, and long leather gloves to protect their hands and arms from the hot sugar. Every few minutes a boy with a pail threw water over the workers to help them keep cool. Small things but a mighty improvement on what the brutes' slaves suffered.

'A simple plant, in demand everywhere just because it's sweet. I wonder what other plants there are that can so easily be turned into gold,' mused Thomas.

'Many, probably, as long as the labour's cheap enough. Or free,' said Patrick. 'Tobacco and cotton in Virginia, grapes in Spain.'

'Yes. I suppose it's really you and me making men rich, Patrick, not the cane. Indentured or slave, we're much the same. A means to an end.'

'Exactly. Although some of us have been treated better than others,' said Patrick. 'Now, did you look at the brutes' curing house?'

'If that is where earthenware pots drip brown liquid into pans, yes I did. Although I suspect that will not stop you showing me another one.'

Having kept the brutes' ledgers for more than seven hundred days, Thomas knew very well what the curing house was and what happened to the sugar and the molasses after they had been cured. He just preferred not to think about it.

'Really, Thomas, you should take more interest in the process. You can't devote your time only to matters of philosophy.'

'Yes I can. And if it weren't for sugar cane, I wouldn't be here. Couldn't we look at something else?'

'No. The curing house it is.'

The curing house was much like the brutes'. Pots of drying sugar stood over earthenware pans which caught the brown liquid dripping from holes in their bases. To avoid the heat, they stood outside and peered in.

'Pay attention, Thomas,' said Patrick sternly. 'You may be tested on your knowledge later.'

Thomas rolled his eyes and sighed. 'Very well, sir. But please make the lesson brief as my attention will soon waver.'

'On this estate we make what is known as muscovado sugar,

which is further refined when it reaches England or Holland. Colonel Drax started making white sugar, using clay pots, but that takes longer.'

'Then why did he do it?'

'Soft white sugar fetches much higher prices than muscovado. Mr Lyte thinks we will all be producing it one day. Here we allow the sugar to cool for twelve hours after boiling, then we pack it in these pots and let it cure for a month. The brown molasses which drips out goes to make rum. When the pots are emptied, the sugar is hard. The middle of the loaf is packed into barrels ready for shipment and the ends are reboiled.'

'And the molasses?'

'Ours goes to a new distillery outside Bridgetown. Some planters make their own rum from it. What did the Gibbes do?'

'Drank the stuff. Is the lesson over now?'

'You are a miserable student, Thomas, and I shall waste no more time on you. Let us return to the house.'

'An excellent idea. I'm feeling somewhat faint. A glass of wine should revive my spirits.'

Thomas soon started on the Lytes' accounts, which were, as Adam had warned, in a sorry state. Piles of paper had to be converted into entries in their ledgers, columns of figures added up and made to balance and the totals reconciled with the records of money in hand and deposited with their agent in London. Not difficult work, but slow and painstaking.

When he was not walking with Patrick or working on the accounts, Thomas took advantage of the Lytes' books. He was sitting in the parlour with a copy of Bacon's *The Wisdom of the Ancients*, when Mary came and sat beside him.

'Thomas, I'm pleased to see your recovery continues. Able to read serious books and plump enough to wear my brother's shirt. Patrick must have been taking good care of you.'

'Indeed he has. He's a skilful physician and an excellent cook and I have much to thank him for.' Thomas touched his cheek. 'Even my scar is fading. I do believe he feels guilty that he has been so much better treated than I have.'

'Perhaps he does. But at least you are alive.'

'The thought of getting home has kept me alive for the better part of two years, madam.' Thomas paused. 'Have you thought further about my position?'

'We have, but as yet without finding a solution. Adam is a cautious man and will not rush to a decision. And while you have been recovering there has been no urgency. Rest assured, however, that we shall do whatever we reasonably can to help you. It would grieve me greatly to send you back to the Gibbes. Patrick tells me you called them the brutes.'

'Yes, madam, red brute and black brute. And I wrote a list of adjectives to describe them. It reminded me of being at school when we gave the teachers names. It's odd how the mind works in such situations.'

'Not so odd, I think. A matter of survival. I believe I might have done the same thing. And while you are our guest, we hope you will use our given names. In Barbados there is less formality than in London.'

'Thank you. But are you not in danger by my being here?'

Mary laughed. 'Put it out of your mind, Thomas. You are safe enough here. Adam will think of something and if we suffer an attack by runaways, you will be needed. Now say no more on the matter.'

'Very well, Mary. Tell me, instead, how you came to the island. Patrick told me you were not born here.'

'Neither of us was. I was twelve years old when we arrived, Adam four years older. At first I found it hot, humid, uncomfortable and frightening — not a bit like Dorset, which was the only other place I had known. When both our parents died of the cholera just before the battle at Kineton, I expected to be put into the care of relatives but Adam would not hear of it and insisted on taking responsibility for his younger sister. Restless and ambitious and much taken with travellers' tales of the fortunes to be made in the Caribbean islands, he wasted no time in putting our family home up for sale. To those who accused him of callousness so soon after the death of his parents, he replied that a war-torn England was no place for him or me and that we would seek a better and safer future in the new colony of Barbados.'

'He must have been a determined young man, and a brave one.'

'He was. A neighbour, Sir Lionel Perkins, tried to dissuade him, having his eye on me as a future bride for his son Richard. They agreed in the end that I would return to marry Richard in the event of Adam's untimely death, in return for Richard having the right to my hand when I reach twenty-one years of age. I do not look forward to that day. Adam purchased our passage on a trading ship leaving Southampton for the Caribbean and we arrived here in the spring of 1643, with a few hundred pounds and the intention of turning them without delay into a large fortune.'

'Which, if I may say so, you have done. A remarkable achievement.'

'We were lucky in finding this estate available at a good price and we have worked hard to develop it. There is only one aspect of our business we dislike.'

'What is that?'

'We do not like slavery.'

'Yet you have slaves.'

'We do. When we bought the estate the slaves came with it. We were faced with keeping them or turning them out to fend for themselves. We decided that the latter would be more cruel than the former. We try to treat them well and have acquired no more. When we need more labour, we find indentured men and only those who chose to be indentured or were found guilty of some petty crime such as poaching. As far as we know, we have no robbers or murderers.'

'What happens to them when their term is up?'

'We have promised all of them the purchase price of ten acres of land or their passage home. So far, all have stayed. Having made the promise we shall keep it, although with the price of land rising daily we shall have to sell many tons of sugar to do so. Adam tells me that good land is now selling for as much as thirty-two pounds an acre. Not only that, but the war in England has depressed the price of muscovado. What money there is, is being spent on swords, not sugar.'

'Another reason to hope for peace. Still, if the estate is attacked the men will no doubt be willing to help defend it. That would not be the case everywhere.'

'Indeed it would not. In fact, Adam and I have chosen quite a different path to almost all other landowners. While they have moved from imported cheap labour to bonded men from Brazil and Guiana to convicts to African slaves, we are moving from slavery to voluntarily indentured servants. And we do believe our men will stay loyal. They know that they are much better off here than as runaways in the woods.'

'And what of Patrick?'

Again, Mary smiled her beguiling smile. 'Patrick is special. His father was white, his real mother died in childbirth. At birth he was put in the care of the woman he calls his mother. They were here when we bought the property. It was obvious that he was extremely intelligent so we took him into the house as a servant.'

'His knowledge is considerable.'

'For that, thank our books and my brother. Adam has done everything he could to teach Patrick about the world. They discuss politics, philosophy, literature, everything. Patrick has become Adam's adopted brother.'

'He's a fortunate man and he knows it. There cannot be many like him in Barbados.'

'None, I should think. In Europe, however, I believe such a relationship is not uncommon. Master and slave become father and adopted son, or something very like it.'

'Adoptions of that sort also happened in ancient Rome, so it's not exactly a new idea.'

'Which reminds me, Thomas. We are visiting our neighbour Charles Carrington tomorrow to look at his new windmill. Would you care to come?'

'I would. Thank you, Mary.'

'And, Thomas, rest assured that we will do what we can to help you.'

Thomas did not doubt it. The question was: what, given Adam's position, could they do?

At breakfast the next morning, Adam raised the one subject on which there was sure to be an argument. He did not seem to care that Thomas was with them. 'I heard from Sir Lionel Perkins yesterday. A letter came with a cargo ship. He asks after you and confirms that Richard is still unmarried.'

Mary rolled her eyes and sighed. 'Sir Lionel Perkins. Trust him to spoil my day. You know my feelings, Adam. I don't want to go back to England, Richard Perkins or no Richard Perkins. This is my home now.'

'You're only nineteen, my dear. Time enough to consider the matter.'

'Adam, you pompous ass, you raised the subject, not I,' said Mary testily. 'I don't want to return to a country I don't know to marry a man I don't know. This is our home now and our livelihood. I do not wish to leave Barbados. Now let us talk of something more agreeable lest we embarrass Thomas further.' Perhaps I should offer to marry Perkins, thought Thomas, that would solve both our problems.

After breakfast they went to visit Charles Carrington's new windmill. The Carrington house came as a surprise. More medieval castle than plantation house, complete with battlements and fortifications, it would resist anything less than heavy cannon. Thomas could just see Charles tipping boiling oil or hurling stones from the roof down on to an attacker. He was waiting for them when they arrived. He waved a greeting and walked out to meet them.

'Adam, welcome. And Mary, always a delight. And, if I'm not mistaken, Thomas Hill, about whom I have heard a good deal.'

'A pleasure to meet you again, sir,' replied Thomas, 'and especially not in the company of the Gibbes.'

Charles laughed loudly. 'Those creatures. Well done escaping their clutches, although you do seem to have fallen into other clutches. I trust they are more friendly.'

'Charles, you are a pig,' said Mary.

'I find myself in excellent clutches, sir,' said Thomas, thinking that the way he looked at Mary suggested that Charles Carrington would like to find himself in the same clutches without further ado. And judging by the colour in Mary's face, she would not discourage him. No wonder talk of the Perkins family had upset her.

'Now, Charles,' said Adam briskly, 'to business if we may. How is the windmill performing? Are you happy with it?'

'Adam, my dear fellow, all in good time. First I want to know what news there is from England.'

'Adam had a letter from England yesterday but it told us little, did it, Adam?' There was an edge to Mary's tone.

'Not much, certainly. Cromwell rules by fear, but we knew that.'

'And the Perkins? What news of them?' Mary looked up sharply at this but Charles had carefully addressed the question to Adam. He must have guessed who had sent the letter.

'Sir Lionel complains of gout but Richard is well. Still un-married and helping to manage the estate. He'll be a wealthy young man one day.'

Mary glared at her brother and changed the subject. 'How is the crop, Charles?'

'We should get over two tons an acre. The weather's been kind and the old leaves we dug in seem to have helped.'

'That's interesting. We must try it ourselves, Adam, don't you think?'

'Indeed. We could mix the debris from the mill with horse manure. It might serve.'

Intricate discussion of animal manure and vegetable matter

could only occupy them for so long and soon Mary said brightly, 'Now, Charles, I believe I'm ready for the windmill. Will you escort us?'

She took Charles's arm and they chatted amiably as they walked.

'I suppose I have the revolting Gibbes to thank for the windmill. It was theirs that persuaded me. It was a big investment and I did not think I could do it until a Dutch merchant persuaded me. No fools, those Dutch. He lent me the money in return for a discount on the price of all the sugar I produce until the loan is cleared. It won't take long.'

'I imagine not,' said Adam, 'not with demand in Europe growing as it is. Very shrewd of you, Charles.'

'It was the merchant who was shrewd. He's making more profit and getting more sugar from me. He told me that windmills are used by most of the Brazilian planters. They don't eat like cattle do.'

'But they need wind.'

'There's plenty of wind up here. The sails turn day and night when we're harvesting.'

Sure enough, when they reached the windmill there was a good breeze and it was hard at work. A gang of men, black and white, was feeding cane through the rollers to extract the juice.

Charles proudly explained the windmill's workings and answered their questions with aplomb. It was an impressive device but the cane still had to be fed in by hand.

'Alas,' said Charles, 'I wish there were another way but I can't think of one. I tell the men to take care but accidents happen and fingers are mangled. We have to send for Sprot, who removes the fingers and pockets my sovereigns.'

'I wonder what he does with the fingers.'

'I've heard that he sells them for fish bait. A guinea a dozen, I believe.'

Mary grimaced. She took Charles's arm again and allowed him to lead her back down the path. 'It's time you were married, Charles. Anyone in your sights?' she asked loudly enough for Adam to hear.

'Good Lord, no. Can't imagine anyone would have me. A younger son with no prospects and forced to try and make his way in the Caribbean. And we're rather short of eligible ladies at present.'

If I could read your mind, Mr Carrington, thought Thomas, it would say something like 'a pox on Perkins', and I don't blame you. Marry her at once is my advice, and damn the consequences.

'Most impressive, Charles,' said Adam, when they had returned to the house. 'Will you give me the name of the Dutch merchant?'

'Of course I will. In exchange for an invitation to dinner.'

'I invite you, Charles,' said Mary quickly. 'Would a week today be convenient?'

'It would. Very.'

CHAPTER 17

Tobias Rush hated being stuck on a ship and out of touch with his affairs. For six weeks he had paced the deck, barked at the crew and drunk more than he normally did. When eventually they docked in Southampton he found a carriage to take him straight to Romsey, where he would deal with the tiresome matter of the message before travelling on to London. He had an idea and another visit to Seething Lane was called for.

After an uncomfortable journey to Romsey, Rush was in an evil temper. When he found the door to the bookshop in Love Lane bolted, he rapped on it with his cane. Nothing happened so he picked up a stone and beat it with that. Still nothing happened so he beat it again. He was on the point of giving up when he heard the bolts being slid open. The door opened a few inches and he pushed his way in. The two girls who stood staring at him must be Hill's nieces. Apart from their fair hair they favoured their mother. They were pretty children. 'Where is your mother?' he demanded.

The older one answered. 'She is at the market, sir. She will be back soon.'

'Who are you, sir?' squeaked the younger one. 'We should not open the door to strangers when our mother is out. She said so.'

'I am Tobias Rush. Has your mother mentioned me?'

The girls looked at each other and shook their heads. 'I don't think so, sir,' replied the older one. 'Are you a friend of hers?'

Rush relaxed. The woman had held her tongue. 'Indeed I am. And I shall wait here for her to return. I have an important matter to discuss with her.' He walked around the desk and sat on the chair behind it. 'Why don't you come and sit beside me?' Again the girls looked at each other.

'You go upstairs, Lucy,' replied the older one, 'I will wait with Master Rush.' Lucy did not need a second bidding. She disappeared through a door at the back of the shop and ran up the stairs. 'May I fetch you anything while you wait?'

'Nothing, child. What is your name?'

'Polly Taylor, sir. If you are a friend of our mother, did you know our uncle, Thomas Hill?'

Rush suppressed a grin. The woman had done as she was instructed and told them he was dead. 'I did not.'

The door opened and Margaret walked in carrying a basket. She took one look at Rush and immediately put herself between him and Polly. 'Where is Lucy?'

'She is in the bedroom,' replied Polly from behind her. 'Master Rush wanted to wait for you.'

'Go and join her. I will speak privately to Master Rush.' When Polly had gone, Margaret continued, 'Have you brought the word?' Rush took the torn-out paper from a pocket and handed it to her. Margaret looked at it and, satisfied, tucked it into her basket. 'So he is alive.'

'He certainly was when I last saw him, and being well looked after.'

'Rubbish. As an indentured man he will be treated like a slave. It is all I can do not to kill you where you sit.' She took the pistol from her basket and aimed it at Rush's forehead. He did not move.

'If you do, you will never find out where he is.'

'I know he is in Barbados.'

Rush smiled. 'In fact, you do not. It is true that he was taken there, but there are other colonies crying out for indentured men — Jamaica, Virginia, Grenada — and he might have been sold on to a planter in one of them.'

Margaret was horrified. Thomas 'sold on' like an animal and the little knowledge she had of him now in doubt. 'Has he been?'

'Perhaps. Why not make more enquiries? You were so clever before.'

Margaret replaced the pistol in the basket. Much as she wanted to, killing the creature would not get Thomas back.

'Very wise.' Rush stood up. 'Such a pleasure to meet your daughters. Delightful children. Do take care of them, won't you?'

Without waiting for a response, he opened the door and was gone.

Margaret went to the kitchen and wept.

Since Rush had been away London had become quieter. The war had taken its toll — shops had closed, the streets were empty and there were few vendors hawking their wares. He had been clever enough to profit from the war, others had not. Now, however, he must look for pastures new. The only serious fighting going on was in Scotland, so demand for soldiers' woollen jackets had dried up, and land prices had yet to recover their former levels. They would, of course, and his venture in Barbados was doing splendidly. Nevertheless it was time to try something new.

When his black carriage drew up outside the house in Seething Lane, Rush ordered the coachman to return in an hour and jumped out. He was admitted at once and shown into the living room. No fire had been lit but the thin-faced man sat in the same chair in front of the hearth, smoking a pipe. 'Tobias Rush,' he said, without rising, 'to what do I owe this pleasure?'

'I have a proposition for you.'

'And what might that be?'

Rush took the seat opposite him. 'I have recently returned from Barbados, where sugar is making men rich.'

'So I believe. Excellent sugar it is too. Greatly superior to the Egyptian stuff.'

'Quite. Demand for it increases by the week. There is only one thing preventing the planters from getting even richer.'

'And what is that?'

'The useful life of an African slave or an indentured man is short. The work breaks them quickly. There is profit to be had from supplying them with younger bodies.'

The man scratched his chin. 'I can see that. Boys who will adjust more easily to the work and last longer. But this is not my sort of work. What do you propose?'

'I would prefer not to be personally involved in the harvesting. I propose that you hire a man who will assist us and that we share the profits of the venture. Do you know such a man?'

'Perhaps. Let us discuss terms.'

For an hour they thrashed out an agreement. When Rush rose to leave, they had agreed a price he would pay for each healthy boy between eight and twelve years old harvested from the streets of London. The boys would be loaded on to a ship at Rotherhithe and held on it until the cargo was complete. Rush would arrange the transportation and disposal of the cargo in Barbados. It was a venture with great potential.

CHAPTER 18

The first news of serious trouble came on the day of the dinner
party, when Charles arrived at the Lytes' house to find
Thomas sitting in the parlour with Adam and Mary.

'There's been a raid on the Morgan estate in St Lucy,' he
reported, 'a bad one. Three men killed and two house slaves with
their throats cut. Three heads left impaled on stakes. Morgan was
away. They took muskets and powder. One of Morgan's men
reported that there were about thirty of them, armed with everything
from flintlocks to bill hooks.'

'It was bound to happen,' said Mary. 'Private militias,
unguarded estates, runaway slaves. We've only ourselves to blame.
Swearing oaths, indeed. What's the point? Walrond's caused
nothing but trouble and trouble breeds trouble.'

'It could easily happen to us. We must be prepared.'

'What are you doing about defences, Charles?' asked Adam.

'As you know, after the rebellion three years ago I took certain
precautions and I've posted sentries around the estate and made

sure my men are adequately armed. I am content to leave matters in the hands of my steward, who is so ferocious that I suspect he was once a pirate. You're much more vulnerable and there's Mary to think of. These men are vicious.'

'What do you suggest we do?'

'I suggest that as soon as we've finished the excellent dinner that I can smell cooking, we make plans. Then we can get to work tomorrow. No time to lose with those savages on the loose.'

While they enjoyed Patrick's roast leg of lamb, they talked of Walrond and the Assembly, of his absurd insistence on oaths of loyalty, of the inevitability of the island now being dragged into the war at home and of the likely effects on trade.

'The man's a dangerous lunatic,' said Charles, mopping up claret sauce with a hunk of bread. 'He's putting it about that anyone who opposes him is plotting to murder every Royalist on the island and turn us into some form of Parliamentary tyranny. He's even accusing Drax and Middleton of being in league with Cromwell.'

'All he's done,' agreed Adam, 'is to set landowner against landowner, freeman against freeman and servant against servant. What's more, landowners leave their estates to take up arms and their slaves and indentured men run off into the woods.'

'And attack the rest of us,' said Mary. 'What do you make of it, Thomas?'

'At Newbury I saw two armies blasting and hacking each other to pieces for no obvious reason. When they'd finished, the king went back to Oxford and Essex marched on to London. All was much as it had been a few weeks earlier except that several thousand men had been killed or wounded. For such a thing to happen on an island as small and as prosperous as this would be even more absurd.'

'No doubt you are right, Thomas,' agreed Adam, 'but war will not be averted by such sentiments. We need common ground and common sense. Alas, I fear that the Walronds have no interest in either.'

'Our immediate concern is Thomas.' Mary smiled at him. 'And if there is to be bloodshed, the sooner he goes home the better. Have you made any progress, Adam?'

'Not yet. I have been busy. He is safe here for the moment.'

'Not only safe. The food is good and the company excellent. Apart from my family, I could not ask for more,' replied Thomas, thinking that he would trade both for news of Margaret and the girls.

'None of us will be safe if we're attacked by runaways,' said Charles. 'Now let's discuss what's to be done. What arms have you got?'

'Not much,' admitted Adam. 'A few matchlocks, powder, shot, a sword or two.'

'Right. I shall visit a Dutch friend in Bridgetown. He will equip us.'

'What shall I do?' asked Mary.

'You, my dear, shall be our quartermaster. Or should that be quartermistress?'

'What does a quartermistress do, Charles?'

'She lays in ample stocks of food and drink in case of a long siege. She also prepares bandages and splints for wounds and sets aside a room where the wounded can be tended.'

'Thomas will assist me in planning our defences,' said Adam. 'Guard posts, lines of fire, barricades, that sort of thing. What do you think, Thomas?'

'Of course I should be pleased to,' replied Thomas. 'Perhaps

Patrick and I could also help Mary with the wounded, if there are any.'

'Thank you, Thomas,' replied Mary, 'I should be glad of your help. Otherwise we might have to send for Sprot.'

'Couldn't we recommend him to the enemy?' asked Charles. 'He'd soon render them incapable.'

'What about our men?' asked Adam. 'Who will train them?'

'My job, I think,' said Charles. 'I'll soon have them up to standard.'

'And I will remain here until the danger has passed. The Assembly will have to manage without me.'

Preparations began immediately. Thomas and Adam surveyed the ground and Charles visited the Dutch merchant who was delighted to provide muskets, powder, shot and swords, and confided that business was brisk. So brisk, in fact, that he thought he might spend a little time in Holland until things had quietened down.

'Wealthy is good,' he told Charles, 'but healthy is better. In Holland I can be both, but here in Barbados, who knows? I must have armed the whole island by now.'

What was more, he had wisely imported a consignment of new French flintlocks which were an advance on matchlocks and wheel locks. He had not been able to obtain any of the new cartridges which came already primed, so powder still had to be measured out and tipped in, but the chances of a misfire were greatly reduced.

Naturally, they were more expensive, but 'How much is a life worth, Mr Carrington? You'd not want to take a risk for the sake of a few shillings.' No, Mr Carrington told him, he'd not want to and happily parted with the extra shillings.

Within a week the Lytes' storeroom was full. Not another sack of flour or salted piglet or box of eggs or churn of butter could be squeezed in. Barrels of water stood in rows in the parlour and turkeys and chickens, newly bought, scratched about in a pen beside the house. Mary had promised that 'Muskets might kill us, but hunger won't.'

Having thoroughly inspected the ground, Adam and Thomas worked out a strategy. They would bring in all their men and their families from their quarters and set up fortifications around the house. The men, fully armed and provisioned, would have to sleep in the open. The women and children would be quartered in the house.

While they worked, Adam and Thomas also talked of other things. They spoke of sugar and trade, of king and Parliament, of peace and war. Most of all though, they talked of people. Of men and women, some born to wealth and luxury, others to poverty, misery and an early death. And others still to slavery. 'If I'd been taken forcibly from my home, shipped to a strange land and worked to death with no hope of ever returning to my family,' said Thomas, emphasizing the 'ever', 'I too would try to escape. I might even be driven to maim and kill. An eye for an eye, a tooth for a tooth, a life for a life.'

'I doubt our Africans are familiar with the Old Testament, Thomas,' replied Adam, 'and many were born here.'

'Like Patrick, yes. Well treated, healthy and happy. And unusual. Most are not. They're here against their will. I almost feel one of them.'

'Would you join them, Thomas?'

'Had I still been at the mercy of the Gibbes, I might have. My lot was not so different from theirs. And imagine, if you can, that you had been shipped to Africa to be the slave of an African merchant. What would you have done? Thanked him warmly for his kindness or done whatever you could to escape? Killed him if necessary?'

'Thomas,' said Adam with a sigh, 'I cannot conceive of such a thing. Please tell me that you will help us defend ourselves against those who threaten us.'

'I will. A man must be allowed to defend himself and his family, whatever the circumstances. And I owe you and Mary my life. That is enough to overcome my scruples.'

When they met again at the Lytes' house for what Mary now disparagingly referred to as their 'council of war', Charles reported first. 'We have a total of twenty-eight men at our disposal, including indentured servants, loyal slaves and ourselves. Not many.'

'Twenty-eight willing men are better than a hundred pressed into service. What will they be like when you've trained them, Charles?' asked Adam.

'Oh, first class, my dear fellow. Highly trained infantrymen and excellent swordsmen, every one. The king would have been proud of them.'

'Yes, Charles. If you say so.'

'Oh, come, come. I'll soon knock them into shape. One look at them and the enemy will turn and run.'

'I have purchased enough food for fifty men for a year,' said Mary. 'If the enemy turn and run, you will have to tell me what to do with it.'

'And Thomas and I have worked out a defence strategy. Let me show you.' Adam picked up a stick and drew a square in the dirt with a semi-circle at each corner.

'This is the house,' he explained, pointing at the square, 'and these marks are the redoubts. As you can see, each is in the shape of a semi-circle, giving a clear line of fire all around the house. We'll set them twenty yards out, which will leave some thirty yards further to the tree line. Anyone trying to reach the house will have to cross open space with fire coming at them from both sides. I suggest we put four men with muskets behind each one with instructions to fire in pairs. That way the pair reloading will always be covered. We haven't any pikemen to cover them and they wouldn't be much use if we had.'

'Excellent, Adam, you should have been a colonel. Or is the plan Colonel Hill's?' Charles was enjoying himself. 'But that accounts for only sixteen men. What about the others?'

'We'll need to see how the training goes but I had thought we would keep them in reserve, with orders to fill any gaps that might appear.'

'A good plan. Casualties have a habit of occurring in battle. Damned nuisance but there it is. We're fully armed, thanks to my Dutch friend. And so, according to him, is everyone else. He has practically nothing left to sell. Better get on with training the infantry, then. I'll start immediately.' Charles sounded as if he could hardly wait.

They soon found, however, that the training was not easy. Assembling the slaves and servants in sufficient numbers to make an exercise worthwhile was the first problem. The cane would not wait for a convenient moment to be ready for cutting and once cut, it had to be milled, boiled and cured without delay, or it would rot. Even with the cooperation of Adam and Mary, Charles had a frustrating time of it. Watching from a discreet distance, Thomas saw that endlessly repeating himself to groups of two or three had become thoroughly irksome.

Charles had divided the troop into three platoons. The first two, each consisting of eight indentured men, he named red platoon and green platoon. The third, the slaves' platoon, with twelve men, he had rather unimaginatively named black platoon. Mary and Adam's slaves, who had all been born in Barbados, were likely to be loyal, especially when they realized that they would be just as vulnerable in the event of an attack as anyone else. They would simply be treated as the enemy, and marauding parties of militiamen, Irishmen or Africans would take no prisoners. Discipline came easily to black platoon, less so to red and green.

'If your commander orders you to run to those trees over there,' Charles tried endlessly to drum into them, 'he means you to run NOW. Not after you've scratched your backside or had a piss. By then you might find yourself pissing out of a new hole. If he says run, RUN.'

It was the other way round with flintlock training. Poachers and countrymen were used to muskets and pistols and some were deadly with them. Bringing down a rabbit or a pheasant called for speed and skill. And as he was told more than once, 'Once you've got it, Mr Carrington, you isn't going to lose it.'

He had tried teaching black platoon how to prime and load a musket but it was no use. The main problem was that with no experience of muskets at all, in the excitement of battle or even imaginary battle they lost track of the amount of powder they had tipped in. Sometimes they forgot to tip any in at all and had to start again, by which time they might have been skewered; sometimes two or even three times the required charge disappeared down the barrel. There had been the inevitable accidents — so far, two badly burned hands and a blinded eye – and the platoon strength was already down to nine.

Unwilling to risk more casualties, Charles had converted black platoon into swordsmen and chosen to command them himself. At this, they quickly proved themselves more adept. Wielding a heavy sword was not so different from wielding a machete in the cane fields, although the cane was unlikely to fight back, and these were strong men, accustomed to hard work and slow to tire.

Under Charles's expert eye, they had learned the rudiments of thrust and parry, how to strike at an enemy's weak spot and how to slash at his ankles and hands. They would never be accomplished with the rapier but, on balance, Charles thought he'd rather be with them than against them. He would hold them back while the musketeers were in action and only throw them at the enemy if needed.

Charles himself was seen practising with a sword in either hand. When Thomas asked him about this, Charles told him proudly that from the age of twelve he had been schooled in the art of swordsmanship by one of the finest fencing masters in England and his daily regime of practice and training would have put any of the king's lifeguards to shame. The skipping rope had encouraged nimbleness of foot, lifting clay bricks and holding them for long periods in outstretched hands had strengthened the wrists and forearms and thrusting the rapier repeatedly at targets no larger than a man's fingernail had sharpened the eye.

'Above all,' said Charles proudly, 'I practised and practised with rapier and sword against older and stronger opponents until, by the age of eighteen, I could best my tutor.' And, he said, he could do so with either hand. His father had insisted that his son be equally adept with left hand or right, to the point at which he could easily interchange and his opponent would not know from which direction the next attack was coming.

'What's more, my boy,' the old man had told him encouragingly, 'should you be unfortunate enough to lose one arm in battle, you will still have the other to fall back on.' Charles chortled at the memory and returned to his practice.

Adam and Thomas, meanwhile, were busy building their defences. They set up lookout posts from which an advancing enemy would be seen well before he was within musket range, for which red and green platoons would provide a rota of sentries. At the first sign of trouble, the lookouts would fall back to the redoubts and take their places among the defenders. The redoubts were constructed of heaped brushwood, logs, rocks and a pair of beds chopped up for the purpose. Mary's objections to this had been ignored.

Mary and Patrick had sewn pieces of material of the appropriate colour on to the right sleeve of each man's shirt, so there was no excuse for any man to forget which platoon he was in. They also made sure the pork and flour were kept dry, the eggs were stored safely and the chickens and turkeys fed daily. And Mary had cut up her petticoats and dresses to be used as bandages. When they simply could not think of anything else to do, Mary had offered their services to her brother.

'The food and water are stored and ready. We have rags for bandages, needles and threads and sharp knives for surgery, although heaven forfend that we shall have to cut off anything or extract any musket balls, and strong rum for the patients. We're as ready as we shall ever be. Is there anything else we can do?'

'Well now, sister,' replied Adam, 'I'm reluctant to put you in danger, but it would greatly assist our gallant musketeers if they had a continual supply of primed and loaded muskets. Thanks to

Charles, we have plenty of flintlocks so if you're willing, you could take up a position inside one of the redoubts and replace each fired piece with a loaded one. That would quicken the speed of fire. But you must keep well down — lie on the ground if necessary — and on no account offer your head as a target.'

'We shall need instruction, Adam, but of course I'll be a loader. And so will Thomas. It'll be more exciting than handing out rations. Charles will teach us, won't he?'

'I expect he'll be delighted. Let's go and ask him.'

Charles was indeed delighted. 'It will be an honour, my dear,' he said, smiling hugely, 'and I'll wager you're better pupils than the maggoty lot Adam's sent us so far. Shall we begin at once?'

At a safe distance from everyone, they had their first lesson in the art of preparing a flintlock. Charles was an assiduous teacher, taking care to explain in detail the way to measure powder into the powder horn and how to load the shot. They both picked it up easily and by the end of the lesson could prime and load a flintlock in under a minute. Their teacher was impressed but still insisted on a second lesson the next day.

'You must be entirely confident,' he advised. 'Practice, practice and more practice, that's what Cromwell preaches to his Model Army, and we'll do well to take heed. Parade tomorrow at nine, if you please.'

'Very well, Charles, if you insist, but we do seem to have got the essence of it, don't you agree, Thomas?'

'I do. But perhaps Charles expects us to load two muskets in a minute.'

'That would be excellent.' He sounded as if he meant it.

The next morning, however, when they presented themselves for further instruction Charles had other ideas.

'Priming and loading is all very well but if you can aim and shoot you'll be even more help. Here are the flintlocks, here is a bag of powder with a horn each, here is a rod and here is the shot,' he said. 'And over there,' pointing to a tree about twenty yards away, 'is your target.'

On the trunk of the tree, Charles had carved the head of a man about five and a half feet up from the ground. He was evidently a better soldier than artist because one eye was twice the size of the other and the grinning mouth stretched from left ear to right.

'Why, Charles,' said Mary, 'I had no idea you were such a fine woodcarver. What an interesting head you've made. Are we now to destroy it with shot?'

'You are. Exactly. You'll be shooting its eyes out in no time.'

'The left one will be easier, I fancy, than the right,' observed Thomas.

'Enough of your insolence, Thomas Hill. Just for that, you will go first. Have you ever fired a musket?'

'I have not, although I have attended a battle.'

'Newbury, wasn't it?'

'It was. I sat in a tent near the king and watched men and animals being killed and maimed. I sent out the king's orders and received reports from his commanders. Some had to be encrypted or decrypted. I was his cryptographer.'

'Well, well, Thomas. A cryptographer, eh? Codes and suchlike.'

'Exactly. Codes and suchlike. I did no fighting.'

'Well, I don't imagine we'll need codes so best have a go with a flintlock.'

Thomas stepped forward and with an unloaded flintlock was shown how to take up a firm stance with his feet apart, how to hold it firmly in his left hand and how to squeeze the trigger with his right, while squinting down the barrel at his target. It was not difficult and Charles had only to show him once and then suggest minor changes.

When it was Mary's turn, however, Charles was displeased. 'No, no, Mary, that won't do at all. If you don't fall over you'll be lucky and you won't hit a forest, let alone a tree, like that. Come, allow me.'

Slipping round behind her, he delicately adjusted the position of her left hand and the set of her shoulders. To be sure of her aim he placed his head beside hers and squinted down the barrel. 'There, how does that feel? Better, eh? Should hit him like that.'

Mary wriggled a bit. 'Very comfortable, Charles. Will we be standing like this for long?'

It was exactly at this point that Adam arrived to check on progress. He coughed loudly but Charles and Mary were too intent upon their lesson to notice.

'Good morning, Charles,' called out Adam, 'I see I find you engaged. Closely engaged by the look of it. Please do proceed. I wouldn't wish to interrupt.'

Charles stepped back sharply. 'Ah, Adam, good morning. Yes, engaged we are. In target practice indeed. You are just in time to observe our first efforts at hitting the target.'

'No doubt Mary at least will have no difficulty in doing so. Few pupils can have enjoyed such intimate attention from their teacher. Was Thomas so fortunate?'

'Don't be silly, brother. Charles was simply pointing out the deficiencies in my technique. Thomas had no need of such help.' Mary was blushing.

'Quite so. Though I do hope he's not expecting you to take a position in the front rank of the infantry. It is uncommon for ladies to do so.'

'No indeed, Adam. Certainly not.' Charles feigned shock. 'Our lesson is purely for the purposes of self-defence, no more. Mary has been instructed to take no risk at all. In the event of an attack she will be under cover at all times.'

'I'm heartily glad to hear it. Now shall we watch some target practice?'

The first attempts of the pupils might have damaged a monkey unlucky enough to be asleep in the branches of the tree but would not have slowed the advance of an enemy. An hour later, however, there was little left of the grinning face and both Adam and Charles pronounced themselves satisfied.

'We deserve a reward after that,' said Mary. 'Let's open a bottle or two of claret. I'll fetch them. And I'm starving.'

Charles followed Mary into the house. By the time they returned, Patrick had put food and wine on the table.

'There's news from Bridgetown,' Adam told them, 'and not good. Walrond is making warlike noises and there have been more banishments. Worse, several estates in the south have been attacked. We must call everyone in at once. It's not safe any longer outside the ring. The men can go out to cut the cane but they should be armed and they must spend the nights here. The women and children must stay here all the time. There are only a few of them, after all. We mustn't be caught off guard.' Adam had made up his mind at once. They would take no more risks than absolutely necessary.

'I agree,' said Charles. 'I'll be off to Speightstown now to see if there is any news from the north.'

'Let us hope we're left alone,' said Mary. 'I don't believe I could bear the smell of more powder on my hands and clothes. It's not a perfume I favour.'

'Speaking of which, Mary,' said Charles, with a sideways look at Adam, 'I'm struggling with my new paintings. I can't seem to hang them right. It needs a woman's touch, I fancy. Might you be free tomorrow?'

'I might. Would midday be convenient?'

'It would. Very.'

By that evening, all the men in the fields had been armed, blankets had been laid out for them in the redoubts and the women were watching their children playing games outside the house. All the children but one were small — Thomas guessed less than six years old. The exception was a boy of perhaps twelve who sat alone, cross-legged and silent. He was an orphan named Daniel who helped in the curing house. Mary called him over. 'Daniel, if there is an attack I want you to stay inside the house to help with the children. They must be kept under cover with the women. We don't want any of them running out to see what all the noise is about.'

'Yes, Miss Lyte. Who is going to attack us?'

'There are bands of men attacking estates in the south. It might happen to us.'

'Are they white men or black men, Miss Lyte?'

'Both. They are armed and dangerous. That is why we are taking precautions. Remember, please, what I have told you.' Mary looked hard at him. There was something unsettling about this boy. But she had things to attend to. Daniel would have to fend for himself.

Just before dusk the men came in from the fields, singing as usual and carrying their muskets and swords over their shoulders.

Thomas and Adam showed each one where he would sleep and posted two sentries at the spots they had chosen. 'What do you do if you see or hear anyone approaching?' Thomas asked them for the hundredth time.

'We run back here and tell you how many there are and which direction they are coming from.'

'Good. Run fast, don't shout and try not to be seen. Off you go, and don't dare fall asleep. Any man who does will be put on sentry duty all night for a week. I'll be checking during the night.' He would be doing no such thing, but it did not hurt to frighten them a little. It might be someone else's fight, but he was caught up in it and he would play his part.

The first alarm came sooner than anyone expected. It was about midnight when the two sentries arrived. Adam heard them coming and went out to meet them.

'Mr Lyte, someone's coming. I heard the sound of a horse,' said one.

'So did I,' agreed the other, 'but it was more than one. They were making a lot of noise.' A horseman, or even horsemen, making a lot of noise did not sound like an impending attack, but there was nothing to be gained by taking chances.

'Wake all the men and tell them to take up their stations. No firing without my order. Make it clear.' Adam went back to tell Mary to stay inside and to keep out of sight until he called for her, then took his flintlock and waited in the shadows in the parlour, where Thomas and Patrick joined him.

Within a few minutes they heard the horse or horses, which seemed to be coming up the path from the road, and took aim at the opening in the trees where it joined the clearing around the house. The moon was full and it was light enough to see a mounted figure emerge. The rider was alone, and over the songs of the frogs Adam could hear him quietly whistling.

'Who's there?' he called. 'Stand and be recognized.'

The rider laughed loudly. 'Can you not recognize me by my excellent and tuneful whistling?'

Adam put down his flintlock and shouted to the men to do the same. 'Charles, you clod. We might have shot you.'

'That would have been unfortunate. I'm on your side.' Charles dismounted unsteadily and led his horse forward.

'Then why have you come under cover of darkness?'

'I would have returned earlier but another, ah, pressing matter detained me. Still, here I am and at your service. Any room at the inn?'

'Come inside and we'll find a place for you.'

The two sentries were looking sheepish. 'Try and count numbers next time but you did the right thing in coming to warn us,' Adam reassured them. 'Now back to your posts and stay alert. Our next visitor might not be so friendly.'

Ignoring Adam's instructions, Mary had been watching from the doorway. 'Good evening, Charles. Always a pleasure to see you although this is an unusual time to call on a lady.'

'My apologies, madam,' replied Charles, with his deepest bow and the most extravagant sweep of his hat that he could manage without falling over. 'Circumstances conspired against an earlier arrival. I crave your pardon.'

'Circumstances in a bottle or petticoats, I daresay. Or both. Now that we are awake, come inside and tell us your news.'

They sat round a small table on which Mary had lit candles. 'The news everywhere is not good,' began Charles, slurring his words only a little. 'Walrond continues to insist on oaths of loyalty to the king from all landowners. His men are still calling on anyone who has not sworn and leaving them in no doubt about their duty. Have they been to you yet?'

'Oddly enough, no. I'd swear the oath but Walrond must have overlooked me. Or perhaps I'm not important enough.'

'The Gibbes brothers were important enough,' said Thomas, 'and signed happily. It meant nothing to them as it won't to others.'

'And what of Drax?' asked Adam.

'He's refused to swear and so have Alleyne and Middleton. Walrond will announce tomorrow that they are to be banished and their estates sequestered. He'll say the estates are to be sold for the public purse but I'll wager he either takes them over himself or gives them to his friends. I don't trust the man.'

'If he does, he'll end up with half the island. Those three have over two thousand acres between them.'

'Drax has issued a warning that if his estate is stolen from him, he will persuade Cromwell to send a fleet and will come back with it to reclaim what is his. It reads like a declaration of war. Walrond has changed him from peaceful and moderate to bellicose and angry. Likewise Alleyne.'

'Are there any other militias appearing?'

'A few. Unlike the Gibbes, some landowners are refusing to sign. They're at liberty for now but they've been taking precautions. It's adding to the tension.'

'Meanwhile,' said Mary, 'slaves and servants are running away from unguarded estates all over the island.'

'And they're getting bolder and more dangerous,' agreed Adam, 'yet Walrond seems reluctant to do anything about them. He'll have to act soon.'

'He will, and he knows it. Let's hope it's soon enough.' Charles paused. 'There is one bright light on the horizon. There is word from England. Lord Willoughby planned to set sail from Southampton at the end of March. If he did, he will be here soon.'

'Do you think he can do anything about Walrond?'

'If anyone can, he can. Having known him for twenty years I have great faith in his abilities, even if he did start off on the wrong side.'

Mary rose. 'With that happy thought, gentlemen, I shall retire. Again. Adam will find you somewhere to rest your head, Charles. It must be heavy.'

'Thank you, my dear. Until the morning.'

Next day, Charles went home to collect clothes and a few possessions. He was back at the Lytes' house by mid-afternoon. 'My estate is secure and my steward is in full charge. He will call me if he needs me. Until then I shall stay here,' he announced, adding, 'assuming you wish me to, of course.'

'Thank you, Charles,' replied Mary. 'We do wish you to.'

'I thought we should have a roll-call of every person on the estate each morning and evening, just to make sure everyone is accounted for. Thomas did the first one this morning. There's one slave missing,' said Adam.

'And who's that?'

'The orphan boy, Daniel. He was here last night but this morning he's disappeared. We've searched and there's no sign of him. It looks as if he's run off.'

'I fear so,' said Mary thoughtfully. 'Let's hope there are no more.'

CHAPTER 19

Thomas was adamant. 'I do not care what you think, Patrick, I have barely left the estate for weeks and I am coming with you.'

'Mr Lyte might object.'

'You will persuade him otherwise.'

'The Gibbes are still thundering about the island looking for you. It's a wonder they haven't come here.'

In view of Adam's failed attempt to buy him, Thomas found it rather surprising. Perhaps their brains had finally succumbed to the drink.

'I doubt if they would recognize me now that I am well fed and well dressed. If they do, I will depend upon you to protect me. Have you got a musket?'

'No, Thomas, slaves do not carry muskets. But I will speak to Mr Lyte. He might take pity on you.'

It took twenty men to manhandle eight hogsheads of muscovado up ramps on to four carts. Each cart was drawn by a pair of oxen and driven by one of the six slaves chosen for the job, with an assistant beside him to keep an eye on the barrels. They had been securely tied down with thick rope but as each one was worth over twenty pounds, a watchful eye was needed. Adam and a grateful Thomas rode in the fourth cart at the rear of the line. Thomas had the job of barrel-watcher.

It was the first time he had visited Bridgetown, which that morning was bustling. They approached the harbour along the coast road from the north, crossing an ancient bridge over the narrow river which emptied into the port, and entering the main square in which the Assembly House stood. The bridge was a crude construction, originally built by the native Indians who had once inhabited the island and reinforced with stout timbers.

Built of dressed pink coral stone, roofed with grey slate tiles and with tall latticed windows, the Assembly House was by far the most impressive building on the island. A flight of wide stone steps led up to the entrance where four armed guards stood watch. Governor Walrond was taking no chances.

Planters and merchants milled about in the square, exchanging news and concluding business. The Dutch merchants would be negotiating prices for the sugar they had agreed in advance to buy and the planters would be demanding lower charges for its transport to London or Amsterdam. As the little procession of carts followed the road around the harbour to a jetty at the southern end, two or three raised their hands in greeting to Adam.

The harbour was a natural semi-circle with a stone wall built around it and unlike Oistins harbour the water was deep enough for a frigate or trading ship to tie up at the jetty. That morning, a squat vessel was being loaded with hogsheads of sugar. Looking out into Carlisle Bay into which the harbour opened, Thomas saw three more ships waiting their turn to come in. Down in their holds, frightened men, both black and white, would be waiting to discover their fate. The lucky ones would work for Charles Carrington, Adam Lyte or another like them. The unlucky ones would end up at the Gibbes's, or worse. Once they were ashore, the men would be replaced by hogsheads of sugar and barrels of rum and the ship would set off back across the Atlantic. Sugar, slaves and convicts were making planters and their suppliers very rich men.

Thomas pointed to the ship at the jetty. 'There's a likely vessel, Adam. When you are not looking, I could slip on board and hide.'

'I wouldn't recommend it,' replied Adam. 'I have met the captain of that ship, who might well be descended from Barbary pirates. He'd steal the shirt off your back and toss you overboard the moment he found you.'

Between the harbour wall and a row of harbour buildings they weaved their way slowly through and around heaps of rope, stacks of timber, barrels, canvas and boxes of provisions. Screeching gulls swooped and fought over scraps of food, spilled sugar and the catch being unloaded from a small fishing boat tied to the wall.

The harbour buildings were mostly wooden and in need of paint. Wedged conveniently between a brothel and the Francis Drake inn, the harbour master's house stood out as the grandest, with an overhanging upper storey, glazed windows and rendered walls.

The Drake was busy, with noisy drinkers overflowing into the street. Outside the brothel an enormous woman with a red cloth tied around her head and skin the colour of coal sat on a low stool, watching the passers-by. Although its door was closed and its windows shuttered, the brothel would also be busy. A ship in port would keep both establishments hard at work and with three more waiting to come in, the landlord and the brothel owner would be doing very handsomely.

Thomas's sensitive nose wrinkled. He smelled sweat, sugar, ale, salt and heat. Barbados had a smell all of its own — thick, sweet and heady. He had noticed it on his very first day on the island and it had never left him. At the Gibbes's and at the Lytes' he had grown used to it but here it was different, enriched with the smells of the sea and of a busy port about its business. Thomas closed his eyes and inhaled. The mixture was not unpleasant but he would rather be breathing the cool, salty air of Southampton.

Near the jetty stood two large timber warehouses in which planters stored their barrels of sugar until they were loaded on board ship. It was more practical to do as Adam had done and bring the hogsheads down regularly in manageable numbers than to keep them on the estate.

Gangs of slaves were rolling the barrels out of one warehouse to the edge of the jetty, where they were attached to a hoist and lifted on to the ship. It was work for big, strong men and, glistening with sweat, the slaves were stretching and straining their muscles with the effort. An overseer with a whip stood over them, occasionally encouraging a man to greater endeavour with a flick of its tongue. It was the sugar trade at work. Tons and tons of sugar, free labour and a ready market. Even the Gibbes could do it.

They drew the carts up to one side of the warehouses while Adam went to make the necessary arrangements to have their load stored. He was not long in returning. 'We'll have to wait a while,' he told the men. 'Stay here and watch the carts. We'll be in the Drake. Come on, Thomas.'

Thomas jumped down and followed Adam back around the harbour to the inn. They were soon sitting at a table inside with wooden tankards of ale in their hands. Among the drinkers Thomas noticed Robert Sprot. As ever, immaculately turned out and with his battered satchel to hand, Sprot sat alone in one corner, politely tipping his straw hat to any customer or potential customer he recognized. With sailors in port and heavy barrels being carted about, it was as good a place as any to do business. A crushed foot or a broken head and Sprot would be ready with his tools.

'At least it has not dawned on the Gibbes where you might be. A little surprising considering that I offered to buy you,' said Adam.

'Indeed. It would be awkward for you if they did discover where I have been hiding. I should not want you or Mary to be embarrassed.'

Adam laughed. 'Embarrassed we could manage. Violence would be more unpleasant. And they are a violent pair.'

'I kept a list of adjectives when I was there. Every ten days I wrote down a new one to describe them. I remember filthy, repulsive and carnivorous. I don't remember violent but it would have occurred to me eventually.'

'I do hope you're not keeping a list about us, Thomas. That too would be embarrassing.'

'No, no list about the Lytes.' Thomas paused. 'Adam, what do you think will happen if Lord Willoughby does arrive?'

'It's hard to be sure. Willoughby, by all accounts, is a formidable man and if he carries the commission of Charles Stuart, he will insist on discharging his responsibility. But Walrond won't go easily. Having swept Bell aside, he won't be easy to shift.'

'And Cromwell won't turn a blind eye either. Until the king

was executed, the island enjoyed peace and prosperity, now nothing but fear and danger. If only—'

There was a cry of alarm from the harbour and at almost the same moment Thomas smelt smoke. Every man in the inn jumped up and rushed outside. The smoke was billowing towards them from one of the warehouses and they saw flames playing around its timber walls.

In the short time it took them to run around the harbour the flames had stretched up to the roof. Several men ran out of the warehouse, their arms over their faces to protect them from the heat and their clothes and hair on fire. Some jumped into the water, others collapsed to the ground screaming. Two quick-thinking sailors found buckets, filled them with seawater and threw them over the burning bodies. Still screaming, the burned men were dragged away.

In seconds the whole warehouse was ablaze and the heat had forced everyone back. Timber walls, timber barrels, rum and sugar fed the flames. There was little anyone could do but watch and hope the fire did not spread to the other warehouse.

Having sensibly driven their carts well away from the fire, Adam's men returned to join the watching crowd. He and Thomas stood with them. 'Did everyone get out?' Thomas asked the man beside him.

The man shook his head. 'Don't know, sir. Perhaps not.'

'How did it start, do you think?'

'Runaways, I should say, sir.'

At that moment a blazing figure emerged from the inferno and staggered towards them. More torch than man, he stumbled and fell. Thomas jumped forward and threw himself on top of him, trying to smother the flames. It was a vain effort and he would soon have caught fire himself had Adam not stepped forward with a pail of water and thrown it over them. It was enough to extinguish the flames, and Thomas rolled off.

Adam bent to examine the man, then shook his head. 'Dead. His face and body burned to cinders. Take him away.' Two of his men stepped forward, picked up the corpse and carried it off. The coroner would do the rest.

The warehouse was still burning. A gang of men had formed a line to the water and were passing buckets up and down as fast as they could. The man at the top of the line threw the water over the flames but to very little avail. Thomas hauled himself to his feet, checked that the burns on his hands were no more than superficial and wiped his face with his sleeve.

'Wouldn't it be wiser to use the water on the other warehouse?' he asked Adam. 'This one's beyond saving but if we dampen the walls of the other, it might prevent them catching.'

Adam nodded, strode up to the man at the head of the line and shouted above the flames. The man immediately moved over to the second warehouse and the line followed him. He threw the water over the walls, heaving it up as high as he could. Soon water was dripping down as if there had been a sudden rainstorm and when a tongue of flame did leap across from the fire, it spluttered and died without doing any damage.

The line kept up its work until the fire had burned itself out. The timber had been so dry and the fire so fierce that it did not take long. A black heap of charred wood and ashes was all that remained of the warehouse; everything in it had been destroyed and at least one man had died. Among those who had thrown themselves into the water there might have been more deaths and gruesome evidence of others might yet be found in the ashes.

Adam and Thomas sat on the harbour wall and gazed at the scene. 'Are you injured, Thomas?' asked Adam.

Thomas held his hands out for inspection. In places they were red and raw but nothing worse. 'Nothing one of Patrick's salves won't cure.'

'It was brave of you to try to save the man.'

'Brave? Not really. More instinct than courage. Thank God more men were not killed and we saved the second warehouse. Who will bear the cost of the other one?'

'The Dutchman who owns the warehouses will have to rebuild at his own expense and replace the lost sugar. He will be insured, I expect. Fortunately, I had no more than a few hogsheads in the one that burned.'

'I wonder if the Dutchman will rebuild in stone.'

'He will have to after this. His customers will not want to risk another fire, especially with bands of runaways on the loose. No fools, the Dutch. While we strive and strain to plant and grow, pausing only to fight each other, they provide finance, buy our sugar cheaply, warehouse it, ship it, sell it to eager buyers in Europe and pocket the profits. While England has been tearing itself to pieces, Holland has grown fat and prosperous.'

'What shall we do with the sugar, Adam?' asked Thomas.

'I think we'll take it home and thank God we did not come yesterday.'

They rose and walked towards the waiting carts. As they did so, the black-clad figure of Sprot appeared from the Drake, satchel over his shoulder and making for the group of men who had jumped into the water. Sprot, at least, would be happy. A burned finger or two to remove, perhaps an arm or a leg and he would have had a good day's work.

The journey back to the estate was sad and silent. Only Thomas had suffered any injury but all were affected. The cost in life and money was great. Indentured man or slave, they were better off with peace and trade than death and destruction, and they knew it.

Mary saw the loaded carts returning and came out to discover what had happened. Adam asked her first to fetch Patrick to tend to Thomas's hands, ordered the placing of the muscovado back in their own store and then sat down with her to tell the story.

When it was done and Thomas's hands had been anointed with a thick salve and bandaged with clean cloths, Mary said only, 'I thank God you are all safe. But we are in danger. If runaways will do this, who knows what else they are capable of?'

'Where is Charles?' asked Adam.

Mary blushed. 'He is asleep. The heat, I fancy, was too much for him.'

CHAPTER 20

The attack came just before dawn. A sentry in the woods to the north was found with his head dangling by shreds of skin. His terrified replacement took one look, then turned and ran, yelling loudly enough to wake the household and rouse the men.

While sleep was being rubbed from bleary eyes and shaken from fuddled minds, Adam forced some sense out of the man and began calling out instructions. Despite the urgency in his voice the men moved slowly, perhaps suspecting another false alarm. His orders for all weapons to be checked and ready were largely ignored until he and Charles booted the slowest backsides and cuffed the dullest heads into action. By the time the other sentries had returned, red and green platoons were more or less armed and in position and Charles had marshalled black platoon around him in the parlour, where they crouched behind a heap of upturned tables and chairs. Each man with a sword looked eager to put its edge to the test. Charles cautioned them to keep quiet and stay out of sight. Adam took the place of the dead sentry behind a red platoon redoubt. Mary sat inside with the women and children, huddled together away from the door, while Patrick and Thomas kept watch out of the windows. Thomas's hands were not up to reloading muskets.

'Observation and casualties, for us, Patrick,' said Thomas. 'Let's hope the only casualties we observe are the enemy's.'

The first shots were fired the moment it was light enough to see. Patrick had predicted this. He said it was the Africans' way. They came from within the tree line on the north and east sides of the house. Calculating that the attackers were trying to gauge their strength before showing themselves, Adam shouted at the men to hold their fire and keep their heads down. Musket shot whistled all about, but behind the redoubts and the pile of furniture they were safe from anything other than an unlucky ricochet.

After several unproductive volleys, a dozen men, frustrated at having failed to tempt the defenders into a response, emerged cautiously from the woods to the north. Peeking through the window, Thomas saw that they were armed with muskets, axes and bill-hooks, and that unless there was an African people with white skin and red hair, they were not escaped slaves. These were convicts — Irish and Welsh probably.

As he watched, half of the attackers split off and circled around to the west. Assuming they planned to advance from all quarters, he looked to his right. There too a dozen men were creeping forward, bent double in the manner of hunters nearing their prey, but these were black men. They also split up, six of them edging around to their left in order to attack from the south. Twenty-four men with muskets and machetes and coming from all directions. Not too alarming unless there were many more in the trees, but time to act. He shouted his report to Adam.

Adam called for the first volley, stood and fired at a head. It was a red one and he might have hit it, but Thomas could not be sure. From behind each redoubt, two men rose, aimed and fired. When they ducked down to reload, two others stood and repeated the process. Three bodies lay on the ground, one squirming about holding his stomach, the other two motionless.

But the attackers had had time to find cover and were returning fire. A musket shot whipped past Adam's left ear and he dropped hastily. Cupping his hands, he took a breath and shouted as loudly as he could. 'Casualties? Red?'

'One minor.'

'Green?'

'One in the head.'

'None here. Enemy down?'

'Two.'

'Uncertain. One perhaps.'

'Two or three for us. Get the wounded into the house.'

At this order Thomas and Patrick darted out to the two wounded men. The first, from red platoon, walked unaided, holding one bloody hand in the other, but the second had to be carried. His eyes were closed and he was sobbing quietly. There was blood on his throat and face and Thomas feared he would be their second fatality. They took him into the house where Thomas left him to Patrick's care and returned quickly to his post at the window.

From his hiding place in the parlour Charles had been watching impatiently. It would not do to unleash his swordsmen too soon, desperate as they were to get into the fray. He held his finger to his lips for silence and signalled for calm. They stayed under cover while the two wounded men were brought back into the house.

The second volley came immediately. Again the shots were fired from behind the tree line and again Adam shouted at his men to keep low and hold their fire. The enemy would have to cross thirty yards of open ground to reach the house and he fleetingly hoped they would think better of trying again. But the incoming musket fire this time was heavier and better directed. The barricades and the parlour where Charles and his swordsmen still hid were peppered with shots. Two screams of pain signalled two casualties, probably from ricochets or flying splinters.

At the window, Thomas was watching the trees. When the first of the attackers emerged flat on the ground, holding their muskets across their faces and using their elbows and knees to crawl forward, he shouted a warning to Adam. This was not a tactic Thomas had seen at Newbury. Musketeers and pikemen certainly did not use it. But he soon saw the sense of it. Hitting a man crawling on his stomach, even from under thirty yards, would be a much more difficult proposition than hitting him standing up. He suspected it was a tactic imported from Africa or America, where men with spears had learned ways of fighting men with muskets.

Behind the crawling front line – thankfully moving at a cautious pace – a second group emerged, took up kneeling positions and began to launch volleys over their heads. If the crawlers reached the redoubts under this covering fire, anything could happen. Again Thomas yelled a warning. Calling for another volley, Adam rose and took aim at a kneeling man. Red and green platoons did the same.

When they ducked down, Adam shouted for Charles. 'Off you go, Charles. Start with the wriggling worms.'

Black platoon needed no prompting. An enemy lying invitingly on the ground, his back exposed to the point of a sword or the blade of an axe, was the very enemy a man might wish to encounter. Even if he had wanted to, Charles could have held them back no longer. They leapt out of hiding and ran past the redoubts, screaming their battle cries and raising their weapons to strike.

'Thank God I'm on their side,' Thomas said out loud. The nearest of the crawlers did not even have time to roll over and face them before being skewered and sliced, and the ones who did simply had a better view of their own ends. Black platoon, Charles Carrington at its head, moved so fast that it sped right around the house killing worms before any could escape. If the first strike did not kill, the second did. In no time, the ground had turned red. Butchered bodies lay everywhere; some lacked limbs or heads, others had been filleted.

But kneeling musketeers were still firing from the tree line and two swordsmen went down. Mary and Thomas ran out of the house towards one of them. Musket fire whistled around them and Adam shouted at them to get back. They ignored him and dragged the man by his arms to the safety of a redoubt.

They returned for the second man. Again they took an arm each, but this man was bigger and heavier and Mary was struggling. Musket fire rang out and she went down. Thomas immediately dropped the wounded man's arm, picked her up and staggered back to the house. Blood from her right thigh was soaking her dress and Thomas feared an artery wound.

'Thank you, Thomas,' she whispered, 'my brother might have helped but I daresay he's busy.'

'Ssh, Mary. You're losing blood. Lie there and Patrick will see to you.' Thomas left her to Patrick and went back outside. This time, the enemy were waiting for him and he was met by another volley of musket fire. Crouching low, he turned himself into as small a target as he could, made it to the wounded man, grabbed his legs and tried to pull him back to the parlour. Until then, Thomas's raw hands had stood up well. But this man was too heavy, and Thomas could not move him. He was a sitting duck. He was about to abandon the attempt when Patrick appeared beside him and took hold of the man's leg. Together, they managed to drag him to the safety of the house, made him comfortable and went over to Mary who was lying in a corner.

'If you will permit it, Miss Lyte, I'll take a look at your wound,' said Patrick. Mary said nothing, but reached down and pulled up her skirt and petticoat. Patrick wiped away blood from her thigh and peered closely at the injury. They were in a battle and there was no embarrassment.

'A musket ball has gone straight through, Miss Lyte. There's cloth from your skirt around the wound. I'll have to make sure there's none inside before I clean it.'

'Is there any sign of bone?'

Patrick peered again at the wound. 'No, but this will hurt.'

Mary sighed with relief. A shattered bone or a pierced artery could kill her. 'Then thank God it's you, Patrick. Sprot would have had my leg off as soon as look at it. Take my hand, Thomas, if you please. I'm ready. Now do it quickly.'

With a silver salt spoon Patrick probed the wound and extracted two small pieces of cloth. Her face ashen and her teeth clamped around her knuckles, Mary uttered no sound but low groans of pain. She squeezed Thomas's hand until it hurt.

'It's done,' said Patrick at last. 'Lie still please and I will clean and bandage it.' Mary opened her eyes and nodded. Then her grip slackened and she passed out. Patrick wiped the sweat from her face and bound the wound. They would soon know if it was poisoned.

Thomas returned to the window and watched the trees. Having despatched the wriggling worms, Charles and his platoon had launched themselves at the rest. The rest, however, were rather more numerous than expected. When Thomas saw a dozen men, again a mixture of white and black, emerge, he shouted an alarm.

These men were led by a flame-haired giant wielding a long-handled axe. Good God, he thought, Africans and Irishmen and now Vikings. The devil alone knows where he came from. Then he remembered the huge Irishman from the ship, the one whom the guards had pulled off Thomas. Not only had he survived, he was intent on revenge.

While black platoon, now reinforced by red and green armed with swords or using their muskets as clubs, cut, stabbed and swung at the enemy, Charles had decided to make the Viking's acquaintance. He spotted a sword impaled in the stomach of a dead slave, tugged it out and advanced upon the Viking with a blade in each hand.

Truth to tell, the Viking had not done much so far. He had merely kept an eye on the ebb and flow and looked as terrifying as he could. He had yet to swing the long axe in anger. But seeing a tall dark-haired man with two swords closing at speed, the Viking raised his weapon and let out a blood-curdling battle cry.

Unimpressed, Charles did not check his stride but advanced to duelling distance, shot out his right hand and drew blood from the Viking's neck. The man let out a howl and brought down his axe with savage force. Charles had stepped deftly back and the axe passed harmlessly by. Before the Viking could recover his balance, he moved in again and this time sliced the man's right arm with the sword in his left hand. Another howl of pain and fury and another fruitless swing of the axe.

Thomas knew that Charles could finish his man off with ease. Rather than move in for the *coup de grâce*, however, Charles stepped back to admire his handiwork. Then, to Thomas's horror, he stumbled on a stone and was down on one knee, knuckles and swords on the ground. He would surely have been up again in an instant but the Viking saw his chance and leapt forward to strike with the axe. One well-timed blow would remove an arm or a leg but he aimed instead for Charles's neck. That was his mistake. A side-swipe at an arm could not have been deflected, but in raising the axe above his head the Viking allowed Charles just enough time to hop forward like a rabbit and thrust a sword up between his legs. Such was the shock that the Irishman uttered no sound, just fell face forward into the dirt, the sword sticking out grotesquely behind him. Charles scrambled to his feet and, as if to atone for his earlier indiscretion, plunged the other sword into the man's back.

Absorbed as he had been in Charles's duel with the Viking, Thomas had not observed progress elsewhere. By the time he looked about, the ground was strewn with the bodies of their attackers mingled with a few of their own, and the battle was over. Any who had escaped the swinging swords and hacking machetes had run for their lives. It was time to count the cost and tend to the wounded, who were already being carried into the house by their colleagues.

'Well, that presented no great difficulty,' observed Charles, wiping his sword on his leg. 'A poorly trained lot, although with an interesting new tactic of advancing along the ground. Might have worked against muskets, but not sharp blades.'

Adam looked about. 'Irish and slaves, I'd say,' and seeing Charles's victim, as large in death as in life and still holding his long-handled axe, 'and a Viking or two, it seems. What an unholy trinity.'

'A stupid Viking fortunately,' replied Charles, 'or I might have been his dinner. The Vikings did eat their victims, didn't they? Or was it the Huns? Damned if I can remember.'

'Neither, I think,' said Adam. 'Now we'd better deal with this mess before the dogs arrive.' He threw up his hands. 'My God. Mary. She was hit.'

Followed by Charles, he ran to the house. There they found the women and children on their feet, milling about wondering what to do next, and a very pale Mary sitting in a chair in the corner, guarded by Thomas and Patrick who would not let anyone near their patient.

'My, my. Two more gentlemen to see me. I must be wounded more often.'

Adam turned to Patrick. 'Patrick, how bad is Miss Lyte's wound?'

'A musket ball passed through her thigh, sir. I've cleaned and dressed it and Miss Lyte has taken a little brandy.'

'Her thigh, eh? Wish I'd been here to do the cleaning and dressing.'

'That would have been a comfort, Charles, but I gather you were otherwise engaged.'

Adam needed reassurance. 'Are you sure it didn't touch the bone, Patrick? And the shot has gone right through?'

'Quite sure, sir. I removed two pieces of her skirt from the wound. There was no sign of bone but we must watch for poison. Now she should rest. I will clear everyone out.'

'Good. And please make sure the wounded are taken care of. I'll come and help in a moment.'

When he had left, Charles said, 'I do hope Patrick was discreet in his attentions. It must have been embarrassing for you, my dear.'

'Tush, Charles Carrington. It had to be done and that's that. Don't be such an old woman.'

Charles smiled broadly. 'I know. Merely jealous.'

'Good,' said Mary, the brandy bringing colour back to her cheeks. 'Now, gentlemen, before I go to lie down please give me an account of the affair. I'm sorry that Thomas and I were unable to put our excellent training to good use but I suppose that's the way of soldiering. You may start from the point at which I was hit. I observed the earlier exchanges.'

Adam described what he called 'the worms' advance' and the swift work of black platoon, and praised red and green platoons for their steadiness under fire.

'And you, Charles?' asked Mary. 'What did you make of it?'

'Our troops, as Adam said, gave a good account of themselves and I doubt we need worry ourselves about any more attacks from that quarter. And if there is another, we have plenty of provisions.'

'And yourself? You were in the thick of it, I'm sure.'

'As a matter of fact, my dear, I did very little. Hardly needed at all. More of a strategic role, I fancy. Barely wetted my sword.'

'Or swords, Charles.' Adam had seen him dispose of the Viking. 'And you are too modest. That axeman could have caused trouble.'

'Axeman?' Mary looked at him enquiringly. 'I do hope he didn't inconvenience you.'

'Oh, not at all, my dear. He was a clumsy oaf.'

'But not too clumsy to have made a hole in your breeches, I see. I couldn't but notice it when you turned around. Quite large, I fear, and rather revealing. Perhaps a gentleman should wear undergarments in battle. They might save his blushes.' Mary smiled but her voice was weak.

Charles, who'd had no idea that part of his backside was on public view, went bright crimson, and retreated briskly towards the wall.

'Now, Charles,' laughed Adam, 'nothing to be ashamed of. It could have happened to anyone and I'm sure you didn't turn your back on the enemy. Have you counted the casualties?' he asked when Patrick reappeared.

'I have, sir. We found eighteen of the enemy dead. No wounded.'

'None?'

'None. Black platoon did not care to take prisoners.'

Adam blanched, but, breeches forgotten, Charles was much cheered by this news. 'Eighteen dead, eh? Out of no more than twice that number. A good day's work. Unnecessary violence I deplore, but when necessary it should be swift and decisive.'

'Of our own men, two are dead — the man hit in the head and the sentry — and we have seven wounded. Two from wood splinters, two hit by musket balls and three with slashes from blades. One may lose an arm, another a leg. The others will heal,' said Patrick.

'We were fortunate, then. I will arrange for our men to be buried properly and we will dispose of the other bodies. I will come and see the wounded when I have attended to Mary.'

'One more thing, sir,' added Patrick. 'One of the dead is Daniel, the orphan who went missing last month. He must have run off to join them.'

'I am sorry to hear it,' said Mary. 'He was no more than a boy.'

'And I,' agreed Adam, 'but it might have been Daniel who led them to us. Now, Mary, I shall take you to your bed and you are to stay there until I say otherwise.' He picked up his sister very gently and carried her to her bedroom.

Charles, squeezed into a borrowed pair of breeches, assisted Patrick and Thomas with the wounded. Bottles of rum were circulating freely. Already, jokes were being told and stories exchanged. How extraordinary, thought Thomas, listening to them: no more than an hour had passed and brushes with death were reduced to ribald humour and vain boasting.

The two dead men had been taken to the small graveyard beside the servants' quarters. Of the wounded, a shin bone had been shattered and an arm badly gashed. The two men struck by flying splinters had suffered the murderous things being pulled out, one from his upper arm, the other from his stomach. The others — one musket ball and two slashes — were not serious. Adam knew that they had escaped lightly.

'Their women will stay with the slaves, Mr Lyte,' said Patrick, 'and I will take care of the others. I fear we shall need Mr Sprot.'

'I will find him when I ride to Bridgetown to inform the governor of the attack.'

'You should post sentries, Adam, and keep the women and children here,' advised Charles. 'They may come back.'

'Oh come now, Charles,' exclaimed Adam, 'surely we've seen the last of them. We gave them a good hiding and they won't want another.'

'I daresay. But we don't know how many more of them there may be. Better to take no chances.'

'Very well. We'll post sentries and keep the women and

children here tonight. But breakfast first and I'll do the cooking.'

Half an hour later, the three men were seated around the Lytes' table with plates of bread, eggs, cold chicken and mutton chops, and big wooden tankards of beer. Adam was a cook with a generous eye to quantity if not quality. 'I wish the silly girl hadn't disobeyed my orders and run out to the wounded men,' he said when they had finished. 'Couldn't you have stopped her?'

'I was too slow. And there was much going on to hold my attention elsewhere,' replied Charles.

'She's a courageous lady,' Thomas said quietly.

'She certainly is,' agreed Charles. 'Brains, beauty and bravery. Perkins is a lucky man.' He paused. 'What about Patrick?'

'He did well. He dreaded having to kill someone, especially an African, but thankfully it didn't happen. Thomas too. He rescued Mary and two men. You don't have to wield a sword to be brave, or even two.' He rose. 'Now I shall go to Bridgetown. The men can go back to the fields this afternoon but they should be armed.'

'Leave it with us, my dear fellow,' said Charles, patting his stomach. 'You be off and tell Walrond to deal with these attacks once and for all and we'll take care of matters here.'

Adam did not return until the next morning, having spent the night in Bridgetown. Charles had stayed to help Thomas and Patrick. If there was any impropriety in this, it had been over-looked in the interests of safety.

In addition to Sprot, Adam brought news. 'Willoughby's ship is in the bay,' he reported, 'and he's been sending messages to Walrond. As we thought, he carries Charles Stuart's commission to take over as governor.'

'I knew Willoughby would come,' said Charles.

'Let us talk about it later,' said Mary impatiently. 'First Mr Sprot must see to the wounded men.'

'I can take him to them,' offered Thomas.

'No, Thomas, you stay here. I shall do it.' Mary was insistent.

Overdressed as always, shirt and stockings drenched in sweat, Sprot was delighted to be of service to the Lytes.

'Thank you, madam,' he said, with a grand sweep of his straw hat. 'I have all my instruments with me and a good supply of bandages, hardly used. We shall need rum. Limbs, like branches, are best pruned when their owner is dormant. I will do everything modern medical practices advise and it will not on this occasion be necessary to request payment in advance.'

'Well, that's something anyway.' Charles did not hold a high opinion of Sprot.

'Come with me, Mr Sprot,' said Mary, who could only hobble along on Patrick's arm. 'We'll visit the slaves first. One has a shattered leg, the other a gashed arm.'

'As you wish, madam. Lead on and I shall follow.'

'There's no need for you to go, Mary,' said Adam, 'you should be resting. I'll go with Sprot.'

'Nonsense. We'll manage. This is a woman's work. Come, Mr Sprot.' And, leaning heavily on her escort, she led the beaming surgeon off towards the slave quarters.

'So,' said Charles, when they had sat down, 'it's Willoughby. I wish he'd come earlier. He might have prevented the banishments and sequestrations. We don't need James Drax as an enemy but that's what we've got. Still, it's a relief. I am not an admirer of Walrond, to say the least.'

'Nor I. But he has yet to be persuaded to recognize

Willoughby's claim. Now he has power, he's reluctant to give it up. Hardly a surprise, I suppose.'

'If he does not receive Willoughby, won't he be accused of disloyalty to the crown?' asked Thomas.

'That's possible. And Willoughby's a clever man. He'll find a way to keep Walrond happy. And don't forget he has a royal commission for other islands, St Kitts and Antigua among them. He won't stay here all the time.'

'Let's hope he stays here long enough to bring some harmony. We don't want any more attacks and we don't want threats of revenge from dispossessed landowners. Willoughby's commission will mean nothing to them.'

There was a scream from the direction of the slave quarters. 'Ah, the leg, I fear,' said Adam. 'I do hope Mary will make certain that's the only limb lost today. You can never be sure with Sprot.'

Happily, when Mary returned with Sprot, it was. They had left Patrick with the wounded. 'He's a strong man,' said Sprot, 'and I am confident that he'll make a good recovery. I am quick with the saw and your men rendered valuable assistance.'

'Good, Mr Sprot. And what of the arm?'

'I was inclined to bleed it or remove it,' said Sprot, 'on account of bad blood. It's a grave risk in such cases. But Miss Lyte insisted that we give the limb more time to heal, so I have applied a remedy of my own devising and bandaged the wound. It may serve, but you should summon me in the event of any deterioration in the condition of the man.'

'You may be sure that we shall, Mr Sprot. May we take it that the other injuries are also now attended to?'

'You may, sir. They are comparatively minor, although the splinter wounds could yet fester. I have probed for fragments with the Saviour as you may have heard, but if any remain you will need me again. I will attend tomorrow in the hope of seeing laudable pus, a sure sign of recovery.'

'Our thanks, Mr Sprot. Now come inside and I shall see to your fee.'

'Most kind, Mr Lyte, Miss Lyte.' Ever courteous, Sprot tipped his hat to Mary. 'An honour to be of service. But would you not wish me to examine your own injury, Miss Lyte?'

'That won't be necessary, Mr Sprot. It's only a graze.'

'As you wish, madam.' Sprot was clearly put out.

Mary sat down in the parlour with the men. 'Thank God that's over,' she said when they were out of earshot. 'The wretch wanted to bleed the arm. Bleed it, for the love of God. He said something about bad blood in the wound. What rubbish. The poor man's lost quite enough blood as it is, without Sprot taking more. I forbade it.'

'And I'm quite sure you were right, my dear,' said Charles, although, in truth, he had no idea whether she was or not. He cared for neither Sprot nor medical matters, especially when they involved saws and knives.

Adam saw Sprot to his horse and came back to join them. 'We got off lightly and I trust we shall not be called upon to do it again. It was quiet last night, I take it?'

'It was,' replied Thomas. 'We posted sentries but there were no alarms.'

'And now that you're back, Adam, I shall take my leave,' added Charles. 'I must see that all is well at home. I'll bring news if I hear any.'

'We are both in your debt, Charles,' said Mary. 'I don't know what we should have done without you.'

'Nor I,' agreed Adam. 'I wouldn't have liked to tackle that Viking myself.'

'All in the course of duty,' said Charles, adding with a bow to Mary, 'and pleasure, of course.'

Adam shook his hand, and Mary reached up to kiss him on the cheek. 'Thank you, Charles. Go well.'

For the love of God, tell Adam you wish to marry her, thought Thomas. Challenge him to a duel if you have to. With two swords.

By that evening, Mary's wound was worse and she had a fever. Adam put her to bed with a sleeping draught and she was still asleep when Sprot bustled in the next morning. Thomas was sitting at her bedside, where he had been for most of the night.

Having checked on the wounded men, Sprot insisted on visiting Mary and was tut-tutting about not having been permitted to examine her wound the day before. 'It is never wise to decline the services of an experienced surgeon when they are offered,' he admonished them, 'and one's fee must reflect any difficulties occasioned by delay.'

'Damn your fee, Sprot,' barked Adam, 'my sister's leg is my concern. Kindly examine it and give us your opinion.'

Sprot peered closely at the wound, pursed his lips and shook his head. 'It is as I feared, sir. There is no sign of suppuration. The wound cannot heal without laudable pus being expelled. It is essential to healing. There is no sign yet of the patient sinking into delirium but it will come as surely as night follows day. In such cases I have learned from long experience that it is the lesser of two evils to remove the damaged limb at once.'

Adam was horrified. 'Are you sure, Sprot? The leg looks strong. Is there no alternative?'

'I fear not, sir. The wound should by now be suppurating freely.'

'I cannot believe that is necessary,' said Thomas, with as much conviction as he could manage. In truth, he had no more idea about suppuration and laudable pus than he had about the workings of the heart. Like Charles, he simply did not trust Sprot.

Sprot peered at Thomas. 'Have we met, sir?'

'I think not,' lied Thomas.

'Well, sir, your medical knowledge may be superior to my own,' observed Sprot, clearly offended that his opinion was being questioned, 'but I doubt it. The leg must come off.'

'Good God. Then it had better be done quickly,' said Adam.

'Very well.' Sprot opened his satchel and took out a small hand saw. 'The patient should be bound tightly and her arms restrained. We must keep her as still as we can during the cutting.'

Adam called for Patrick. 'Patrick, it's necessary to remove Miss Lyte's leg. Bring a bowl of hot water, cloths, rope and brandy. And a bucket for the blood.'

Patrick too was horrified. 'But there's no poison, sir. The leg can be saved. Let me try my mother's remedy, I beg you.'

'There is no time for it to take effect, Patrick, even if it does have healing properties. Kindly do as I ask.' The look on Adam's face told Patrick that further argument would be useless. He went to collect what was needed.

While Adam and Thomas were tying her hands to the bed-posts, Mary opened her eyes. Groggy from the sleeping draught, she did not immediately take in what was happening. The sight of Sprot, bloodstained coat removed and brandishing his saw, however, brought her to her senses. She screamed. 'Adam, Adam, what's happening? Why is Sprot here?'

'Hush, sister. We need to act quickly.'

'For God's sake, no.' It was a cry of anguish. 'I forbid it. I will not have my leg off. Send Sprot away. Get Charles. Thomas will stay with me.'

'Mary—' began Adam.

'*No*, Adam. I will not suffer it. Get Charles.'

'Why Charles?'

'I need him. Kindly send for him at once.' Mary struggled but Thomas held her gently until she subsided on to the bed.

'I will be here until Charles arrives,' he said. 'Mary will come to no harm in that time.'

Adam knew his sister. 'Mr Sprot, be so good as to wait outside. I will fetch Mr Carrington. Patrick will give you food and drink.'

'As you wish, sir,' replied an unhappy Sprot, 'although I cannot condone the delay. Every minute may be crucial.' He peered again at Thomas. 'Are you certain we have not met before, sir?'

'Quite certain, Mr Sprot,' replied Thomas. Then, doubtless consoling himself with the opportunity further to increase his fee for the time wasted, Sprot disappeared.

'Mary,' said Adam quietly when he had gone, 'I too dislike Sprot and I would not have sent for him if I thought there was any other way. Your wound is not suppurating. Sprot is the only surgeon on the island. We have no choice.'

'There's always a choice, Adam. It's my leg and I choose not to let Sprot near it. Now kindly fetch Charles. I want him here.'

Adam nodded and left. Charles would have to be fetched before Mary would permit anything else to be done.

Thomas sat with Mary while they waited. He used a damp cloth to wipe her face, which was frighteningly hot to the touch, and encouraged her to sip water. 'Well, Thomas, what do you make of this? Sprot wants to take my leg off, Patrick says it can be saved without endangering my life. What would you do?'

'My instinct would be to do the opposite of what Sprot says. I think the man's a charlatan. He'd like to take a leg off everyone and return to England a wealthy man.'

Mary smiled weakly. 'I rather think Charles will agree. And besides, between you and me, he likes it when both my legs are wrapped around him. One wouldn't be the same at all.'

'Mary, I've seen the way you look at each other. Can you not marry him and forget about Perkins?'

'I wish I could. Adam, however, feels duty bound to honour his promise. If Sir Lionel demands it, he will send me home to marry Richard and I will spend the rest of my days in misery.'

'So you must defy your brother or suffer a loveless marriage to a man you don't know. Shouldn't your wishes be taken into account?'

'Of course they should. But Adam is old-fashioned in such matters. Debt of honour, duty, chivalry, all that sort of thing. Thankfully, Barbados society is more open-minded. I think it comes from the island having no history. After all, it's less than twenty-five years old.'

'It must have a history, I suppose. Just not one we know about,' said Thomas thoughtfully.

The door was thrown open and in strode Charles, with Adam not far behind. 'What's all this?' he demanded. 'Adam says Sprot wants to take your leg off. I've never heard such nonsense.'

'He spoke of suppuration and laudable pus.'

'Too much or too little?'

'None.'

'The man's a dangerous fool. What does Patrick say? He knows about this sort of thing.'

'He says that his mother's remedy will save the leg.'

'For the love of God, why then are we taking notice of Sprot? Send him away and fetch Patrick at once.'

Mary and Thomas exchanged a glance. Adam shrugged and went to give Sprot the news. The wretched man would not be happy. His opinion rejected in favour of that of a slave and no fee. A bad day for Robert Sprot.

'Thank the Lord for that,' said Mary with a sigh. 'I was afraid that you might tell me to be sensible and leave it to the surgeon to decide.'

As soon as a disgruntled Sprot had been sent on his way, Patrick was summoned to begin his treatment. The three men watched with interest.

'I shall apply the remedy six times each day,' said Patrick, when he had coated the wound. 'You must lie still, conserve your strength and eat all that I bring you. We'll know within two days if the leg is safe.'

'And I shall visit frequently to make sure that, for once in your life, you're doing as you've been told,' added Charles.

'Mixture, food, visitors. I shall be quite exhausted. Now go away, all of you. I want to sleep.'

Charles, as good as his word, rode over three times to see what progress there had been. Each time he asked Patrick what he thought. Patrick had no doubts.

'Miss Lyte's leg will be as good as new, sir. Mr Sprot's opinion of the healing process is not one my people share. A suppurating wound is to be feared, not desired. Thankfully, there is no sign at all of pus in Miss Lyte's leg. She has no fever now and she is eating well.'

'Let's hope your surgeons are wiser than ours. Or at least wiser than Mr Sprot.'

'Of that I am sure, sir.'

Patrick would let no one near his patient while he was treating her, so Thomas had to rely upon his progress reports. Having experienced Patrick's aloe mixture, he expected Mary to make a full recovery. Nevertheless it was a relief when she emerged from her room to sit in the parlour. Seeing him throwing scraps to the chickens, she called him over and asked him to sit with her.

'Thomas, how are you? None the worse for your experience, I trust?'

'No, Mary, thank you. I am quite well. But more importantly, how are you?'

'Very much improved, thank you. And thanks to Patrick I still have two legs. Really, I think Sprot should be banished. The man knows nothing.' Thomas nodded in agreement. 'And I have you to thank for being here at all. My brother and I owe you a great debt.'

'There is no debt, Mary. If it weren't for your kindness I wouldn't be here either.'

'And I promise we shall find a way home for you. While I was recovering Patrick told me more about your family and what happened to you. Is it true?'

'It is. I was arrested on a charge trumped up by a certain Tobias Rush, the most vicious man the devil ever made, deported without trial and indentured to the Gibbes. He arranged the whole thing because I exposed him as a traitor when I was with the king in Oxford. I thought he was dead until he appeared at the Gibbes's estate. It was only then that I realized they were in his pay. He had me whipped and gloated that he had taken my house and that Margaret and the girls were living happily with him.'

'Did you believe him?'

'That he has taken my house, yes. That he has forced them to live with him, perhaps. That Margaret has suffered him to lay a finger upon her, no.'

'And your nieces?'

'I weep for them every day. Still children, children with neither father nor uncle, and living in the same house as Rush.' Thomas shuddered at the thought.

'That is much as Patrick told me. Adam and I are resolved. You must not return to the Gibbes. We must get you back to England just as soon as we can.'

CHAPTER 21

1651

On the day the Assembly voted to receive Francis, Lord Willoughby of Parham as their next governor, Adam returned in a state of such excitement that even Thomas was caught up in it.

Walrond had been under pressure from the Assembly to acknowledge Willoughby's claim or be vilified for disloyalty. As the most ardent Royalist on the island, that was something he could not tolerate and he was persuaded to agree to continue as governor for no more than three months while Willoughby settled in on the island.

Charles had managed to have himself rowed out to his lordship's vessel to speak to his old friend. He had brought back the news from England and an assurance that Willoughby would not leave before he had carried out his commission and been appointed governor of Barbados. Charles had complete confidence in Willoughby's doing exactly what he said.

Charles's faith was justified. When, two days later, Lord Willoughby stepped ashore at Bridgetown harbour to a fanfare of trumpets, Adam, Mary, Charles and Thomas were in the crowd awaiting him. As he had when they had taken sugar to the warehouse, Thomas had insisted on coming in spite of the risk and Adam, to Thomas's surprise, had chosen to stand with them rather than with the other Assembly members. Skulking on the estate would not get him home any quicker and Patrick had reported no more drunken rages in Speightstown. Fear of the Gibbes had receded.

A guard of the governor's own militia lined the short route from the harbour to the Assembly House where the members, led by Humphrey Walrond, waited to welcome him. His lordship was dressed in a sparkling white cotton shirt, ruffled at the neck and wrists, blue velvet jacket and breeches and white silk stockings. His greying hair curled around his neck, the buckles on his shoes were gold and the feather in his hat had once belonged to a peacock. Accompanied by his personal bodyguard of halberdiers, Willoughby walked at a carefully measured pace, turning this way and that and acknowledging the cheers of the crowd with a beaming smile and a wave of his hand. Lord Willoughby of Parham was not a man to let an opportunity for ceremony slip by.

When he reached the steps of the Assembly House, Willoughby stopped and, with an extravagant sweep of his hat, bowed low to the welcoming party. The halberdiers lined up behind him to prevent the crowd pushing forward and Walrond came down the steps to greet him. They shook hands, spoke a few words, and then Walrond led him up to where the other members waited. Willoughby greeted each of them and turned to face the crowd.

'If appearances are anything to judge by,' said Mary quietly, 'this is an impressive man. Let's hope the substance matches the looks.'

Charles smiled. 'I assure you it does, my dear. I'll wager it won't be three months before he takes over. Less than half that, I'd say.'

'We shall see,' said Adam. 'But he's here and that's a start.'

In a deep voice which carried even to the back of the crowd, his lordship started to speak. He spoke of the honour Charles Stuart, the future king of England, had conferred upon him, his pleasure at being on such a beautiful and prosperous island and his determination to govern fairly and in the interests of all. He spoke too of his belief in political and religious tolerance and hinted, no, more than hinted, at the possibility of the sequestrations being reversed. He expressed his gratitude to those who had supported him and who had worked to effect an easy transition from one governor to the next. Without mentioning Walrond, he managed to convey his disapproval of the way in which Sir Philip Bell had been treated.

It was a fine performance from a man well practised in the art of understanding an audience and delivering what it wanted. Willoughby also knew that good speeches, like good sermons, do not tax the patience of the listener. He wasted no words.

The applause was long and enthusiastic as Willoughby turned to follow Walrond into the Assembly House. He was on the point of entering when a small man, dressed in black and carrying in his right hand a battered Bible, squirmed through the crowd and past the line of guards to plant himself on the steps. Holding up the Bible, he turned to the crowd.

'I am the Reverend Simeon Strange,' he began, 'and I am

here—' On this occasion, however, his congregation did not learn why the little reverend was there. Before he could enlighten them, two burly guards had stepped forward and picked him up by the arms. They carried him down the steps and threw him roughly into the crowd. There he lay for a moment, shaken but unharmed, before rising and making as if to try again. Fortunately he was restrained by those around him. The reverend had to content himself with clasping the Bible to his chest and trying to look dignified. To a chorus of coarse laughter that cannot have been easy. It was as well for the little man that only one member of his audience knew the truth about him, and that man would not be saying anything.

As the crowd dispersed, Mary found herself being accompanied by her three companions towards the other side of the square from the Assembly House. Patrick's remedies had worked their magic and apart from the slightest of limps she had quite recovered from her wound. Charles led the way. 'There's a tolerable inn I know just over here. I don't believe Mary will be embarrassed by it and it's time for a little sustenance.'

'I daresay I can manage as long as I have three gallant escorts,' said Mary, 'but kindly stay sober and protect my virtue at all times.'

'We certainly shall,' Adam assured her, 'and we have the finest swordsman on the island to defend us should we have need of him.'

The inn was dark but a cut above most, its customers being landowners and merchants who valued a quiet place to refresh themselves while talking business. Adam and Charles recognized several faces and nodded politely. They chose an empty table in a small alcove at the back, where they were partially hidden from the rest of the room and could make sure that Mary was not in any way discomfited.

'So this is where you spend your days, Charles,' Mary said brightly, when food and drink had been brought. 'I wonder that you can haul yourself away to visit us from time to time.'

'Not at all. I come here infrequently and then only in pursuit of information. Some of the merchants are to be found here and they are always the first to hear news from England and Europe. If their ships could sell the information they carry, they would be even wealthier than they are.'

'Will Cromwell send a fleet to the Caribbean?' asked Thomas.

'Willoughby's view is that if Drax and the others hadn't been sent back to England, we might have been left in peace. Cromwell has enough on his hands in Ireland and Scotland. But Drax and Alleyne will demand the restoration of their estates and they are not without influence.'

'If he does send a fleet we shall have to decide how to meet it. Would Willoughby fight, do you think?' Mary sounded worried. War on the island would be disastrous.

'I'm sure he would prefer almost anything else but there may be no choice. A landing by hostile troops would have to be met with force. Willoughby would not surrender the king's commission without a fight.'

'Then let's hope that Cromwell decides we're not worth the trouble and leaves us be.'

'Indeed, let's hope so. Or at least that Thomas is safely on his way home before he acts.'

The door of the inn was thrown open and a rough voice demanded rum. 'Rum, man, and look sharp. My throat's as dry as a nun's cunny.'

Charles looked up sharply. 'God's wounds. It's the Gibbes.' The others followed his eyes. The Gibbes brothers, dishevelled, truculent and obscene, had planted themselves at a table at the front. Samuel threw a pile of papers on to the table, ignoring the few that fell on the floor.

'Under the table, Thomas, quickly,' whispered Adam.

Thomas slid off his chair and beneath the table. The others shuffled their chairs together to hide him. The Gibbes drained two glasses of dark rum and shouted for more.

'So those are the Gibbes brothers,' said Mary, leaning across Charles to see them. 'I do believe the red-haired one is the most revolting man I have ever laid eyes upon. You did not exaggerate in your description, Adam.'

Thomas peeked through Adam's legs. The Gibbes sat facing each other and were too intent upon slaking their thirst to have noticed the group at the back of the room. As both were illiterate, he wondered what the papers could be. New material for the privy, perhaps.

With each glass of rum, they became louder. 'If you hadn't let the little worm run off, we wouldn't be in this mess,' growled Samuel, thumping his fist on the table.

'If he hadn't tricked me and hit me from behind with a stone, I wouldn't have.' John was angry. Thomas smiled. He did not remember a stone.

'We'd better find him. Tobias'll throw us to the dogs if we don't.'

'Perhaps Tobias won't come back.'

'He'll come for his money.'

Thomas was wondering how long he would have to stay under the table when the door opened and in walked Robert Sprot.

Battered satchel over his shoulder and straw hat in his hand, he called for a mug of ale, saw the Gibbes and sat down at the table next to them.

He greeted them affably. 'Good morning, gentlemen. What do you make of these developments?'

The Gibbes stared at him. 'What developments, Sprot?' asked John.

'I refer to the arrival of Lord Willoughby.'

Samuel grunted. 'Lord Willoughby can go and fuck himself and so can all his friends. It makes no difference to us who's governor and who's not. A pox on the lot of them.'

'It seems to me that it will make a difference to Cromwell. I daresay we'll see his fleet in the harbour before long.' Sprot sounded delighted at the prospect. Fighting meant casualties and casualties meant business.

Samuel ignored him. He took a paper from the pile and handed it to Sprot. 'We're looking for this man,' he said, 'Thomas Hill. He's run off.'

Sprot studied the paper. 'Hill. Your indentured man, was he?'

'Still is, Sprot,' spat John, 'and when we find him, we'll cut off his balls and feed them to the dogs.'

Sprot looked again at the paper. 'A hundred guineas' reward, eh? A considerable amount for one man. Five and a half feet tall and skinny, you say. Where do you think he might be?'

'If we knew that we wouldn't be sitting here, Sprot,' spluttered John.

'No, no, indeed not. I merely wondered if I might be able to assist in your search. I could ask around while I'm about my work. I meet many people in the course of business.'

Samuel leaned over and thrust his face into Sprot's. 'Do that,

Sprot, but don't expect a hundred guineas unless you bring the fairy to us. And we want him alive.'

'Oh quite, quite. A smaller amount will suffice for information regarding his whereabouts.' He paused. 'Shall we say twenty guineas?'

'Ten. And only if we catch him.'

'Ten it is. You may rely upon me, gentlemen.'

Thomas felt a nudge on his backside. 'Stay there,' whispered Charles, who pushed back his chair and strolled over to the Gibbes. Thomas took another peek.

'Good morning, gentlemen,' said Charles, ignoring Sprot. 'I couldn't help overhearing your discussion and I think I might be able to help.'

The Gibbes eyed him suspiciously. 'And you'll want our money too, Carrington, won't you?'

'Indeed not. We may have had our differences but I abhor runaways and my reward will be in seeing one brought to justice. As you may know, Adam Lyte's estate was recently attacked by runaways. I happened to be there and recognized Hill among them.'

'Did you kill him?'

'I tried but the coward ran off. He'll be hiding in the forest.'

'If you're lying, Carrington, you'll be sorry.' Samuel spat out the words.

'Why would I lie? My advice is to gather a group of land-owners to search the woods in St Lucy. That's where the runaways are hiding.' He paused. 'In fact, why not start immediately? The square is full of men who would be willing to help. You could recruit a regiment if you look sharp.'

The Gibbes exchanged a glance. Samuel grabbed the papers

and stood up. 'Come on, brother. It'll be better than sitting on our arses and we'll work up a good thirst.'

'Allow me to accompany you,' said Charles. 'Three heads are better than two.'

When they had gone, Adam and Mary left Thomas under the table and went over to Sprot. Thomas risked another peek. Sprot stood up when he saw them. 'Mr Lyte, Miss Lyte, I did not see you there.' He scratched his head thoughtfully, as if trying to remember something. Whatever it was, it did not come to mind. 'And how is your leg, Miss Lyte? Would you care for me to examine it?'

'What a good idea, Mr Sprot,' she replied, 'and how fortunate to have met you here. Let us find a suitable place outside where the light is better.'

'A pleasure, madam.'

Adam took Mary's arm and opened the inn door. Sprot followed them. Thomas waited two minutes, then rolled out from under the table. Ignoring the looks of the other drinkers, he walked quickly to the door and looked outside. Mary had found a wooden crate on which to sit and had positioned herself so that Sprot's back was to the door. There was no sign of the Gibbes.

Thomas slipped out and made his way to Adam's carriage, where he found Charles with a smug grin on his face.

'What did you think of that, Thomas? Rather skilful, although I say it myself. I should have been an actor.'

'I suppose I owe you my thanks, Charles, although was it necessary to call me a coward?'

'All part of the deception, my friend. Worked well, I fancy.' He looked about. 'Where are Adam and Mary?'

'Sprot is examining Mary's leg.'

'Good God. He hasn't got his saw with him, has he?'

'I doubt it will come to that. It was just a way of getting him out of the inn so that I could escape. What have you done with the Gibbes?'

Charles laughed. 'The square was quiet so I sent them to find men in Oistins. They really do want to find you, Thomas.'

'I know. They're terrified of Tobias Rush, and with good reason. He'll skin them alive if he finds out that I have escaped. Ah, here are the Lytes.'

Mary was hanging on to her brother's arm and giggling. 'The man's absurd,' she said when they had settled into the carriage. 'He told me that although my leg is quite healed and as strong as it ever was, there may still be poison inside it.'

'Did he want to remove it?' asked Charles.

'He thinks the poison will appear and that when it does, the leg should come off. I could hardly stop myself from laughing out loud.'

'Well, Thomas,' said Adam, 'I shall redouble my efforts. We must find you a safe ship without delay. I for one have had enough of the brothers Gibbes.'

CHAPTER 22

Tobias Rush had chosen his house for its discreet location and modest size. It stood at the western end of Cheapside, not far from St Paul's, and had no distinctive features. Like its neighbours, it was narrow-fronted, half-timbered and shuttered. A man might walk past it every day for ten years and not give it a second glance. That was just as Rush liked it. He maintained a small staff and seldom entertained visitors. Visitors had a habit of asking questions and he did not like questions. He preferred his own company.

But for the two gentlemen he had invited to dine he had made an exception. James Drax and Reynold Alleyne, both recently expelled from Barbados for refusing to swear an oath of loyalty to the king, were two of the island's largest landowners. Drax was almost certainly the largest of all. For them he would not only make an exception, he would offer them the very finest food and wine to be found in London.

They arrived punctually at six o'clock and were shown into

the living room by Rush's steward. Rush greeted them warmly. 'Gentlemen, it is an honour to welcome you here. I thank you for coming.' He had met neither of them before. His letters of invitation had been delivered by messenger and had hinted at a matter of mutual benefit. He knew how to interest men of business.

'Good evening, Master Rush,' replied Drax. 'We were intrigued by your invitation.'

'Indeed we were,' agreed Alleyne. Unlike the tall, elegant Drax, Alleyne was a small, plump man, with shrewd eyes and a small mouth.

Rush led them to the dining room where they sat around his modest oval dining table. When his steward had filled their glasses Rush proposed a toast. 'To our prosperity,' he said, raising his glass, 'and to your swift return to your estates.' It was well calculated. James Drax and Reynold Alleyne had suffered the outrage of being deprived of their estates and their livelihoods and they wanted them back.

While they were served seven courses, starting with an onion soup and ending with dishes of dried fruit marinated in Barbados rum, the three men talked of Cromwell's victories at Drogheda and Wexford in Ireland, and his likely assault on the Royalists in Scotland. They spoke also of Barbados and the damage done to the island by the Walrond brothers. Drax described them as 'a thieving pair of cutpurses' whose aim had always been to appropriate for themselves the estates of the landowners exiled. Alleyne ridiculed the notion of an oath of loyalty, pointing out that the island had been deprived of some of its most honourable and successful landowners and been left with the most unscrupulous. Naturally, their host agreed.

*

When the meal was over, Rush ordered his steward to leave them. 'Now, gentlemen,' he began, 'to business. I have a proposition for you. I too have interests in Barbados and am aware of the need for efficient labour.'

'Efficient and cheap,' interrupted Alleyne.

Rush bit his tongue. He did not care to be interrupted. 'Quite so, sir. And that is exactly why I have invited you here. I have established a source of good, young labour, which I will transport to Barbados and will sell you at a price I am sure you will find agreeable.'

'African slaves we can buy,' said Drax testily. 'What are you offering?'

'Healthy boys of eight years or more.'

'Where will you find them?'

'The streets of London are awash with them. It is the same in Norwich and Bristol. War orphans, most of them.'

His guests had no reservations about the proposal. It was too good a solution to a problem for them to allow scruples to get in the way. It did not take long for them to reach agreement. The only question was when they would be back at their estates and ready to do business. 'As to that,' said Drax, 'Reynold and I have been busy petitioning Cromwell and his council to send a fleet to take the island. Naturally, he can see the sense of it. Willoughby trades freely with the Dutch. Cromwell wants our sugar to be shipped to London, not Amsterdam.'

'And when do you suppose such a fleet might sail?' asked Rush.

'We are pressing for it to sail this year. Once Sir George Ayscue has taken the Scilly Islands, we believe he will be sent to Barbados with his fleet.'

'As long as Charles Stuart does not cause trouble,' added Alleyne. 'There is always the chance of the young fool trying to invade from France. Cromwell would want all his ships at his disposal if that happened.'

Before they left, Rush had a request. 'The widowed sister of an old friend has asked me to escort her and her two daughters to Barbados to join her brother there. I would not wish to put them at risk without the protection of a fleet and hoped we might travel with you.'

Drax and Alleyne exchanged a glance. 'That should present no problem.'

CHAPTER 23

Charles Carrington was right about Lord Willoughby. Within six weeks he had so impressed Assembly members with his intellect and charm that they had voted to appoint him governor without further ado.

Walrond had no alternative but to accept their wishes. There had been no serious threat of trouble from anti-Royalists and since Willoughby had issued a cogent rebuttal of a law recently passed by the English Parliament prohibiting trade between Barbados and the Dutch, the island had been peaceful and industrious.

Much had been done to strengthen its defences — heavy cannon had been acquired and set to face the approaches to the two principal harbours at Bridgetown and Oistins, new fortifications had been constructed around both harbours and the governor's militia had been reinforced by the recruitment and training of five hundred regulars. Many of these had faced Parliamentarian forces before at Marston Moor or Naseby, where they had been captured and despatched to the Caribbean.

Willoughby had brought some of them over from Antigua and Montserrat. Garrisons had been posted at Holetown and Speightstown as well as at Bridgetown and Oistins. If a Parliamentary fleet did come it would find the island well prepared to defend itself.

Meanwhile, prices for Barbados sugar continued to rise, more and more land had been put to growing cane and improved techniques for planting, harvesting, milling, boiling and curing were being developed. The attacks by runaways had all but stopped and the Lytes' estate had returned to normal. Adam had brought regular reports of Willoughby's skill in handling the Assembly members, even Walrond's supporters, and had developed a respect for the man almost as great as Charles's.

Better still, Adam had at last found a ship whose captain he trusted to take Thomas home. It would arrive in Barbados at the end of October and depart for the return journey two weeks later. As he had warned, finding a safe passage had not been easy. Most of the trading ships were Dutch, heading for Amsterdam, and the English captains were villains who would think nothing of selling an unaccompanied passenger to an agent on another island or feeding him to the sharks. Adam had been reassured that an old friend would also be a passenger on the ship.

Now, at last, the waiting was almost over and Thomas would be going home.

The invitation to Lord Willoughby's banquet arrived by special messenger at the Lytes' house. His lordship requested the pleasure of the company of Adam and Mary Lyte to celebrate his first year as governor.

'Who else will be there?' asked Mary, studying the invitation.

'Most of the leading landowners, I expect. Probably not the Gibbes.'

Mary feigned disappointment. 'Such a pity. I was so looking forward to making their acquaintance. And it would be interesting to see how Lord Willoughby handles them.'

'With a twenty-foot pike, I should imagine. And even that would be too close for comfort.' Thomas tried never to think about the brutes.

Charles had also been invited to the party and at four in the afternoon on the appointed day he arrived to collect Adam and Mary in a handsome black and gold carriage borrowed for the occasion. Charles himself was resplendent in a sparkling white shirt, a silk coat and silk breeches. Adam suffered nothing in comparison but Mary outshone them both. Her hair fashionably pinned up, her mother's pearls around her throat and her pale blue gown decorated with pink ribbons sewn on to the shoulders and sleeves, she was ravishing.

'You look splendid, my dear,' said Charles in his bluff way. 'I doubt there'll be a pair of eyes not green with envy or wide in admiration.'

'Thank you, Charles, you are most gallant. And what do you think, Thomas? Will I do for the governor's dinner party?'

Thomas, a little flustered at being asked his opinion on such a matter, managed to assure Mary that she would put the other ladies to shame. Looking at her, he thought that it might be just the occasion for Charles to ask Adam for her hand. Insist on it, in fact. He and Patrick waved them off and settled down to their own dinner. While they ate, they talked.

'He is going to marry her, isn't he?' asked Thomas.

'I do hope so,' replied Patrick. 'Mr Carrington worships her and she'd be wasted on Master Perkins.'

'Then we must hope that her brother sees sense.'

After a while, Patrick asked, 'Have you ever thought of marrying, Thomas?'

'Only once. I met a lady in Oxford. Tobias Rush had her raped and murdered.'

'Why?'

'She betrayed him to save me.'

'She must have loved you.'

'I think she did. And you, Patrick? Would you be permitted to marry?'

'The law does not recognize marriage between slaves.'

'But you could have children?'

'Yes, with the Lytes' consent, I could. Perhaps I will.'

When dinner was over, they talked of England, of Barbados, of sugar and of the tricks fate plays. 'In one matter, at least, Patrick, you are fortunate,' said Thomas, lighting a new candle. 'You know what your place is. It is here with Adam and Mary. I am no longer sure where I belong. Royal cryptographer, uncle, prisoner, indentured servant, runaway, guest. I wonder which of them I am.'

'Can you not be all of them and more besides? What about scholar, bookseller, mathematician, brother, friend? We all show different faces to different people, even I. The field slaves do not see me as you do or as Miss Lyte does.'

'I suppose so. It would be tedious otherwise, although Monsieur de Montaigne, as usual, had something apposite to say on the matter.'

'And what was that?' asked Patrick with a smile. By now

he had heard a good deal about Thomas's favourite philosopher.

'He said, "I do not care so much what I am to others as I care what I am to myself."'

'He wasn't an indentured man, then?'

'He was not, although he was something of a recluse.'

It was approaching midnight when the carriage carrying his lordship's guests returned. Judging by their mood and the colour of Charles's face, they had enjoyed themselves. Despite the hour Mary insisted on telling them about the food.

His lordship had admitted that, by the standards of London or Paris, dinner was a modest affair but as few of the guests had dined in either city they had all thought it sumptuous. Crêpes and pastries basted in honey had been followed by mullet in a sweet and sour onion sauce, chicken pies, stewed lamb and pork in a wine sauce with fried beans and carrot fritters. Sweet lemon cream with coconut biscuits had been served as dessert.

'It is several courses fewer than one might serve at Parham,' Willoughby had confided, 'but I trust no one will be disappointed.' He told them that he had taken the precaution of bringing his chef with him. 'I employed him when we were in Holland with the king and have never regretted it.'

'It was excellent,' Mary said, adding hastily, 'although of course no better than Patrick serves.'

'Quite right, my dear,' agreed Adam. 'And his lordship's news was even more excellent. A Dutch ship has arrived. It reports that our new king, having sailed from France to Scotland, marched south and won an overwhelming victory over Cromwell and Fairfax near Worcester and by now will be in London. Cromwell is dead and the people have risen for the king. Is that not splendid news?'

'Splendid indeed,' agreed Charles, 'and there is more. The Parliamentary fleet is no more than a rabble of refugees. The risk of invasion has gone.'

'His lordship has ordered celebrations,' said Mary, 'so celebrations it will be.'

The news was not only splendid but astonishing. How the king could have led an army of Scots to a victory over Cromwell's well-equipped, highly trained New Model Army, Thomas could not imagine. At Naseby the Model Army had crushed the Royalists, including Prince Rupert's celebrated cavalry, so how had they now come to be defeated? 'Is Lord Willoughby sure of this information?' he asked.

Adam was a little put out. 'His lordship would not have ordered celebrations if he were not sure, Thomas.'

'I suppose not.'

'And,' added Mary, 'you will be going home to a country at peace and with a king back on the throne. If that is not a cause for celebrations, Thomas, what is? We must pray for the safe arrival of your ship. Now, gentlemen, it has been a long evening and with your permission I shall retire. Perhaps you would come and assist me, Patrick.'

'Certainly, Miss Lyte. Good night, sirs.'

'Mary's relationship with Patrick is unusual, is it not?' asked Thomas when they had left.

'It is certainly unusual,' replied Adam, 'but my sister and I trust Patrick completely. He himself is unusual and not merely in his intelligence and sensitivity. He is extraordinarily loyal.'

On the last day of October Thomas's ship had not arrived and his spirits were low. He wandered around the estate, watching cane being harvested and taken to the mill, listening to slaves singing while they worked and sniffing the sweetness in the air, but thinking all the while of home. The first frosts would have come, the trees — all but the ancient oaks of the New Forest whose leaves clung to their branches until December — would be bare and the countryside would be closing down for the winter. On this island he missed the seasons of England. No spring flowers, no long summer evenings, no autumn mists, no winter snow. Just a drier season and a wetter season. A man could easily tire of that.

As he walked slowly back to the house, Thomas saw Adam waving from the parlour. He quickened his pace.

'It's here, Thomas,' called Adam. 'The ship arrived this morning. It will take a week to unload its cargo, revictual and load the sugar, and then you'll be off.'

Thomas could hardly believe it. Only seven more days. The Atlantic crossing, England and home. He would find Margaret and the girls and he would do whatever it took to ensure that Rush faced the justice he had avoided for so long. 'Thank the Lord. I was losing hope.'

Adam clapped Thomas on the back. 'Patrick will produce one of his feasts for us tonight. I am delighted for you, Thomas.'

CHAPTER 24

I t was a long week. Much as he would have liked to find something to occupy his mind and tire his body, Thomas dared not
leave the estate for fear of meeting the brutes. With only hours
before he boarded ship for England that would have been un-
bearable. So he passed the days walking and reading, helping
Patrick in the kitchen and in the evenings enjoying the company
of the Lytes and twice of Charles Carrington.

They plied him with questions about his shop and his nieces,
offered generous advice on how to find Tobias Rush and what to
do with him when he did and assured him repeatedly that his
family would be well and overjoyed to see him home safely.
Thomas tried his best to believe them. Charles, ever the man of
action, recommended swift retribution for Rush and suggested a
number of unpleasant ways of exacting it.

'Whatever you do, do not trust the courts,' he advised. 'The
man will bribe them as he bribed his gaoler in Oxford. You must
deal with him yourself, Thomas. If I could come with you, I

would. Would you care for instruction in the matter of swordplay?' Thomas declined politely. Charles was insistent. 'Then have you worked out a plan?'

Thomas had not worked out a plan and did not see how he could until he had some idea of where Rush was and how Margaret and the girls were. He would get home and proceed from there. A disappointed Charles wished him good fortune.

On the morning of Thomas's departure, a cheerful party boarded the carriage arranged by Adam to take them to Oistins, from where the ship would set sail at noon. The carriage rattled down the hill and turned along the coast road. They passed through Holetown, crossed several narrow bridges built over the streams that ran down the gullies from the hills, and were soon nearing Bridgetown. There the road twisted and turned through outlying settlements, before dividing into two branches. They took the left branch which ran in a wide circle around the town and carried on to Oistins. The sky was cloudless and the sea glimmered in the sun. I shall remember my last day in prison as a beautiful one, thought Thomas. It was the first time he had been in Oistins since the announcement of the king's death and it would be the last. He was going home.

They finally came to a halt beside the Oistins harbour master's house on the quayside. There Charles jumped out, followed by Adam and Thomas, and Patrick handed Mary down. A large crowd had gathered around the harbour, most of them gazing towards the horizon. With hands protecting their eyes from the morning sun, they too looked past the few ships anchored in the harbour and out to sea.

'The devil and all his whores,' growled Charles, 'are those warships I see?'

The others followed his gaze. Three ships were anchored outside the harbour. Each one carried cannon and they could just make out the movement of men on their decks. There were hundreds of them. They were certainly warships and they carried marines. A fleet had arrived overnight and the harbour was blocked. If it was a Royalist fleet it would have entered the harbour and anchored there. They must be Cromwell's ships. So much for the Parliamentary fleet being a rabble.

Thomas turned away, unable to look. A day earlier and he would have got away. Now his ship could not sail. He shut his eyes and tried not to weep. He felt an arm around his shoulders.

'Mr Carrington has gone to make enquiries, Thomas. There are only three ships. It may not be what it seems.' There was a catch in Patrick's voice. But Thomas knew that it was what it seemed. He knew it. And when Charles returned, there was no room for doubt.

'They arrived last night,' said Charles grimly. 'Three here and four at Bridgetown. The harbour master has gone out to enquire as to their purpose. He'll be back soon. I fear it's certain, though. Willoughby recognizes one of the ships. It's a Parliamentary fleet.'

'It certainly does not look like a fleet of refugees,' said Mary. 'So Lord Willoughby's information was wrong.'

'I fear so. Either the Dutch were misinformed or Cromwell sent false information to deceive us.'

'Perhaps he will permit Thomas's ship to sail,' suggested Mary. 'It wouldn't do him any harm.'

'I'm afraid not,' replied Adam. 'Ayscue will carry out his orders to the letter and if Cromwell has ordered him to blockade the island, that is what he will do. He's only got two harbours to block.'

'There's a rowing boat coming in,' said Patrick, pointing out to sea. 'It must be the harbour master.'

When the rowing boat tied up at the quay, however, it carried not the harbour master but a young man in the red jacket and leather breeches of an infantry officer. He stepped ashore and spoke loudly enough for everyone at the harbour to hear.

'General Sir George Ayscue begs to inform the people of Barbados that he carries the commission of Parliament to assume the governorship of the island and that he intends to do so immediately. The harbour master will be detained on the *Rainbow* until a satisfactory response is received from Lord Willoughby.' Before anyone thought to stop him, the young officer had jumped into the rowing boat and was on his way back to his ship.

While the watching crowd were milling about wondering what to do, Adam asked Charles to take the others home. 'There's nothing to be done here, Charles. I'll stay and wait for news. I'll be back as soon as I can.' He was right. There was no point in their all waiting at the quay. Thomas's ship would not be sailing that day and they might just as well go home. They climbed into the carriage and left Adam to it.

The journey home was made in silence. Not a word was spoken until they were back at the Lytes' house. 'Patrick,' said Mary brightly, as they stepped out of the carriage, 'please bring out two bottles of our best hock.'

The hock cheered Mary and Charles up enough for Mary to accept his offer of dinner and to accompany him back to his estate, but they weren't the ones whose hopes had been dashed. No amount of wine, however good, could cheer Thomas up. He sat in silence, eyes closed, quite unable to speak. Patrick, knowing that words were the last thing Thomas needed, disappeared into the kitchen and left him to his thoughts. A plate of chicken legs went untouched, as did the coconut biscuits. Eventually, Thomas stirred himself and went to his room. He had not spoken since they left Oistins.

Adam did not return until the next morning. He had spent the night at the governor's house. There had been some communication between Ayscue and Willoughby and he brought news. Patrick woke Thomas gently and helped him dress. Adam and Mary were waiting for them in the parlour.

'Charles Stuart did raise an army in Scotland,' he told them, 'but it was destroyed by Cromwell at Worcester in September. He escaped and is now back in France. The information the Dutch brought us was entirely wrong. When the Assembly met yesterday afternoon and Lord Willoughby called for a vote on how we should respond to Ayscue's demand, we voted unanimously in favour of a declaration of support for Lord Willoughby and agreed to resist any attempt by Ayscue to take the island by force. The waverers were won over by Willoughby's eloquence. He told us that Cromwell had sent his admiral to take control of our island and thereby deprive our king of his rightful dominion but that he had gravely underestimated our loyalty and determination by sending a pitiful armada of only seven ships, carrying barely a thousand men. He reminded us that our strength is much the greater and that we have improved our defences to the extent that any invader would find it impossible to land his troops in any numbers. The members cheered and we voted to authorize the governor to send an appropriate message to Ayscue.'

'And what will happen now?' asked Mary.

'Ayscue will no doubt set up a blockade. Our trade may be

disrupted but the mood of the Assembly is that we will not be dictated to or cowed by the threat of attack.' He turned to Thomas. 'Your ship cannot sail while Ayscue's fleet is anchored outside the harbours. It would be too dangerous. It will have to wait until they leave or an agreement is reached. I'm sorry, Thomas, it's dreadful news. Let us hope that the delay will be short.' Thomas did not reply. He no longer dared hope for anything. 'The estate will carry on as usual. We will store the sugar for as long as we have to. I will be travelling to and from Bridgetown and will bring whatever news there is.'

Mary placed her hand on Thomas's. 'You will go home, Thomas, I promise you.'

Over the next week Adam brought more reports. Messages had been travelling to and fro between Ayscue's ship, the *Rainbow*, and the governor's house. Ayscue had written a long letter to Willoughby, expressing his dismay that the Assembly had refused his demands and claiming that he did not relish the thought of fighting a man who had once been his ally. Nor did he want to bring destruction to the island; control of its government and its trade were his aims, not its ruin. But if Willoughby and his Assembly stubbornly held out against him, he would have no choice but to land his troops and take over by force.

In reply, Lord Willoughby had pointed out that the island's defences were strong, Ayscue's force was easily outnumbered and Barbados could not be starved into submission. What he did not mention was that he had received a demand from a committee claiming to represent the island's leading landowners that he should meet them to discuss the situation. The committee could not claim to represent all leading landowners because neither

Charles nor Adam was included. Despite this, Willoughby agreed to the meeting, which was hurriedly arranged for two days hence and would take place in the governor's residence.

What the planters feared most was a long blockade. Sugar sitting in barrels and going nowhere would do no one any good. If they could not ship it, it would deteriorate and lose its value. And there was a problem with storage. Since the fire, they were having to store more of their cured sugar on their estates where rats and cockroaches got at it. The planters wanted action of one sort or another.

When Adam returned from the meeting he told them that the Walronds were demanding that Willoughby attack Ayscue's fleet. With what exactly was not clear. The others would accept a truce provided they could ship their sugar without hindrance.

'Is a truce possible?' asked Thomas.

'Not while the Assembly supports the governor. With Drax and Alleyne and Middleton gone, there are few voices prepared to speak against him and those that do lack authority. By the way, it seems that both Drax and Alleyne are with Ayscue's fleet, which makes a truce even less likely. They want their estates back and I for one don't blame them.'

'Then what?'

'Apart from the fact that Ayscue is an old colleague, Willoughby wants at all costs to avoid bloodshed. Nor do we have the means of destroying his fleet. All Ayscue has to do is anchor out of range of our cannon and we can't hurt him. On the other hand, as things stand he can't hurt us. An impasse. Is that the right word, Thomas?'

'I fear that it is,' replied Thomas, 'and with no immediate solution in sight. Either Ayscue will be forced to land his troops and there will be bloodshed or he will maintain the blockade until the landowners force Lord Willoughby to seek terms.'

'That is true, but Willoughby believes that although Ayscue would prefer not to fight, he will be under pressure from Drax and Alleyne to do something and will try to invade. Then we shall have to defend ourselves but we will not have fired the first shots and we are confident of repelling any attack.'

'So it's "wait and see".'

'For the present, it is. I wish I had better news.'

The first shells landed in Oistins and Bridgetown four days later. Other than sinking a fishing boat in Oistins harbour and killing a pony tethered outside the Neptune, they did little damage. At the same time parties of skirmishers in longboats landed near Holetown and Speightstown. They too did little damage, concentrating on distributing leaflets to the local people.

Adam showed Thomas and Mary one of the leaflets. It urged the people of Barbados to accept the rule of Parliament and Sir George Ayscue as governor, and warned them of dire consequences if Parliament's demands were not met. Until Lord Willoughby and the Assembly agreed to stand down the Parliamentary fleet would blockade the ports to prevent any vessels getting in or out.

Thomas waited in vain for a glimmer of hope to lift his spirits. There was none. It might be true that neither Ayscue nor Willoughby wanted to fight but Cromwell and the Barbados Assembly were adamant. There would be no compromise.

When Thomas tried to read, he found himself unable to concentrate on the words; when he walked with Patrick he saw nothing; and when he ate he tasted nothing. He knew he was slipping into a deep melancholy but could do nothing about it.

Then there was more news. During the bombardment a merchant fleet of eleven Dutch and three English vessels had arrived in Carlisle Bay. They carried cargoes of horses, cattle, provisions, tools, cloth, muskets and ammunition, and were lightly armed. Ayscue had captured the fleet and taken prisoner all its officers and crew. By a stroke of fortune Ayscue was now equipped to maintain the blockade indefinitely.

Further up the coast larger groups of men were now stealing ashore, making use of the shallow water inside the reef which ran parallel to the coastline and landing on one of the island's many small beaches. They came armed with pistols and swords, and with more leaflets. The latter they nailed to trees and houses where they were ignored or taken down and put to better use in privies, and the former they used to raid hamlets and villages from Six Mens Bay in the north to Freshwater Bay in the south.

Willoughby responded by reinforcing the garrisons at Holetown and Speightstown but left the bulk of his army further south, where large-scale landings were more likely. It was as well that he did because in the third week of November Ayscue risked a major assault and sent sixty longboats carrying three hundred men to capture Bridgetown. It was a rash move and his force was easily repulsed with the loss of fifteen men.

When the Assembly met the next day, Adam reported that Lord Willoughby had addressed them in confident mood.

'Gentlemen,' Willoughby said, 'Ayscue has attacked us with cannon and sword. He has tried to undermine our spirit with threats and falsehoods. In his notices, smuggled ashore by night, he plants among our people the false idea that it is a small minority of us only who support the king, claims that we cannot resist his force and offers pardons to all who declare for Parliament.

He is preventing us from sending our sugar to our customers in Europe. And now he has attempted a full assault. In all these actions he has met with failure and his latest effort was repulsed with ease.'

But Willoughby's confidence was not shared by all and William Byam had risen to speak. 'My lord,' he replied, 'it is true that Ayscue has achieved little of lasting consequence although the incursions around Holetown and Speightstown have caused some loss of life and damage to property, and while he is so outnumbered by our forces any attempt at invasion must meet with failure. But should we not have some concern about intrigue?' Here he had glanced at Thomas Modyford. 'Are there not some in this Assembly who would argue for an accommodation with Ayscue? If there are, I ask you to call upon them to speak. Better by far that the truth be known than uncertainty bring misunderstanding and mistrust.'

Modyford knew that Byam's dart was aimed at him and was quickly on his feet. He claimed that in the present circumstances he was in favour of resisting any attempt to take Barbados by force as the island's strength was more than adequate for it to defend itself. Only if the balance were to change for any reason might it be wise to seek an alternative solution to their predicament.

'It was typical of the shrewd Modyford,' said Adam, 'ruling nothing out and nothing in and giving an opponent little room for manoeuvre.'

It had satisfied the Assembly and the meeting had ended with a resolution steadfastly to continue the defence against incursion or invasion by Parliamentary forces.

Adam, however, having become through Charles's good offices one of Lord Willoughby's inner circle of advisers, knew that although in public he was treating Ayscue with disdain, the governor was privately worrying about what he might do next. Ayscue would not return to England without having at least attempted an invasion and he would have to act soon. Eight weeks was a long time for soldiers to be confined to ships. So heavily out-numbered was he that Ayscue could not risk a single assault and would try to stretch their defences along the coast. And Willoughby was now receiving more representations from planters desperate to load their sugar and see it off to Europe. The blockade had become more serious than he chose to admit.

'If I were Ayscue, I would attack at two points,' Willoughby had told Adam. 'His skirmishes in the north have had some limited effect and he knows where he can land larger forces near Holetown and Speightstown. He might try to take those towns while we are engaged in the south. We will strengthen our defences in the north and prepare ourselves for another assault on Bridgetown. Ayscue will want to take control of the harbour and the Assembly House.'

He decided to send five hundred men to guard the five beaches in the north where landings could be made and asked his old friend Charles Carrington to command them. 'Put a hundred men with lookouts at each place,' he ordered, 'and be ready to move your troops quickly to any point of attack. You will have the advantage of prepared positions and good cover.'

Delighted to be doing something positive, Charles made arrangements for the transfer of five hundred men to his command in the north and issued detailed orders to his captains for their deployment. When he called at the Lytes' house to tell Mary of his new commission, he was met by Thomas.

'Thomas, better news at last,' he said. 'An end to the foreplay and on with the real thing. The sooner we send the insolent beggars packing, the sooner you'll be home.'

'In that case, kindly waste no time in doing so,' replied Thomas with a weak smile, and went to fetch Mary.

'Charles, this is a pleasant surprise. We imagined you were occupied with our visitors in the south. Do you bring news from there?' she asked.

'In part, I do. I had hoped also to speak to Adam.'

'He will be back from the mill soon. What news do you bring?'

When Charles had told her, Mary did not share his enthusiasm. 'You're not a proper soldier, Charles,' she pointed out. 'Why has Willoughby asked you to do this?'

'Matter of trust, I suppose. No danger of my changing sides.' He grinned. 'And I have two swords, of course.'

'I really cannot see what difference that makes. Just don't do anything foolish.'

'Foolish? Me? Come now, my dear, surely you're thinking of someone else.'

Mary was spared having to respond by the arrival of Adam. 'There you are, brother. Captain Carrington has come to give us news.'

'Have you been given a commission, Charles?'

'I have. Willoughby has asked me to organize defences around Holetown and Speightstown. We think it likely that Ayscue will launch assaults in the north as well as on Bridgetown. I have command of five hundred men for the purpose.'

Mary interrupted. 'Has there been no progress towards a peaceful resolution? We have been hoping for better news.'

'I fear not, and Ayscue is running out of time. He will have to attack soon or go home empty-handed.'

'That would not endear him to Cromwell.'

'No indeed. So we are expecting something to happen.'

'And how may I help, Charles?' asked Adam.

'I had thought that now you have men expertly trained and hardened to battle, you might care to augment our force. With you in command, of course.'

'Does one skirmish with a rabble of runaways constitute battle-hardening?'

'Certainly it does. It's more fighting than most of our men have seen. I do not ask for your slaves — you will need them to keep the estate working — but your indentured men would be useful. We shall need all the bodies we can find.'

'Of course we will do as you ask. Just tell us what you want us to do.'

An hour later, Charles had outlined his plan and asked his new commander to bring his platoon to Six Mens Bay, just north of Speightstown, the following day. There it would be deployed in defensive positions. They would all have to come prepared to spend some days in the open and to bring their own rations. Five hundred men reliant upon the goodwill of the local people for food and water would be quite enough. Anyone who could should fend for himself.

'Well,' said Mary when Charles had left, 'runaway slaves and now Roundheads. Do look out for Viking longboats, won't you.'

'Mary, we could hardly refuse him. The island's in danger. What would you have us do?'

'It is hardly up to me, brother, but something not involving swords and muskets would be an improvement.'

'And how, pray, should we do that? Welcome Ayscue with open arms and take an oath of loyalty to Cromwell?'

'Would that be so terrible a thing? And as you've never sworn the oath to the king, I doubt you'd have to swear one to Cromwell.'

Adam laughed. 'Odd, isn't it, that the charming Gibbes brothers had to swear but Charles and I were never asked to? Perhaps Walrond didn't care about us.'

'Perhaps, or perhaps he wasn't as even-handed as he liked to make out. Well, off you go then, both of you. Thomas and Patrick and I will manage perfectly well. There are no runaways left in the woods, so unless we're attacked by a troop of monkeys with loaded muskets we shall be quite safe.'

For the first time since Adam had returned, Thomas spoke. 'Mary, I should like to accompany Adam.'

Mary was astonished. 'Really, Thomas? What on earth for?'

'I cannot sit here any longer and do nothing or I shall lose my wits.'

'Are you willing to fight?' asked Charles.

'Only if there is no alternative. Could I not help with the administration — supplies, orders, that sort of thing?'

Charles pondered for a moment. 'Why not? I shall need a quartermaster, Thomas, and it might as well be you. Consider yourself appointed.'

Chapter 25

For several days neither the garrisons in the south nor Charles's men in the north had much to do but watch and wait. Charles divided his forces into five companies, each charged with defending one of the vulnerable beaches. While he set up his camp at Goding's Bay, Adam and Thomas took their platoon of twenty-five men, now named white platoon, north to Six Mens Bay to join a company led by a Captain Brown. Adam put Thomas in charge of all matters administrative — food, water, shelter, casualties and settlement of the occasional dispute. Thomas had arranged for any casualties to be taken to the Serpent Inn.

Six Mens was the most likely landing place. The seabed was free of rocks for fifty yards out and erosion of the sand meant that the water was deep enough for a longboat to approach within five or six yards of the shore. The skirmishers had used it before and Charles was sure they would use it again rather than risk a landing at a place they did not know.

The men passed their days in musket practice and their nights sleeping among the palms and casuarinas which fringed the beach. On Thomas's advice, they avoided the manchineels. Wagers were made on which of them could climb the palms quickest to gather coconuts for their fruit and water, and fish were caught from an outcrop of rock at the northern end of the bay. Local villagers brought them bread and meat. Lookouts were posted day and night and no boat could approach without being seen long before it was within musket range. Even at night the sea was lit by the moon. Calm and shadowless, it afforded no cover for a longboat.

Charles made daily inspections of the beaches, checking the defences built of rocks and driftwood, recommending improvements and enquiring about the troops' morale. If they had a concern it was that the waiting would dull the men's spirits.

Eight days before Christmas, they met as usual at the southern end of Six Mens Bay. 'White platoon is ready,' reported Adam, 'but no sign of the enemy again today, Charles. Do you think he's heard of our reputation and taken fright?'

'Alas, no. He's overdue for his rendezvous and he'll be here soon, mark my words.'

'I do hope so. I worry for Mary.'

'As would I for my sister. But she's a capable lady and Patrick is with her. She'll come to no harm.'

'Any news from Willoughby?'

'Routine reports only.'

The reports that very evening, however, were anything but routine. About an hour before dark, a breathless rider arrived at their camp, where Charles was sharing a bottle with them. He brought news from Lord Willoughby. 'There has been an attack, Mr Carrington. About six hundred men led by Colonel Alleyne, on the harbour at Bridgetown. They set fire to warehouses and vessels and disabled twenty cannon. There was much damage to property. Colonel Alleyne himself was killed.'

'Was he now? Casualties?'

'Fifty of our men dead, sir, and a hundred taken prisoner.'

'Good God, were they all asleep? How could they take a hundred prisoners? And how did they get into the harbour in the first place? Were the batteries out of action?'

'There was rain this morning, sir. Visibility was poor. They came in under its cover. By the time they were seen, it was too late to prevent them landing. They were trained men who knew their business.'

'Of course they were. What did we expect, a rabble of pirates? Did we take any prisoners?'

'We did, sir. Twenty, I believe. Some were Scots.'

'Perfidious Celts taken at Dunbar, I don't doubt, and now Cromwell's men. It sounds like a disaster. But it's done now. What would Lord Willoughby have me do?'

'He asks that you send two hundred men to replace his losses. He expects another attack directly.'

Charles was not at all sure that reducing his force by two hundred was a good idea, but if Willoughby wanted it he had no choice. 'Tell Lord Willoughby that I will send two hundred men under the command of Captain Skeete at dawn tomorrow. It's too late to march today.'

'Yes, sir.'

Having summoned Captain Skeete and given him his orders, Charles dragged Thomas and Adam to the Serpent for dinner. He was fuming. The garrison commander should be drawn and quartered. Fifty dead, a hundred captured and twenty cannon destroyed.

'Ye gods,' he thundered, 'what chance of defending the island have we if that is the best we can do?'

Despite Thomas's urging him to calm down and consider how best to defend the north rather than worry about the south, Charles was beside himself. 'Michel de Montaigne, a great French philosopher, said that not being able to govern events, he governed himself,' Thomas told him.

'I care not a fig for your Frenchman. They might as well hoist a flag of surrender now and be done with it.' With a pint of claret inside him, it took a long time for Charles to regain his temper.

The first sight of longboats came at dawn the next morning when Captain Brown's watchmen spotted twenty of them about a quarter of a mile out and heading for the beach. A messenger was despatched to Charles, who replied that he would bring fifty men to Six Mens Bay immediately.

At the bay Captain Brown spread his force out among the trees along the length of the beach. Adam and Thomas waited with white platoon at its southern end and watched as the longboats approached.

'I see no Vikings, Adam,' said Thomas, 'but it's a large force. Approaching two hundred.'

'About that. How long before they land, do you suppose?'

'Ten minutes, no more.'

'Right. We mustn't let Charles down. Let's hope he arrives in time to see us in action.'

Watching the boats approach the bay, Thomas thought again of the only other battle he had witnessed. There he had been with the king and never in real danger. Here things would be different. He would certainly not be encrypting messages.

As soon as the leading boats were within musket range, a few lightly armed infantrymen jumped out into water barely as high as their waists. Captain Brown's men held their fire, allowing the first of them to wade to the beach. The captain wanted to keep his men hidden for as long as he could. As expected, the light infantrymen formed up on the sand to cover their more heavily armed colleagues.

The moment they did so, he gave the order to fire. Muskets flashed all along the tree line and perhaps a quarter of the enemy's front line fell. Ignoring the screams of the wounded, the remainder pressed on for the shore, their muskets held over their heads, and, once there, they formed a line. They returned fire but their targets were among the trees and hard to see.

While the attackers were reloading, the defenders fired another volley. Again, several men went down but the volley was far from decisive. By this time the boats were grounded in shallow water and more armoured troops were reaching the shore. They spread out in a double rank and sent their first volley into the trees. The front rank then ran a few paces up the beach and dropped to one knee to reload. The second rank fired over their heads. Two ranks of less than a hundred men each did not reach right along the bay, so they had to take some fire from left and right and their progress was impeded by the seawater that had splashed their muskets and dampened their charges. One in ten misfired and had to be recharged and reloaded before firing. But these were highly trained infantry, their breastplates proof against musket shot, and there was not a hint of panic. With dead and wounded all around them, they maintained their order and kept their line while the advance guard withdrew to protect their means of escape.

At the southern end of the bay Adam and Thomas had been

watching and waiting. Judging the moment to be right, Adam ordered a volley of musket fire and then led white platoon in a headlong charge across the sand. Thomas, ignoring strict instructions not to put himself in danger, charged with them, intending to do what he could to help the wounded.

At the northern end Captain Brown also led a charge. The double attack by screaming swordsmen on both flanks took the enemy by surprise. Some turned to meet the threat and three swordsmen fell before they reached the line, but Adam had impressed upon their men the need for speed over the ground. Keeping to the firmer sand near the water's edge, they were soon among the invaders.

In a matter of seconds, the nature of the battle changed. Lines of infantry firing at each other from a distance were replaced by slashing, thrusting swordsmen, each one intent upon hacking off an arm or piercing a throat. In the mêlée Adam saw one of his men make a clean kill with a thrust to the heart, only to have his knees cut from under him and his exposed neck severed from behind. The man's blood stained the sand and splattered his killer. The defenders' attack was fast and brutal, yet the rigid discipline of men trained and hardened in Cromwell's army proved up to it. After the initial impetus of their charge, white platoon on one flank and Captain Brown's platoon on the other found their advance blocked.

Thomas moved from body to body, searching for any he could help. It was mostly futile. Bodies, dead and maimed, lay on the beach and in the water and any wounded man foolish enough to call for help was likely to find himself swiftly despatched by an enemy sword. One man who had taken a ball in the leg Thomas was able to assist to the cover of the trees. From there he saw that the landing party were adept at protecting each other by fighting back to back, ensuring that an attack could only come head-on, and that in this fashion they were gradually gaining the advantage. Captain Brown's platoon was losing men and giving ground. The invaders were slashing and hacking their way along the beach, forcing the defenders back. If they gave way, the entire force of the enemy would turn on white platoon and the battle would be lost.

Thomas was about to rejoin the fray when a troop of screeching swordsmen, a familiar tall figure to the fore, charged out of the trees and joined the fight. Crack soldiers though they were, fifty fresh men with fifty-one fresh swords — Charles had judged the situation to warrant two — were too much for the landing party. Retreating hastily, they splashed through the shallow water to find the comparative safety of their boats and Charles was soon able to give the order for his men to disengage. There was no point in risking more lives if the enemy were leaving and could be sent on their way with musket fire. Watching from the northern end, Captain Brown followed suit. His men stepped gratefully back and let the muskets do their work.

Thomas joined the swordsmen who stood on the shore and cheered while the musketeers continued firing. They were more parting shots than anything else but a few hit home as the boats struggled to get back out to sea. Only two were still within musket range when a wild figure, bearded and dishevelled and shouting incoherently, ran out of the trees frantically waving his arms at the departing boats. Adam and Charles watched in astonishment.

'What in the name of God is that?' exclaimed Charles.

'A man either drunk or demented or both. He seems to be trying to reach a boat,' replied Adam, shaking his head in astonishment.

Thomas squinted at the figure. It looked familiar. Shots rang out and the man fell to the sand. 'He won't reach one now. Must have escaped from Bedlam.'

Adam turned to Charles. 'Good of you to join us, Charles, although you were scarcely needed.'

'No indeed. I could see that the battle was as good as won but could not restrain my troop. My apologies, gentlemen.'

'Charles, is that your blood on your shirt or someone else's?' Charles had not noticed that his sleeve was drenched in blood but now realized that he had been wounded. A ball must have taken him in the forearm.

'Here, let me look,' said Thomas, rolling back the sleeve. Charles grimaced. 'It's gone straight through, leaving a neat but bloody hole. It'll hurt and you'll need a sling, but it should mend. I don't think we'll require Sprot.'

'Thank God for that,' replied Charles. 'Now that you've told me it'll hurt, it does.'

The cleaning up began as soon as the departing boats were out of range. Thomas supervised the movement of the wounded of both sides to the Serpent, and of the dead for burial once they had been stripped of armour and weapons. He walked along the beach with Adam and Charles, counting the casualties and giving instructions for their care. Crabs were already emerging from their holes in the sand to examine the flesh and guts that lay all about. They would be feasting for days.

Charles held his wounded arm to his chest. In due course they came upon the bearded lunatic unmoving and face down on the sand. He had taken at least one musket ball in the back. Idly, Adam turned the body with his foot. He had also taken at least one in the front. 'Shot by both sides,' he said. 'Most unfortunate.'

The body groaned weakly. It was still alive. Adam stooped to be sure he had not been mistaken and peered at the man's face. 'God's wounds, it's one of the Gibbes and he's still breathing.'

Charles too stooped to look. 'By God, it is. Samuel Gibbes. And shot front and back. One bird with two stones, you might say.'

Thomas said nothing. It was Captain Brown who called for help. 'This man lives. Take him to the inn.'

One of the soldiers who stepped forward pointed at Gibbes. 'This is the madman who tried to reach the boats. He was shouting something about oaths and sugar. Must have been at the rum. Deserves to be left here to rot.'

'Possibly, private. But take him to the Serpent. He can die there.'

'Well done, captain,' said Charles, clapping the young soldier on the back, 'you did well. When you've cleared the beach, issue a decent tot of rum to the men. And issue one to yourself, too.'

Captain Brown was pleased. 'Thank you, sir. Let's hope that every battle goes as well.'

'I fear they won't. I heard last night that Bridgetown was attacked yesterday. We lost fifty men and a hundred taken prisoner.'

'A hundred prisoners? Did they surrender?'

'I don't know, but Lord Willoughby has ordered me south with two hundred men. I'll send Skeete and as soon as my wound has been attended to I must join him. Your men have done enough, captain. I won't trouble you for a contribution to my company. But keep close watch. There's no saying they won't try again.'

'Depend upon us, Mr Carrington, and good fortune in the south.'

'And what of white platoon, Charles?' asked Adam. 'Are we dismissed?'

'Certainly not. Take Thomas and return to Mary for now. I shall go home and have my steward attend to my scratch. We'll go south in a day or two. I've an idea we'll be needed again.'

Before they left, Thomas went to inspect the wounded and to make an accurate count of numbers. Outside the Serpent they had been laid out in neat rows. A dozen victors to one side and three times that number of the vanquished to the other.

Women from nearby villages moved up and down the rows, offering comfort, swabbing wounds and mopping brows. There was no surgeon among them so there was nothing but rum and water to be done for those with musket balls lodged in flesh or organs. One or two might survive, no more. Sword wounds were more easily treated. They could be cleaned and bound.

If the victors received more attention, the vanquished were not ignored. They too were given what little help there was. Thomas walked up and down the lines, offering advice to the women and counting the injured.

He did not go inside the inn. If he had, he would have found John Gibbes sitting miserably in one corner, tears running down his festering cheeks. Samuel lay outside, not clearly in one row or the other, mortally wounded and unconscious. Without his brother John would be lost. He had never had to fend for himself. He sat in the corner and wept.

A woman had told John that there were three musket balls inside his brother. Two had entered from the front and one from the rear. All three were lodged somewhere in his chest and any one of them could kill him. He had tried to stop Samuel but Samuel would not be stopped. They had a great deal of capital tied up in barrels of sugar sitting in a warehouse waiting for an end to the blockade and Samuel was getting worried. He was also worried that they had sworn the oath. What if Ayscue demanded they pay for their crime? What if he sequestered their estate and took their gold? They had lost enough from the blockade already. They would be broken.

Samuel had convinced himself that he must make contact with Ayscue's men to assure them of his loyalty to the cause of Cromwell and Parliament and had been waiting for the right moment to do so. It had come when they heard musket fire from the direction of Six Mens Bay. Samuel had leapt on to a horse and galloped off, shouting to his brother to follow. They had left the horses in Speightstown and crept up to the bay, where they watched the battle from the safety of the outcrop of rocks.

When the swordsmen had arrived and the invaders had to retreat, Samuel feared their chance had gone. He had left his hiding place in the rocks and run out along the beach. John had seen him fall but, fearing for himself, had stayed hidden until the battle was over. He could see where his brother lay and assumed he was dead. With no better idea of what to do, he had sloped off to the Serpent. He would find Samuel's body later. He would not leave it to the crabs.

But Samuel was alive and had been brought up to the inn with the others. A woman had said he would be dead before dusk. Thomas did not notice two women among those tending to the wounded, much alike in looks, both with auburn hair and green eyes. They moved from body to body, gently wiping off blood, dripping water on to parched lips and silently assessing each man's chances. When they came to the black-bearded man set apart from the others, they found him alive but unconscious. The older woman looked at his face and jumped back, startled. 'Is it him?' she whispered.

'It is. The other is inside.'

'Stand there,' said the older woman, indicating a spot between the man's head and his nearest neighbour. Then, with a quick look to be sure she was not observed, she bunched a wet cloth and held it tightly over the man's nose and mouth. For two minutes she held the cloth in place. When she removed it the man did not move or utter a sound. She felt for a pulse in his neck and put her hand over his heart. She nodded to the younger woman and they moved on to the next man.

When John Gibbes eventually stirred himself and went outside, his brother was nowhere to be seen. 'Where is the man who was here?' he asked the younger woman.

'He's dead,' she replied with the ghost of a smile. 'The body has been taken. No one claimed him so he'll be buried with the others. The grave's being dug now.'

John Gibbes turned and went back inside the inn.

Six hours later, when the sun was setting, he was still sitting in the corner. He had said nothing, eaten nothing and barely moved except to lift a bottle to his mouth. The landlord thought he must have drunk twelve pints of claret and showed no surprise when he eventually passed out on the floor.

Helped by two strong customers, the landlord dragged him outside with the wounded, and there he lay until morning.

The inventory of casualties taken, Thomas and Adam left for home. Sitting in the parlour, Adam described the battle to Mary, neglecting to mention Charles's wound until the end.

Mary was horrified. 'Wounded? Charles is wounded? Why didn't you tell me this before? Is it serious? Where is he wounded?'

'Calm down, sister. It's not serious. A clean wound in the arm. Nothing much. It'll mend quickly and his steward will take good care of him. You could visit him if you wish.'

'Thank God for that. Good of you to tell me, Adam. Anything else you'd like to reveal?'

'There is one thing. Samuel Gibbes was shot. By both sides. He ran out of the rocks waving his arms about like a lunatic. We didn't know what on earth he was up to. Nor did the soldiers. He'll be dead by now.'

'Now that is good news,' said Mary. 'Any sign of the other one?'

'I didn't see him. Might be dead too, I suppose.'

'I do hope so. It would save us all trouble.'

'One left is more than enough, Mary,' said Thomas, 'but probably not as much as half of two. They fed off each other. John Gibbes on his own is much less of a danger.'

'Indeed. And now I'm going to visit Charles.'

'Take Thomas with you.'

'If you wish. Would you care to accompany me, Thomas? I prefer not to leave the estate alone.'

At the Carrington house, Mary asked Thomas to wait outside while she went in. She thought she might be with the patient for an hour. She did not bother to announce herself in any way and simply walked straight in. As there was no sign of Charles's steward, Thomas led their horses to a tethering post and sat down under a flambeau tree to wait.

Compared to Newbury, the skirmish at Six Mens Bay had been a minor affair but it was the most serious clash yet. Things were getting worse. There had now been two bloody battles and the list of dead and injured could only get longer. Ayscue said he wanted to take control of the island peacefully and Willoughby wanted to keep it peacefully. One claimed the commission of Parliament, the other of the king. Neither wanted to fight but both had to do their duty. It was hard to see a compromise.

After a little over an hour, Mary emerged from the house. She looked elated. 'How did you find him, Mary?' Thomas asked.

'He'll be as good as new in no time. And what have you been thinking about?'

'After long and thorough consideration, madam, I have concluded that I am against war, cruelty and intolerance, and am for peace, good health and good food.'

'What about love?' There was a twinkle in her eye.

'Essential. As often as possible.'

'My thoughts exactly. Although I should be grateful for your discretion.'

'Of course. On condition that you marry him.'

'I intend to, Perkins or no Perkins.'

The following evening, when Adam had taken his platoon to join Willoughby in the south, Thomas dined with Mary and Patrick. Mary preferred not to eat alone, so when her brother was away Patrick joined her. For an hour afterwards they sat and talked. Mary spoke of her love of Barbados and her fear of being sent back to England, Thomas of his love of Romsey and his fear of never getting back to England. Actually doing something more than sit about feeling sorry for himself had lifted his spirits.

Patrick listened and said little. Fond as he was of both these people, he knew only what he had been told of England and he confessed that he could not picture it clearly in his mind. They were interrupted by an urgent knocking on the door.

Mary looked up sharply. 'Patrick, please answer it. More news, I expect.'

But the news Patrick brought was not news any of them expected. 'A man is at the door, Miss Lyte. He gives his name as John Gibbes. He asks to see you.'

Thomas was on his feet immediately. 'Hell's hounds. Surely not.'

'Calm yourself, Thomas. Patrick, please tell Mr Gibbes that it is late and I am not inclined to receive visitors at this hour. He may return in the morning.'

'Yes, Miss Lyte.'

'That will give us time to think of something.'

Patrick was soon back. 'He is most insistent, Miss Lyte, and not entirely sober. He says that if he is not admitted, he will admit himself. He carries a pistol.'

'In that case I shall get rid of him myself. Come with me, Patrick, please. Keep out of sight, Thomas.'

'Mary . . .'

'Go, Thomas.' Reluctantly, Thomas disappeared into the kitchen. He slipped quietly out of the kitchen door and around the side of the house, to a small window from where he could see and hear without being seen or heard.

When Mary opened the door, Gibbes was standing outside, even more revolting than she remembered him. Matted red beard, carbuncles and warts, bleary eyes, filthy clothes and reeking of something foul. So foul that Mary took a step backwards.

'Mr Gibbes, I am Mary Lyte.' For all her courage, Thomas heard a slight tremble in her voice. 'You are not welcome here.'

Gibbes shuffled his feet and looked at the ground. He clutched in both hands a small sack tied with a length of rope. It looked heavy. 'My brother is dead, killed at Six Mens Bay. That is why I have come.'

'I do not see how that concerns me.'

'I am a rich man.' He held up the evil-smelling bag. 'This bag is full of gold. I have come to give it to you.'

Expecting a demand for Thomas to be handed over, Mary was taken by surprise. 'That is absurd, Mr Gibbes. Why would I wish to take your gold?'

He ignored the question. 'There is one condition.'

'Which is?'

'You will be my wife.'

Mary stared at him in astonishment. Before she could say anything, Gibbes went on, 'You are of marriageable age, I am the owner of a good estate and a wealthy man. Now my brother is dead, I wish to take a wife. Why would you refuse me?' Thomas knew that there were at least a hundred reasons, none of which Mary cared to offer him.

'Kindly leave my estate at once. If you come here again, I shall instruct my servants to shoot you.' Now she was shouting.

'Your servants are away,' said Gibbes slyly.

'This unwelcome meeting is over. Go, Mr Gibbes. Now.'

She made to close the door. But for all the rum inside him, Gibbes moved quickly. Before Mary or Patrick could stop him, he shoved the door open and stepped inside, slamming it behind him. Putting himself in front of Mary, Patrick shot a fist into Gibbes's face. Ignoring the blood streaming from his nose, Gibbes dropped the bag, pulled a knife from inside his shirt, grabbed Patrick's hair and with a single backhand slash opened his throat.

As Patrick fell, blood spurting from the wound, Mary screamed. Stepping over him, Gibbes jammed the knife into the doorpost and reached for her throat. Again she screamed. He got his hands around her neck and thrust his face into hers. 'Now you're going to learn what happens to a woman who defies John Gibbes. If you won't be my wife, you won't be the first whore who's learned her lesson.'

Mary wriggled and struggled and beat at his shoulders with her fists. Blind with rage and lust, Gibbes barely flinched. He forced her on to her back and straddled her. She was pinned under his weight, but her arms were free. Desperately, she thrust both hands into his groin, twisted and squeezed. Gibbes shrieked, but kept one hand around her throat and punched her hard in the face. Again she twisted and squeezed and again he hit her, this time with enough force to knock her senseless.

He got to his knees and pulled up her skirts. 'Filthy whores get filthy treatment,' he spat at her, unbuckling his belt, 'and it's time for yours. You'll thank me later.'

The moment Gibbes stepped inside the house, Thomas had run round to the front door. When he found that Gibbes had shut it violently enough to jam it, he ran back and through the kitchen. Patrick lay in a pool of blood on the floor, his hands clasped over his throat. Gibbes, his back to Thomas, had pinned Mary to the floor and was struggling to get out of his breeches. Mary was not moving.

Thomas cast about for a weapon. He did not see the knife in the door but a silver candlestick stood on the dining table. He picked it up and smashed the heavy base down on Gibbes's head, feeling the impact right up his arms. Gibbes fell to one side, stunned. Mary opened her eyes and tried to focus. Her cheek was livid and swollen and she was shaking. She held out a hand to Thomas. From the corner of his eye Thomas saw Gibbes beginning to stir. He would have to be quick. Gently disengaging from Mary, he reached down, pulled the pistol from the brute's belt, aimed carefully at his eye and pulled the trigger.

There was an empty click. Damp powder. Red brute staggered dimly to his feet and made a lunge for Thomas, catching enough of his shoulder to knock him down. Before he could roll away, Thomas found himself trapped under the weight of the man, his throat being squeezed and his face no more than inches from a fetid, black-toothed hole of a mouth.

'Hill, you little runt. I might have guessed. Run away, would you? Now you'll get what John Gibbes should have given you years ago.'

Thomas felt the pressure on his throat increasing and the strength to fight draining away. His eyes closed and he was on the point of losing consciousness when the weight on his chest lifted, his windpipe opened and his lungs sucked in a gulp of air. Gasping painfully, he sat up. Gibbes lay beside him, felled for the second time by the heavy candlestick.

'Be quick, Thomas. His knife. In the door,' whispered Mary.

His mind clearing, Thomas was on his feet and pulling the knife from the wood. 'You or I?' he asked, holding up the knife.

'Can you?'

'I can.' He stepped over to the unconscious Gibbes. Mary turned away. When she turned back, red brute was impaled by the knife. It had gone through his throat and into the floorboards.

Thomas knelt over Patrick, one hand under his head and desperately trying with the other to staunch the flow of blood from the awful wound. Patrick's eyes were open but all colour had drained from his face. Mary grabbed a cloth from the table and held it over his throat. Blood still spurted out. Patrick smiled weakly and put his hands over Thomas's. Then his eyes closed and his head slumped to one side. Thomas put two fingers to his neck. Patrick was dead.

For a long time, Mary and Thomas sat together in silence.

Eventually Mary asked quietly, 'Thomas, who saved who this time, would you say?'

'A little of each, perhaps? Would that we could have saved Patrick, too. This terrible thing should not have happened. I should have killed them years ago.'

'And been hanged for it?'

'Perhaps. Now you should rest. I will take care of Patrick.'

In no state to argue, her cheek now so swollen that her left eye had closed, Mary did as she was told.

Thomas left the house and ran to the slaves' quarters. The commotion had been heard and the slaves were up and alert. He took two men back to the house. 'There's been trouble. Patrick has been murdered by an intruder. Take him to your quarters and we'll bury him tomorrow. When you've done that, take this man's body and burn it. There must be nothing left. Do it immediately.'

'Miss Lyte? Is she hurt?'

'She's bruised but otherwise unharmed. I will take care of her. Now be quick.' While the two men moved the bodies, Thomas picked up the bag and opened it. As the brute had said, it was full of gold sovereigns. He put it in a corner.

Thomas did not sleep. Neither his mind nor his body could rest and he could just hear the low sounds of mourning coming from the slave quarters. As soon as it was light, he went to Mary's bedroom and found her awake. Her face was like a pumpkin. 'Tell me it was a nightmare, Thomas,' she said.

'Alas, it was not. But it's over. May I bring you anything?'

'Water, please, and a looking glass. I'd better see the damage for myself.'

When he returned, Mary took a sip of water and held the glass up to her face. With a groan, she put it down again. 'Is it done?'

'It is. Gibbes's body will not be seen again. Patrick will be buried this morning. Will you come?'

'No, Thomas. I'll visit him when I'm recovered and able to grieve as I should. He was an unusual man and a brave one. Do it well.' Thomas turned to leave. 'And Thomas, the bag. Is it full of gold?'

'It is. Gold coins of various sorts.'

'Where did it come from, do you think?'

'I'm not certain, but I do have an idea about that. I will tell you when you are stronger.'

'When you've buried Patrick, please send word to Charles. Without Patrick or Adam, we shall need his assistance.'

With the help of the two slaves who had disposed of Gibbes's body, Thomas buried Patrick within the hour. There had been no funeral and there was nothing to mark the grave. Those would come later. He stood alone, thinking of the man who had thought nothing of being born a slave, had nursed Thomas back to health and had given his life for Mary. He found that he could not weep. It would take time.

When Adam arrived back from Bridgetown that afternoon, he had worked himself up into a rare fury. To have been summoned from an important meeting to discuss the crisis was not only most inconvenient but also, judging by what the messenger had told him, deeply alarming. Face the colour of a red pepper and shirt drenched in sweat, he leapt from his exhausted horse and stormed into the house. He found Mary sitting quietly with Charles and Thomas. Charles's arm was in a sling.

'What the devil's been going on here?' he demanded. 'I leave my sister in the care of Thomas and Patrick and now I gather there's been an intruder and Patrick's dead. What have you to say for yourself, Thomas?'

'Good afternoon, brother,' said Mary. 'My face is a little bruised, but I'm otherwise unharmed, thank you.'

'I can see that and am much relieved for it, but why was an intruder allowed into the house? What happened? And what about Patrick? Is it true he's dead?'

'Calm yourself, my friend,' said Charles, rising to greet him. 'Alas, Patrick is dead. He died protecting Mary and so, nearly, did Thomas. No blame attaches to either. Now sit down and you shall hear the story.'

An hour later, the story had been told and Adam had calmed down. 'John Gibbes. I would never have left you if I'd known that creature was on the loose,' he said. 'Don't tell me what they've done with his body. I don't want to know, just as long as he's dead.'

'He's quite dead,' Thomas assured him, 'and I much regret not having done what I did long ago. I find, to my surprise, that taking a life in such circumstances troubles me not at all. In fact, I'm pleased to have done it.'

'Patrick has been buried and we will have a proper funeral for him when I feel stronger,' said Mary. 'I wish to grieve properly and I am not yet ready to do so.'

'Nor I,' agreed Thomas.

Charles broke the silence. 'Now, Adam, as you are here, tell us how matters stand in the south.'

'There has been no further action since Alleyne's landing. Willoughby still believes that Ayscue cannot hope to win while he is so clearly outnumbered and at the disadvantage of having been at sea for so long, but as long as his fleet is there we are blockaded and in some danger. However, there has been one development.'

'What's that?'

'A message has been intercepted. The messenger came ashore alone; he was seen by sentries and shot. He died before he could be questioned.'

'What did the message say?'

'We don't know. It's a cipher. Willoughby's man hasn't been able to break it.'

'What sort of cipher is it?' asked Thomas.

'God knows. It looked like nonsense to me.'

'Would Lord Willoughby like me to take a look at it, do you think?'

'You, Thomas?' Adam threw up his hands. 'My God, of course. I'd quite forgotten. You broke the cipher at Oxford. You must indeed look at it. We'll return to Bridgetown tomorrow.'

CHAPTER 26

Lord Willoughby of Parham prided himself on never being less than immaculately attired, even in the heat of Barbados. His custom was to take breakfast before performing his ablutions and dressing meticulously. If the Assembly were sitting or if he had other official business, he would invariably select a satin jacket over a white ruffled shirt, silk breeches — blue or burgundy — and white silk stockings. He disliked long boots, preferring one of the dozen pairs of black leather shoes with silver or gold buckles made for him by the village cobbler in Parham. His lordship did not care to be rushed when preparing himself for the day ahead and was seldom ready before ten o'clock.

Since the blockading fleet had arrived, he had dressed formally every day. It was a point of principle. When his elderly secretary bustled in with the news that Adam Lyte had returned and was asking to see him, he was still casting a critical eye over himself in a long mirror. 'Well,' he said, carefully adjusting his cuffs, 'it must be something urgent to bring Adam back so soon. Ask him to come straight in.'

When the secretary returned with Adam, Willoughby was quite composed and ready to greet him. 'Adam, good morning. To what do I owe the pleasure at this time of the day?'

'Your lordship, I have with me Thomas Hill who is presently a guest at our estate,' replied Adam breathlessly. 'He's a crypt-ographer who was at Oxford with the king. He broke an enemy cipher which revealed a plot to capture the queen.'

'Did he now? And how does he come to be your guest?'

'Better I let him tell you that himself, your lordship. May I ask him to come in?'

'Please do. I shall be pleased to meet such a clever man. Show him to the library.'

Scrubbed up and finely turned out, Thomas was waiting nervously in an antechamber. A man who has met a king should not be nervous of a mere lord, he thought. As usual, he turned for support to Montaigne. '*Au plus eslevé throne du monde, si ne sommes assis que sus nostre cul*' — 'Upon the highest throne in the world, we are seated, still, upon our arse.' He would try to keep it in mind if his lordship summoned him. And when Adam, beaming broadly, came striding out of his lordship's room, he knew that he had done so.

They were shown by the secretary into the library. There Lord Willoughby was seated on his *cul* in a big library chair, a decanter of claret and three glasses on a small table beside him. He did not rise, but smiled amiably and invited them to sit. The secretary poured the wine and left.

'Now, Master Hill,' began Willoughby, 'Adam tells me that you are something of a cryptographer, that you are his guest and that you served our late king at Oxford. What else is there that I should know about you?'

Twenty minutes later, Lord Willoughby knew a great deal about Thomas Hill. He knew that he had studied mathematics and philosophy at Oxford, that he owned a bookshop in Romsey, that the king had summoned him to Oxford and that he had broken the Vigenère cipher. He knew about Tobias Rush and about Margaret and her daughters. To his astonishment, he also knew about Thomas's arrest and indenture to the Gibbes brothers. He listened to the story without interrupting and when Thomas finished, his only comment was that Barbados was certainly a better place for being rid of such men as the Gibbes.

'Very well, Master Hill,' said Willoughby, 'let us see what you can do. This message has defeated my advisers and may defeat you. But you shall try. Is there anything I can tell you that might help?'

'Context is always helpful, my lord. And possible names, although military messages seldom carry names, as you will know. Could you tell me what the message might be about? That would help.'

'The names Modyford or Hawley might appear. It might contain dates and place names. There again, it might not. Is there anything you will need to help you?'

'Just paper, quills and ink, my lord. Plenty of them, if you please.'

Willoughby summoned the secretary and told him to provide Master Hill with a quiet room in which to work, all the materials he needed, whatever refreshments he requested and the intercepted message. 'Have you any idea how long this will take?' he asked Thomas.

'None, your lordship. It will depend upon the nature of the cipher. I may not be able to decipher it at all. I will be able to say more when I have seen it.'

'In that case, kindly report to me this evening on your progress or immediately if the cipher begins to reveal itself. This could be a matter of the greatest importance.'

Alone in his room, Thomas studied the message.

SSKSOOBSQFISLHFWKXSWURCYDSBOMZQHMWIGAROXSBSG
MHQGAFFRUXRSTWJBLFFRCXWLJPBSJPMEFQKGOLAYUPYBBYUW
YSTWOGIPAWAYFSLEUXDBJPDBVGSKUBOAARSBCGMHLZKCUWRB
LFCSOEFPJLLJWGRKAPJTQGVBFPAORDTG

So, 172 letters in four lines, with neither breaks nor numbers. He began as he always had, by trying to envisage the sender of the message. What kind of man was he? Was he fat or thin, short or tall? How old was he? Where might he have learned the science of encryption?

Nothing much came to mind, probably because the message was short and there was nothing distinctive about the hand. He wondered if it contained misspellings or nulls. Probably not, due to the length. He studied it again, trying to work out a way into the cipher. He noted the two double F's and three instances of JP, but little else. Time to count letters. He wrote out a chart and began.

When he had finished, he had:

A B C D E F G H I J K L M N O P Q R S T U V W X Y Z
9 13 5 4 3 11 10 4 3 7 6 9 5 0 9 8 5 9 16 4 7 2 10 5 6 2

Sixteen of S, thirteen of B, eleven of F and ten each of G and

W made them good choices for E, A and T. As there were double FF's, in a simple substitution cipher F could not be A, so it should be E or T. N, with no appearances, would be Z or X. He would work from there.

By that evening, his head ached, he had cramp in his right hand from holding the quill and, having eaten nothing since breakfast, he was starving. He knew very little more about the message than he had eight hours earlier, except that it had not been encrypted with a simple cipher. None of the standard techniques had worked, but before trying a new approach he needed to rest.

First, though, his lordship expected a report. Again the secretary showed him into the library. 'Ah, Master Hill,' said Willoughby, 'what do you have to tell me?'

'Other than that I have eliminated the most obvious cipher systems, very little, I fear, my lord. It is more complicated than I had expected. I suspect a double or triple substitution cipher. I will break it but it will take more time.'

'Only to be expected, I suppose. Ayscue's no fool. He won't know about you but he'll assume we have some expertise in these matters.'

'Quite so, my lord. I shall resume first thing tomorrow.'

'Good. This could be vital, Master Hill. It might just tip the scales sufficiently for Ayscue to go home. We must read the message. I depend upon you.'

After a frugal supper – he had always tried not to overindulge while working on a problem – Thomas went reluctantly to the bedroom prepared for him. He did not expect much sleep. A mind stimulated by eight hours of thinking and figuring does not readily submit to sleep and it was not until the early hours that he eventually nodded off.

He was awoken at dawn by a knocking on the door. Squinting against the morning light, he managed a gruff 'Enter' and was rewarded by the sight of a plump girl bearing a tray.

'Good morning, sir. I'm Annie. I've brought your breakfast. Shall I put it on the table?'

'Thank you, Annie.' Annie put the tray down, and came over to the bed. It was a large bed, equipped with cushions for the head and a light cotton sheet. In Barbados, no more was needed.

'His lordship says I'm to ask if there's anything else you might want,' said Annie. Thomas opened his eyes fully and looked at her. His lordship says that, does he? he thought. Whatever can he mean? She was pretty enough in her way. About twenty, blonde and buxom. Built for comfort rather than conversation.

Annie smiled encouragingly. 'Anything that might help with your work, he said.'

Thomas hesitated. 'I am, er, a little unpractised, Annie.'

Annie giggled. 'Don't you worry about that, sir. Just you lie back and let Annie take care of things.' And having slipped out of her smock, Annie joined Thomas on the bed.

An hour later, breakfast forgotten, Annie had carried out his lordship's instructions with the utmost diligence. 'Well, Annie,' said Thomas, stretching out while she dressed, 'let's hope your contribution to our efforts proves successful. I certainly feel better for it.'

'That's good, sir. If you need any more help with your work just send a message to the kitchen. Now better eat your breakfast. Goodbye, sir.'

By the time he had eaten two cold cutlets, a chunk of bread and a piece of cheese, all washed down with good ale, Thomas was ready to return to the message. Something was nagging at his mind. What was it? He thought of Abraham Fletcher, cruelly murdered by Rush. Abraham and he used to amuse themselves by sending each other encrypted and coded messages and challenging the other to break them. Was this a cipher one of them had used? Or had he come across it elsewhere?

He looked again at the text. He would begin on double substitutions, each letter being encrypted alternately with each substitution. A double substitution would render the double FF's and the repetitions of JP irrelevant, and would be laborious to unravel. A shortcut would be useful. As he had told Lord Willoughby, military messages seldom carried names but if this one did, it would most probably be the name of the sender and would appear at the end. He should have thought of it earlier; it was worth a try. He would assume that the letters AORDTG were AYSCUE, and proceed from there. If he was wrong, he would soon find out and not much time would have been wasted.

It took all day, but, by evening, he had done it. The letters AORDTG did indeed represent AYSCUE and two substitutions had been used. No nulls and no misspellings.

Thomas's second chart revealed the substitutions:

```
A B C D E F G H I J K L M N O P Q R S T U V W X Y Z
a e i o u b c d f g h j k l m n p q r s t v w x y z
b c d f g h j k l m n p q r s t v w x y z a e i o u
```

A double Caesar shift, named after the man who had used it to send reports home to Rome when on campaign in Gaul or Germania, using the five vowels to make the shift, in the first substitution at the beginning of the alphabet and in the second at the end. Easy to remember and for the sender and recipient easy to encrypt and decrypt. His lordship's advisers could not be very experienced cryptographers and he was cross with himself for not having thought of this cipher earlier.

He went to find Willoughby's steward, who showed him into the library where his lordship was enjoying some refreshment. 'Master Hill, good evening. Will you take a glass of madeira? Better news, I trust.'

'Thank you, my lord, I should enjoy a glass. And better news there is.'

As the steward poured his drink, Thomas handed Willoughby the message written out in plain English text. His lordship read it aloud.

'*To Modyford. Confirm strength of your force and state of readiness. Our landings will follow immediately after your declaration. We shall have the advantage of numbers and, God willing, we shall prevail. Ayscue.*'

'Are you sure of this?'

'Quite sure, your lordship. It turned out to be a double substitution based upon moving the vowels to the beginning and the end of the encryption alphabets.'

Willoughby beamed at him. 'Then you have done us all a considerable service.'

'I regret that it took so long, my lord. I was a little out of practice.'

'No matter. This has come as no surprise. Colonel Modyford's loyalties have always been in doubt. At least now we know where we stand and we have time to take steps. Had it been otherwise we might have found ourselves trapped.'

'I am pleased to have been of service, my lord.'

'And you shall be rewarded for it. You shall dine with me tonight and return to the Lytes tomorrow,' he said, adding with a discreet cough, 'I do hope you've found our hospitality to your liking.'

'Indeed, my lord. A little more of the same would be most welcome.'

That evening, an effusive Willoughby promised to help him find passage home as soon as possible and appointed him in the meantime to the position of principal secretary to the governor. Taken by surprise, Thomas delicately enquired as to the position of the present principal secretary.

'I find that one can't have too many secretaries, Thomas. Rest assured, I shall find you plenty to do and I shall send for you when I need you. My valet has selected some appropriate clothes for you. After dinner you must try them on. We have a seamstress who will alter them for you, my figure being somewhat more substantial than yours.'

After an excellent dinner, a restful night and more help from Annie, Thomas, now principal secretary to Lord Willoughby, rode back to the Lytes' estate. With Willoughby's personal support, surely there would be no more disappointments and it would not be long before he boarded a ship for England.

CHAPTER 27

1652

The news of Colonel Modyford's declaration for Parliament was not long in coming and when it did it altered the balance of power, giving Ayscue a small advantage in numbers.

Willoughby immediately sent word to Captain Brown to hurry south with the three hundred men under his command. He did not now have the resources to split his strength and the defending army could no longer hope to hold its line in the south. It withdrew speedily to a position prepared on a plateau between two ridges above Oistins.

From the plateau, Willoughby could look out over Oistins to the sea beyond. Low hills protected his east wing and a sharp drop down to the town protected his west wing and rear. The enemy could only attack from his front. When Thomas had decrypted the message, Willoughby had made sure that he controlled the road from Bridgetown, thus preventing Modyford from cutting off his withdrawal. Had he been trapped in the town there would have been no escape. Bridgetown and Oistins harbours had to be left undefended, enabling Ayscue to land his troops the following day. He was met by Modyford and together they marched to face Willoughby.

When both sides had assembled, a force of about eighteen hundred men and two hundred horse led by Francis, Lord Willoughby of Parham, faced another with two thousand men and three hundred horse under the command of Admiral Sir George Ayscue.

The armies were encamped in close formation, their horses and baggage trains being held in the rear. Fires burned outside tents, there was constant movement of men and animals and a continual hubbub from both camps. Nearly four thousand men and five hundred horses were making a great deal of noise. Furthermore, their preparations were not being helped by a flurry of unseasonal rainstorms which were turning the ground, already churned up by horses and artillery, into thick mud.

On the second morning, Willoughby sent for his new principal secretary, Adam Lyte and Charles Carrington. The four men met in a cottage behind the Royalist lines, where Willoughby had set up his headquarters. The owner of the cottage had obligingly abandoned it to join Sir George Ayscue, leaving his roof, bed, furniture and kitchen at the disposal of his lordship.

'Gentlemen,' began Willoughby, 'I have taken the unusual step of inviting you here without other Assembly members present because I trust each of you implicitly. Regrettably, I can now trust almost no one else. Thomas is here as my secretary and will record our decisions. And, of course, we may need his particular talents again.' Thomas, a little self-conscious in one of his lordship's pale blue silk shirts and a pair of his embroidered cotton breeches, inclined his head in thanks. Willoughby continued, 'The very thing we wanted to avoid is now upon us. Modyford has acted in what he thinks are his own interests, without the inconvenience of principle. We are outnumbered and outgunned and we face a battle far out of proportion to the size of our island. There are a little above forty thousand souls in Barbados, of whom four thousand are about to start killing each other. I do believe we are mad.'

'Put like that, Francis, I do believe we are,' agreed Charles. 'Everything that's been achieved since the Powells first arrived here is about to be destroyed. Peace and prosperity are being sacrificed in the name of politics. Cromwell is determined to take the island at any cost, even that of its future.'

Willoughby looked thoughtful. 'The question is, should we resist him or should we not? We are unlikely now to win a pitched battle but I have sworn to defend the island in the name of Charles Stuart, our rightful king.'

'What does Walrond say?' asked Adam. Immediately after the skirmish at Six Mens Bay, Humphrey Walrond, still licking the wounds suffered from having to relinquish his hard-won governorship, had swallowed his pride and led a troop of three hundred militiamen to support Willoughby.

'Walrond of course wants to fight. He is not a man hampered by self-doubt or by subtlety of mind. He knows he is right and that as a consquence he will prevail. It is not a view I share.'

'My lord,' said Adam, 'other than the Walronds, I doubt there is a landowner on the island who really wants to fight. Demand for our sugar has never been greater, we are learning new ways of producing it and land values are rising. The last thing we need is for it all to be put at risk.'

'The king, however, expects me to hold the island.'

Charles looked out of the window. 'If it goes on raining like this, we shall need ships, not cavalry. It is most unusual for January.'

'Gentlemen,' said Willoughby, standing up, 'we need to think more before acting. Please remain in the camp for the present. I shall have further need of your advice.'

For another tedious day, the two armies faced each other. The rain fell steadily and both camps were rapidly becoming little more than sodden bogs. Water gushed down the hillside while officers on both sides shouted frantic orders to drenched soldiers to get muskets and powder under cover and to protect their cannon with whatever they could find. Cooking fires spluttered and died, miserable soldiers huddled in tents and under trees and horses hung their heads and turned their backs to the wind.

Charles pitched his tent at the rear of the line where the ground was a little firmer. Adam and Thomas were sharing one beside him. Other than try to keep dry and warm, they had little to do. Their sole diversion came from one of the low hills overlooking the plateau, where a group of Ranters, their numbers recently swelled by an influx of new recruits from both armies, were watching the scene unfolding below them.

Lord Willoughby's camp had been visited by a deputation of Ranters led by Catherine. She and her helpers had used their skills to entice several dozen soldiers up the hill to their camp. The more reluctant of the men had been persuaded by a taste of what life with the Ranters had to offer.

From time to time, their leader started up on his flute and the Ranters, holding hands and singing, danced naked around him.

One of the dancers was the Reverend Simeon Strange. Both the flautist and the dancers appeared impervious to the rain and to the ribald shouts of encouragement from their audience of dripping soldiers.

After two days of rain, Thomas was sure that it could not go on and that they would wake the next morning to a cloudless sky and a blazing Caribbean sun.

But it could go on and it did. It rained all night and all the next morning. By noon, all attempts to keep men and equipment dry had been abandoned and morale had collapsed. Even Colonel Walrond's troop had been depleted by men disappearing back to their homes and families under cover of darkness.

'And who can blame them?' asked Charles miserably. 'Three days of wretchedness waiting for a battle they don't want to fight, or a dry bed and a warm wife. Which would you choose?'

'If this goes on,' said Adam, 'neither side will have any men left. Warm wives and dancing Ranters will have taken them all.'

'I rather think that the Mermaid has also taken some,' said Thomas. 'I noticed a party heading down the hill yesterday.'

'Did you now? Perhaps we should make sure that they haven't come to any harm.' Charles sounded more cheerful. 'What would you advise, Adam?'

'On such a matter, I would defer to the governor's principal secretary.'

'So would I.'

'In that case, if you care to follow me, gentlemen,' said Thomas, 'I will show you the way.'

It's an ill wind, thought Thomas, as they pushed their way into the Mermaid. Despite the early hour, the inn was heaving with drinkers, too intent upon getting their mugs refilled by one of the landlord's cheerful serving girls to notice the new arrivals.

Charles managed to catch a girl's eye and called for a bottle of their best claret and three glasses. 'Confusion to our enemies,' he said, raising his glass.

Adam followed suit. 'And prosperity to our friends.'

Thomas took a sip and looked around. He saw familiar faces to which he could not have put names and heard voices whose origins he could not have placed. He heard snatches of tales of wet clothing, leaking boots and rotten meat, and watched bedraggled men swallowing as much drink as they possibly could before having to return whence they came.

To his surprise, some of the voices were Scottish. And when he listened carefully, he realized that they belonged to men whom, only two days earlier, they might have faced in bloody battle. Ayscue's men had also found the Mermaid. He pointed this out to his companions. 'More Scots,' said Charles, unconcerned that they were sharing an inn with the enemy and ordering another bottle.

Squashed together as they were, it took no more than a drink and a half before the men of Parliament and the men of the king were happily arguing, comparing conditions in their camps and cursing their respective lots. The Scots complained about the lack of whisky, the English about the lack of beer. When told about the old 'turkey and shoat' law, the Scots made a point of shouting Roundhead and Cavalier as often as possible. The Roundheads swore that they were treated worse by their officers than the Cavaliers were. The Cavaliers claimed to be owed months of pay. Within an hour, with but one exception, there was neither a sober nor an unhappy man in the inn.

The exception sat alone in a corner. Having spent the best

part of two days in the Mermaid waiting for news that battle had commenced, Robert Sprot looked less than his usual smiling self. No doubt he imagined that four thousand men trying to kill each other would provide plenty of lucrative work for a skilled surgeon without particular political affiliation, but judging by the mood of these men a battle was now unlikely.

Perhaps, thought Thomas, he's hoping for a fist fight to break out, providing at least a broken bone or a bloody nose. But there was no mood that day for fighting. These were men who wanted to laugh and drink, not fight. Before long Sprot picked up his precious satchel and left.

The singing broke out soon after Sprot had gone. A tall Scot, encouraged by his comrades, hoisted himself on to a table and launched into a revolting song about the ladies of Fife. He was followed by a fat planter who used much the same words to describe his experiences in Holetown and before long the whole inn was in lusty voice. The singing continued while the serving girls sloshed drink into mugs and glasses, fended off unwelcome hands and collected whatever coins they could from the drinkers.

By two o'clock, however, the Mermaid was deserted. The landlord had run out of beer, wine, ale and rum, and Adam Lyte, Charles Carrington and Lord Willoughby's principal secretary, none of them entirely sober, had followed grown men splashing like children through puddles in the streets of Oistins, singing as they went and for once not minding the soaking they were getting from above and below. Some walked arm in arm, others held on to each other for support.

When the party reached a fork in the road at the bottom of the hill, one of the Scots was so enamoured of his new friends that he tried to accompany them back to their lines rather than his own.

Only with great difficulty, and a clout on the head with a bottle, was he persuaded by his colleagues to stay with them.

The dripping sentries turned blind eyes to the returning soldiers. Many did not try to locate their platoons but simply lay down under the trees near the cavalry horses at the rear of the camp and went to sleep in the rain. Having reached his tent, Thomas's last thought before passing out was that men who drank and sang together would not relish blowing each other's heads off or sticking swords into each other's stomachs.

The next morning, Willoughby sent for the three of them again. Heads covered, they splashed their way past artillery pieces stuck fast in the mud, abandoned muskets and sodden barrels of powder to his cottage, where they were given breakfast. His lordship had news.

A squadron of six ships had been sighted approaching from the north-east. They were too far away to be identified with certainty but from their look they might have come from Virginia. If so, they were either settlers or reinforcements for the blockading fleet. Lured by the promise of prosperity in a more agreeable climate, settlers from the American colonies were arriving in numbers to start new lives in the Caribbean. Barbados, for its society and its wealth, had become their most favoured destination. But Cromwell might have sent a fleet to take control of Virginia and having done so, it might have had orders to join Ayscue. The squadron had anchored outside Oistins harbour.

'We must find out who they are,' declared Willoughby. 'If they are reinforcements, Ayscue will be even more reluctant to agree a truce. I imagine there is no risk of his being able to attack today any more than we could?'

'None,' replied Charles. 'If anything, he's even wetter than we are. Modyford's troops came ill-prepared and have been sleeping in the open. Their rations are poor and if they haven't drowned, they certainly won't be up to fighting.'

'How do you know this, Charles?'

Charles coughed lightly. 'Information to that effect fortunately came to our notice.'

'Have you heard any more from Colonel Walrond, my lord?' asked Adam, quickly. None of them wanted to be drawn on the source of the information.

'He's as bellicose as ever,' replied Willoughby. 'He asked my permission to lead a troop of two hundred men in a surprise attack on their flank. I refused it. Ayscue may yet change his mind and we should do nothing to provoke him. Are we still adequately provisioned, Charles?'

'For the present, yes. Supplies are brought daily from Oistins and Bridgetown. The meat is not always fresh and the bread often stale but as long as it continues to arrive, we need have no fear of starvation. Of water, we have an abundance.'

'What about the enemy? Who's supplying them?'

'Much the same merchants, I daresay. I doubt they're particular about their customers, as long as they can pay.'

'Is there any more we can do?'

'Other than keep dry, I can think of nothing.'

'My lord, if you will forgive me, would it not be wiser to seek a settlement?' ventured Thomas. 'Once we've started hacking each other to pieces, it might be difficult to stop. And our position will be gravely weakened if we suffer heavy losses.'

'What do you suggest?'

'If I may, my lord, that we send a message to Sir George

Ayscue to the effect that we are prepared to fight but would rather find a peaceful solution. His response may tell us more about the squadron.'

'It would have to be done in secret. Walrond must not hear of it.'

'That, my lord, is why I, not Charles or Adam, should carry the message. Colonel Walrond will not note my absence. With your consent, I will go tonight.'

Willoughby considered. 'I am not happy about this, Thomas. You might be in danger.'

'That I am quite used to. I have found Barbados to be a dangerous place.'

'Are you sure?'

'Unless there is a better idea, my lord, quite sure.'

Willoughby looked at the other two, who both shrugged. 'Very well, Thomas. The Lord had a purpose when he sent you here. Again it is you to whom I turn for help. I shall await your report.'

Thomas approached the Parliamentary lines from the direction of Oistins. He had taken a path which wound round below the plateau and climbed the hill behind them. He was unarmed. The first sentries he met were stationed in bushes fifty yards down the hill. In answer to their warning, he gave his name, stated his purpose and asked to be taken to Sir George Ayscue. The sentries made him wait while one of them went to deliver the message.

The man finally returned to say that Sir George Ayscue was at dinner with Colonel Modyford and Colonel Drax and that he was to escort Master Hill to them.

At the rear of the Parliamentary lines, Thomas found the

three men seated at a small table in Ayscue's tent, working their way through a hearty dinner. Modyford's comfortable house had been abandoned as battle headquarters in favour of a tent on the plateau. They looked up when he entered.

'Thomas Hill, sent by Lord Willoughby, I understand,' said Ayscue, 'and for what purpose, pray?'

Thomas presented the document he had himself written and which Lord Willoughby had signed. It confirmed that Master Thomas Hill, principal secretary to Lord Willoughby, had come at his lordship's command. 'Lord Willoughby wishes me to advise you that he carries the commission of the king to govern Barbados and that he does not intend to relinquish it.'

Ayscue's response was sharp. 'We recognize no authority but that of Parliament. Charles Stuart, the man to whom you refer as king, is at present in Holland and holds no sway in England.'

'Lord Willoughby believes otherwise and if necessary will fight in the name of King Charles.'

Modyford shrugged. 'There's nothing new in this. It's what Willoughby has been saying for weeks. It's got us nowhere, which is why I have allied myself to Sir George. With the Virginia squadron we now easily outnumber you. Willoughby must know that he cannot defeat us and would be well advised to sue for peace. The terms would be more favourable now than after he has been defeated.'

'His lordship does not entertain the possibility of defeat. Nevertheless, he would prefer, as he believes you would, to avoid bloodshed and invites you to meet him to discuss a truce.'

Drax had been chewing a chicken leg. He threw it down. 'No one tried harder than I to avoid bloodshed. I spoke often for peace and tolerance. I did not follow suit when Walrond raised a militia although it would have been a simple matter to do so. I put my estate and my wealth at risk in the interests of harmony. And how was I repaid for this? I was banished. Summarily despatched and without compensation. Do you wonder that I do not now care to listen to pleas for peace? Walrond and his like have brought this upon themselves. Tell Willoughby that the time for talk is over. Surrender or fight. I have nothing more to say.'

Thomas tried again. 'This is a small island. A battle would be a catastrophe. The losses on both sides would be great, differences of opinion would become lasting enmities and the prosperity of all would suffer for years to come. Lord Willoughby believes that you do not want this any more than he. If there are terms upon which you would be willing to discuss a truce, he asks that you inform him of them.'

Ayscue's voice rose to a shout. 'Of course there are terms. I have made them clear. Lord Willoughby will step down, I will take over as governor and the Assembly will acknowledge the right of Parliament to direct its actions. If Willoughby wishes me to put this in writing so that there may be no mistake or misunderstanding, I will do so.'

Thomas could do no more and turned to leave. As he did so, a figure entered the tent. Thomas froze. He was black-hatted, black-cloaked, and carried a silver-topped cane. For a long moment the two men stared at each other. Rush spoke first. 'Thomas Hill. Well, well. I'm indebted to you. You have saved me a great deal of trouble by coming here.'

'Do you know this man, Tobias?' asked Ayscue, in surprise. 'He's Willoughby's secretary.'

Rush laughed. 'Ha. Is that what he told you? Willoughby's secretary indeed. This man is a common criminal, sent to

Barbados as an indentured servant. He has probably murdered his masters and stolen their money. Or, rather, my money.' The black eyes held Thomas's. 'Guards, take this man.'

Two guards immediately appeared from outside the tent. Each took one of Thomas's arms. He stood pinioned between them, still staring at Rush. The three men at the table rose. 'Is this true, Hill? If it is, you're a spy.'

'I am neither a murderer nor a thief, sir,' replied Thomas steadily, 'nor a spy. I am principal secretary to his lordship and am here on his orders.'

'And are you an indentured man, Hill?' asked Modyford suspiciously.

'I was until my masters died. Then I was appointed by his lordship.'

'How did they die?'

'They were killed at Six Mens Bay.' The lie was secure. Rush could not know otherwise.

'And how did an indentured man come to be appointed to such a position?' asked Drax.

Before Thomas could answer, Rush interrupted. 'No matter how. I know this man. He's not to be trusted. He's a spy. He should be hanged without delay.'

'And what about his letter of authority?' asked Modyford, handing it to Rush.

Rush barely glanced at it. 'Forged. I have seen this man forge documents before.'

Ayscue hesitated. Arresting Willoughby's secretary would be a serious breach of convention. 'How do you come to know this man, Tobias?'

'It's a long story, Sir George. I would not wish to detain you with it now. Instead, I'll give you proof. Remove your shirt, Hill, and turn round.' Thomas had no choice. 'There, gentlemen. Unmistakable signs of the whip. Who but a criminal would carry those?'

Still unconvinced, Ayscue said, 'Hardly proof, but evidence of something odd. What have you to say, Hill?'

'I was whipped by my masters, sir. It was their pleasure to do so.'

'Lies!' shouted Rush. 'You're a traitor and a spy. Sir George, you have my word on it. This man is dangerous. He must be hanged.'

'I trust Tobias,' Drax assured them. 'If he says this man is a traitor, then he is a traitor.'

'Very well,' replied Ayscue. 'Hill, if you are not who you say you are, you will be hanged. Until then you will be our prisoner. Take him to the *Rainbow* and lock him up.'

Escorted by the two guards, Thomas was marched out of the tent and down the hill to the harbour. There he was put on a long-boat guarded by six soldiers and rowed out to the *Rainbow*, where he was taken below and locked in a tiny cabin.

It had all happened so quickly that Thomas had barely had time to think. Once in the cabin, he sat on the narrow cot which was the only thing in it, and wondered what else fate might have in store. This was hardly the ship he had in mind to take him home. Not that going home looked likely. The end of a rope or worse was what lay in store now. Rush. If the monster was here, where were Margaret and the girls? Left at home under guard or despatched to the poorhouse? Or had he murdered them too? And how did he come to be with Ayscue? Talked his way into a lucrative position as adviser of some kind probably and expecting rich pickings when Ayscue took over.

It was a sleepless night. By morning, he had come up with scores of questions and no answers. His mind was scrambled, he was stiff and cold and he wondered if he had been condemned to death by thirst and hunger. Soon after dawn, however, the cabin door was unlocked and a grizzled old man entered with a plate of bread and chicken and a cup of water.

'Good morning, sir,' he said with a toothless grin, 'I'm Ned. I'm to look after you. Make sure you get food and water and don't run off.'

'Where would I run to, Ned? I can't walk on the sea.'

Ned managed a throaty gurgle. 'No, sir. And lucky for you, because it means you're allowed an hour on deck each day. I'll fetch you this afternoon. In the meantime don't go getting ideas. There's two guards outside the door and both of them is a mite hasty with a knife.'

Thomas passed the morning dozing and thinking. He wondered what had induced him to volunteer to act as Willoughby's envoy and what lies Rush had been telling Ayscue about him. He wondered about Margaret and the girls. And he wondered how Willoughby could avoid a battle which he must surely lose.

That afternoon, having walked ten times round the ship with a cloak provided by Ned over his head, Thomas was about to go below when a longboat emerged out of the rain and spray and came alongside. Out of curiosity he waited to see what it brought, expecting barrels of food and drink to be manhandled up to the *Rainbow*.

To his surprise, however, the first person who clambered up the ladder and on to the deck was a woman. She was followed by eleven others, all complaining noisily about the scabby soldiers and the leaking boat that had brought them there. After the women came the marines, each armed with a pistol and a cutlass. These were tavern women, doubtless offered a few shillings to boost the morale of men who had been more than ten weeks on the *Rainbow*.

The marines set about herding the women towards the bow, where a short ladder led down to the deck below. Thomas followed them down. At the bottom of the steps, the woman in front of him stumbled. Thomas put his hand under her elbow to steady her. The woman turned. It was a face he recognized at once. Snub nose, green eyes, auburn hair. The last time he had seen her, this woman and her mother had just been savagely raped by the brutes. He had never forgotten the hatred on their faces.

Seeing Thomas, the woman smiled. Without speaking, she touched his face, just as she had once before. Thomas was about to say something when there was a shout from in front of them and the woman hurried off to begin her night's work. He watched her go, then went to his cabin. It was her, beyond doubt, and she had recognized him. So she had survived; as, he supposed, had he. Survivors both.

The second of Thomas's daily meals came at six o'clock. When it arrived, Thomas said, 'Looks like you'll be enjoying yourselves tonight, Ned. Twelve women I counted.'

Ned grunted. 'No use to me, sir. Long past it, I am. Caught the pox in Jamaica and lost interest years ago. It's the bottle keeps me company now.'

'The young men'll have a good time, though. How long will the women stay?'

'The boat'll be back before the eight o'clock bell. That's our orders.'

'Do they visit all the ships?'

'Must do. The sailors are bad enough but those Virginia farmers are worse. They expect a new woman every day.' Farmers, not soldiers.

'Do they now, Ned? Farmers, eh? Must be all those bulls they keep making them lusty.' Ned laughed and left Thomas to his dinner.

Now Thomas knew the truth of the newly arrived fleet, he must get a message ashore, but how? He sat and thought.

When Ned returned for Thomas's plate, he had decided that a risk must be taken. 'It's been lonely down here on my own, Ned, even with you for company,' he said. 'Could you find me one of the girls for half an hour?'

'I don't know about that, sir. I'd be in trouble if I was caught.'

'A shame, Ned. Just what I need, a woman, especially if she has the Irish look about her. Red hair and green eyes are what I've always had a weakness for. Are there any like that, do you know?'

'There might be, sir. I couldn't rightly say.'

'Could you take a look, Ned? There'll be five sovereigns in it for you when I'm released.'

'If you're released, sir, as I hope you will be. Five sovereigns, eh? You must be lonely. I'll see what I can do.'

'Thank you, Ned. Don't be too long, mind. I might fall asleep.'

Before long, Ned was back. 'You're in luck, sir. There's one just as you like 'em. Young, too. She's busy now, so I'll bring her along when she's free.'

An hour later, there was a knock on the cabin door and Ned ushered the woman in. 'There you are, sir. Red hair and green eyes, as ordered. I'll be back for her when the boat arrives.'

The woman stepped into the cabin. Her hand went to her mouth.

'Don't be frightened,' he said gently. 'What's your name?'

'Agatha.' It was the first word she had spoken to him.

That was promising. 'Agatha. It means good. Did you know that?'

'No, sir, I didn't. But I remember you, sir. You helped us. Are you wanting something in return?'

He smiled. 'Not in the way you mean, Agatha. I'm glad to see you alive. And your mother?'

'You knew she was my mother? Yes, sir, she's alive. One of them is dead, though, thank the Lord. He was wounded. We made sure.'

'So is the other. I killed him.'

She nodded. 'Both dead. I thank God.'

'There is one thing I would ask of you, Agatha. It won't be easy and it might be dangerous. Before I tell you what it is, I must know if you will do it.'

She grinned. 'It won't be the first time I've done something dangerous. And but for you, sir, we might be dead. I'll do it if I can.'

'Good. First let me explain how I come to be here.' While Thomas told his story, Agatha sat silently beside him and listened. She was no stranger to injustice so she believed him when he told her of his arrest and indenture and of his treatment by the Gibbes, of his escape and rescue and of the deaths of his friend Patrick and of the brutal Gibbes brothers. He paused in the telling. 'Before I explain what I ask of you, have you any questions?'

'No, sir. Though I'm sorry for the loss of your friend.'

Not just a cold-hearted whore, he thought, she must have

heard it in my voice. A deep listener, just like the Ranters. 'Thank you, Agatha. Now here's the important part. I was promised my freedom and passage home in return for a service I provided and for acting as envoy from Lord Willoughby to Sir George Ayscue, who commands this fleet. As you can see, the plan hasn't worked and here I am a prisoner. However, I do now have some information of great importance which I must get to Captain Charles Carrington, who is with Lord Willoughby's army. Will you take it for me?'

'Where will I find him, sir?'

'First, Agatha, tell me that you will take the message.'

'I will, sir, if I can.'

'Good. The message is "Thomas Hill, on the *Rainbow*, says they are settlers from Virginia, not soldiers."'

'"Thomas Hill, on the *Rainbow*, says they are settlers from Virginia, not soldiers." Who do I give it to, sir?'

'Charles Carrington. Find Lord Willoughby's army and you'll find him. Ask around but do not give the message to anyone else. No one, Agatha.'

'Charles Carrington. What if he doesn't believe me? Will I be hanged?'

'No, Agatha, you won't be hanged. If Mr Carrington asks for proof, say "The Gibbes are dead."'

'"The Gibbes are dead." I can remember that, sir.'

'Good. Now repeat the message, please. It must be exactly as I have said.'

But before Agatha could repeat the message, there was a loud knock on the door. 'It's Ned, sir. The boat is here.'

'Come in, Ned. All ready for you.'

'That's a relief, sir,' said Ned, opening the door. 'I was afraid you'd be half-cocked, if you know what I mean.'

'Fully cocked, Ned, thank you. Here she is.' With a quick smile, Agatha followed Ned up to the deck.

Thomas lay down and closed his eyes. It's a slim chance, he thought. She has to find Carrington, she has to deliver the message accurately and she has to be believed. I wouldn't put a guinea on it.

That night he lay awake, imagining how Agatha would go about her task or, indeed, if she would go about it at all. True, he had probably saved her life and her mother's, but the prospect of making her way up the hill to Lord Willoughby's lines, finding Charles Carrington and convincing him that the message was genuine might be too much for her. She might forget her debt and go home. Why would a whore do otherwise? If she did try, how would she persuade the sentries to let her past? The only way she knew how, he supposed. And if she did find Charles, would he see her and, if he did, would he believe her? If, if, if. Would that he could have thought of another way to send word.

Word from the longboats the next day was that battle had not yet commenced and that both sides were still sloshing about waiting for a break in the rain. Thomas could only sit in his tiny cabin and think about Agatha. Even if the girl had found Charles, which was a tall enough order, he would have been quite justified in thinking that under threat of torture Thomas had sent false intelligence and that the fleet really were reinforcements. Willoughby would then have no choice but to agree to Ayscue's demands, Ayscue would be appointed governor and Rush would demand Thomas's immediate execution as a spy.

And the message was not his only worry. As far as he knew the deception had not been discovered — he was being treated well enough — but the arrival of any one of the longboats might bring an order for his death. Even if the message went undetected, Ayscue had made his fate quite plain if he were revealed to be a spy and an indentured man pretending to be the governor's secretary was certainly a spy. Thomas lay on his cot and listened to the rain.

After a long day with only a brief turn on the deck and an interminable night of worrying and wondering, Thomas was eating his breakfast when the young captain who had first received him on board knocked on his cabin door, entered without being invited to and read out the order. 'Thomas Hill,' he announced importantly, 'this order commands me to have you taken at once to the Assembly House, where you are awaited.'

'Awaited by whom, captain?'

'It does not say, but the order is signed by Sir George Ayscue.'

'May I see it?' The captain held out the order. The signature was indeed that of Ayscue. 'Has there been a truce?'

'That I do not know. Now kindly make haste. The longboat will take you ashore. You will have an escort.'

Accompanied by two armed sailors, Thomas descended the rope ladder and settled into the boat. It was still raining and the sea was choppy, but he hardly noticed. An order from Sir George Ayscue did not augur well. If Willoughby had capitulated, Agatha had not delivered the message or it had been disbelieved and his principal secretary would hang. Rush would get his way.

The trip to the harbour did not take long. Thomas was helped on to the quay by his escort, put into a carriage with two guards and taken to Bridgetown. At the Assembly House they left him in charge of another guard, who showed him to a small antechamber, closed the door and stood to attention outside it. Thomas sat down and waited to learn his fate.

When he heard voices approaching, he stood up. The door was thrown open and Lord Willoughby, resplendent in full ceremonial dress and followed by Charles Carrington and Adam Lyte, swept in. 'There you are, Thomas Hill. I am much relieved to see you safe.' His lordship offered his hand. Thomas's mind went blank and he only just managed not to kiss it.

'Your lordship, my relief is greater even than yours. I understood that Sir George Ayscue had ordered me to be brought here and feared the worst.'

'Indeed he did. The *Rainbow* is, after all, his ship. I doubt that his captain would have paid much heed to an order signed by me.'

'Stop looking as if you've seen a ghost, Thomas,' said Charles, 'or I'll have you sent back to the ship.'

'And you've got work to do,' added Adam, 'so collect your wits.'

'Is there another message to be decrypted?'

'No, no, nothing like that,' replied Willoughby. 'As my secretary, you are needed this afternoon for an important task.'

'May I enquire what the task is?'

'You may. At two o'clock this afternoon, Sir George Ayscue with Colonels Drax and Modyford will present himself here to discuss and agree the terms of a truce. A condition of the meeting was that my principal secretary be released immediately so that he could record it properly.'

'When Ayscue objected, I advised his lordship to throw you to the wolves,' said Charles with a grin, 'or should that be the sharks? Luckily for you, his lordship ignored my advice and pressed the point. Ayscue eventually decided that Tobias Rush would not get his way.'

'And here you are,' said Adam. 'Mary will be pleased. I had sent word that you were a prisoner with little hope of escape.'

'I thank you all, gentlemen. I am in your debt.'

'You are in no one's debt, Thomas Hill,' replied Charles firmly. 'You saved Mary's life not once but twice, you decrypted a vital message and you managed to get word to us about the squadron. It is we who are in your debt.'

'So Agatha found you. I doubted she would.'

'She did, and, armed with the information that the squadron carried settlers, not reinforcements, we were able to persuade Ayscue to agree a truce. Clever of you to tell her to mention the Gibbes. I might not have believed her otherwise. And the message also told us where you were.'

'I won't ask how you managed to persuade her, Thomas,' said Adam. 'You can tell us later.'

'So there's been no fighting?'

'None. The rain saw to that. It hasn't stopped for six days. Any battle would have had to be a wrestling match and a muddy one at that. Then Agatha arrived.'

'Enough of this, gentlemen,' announced Willoughby. 'Let us prepare ourselves for the meeting. The future of Barbados hangs on it.'

Of the seven men who sat down at the table in the governor's study at two o'clock that afternoon, Colonels Drax and Modyford were seated either side of Admiral Sir George Ayscue, Charles Carrington and Adam Lyte opposite them and Thomas Hill beside Lord Willoughby, at the head of the table. Thomas was equipped with a stack of excellent rag paper, half a dozen sharp duck-feather quills and a pot of English oak-apple ink. It had been agreed that he would record the terms of the agreement, which would be enshrined in a 'Charter of Barbados'.

With typical skill Willoughby proposed that they begin the meeting with each man making a brief personal statement. He knew that this would not only allow grievances to be aired and disposed of but would also encourage a spirit of cooperation, as views expressed in private are invariably moderated in public. Willoughby himself then made a fulsome speech thanking Sir George and his fellow officers for attending the meeting and expressing the fervent hope that agreement on all important issues might be reached. He concluded by saying, 'It seems that our Lord did not wish a battle to take place on this island and sent us enough rain to ensure that it did not. Let us try our utmost to heed his wishes.'

Ayscue's reply, although less eloquent, expressed a similar wish. A battle that had looked inevitable had been avoided. Let them try to reach an agreement. Drax spoke again of what he called his betrayal and insisted upon the immediate return of all his property. Modyford made an unconvincing attempt to justify his defection in the interests of peace. And Charles Carrington said that as they wanted to go home, they should reach a speedy agreement and do so.

Four hours later, they had. The Charter of Barbados, written out in Thomas's neat hand, ensured for the island's inhabitants freedom of religious belief and worship, the independence of their courts and Assembly, freedom of trade, the return of all lands and possessions to those unjustly deprived of them, indemnities for past deeds and actions and a ban on future sequestrations without due course of law. It also outlawed incitements to violence, guaranteed that no citizen would be expected to swear an oath of loyalty of any kind, recommended the restoration to Lord Willoughby of his estates in England, guaranteed the safe return of any man banished by previous governors, required the disbandment of all forces and the immediate release of all prisoners on both sides. Finally, it was agreed that the governor of Barbados would be appointed from time to time by the States of England, that the governor would be empowered to choose his Council and that the Assembly would continue to be elected by popular vote. It would be recommended that Sir George Ayscue would replace Lord Willoughby as governor.

By nine o'clock that evening, a final version had been agreed and signed by all those present. It had only to be ratified by Ayscue's Council and Willoughby's Assembly.

Their work done, Ayscue and his two advisers rose to leave. Willoughby and Thomas escorted them to the door and walked outside with them. Their guard stood smartly to attention. 'Thank God that more bloodshed has been avoided,' said Willoughby, 'and just in time.'

'Just in time?'

'You haven't noticed, Sir George? The rain has stopped.'

Admiral Sir George Ayscue, carrying the commission of Parliament to assume the governorship of Barbados, yawned. It had been a long day.

Lord Willoughby turned to Thomas. 'Thomas, unless you would like to stay on as my principal secretary, Adam will arrange for the next available ship to take you to England.'

'Your lordship's offer is a generous one, but my family are in England.'

'So be it,' said Willoughby, extending his hand. 'Is there anything else I can do for you?'

'Just one thing. I would be grateful if you would give Sir George five sovereigns for the man Ned who looked after me on the *Rainbow*.'

As if he were quite accustomed to such requests, Lord Willoughby produced a leather purse from his pocket, counted out the sovereigns and handed them to Sir George Ayscue.

'Thank you, your lordship,' said Thomas. 'I have two more matters to attend to and then I shall be ready to go home.'

CHAPTER 28

The brutes' gold first, then Rush. When he arrived at the track leading to the brutes' hovel the next morning, Thomas dismounted and left his horse in the shade on the corner of the road. For a reason he could not explain he was nervous returning to this place, half expecting the brutes to jump out of the trees and set about him with their whips. Come now, Thomas, the brutes are gone, there's no one here but you and it won't take long to do what you've come for and be away. Taking a deep breath and squaring his shoulders, he strode up the track.

But there was someone there. Tethered to the listening tree was a horse harnessed to a flat cart of the kind used for transporting barrels of sugar. Very cautiously he moved forward, alert to any movement or sound. Hearing a voice, he crept round the hovel, keeping within the cover of the trees. A shirtless man armed with a long-handled shovel was frantically digging at the privy. Thomas smiled. It was the new privy, not the old one where he suspected the gold was buried, and the man was covered in filth. Who the digger was he had no idea but he would not find the gold there.

When he glimpsed movement in the trees beyond, however, his smile disappeared. There was no mistaking the figure in black watching from the shade. And when he spoke, there was no mistaking his voice. 'Get on with it, man. I'm not paying you to dig like an old woman. Bend your back or I'll bend it for you.' Tobias Rush had got there first.

Thomas could see that the filth-covered digger was exhausted and no threats from Rush were going to give him strength. He would soon have to rest.

'I've dug out all the shit,' the man grumbled, 'and there's nothing here. How deep do I have to go?'

'As deep as I tell you,' snarled Rush, 'and be quick about it. I know it's buried down there and I want to be away.'

The wretched man dug for another minute or so, then abruptly stopped. Leaning on his shovel and looking up at Rush, he cursed loudly. 'That's as far as I'm going. There's nothing here. If you don't believe me, dig it yourself. I'll take my money and be gone.'

'Money? You get no money from me, you idle pig. Dig or be damned.'

For a moment, the digger stared at Rush. Then he climbed slowly out of the hole. When he threw the shovel Thomas was just as surprised as Rush. It hit Rush in the face and knocked him to the ground. Rush dropped the silver-topped cane and, in a trice, the man was on him, his hands around his throat. Thomas did not move. There was a pistol shot and the man rolled off Rush. The flintlock must have been primed and hidden somewhere inside Rush's cloak. The man lay still. Rush got to his feet, dusted himself down and picked up the shovel. He left the man where he lay, took off his cloak and climbed down into the hole.

Carefully keeping behind Rush, Thomas moved out of the shadows and crept towards the hole. Twice he thought Rush had heard him and was about to turn round, but he was too intent on his digging to notice anything. Thomas reached the cane and picked it up. He knew this cane well enough. He had another just like it at home in Romsey. Twisting the silver handle, he pulled out the narrow blade and tested the tip with his finger. Needle-sharp, just like its twin.

'You won't find anything there, Rush,' he said quietly. 'It's the wrong privy.' Rush stopped digging and turned slowly towards him. His head was little higher than Thomas's knees.

'Hill. So we meet again.'

'Indeed we do. Now kindly drop the shovel. As you can see, I have luckily come across this swordstick lying on the gound. The blade is made of the finest Toledo steel, you know. Very sharp.' Rush put down the shovel, his eyes never leaving Thomas.

'And now what do you propose, Hill?' asked Rush with a smirk. 'If you kill me, you will never see your sister and her lovely daughters again.'

'Is that so? Now that the truce has been signed, I will soon be on my way back to England. Lord Willoughby is arranging my passage. I shall find Margaret and the girls, whether you're dead or alive.'

Rush snorted. 'Not in England, you won't. They're here, hidden safely away and under guard. The guard has orders to kill them if I have not returned by tonight.'

'I don't believe you, Rush. Why would you bring them here and why would you tell me where they are?'

'If I told you they were in England, I would be of no further use to you and you would kill me. As they are here, I will take you to them in return for my freedom. I brought them here because I thought they might like to see how you were faring with the Gibbes. It would have amused me to observe your nieces' tears. The Gibbes may be dead but at least they'd told me where the gold would be.'

'It seems they misled you. If there's gold, it's in the old privy over there.' Thomas gestured with the sword.

Rush nodded. 'In that case let me suggest a bargain. I will dig out the gold, which we will share. Then I will take you to your sister. She and her daughters will be yours.'

'How do I know I can trust you?'

'You don't. But can you take the risk? Kill me and your sister and nieces will die.'

'And if I don't kill you?'

'You must rely on my word. In truth, I'm a little tired of them. Pastures new for Tobias Rush, I fancy.'

Thomas considered the proposal. Rush's word was worthless but could he take the risk? He would have to find Margaret before nightfall. 'Very well, Rush, I agree.' He stared at Rush, watching his reaction. 'With one small change.'

'Which is?'

'You will first tell me where they are, then you may climb out of that shithole.'

'How do I know I can trust you?'

'You don't.'

'Touché.' Rush thought for a moment. 'As you wish. Your sister and her daughters are at a house on Long Bay, to the east of Oistins. I will take you there when we've found the gold.'

'If you're lying, Rush, I will kill you.'

'I know. That is why I have told you the truth.'

'Then you'd better start digging. Long Bay is a good fifteen miles away,' said Thomas, stepping back to allow Rush room to clamber out.

Rush threw the shovel out and hauled himself up until his knees were clear of the hole. He knelt on the ground, as if to catch his breath. Thomas's eyes never left him and did not miss the hand slipping under the shirt. Even before it emerged with the dagger, he had the point of the swordstick at Rush's throat.

'You lied, Rush. I knew you would. So did I.' The sword slipped smoothly into Rush's neck. There was a fountain of blood and Rush's eyes widened in shock. Thomas pulled out the sword and used his boot to kick the dying man back into the hole. Then he took the shovel and heaped earth and filth over him until the hole was full.

Panting for breath, Thomas leaned for a moment on the shovel and looked for any sign of movement in the hole. There was none. Rush was dead — but he would have to move fast. He wasted no time in setting about the old privy, shovelling out heaps of soil and muck as quickly as he could.

The first bag was about three feet down, four more just below it. He heaved each one out. If there were more, they would have to stay there. Perhaps some lucky person would find them in a hundred years' time.

It took him five trips to load five foul-smelling bags on to Rush's cart. Rush had been dead an hour when Thomas climbed up and took up the reins. Then a thought occurred. He jumped off the cart and ran up the path to his hut. The door was open and he went in. On the table was the silver inkwell and under the cot was the list of adjectives. He put both in a pocket.

Then he ran on up the path and down to the slaves' quarters.

He knew before he reached the huts that they were deserted. There were no voices and no smells of cooking. The slaves had taken their chance and escaped. Despite the attack on the Lytes' estate, he hoped they would survive in the woods. They had suffered enough. He ran back to the cart and set off for the Lytes' house.

It was midday when the horse, hot and tired from being urged on at a pace he was not used to, pulled the cart up beside the Lytes' parlour. Thomas jumped down and ran into the house. There was no sign of Adam, but Mary was there, reading a book and sipping a glass of wine. She looked up when she heard him.

'There you are, Thomas. I was worried. Where have you been?'

'Mary, my apologies. I thought it best not to tell you in case you tried to stop me. I've been at the Gibbes's estate. There are five bags of gold outside. Could someone help me bring them in?'

'Certainly, although if they smell like the last bag of gold that came here, it won't be me. Fetch one of the men from the kitchen.'

When the bags had been unloaded and put in an empty storeroom, Thomas returned to Mary. 'Is Adam here?' he asked. 'I must be off at once and could do with his help.'

'Adam has gone to Bridgetown. The Assembly meets today to confirm Sir George Ayscue as governor. Why do you need help?'

'Tobias Rush is dead. I believe my sister and nieces are under guard at a house on Long Bay. They will be killed if I don't rescue them by nightfall.'

'Your sister is here?'

Thomas nodded.

'Then we must waste no time. Long Bay is a good ride from

here. Saddle two horses, Thomas, while I change my clothes.'

'Mary, this will be dangerous. I can't possibly allow you to come. Let me take someone else.'

'Nonsense, Thomas. I won't hear of it. And a woman's touch might be just what's needed. Now go and prepare the horses.'

Thomas had heard that tone before. He went to find two good horses.

By the time they had covered half the distance to Long Bay, Mary had heard about Rush's death and what he had said about Margaret and her daughters. There was no certainty that they were at Long Bay but it was all they had. And Thomas suspected that Rush, perversely, had for once told the truth in the expectation that he would kill Thomas before he could act upon it. It was just the way his devious mind would work.

She suggested a plan. 'Long Bay is a wild spot. I didn't know there were any houses there. That's probably why Rush chose it. I'll approach the house from the front, knock on the door and pretend to be lost. I'll distract the guard while you look for a back entrance. Get inside and find your sister. If she doesn't faint when she sees you, keep her quiet somehow. And the girls. No screaming and no shouting. Get them out and run. I'll keep the guard busy as long as I can.'

It was a hasty plan; the guard might be impervious to Mary's charms, there might be more than one of them and Thomas might not be able to keep at least one of the girls from screaming. They'd probably take him for a thief and call for help. After all, it was nearly four years since they'd seen him. But there was no time for a better plan. If the guard really was under orders to kill them, it would have to do.

Long Bay was well named. A narrow strip of sand perhaps

four hundred yards long, it curved elegantly beneath a steep cliff facing out to the Atlantic. Waves swept up the bay, entirely covering the sand, only to wash quietly back to the ocean. It was a lonely place and at first they saw no houses.

They rode along the cliff top almost the length of the bay before a cottage appeared, partly hidden by a stand of trees and no more than ten yards from the cliff edge. Rush had chosen well. It was a good place to hide, easy to defend, and he had probably used it before. Thomas tethered his horse and made his way through the trees to the other side of the cottage. From there he would creep along the cliff top to the back, hoping to find an easy way in.

When Thomas had disappeared into the trees, Mary rode up to the door of the cottage, dismounted and knocked loudly. She had undone two buttons on her dress and hitched it up above her ankles. She hoped the guard was one for the ladies and when a tall young man answered the door, she thought she might be in luck. Dark-haired, brown-eyed and with a scar down his left cheek, he looked promising. Mary decided to play all her cards at once. She gave him a dazzling smile and smoothed her hair with a hand. 'Excuse me, sir. I was out for a ride and seem to be lost. My horse is a little lame too. Could you direct me to the road for Oistins?'

The guard also thought his luck was in. A pretty lady, lost and alone, and in need of help. Just the thing to cheer him up. 'Why don't you come inside, miss, while I take a look at your horse?' he offered.

'That is most kind of you, sir, but I must be on my way. If you could just give me directions.'

The guard had noticed the buttons and the ankles and was not to be put off so easily. 'Come now, miss, a glass of wine will do you good. Step inside for a minute.'

'You're too kind, sir. But would you look at the horse first? I'd like to be sure he's sound.'

'Very well, miss. I'll do that.' He shut the door, carefully locking it behind him, and walked over to the horse. He examined each hoof in turn, ran his hands up and down each leg and patted it on the rump. 'I'd say he's sound, miss. Can't see anything wrong.'

'Oh, good. He seemed to be favouring a front leg. Perhaps I was mistaken.'

'Must have been, miss. Now shall you have that glass of wine?'

Before Mary could reply, there was a shriek from inside the cottage. The young guard, wine forgotten, ran back to the door. The lock delayed him but a moment and he was inside within seconds. Tobias Rush had a way of making a man move very fast.

While Mary had been distracting the guard, Thomas had slipped round the cottage and found a back door. He tried the handle but of course it was locked. The shutters of one window were slightly open. He peered through them and, easing his hand in, managed to reach the catch and push them fully open without making any noise. The window was low enough for him to pull himself up and tumble inside head first.

The room was empty. He tried the door. It was locked. He was locked in the cottage in an empty room and had no idea how Mary was getting on, or how many guards there were. There was no time for thought. He would have to act. He stepped back to the window and launched himself at the door. It creaked but held. He tried again. This time the lock broke and he fell through the doorway. Three terrified faces looked down at him sprawled on the floor and one of them screamed.

He got to his feet and held his finger to his lips. 'Margaret, it's me. There's no time to explain. We must go.' Margaret peered at him. Thomas? She peered again. Older, sturdier and with a faint scar on his cheek, but it was Thomas. Recovering some of her wits, she shepherded the girls to the window.

'Out, girls, quickly.' Margaret pushed Lucy through the window and was helping Polly up on to the window ledge when the guard burst in, his pistol drawn. Polly jumped and Margaret turned to block the window. Thomas stood in front of her. No more than ten feet from the guard, he braced himself for the shot. The guard raised his pistol and fired. As he did so, he was pushed hard in the back by Mary, who had followed him inside. The shot went wide, merely grazing Thomas's arm. The guard lunged past him and got his arm around Margaret's throat. He moved behind her. 'Move an inch and she dies,' he threatened. 'Either of you.'

'Tobias Rush is dead. You have nothing to fear from him,' said Mary, looking the guard squarely in the eye. Margaret looked astonished.

'Rush dead? You're lying.'

'Why would I lie, sir?' Mary continued. 'And how do we come to know about Rush?'

The young guard looked at Thomas, thoroughly confused. 'Who are you?'

'My name is Thomas Hill. The lady you are holding is my sister and this lady is my good friend, Mary Lyte. Her brother is a member of the Assembly of Barbados.' A little shaken by his wound, Thomas managed still to speak with authority. 'Please release my sister. Then you will be free to go. Tobias Rush is quite dead. I killed him.'

They could see that the guard was wavering. Mary reached into a pocket and pulled out a small purse. She took out a sovereign and offered it to him. 'This is for your trouble. It's more than you'd have got from Rush.' The guard released his grip on Margaret and took the coin.

Without a word, Thomas put his arms around Margaret.

'Be on your way, young man,' said Mary. 'You've acted wisely and you have nothing to fear.'

Thomas and Margaret were weeping on each other's shoulder. 'Come now,' said Mary, 'tears later. First we must find the children.'

It did not take long. Polly and Lucy had been hiding in the trees, watching the door. When they saw their mother come out of the cottage, they dashed out. 'We heard a shot,' said Lucy. 'Are you hurt?'

'No. I am quite unhurt. Uncle Thomas has a graze on his arm, nothing more.'

'Is it really you, Uncle Thomas?'

'It's really me,' replied Thomas. 'Is it really you?'

'Of course it is.'

They put Lucy on one horse with her mother and Polly on the other with Mary. Both girls were crying. Thomas had to walk. In Oistins, they found another horse and set off for the Lytes' estate.

When Adam returned that evening from the Assembly, he found Thomas and Mary sitting in the parlour with a lady and two young girls he did not recognize.

'Well now, we have a new governor, and we seem to have new friends!' he exclaimed. The appointment of Sir George Ayscue and the subsequent festivities had gone well and he was in high spirits. 'And who may these lovely ladies be, may I ask?'

'You may ask, brother,' replied Mary, 'and removal of your hat accompanied by a suitably low bow would be in order. These ladies are Thomas's sister Margaret Taylor, and her daughters Polly and Lucy Taylor.'

'Good Lord. Are they really? A most unexpected pleasure,' said Adam, bowing as extravagantly as he could without falling on his face. 'I have no idea how you come to be here but your arrival most certainly calls for a celebration. Would you be kind enough, Thomas?'

By midnight, the girls asleep in Mary's bed and the table littered with wine bottles, jugs of plantain juice, cups and glasses, and the remains of a hastily prepared meal, Margaret knew about the brutes, about Patrick, about Charles Carrington and about Humphrey Walrond and Lord Willoughby. She had heard about the battle that never took place and Thomas's part in it and she had heard about the revolting Gibbes brothers. She knew about the scar, but she did not know, and never would, about the whippings or about the manner of their deaths.

And Thomas knew about Tobias Rush. He was a man for whom pain and power were substitutes for sexual gratification. For three years he had threatened to harm the girls if Margaret defied him but she had been spared anything more. He had, as he had claimed, acquired Thomas's shop and house by forging a contract of sale. She had found out that he was in Barbados and knew he was alive when Rush handed her the torn-out page with the word 'Montaigne' written on it. But that had been two years earlier. For all she knew, he had died since. As for the girls, despite being told that he was dead, they had always believed their uncle to be alive.

The next morning, Adam sent a messenger for Charles. When he arrived and after much of Margaret's story had been told again, Thomas led them all to Patrick's grave. There those who had known him and those who had not grieved together.

Later, unable to resist the opportunity for a little gallantry, Charles insisted on escorting Margaret and the girls around his estate. While they were gone, Adam spoke to Mary. 'Ayscue's fleet brought with it letters from England. Of course, only now have they been delivered. One of them was from Sir Lionel Perkins. His son has died of a fever and you are thus free of any further obligation to his family.'

'Adam, the obligation was yours, not mine. Nevertheless I am sorry for Sir Lionel's loss. Please tell him so when you write back. But I have grieved this morning for a man I knew and cared for and who died protecting me. I cannot grieve for a man I did not know and did not want to marry.'

'Quite so. You are, however, nearly twenty-one, and it's time you found a husband. Do you have anyone in mind?'

Mary looked up sharply and saw the twinkle in her brother's eyes. 'Possibly, Adam. I shall give the matter thought.'

Over the following days, Polly and Lucy, as he expected they would once they were comfortable with their uncle again, demanded to know every gruesome detail of Thomas's voyage and of his indenture to the brutes.

'Was the red one really uglier than Cromwell?' asked Lucy, when they were sitting in the parlour one morning. 'He must have looked like a pig if he was.'

'He behaved like a pig too,' replied Thomas, 'and so did his brother. And they were a good many other things besides. I made a list of all the adjectives I could think of to describe them. Here it is.' He took the torn-out page from the ledger from his pocket and passed it to her. Both girls studied it, laughing at some of the words.

'What does "carnivorous" mean, Uncle Thomas?' asked Polly, looking up from the page.

'Oh, come now, surely you know what carnivorous means. Have you learned nothing while I've been away?'

'Of course we have,' said Lucy.

'What about carnivorous, Uncle Thomas?' asked Polly again.

'Meat-eating. Like a wolf.'

'Or a brute.'

'Exactly. And since you have learned nothing in the last three years, I shall take the opportunity presented by our voyage home to repair at least some of the omission. We will study mathematics, English and Latin. It will help to pass the time on the ship.'

Both girls groaned. Uncle Thomas alive and well was one thing; mathematics, English and Latin, quite another.

One week later, at exactly midday, the ship on which Thomas, his family and two sturdy chests full of the Gibbes's gold were to sail to England raised its anchor and began the long voyage. Among those waving them off was Francis, Lord Willoughby of Parham, who had recently stepped down as governor of Barbados. Lord Willoughby had happily agreed to Adam Lyte's request for two letters to be written and signed by his lordship, and presented to Thomas Hill.

The first gave a brief account of the valuable services Thomas had performed by decrypting the intercepted message and by sending word that it had been settlers, not soldiers, who had arrived at the island. This letter he recommended Thomas keep safely until the day England again had a king. The second letter officially recorded the deaths of Tobias Rush and Samuel and John Gibbes and granted Thomas immediate release from his indenture.

Adam and Mary Lyte were there and so was Charles Carrington. After much embracing and bidding of farewells, they stood on the quay and watched the ship raise its anchor, cast off and sail slowly out of the harbour. Thomas had promised to write to confirm their safe arrival, Mary had instructed Margaret to find Thomas a wife before the year was up and both Polly and Lucy had begged to be allowed to stay in Barbados to marry Charles Carrington. Thomas shook hands solemnly with Adam and Charles before embarking. 'Let us hope,' he said, 'that when we meet again, England is at peace and the king has been restored to his throne.'

'When the king is restored to his throne,' replied Charles, 'you may be sure that I shall be there to see it. Perhaps, by then, with Mrs Carrington.' Thomas looked at Mary and raised an eyebrow.

Having stowed the two chests safely in his cabin and settled the girls into theirs, Thomas and Margaret returned to the deck to watch until first the harbour and then the coastline shrank and finally disappeared behind them. It was a time for tears and sentiment but Thomas found he could manage neither. Barbados had been his prison. After four years he was going home and he had much to do. There was nothing to be gained by looking backwards. But as he stood there, Montaigne whispered in his ear once more. 'Take care, Thomas. Nothing fixes a thing so intensely in the memory as the wish to forget it.'

'I shall take care, monsieur,' replied Thomas silently, 'particularly not to put my name to any more pamphlets.'

EPILOGUE

A little over five weeks later, their ship passed the Lizard and began to make its way up the Channel. The Atlantic voyage had been swift and uneventful, their captain having made good use of the prevailing westerly winds and no other sail having been sighted until they approached the Scillies.

The lessons in mathematics and Latin had lasted a week and then been abandoned in favour of reading and story-telling, and the girls had amused themselves with drawings of Tobias Rush, whom they called 'The Crow'. For these, they used paper taken from the ship's log and supplied by the captain, and charcoal from the ship's cook. They had also learned how to tie a reef knot, a clove hitch and a running bowline, and Thomas had remarked proudly to Margaret that if the voyage had been any longer they would have taken over the navigation and steering.

Thomas and Margaret stood on the larboard side and watched the hazy coastline of England pass by. 'From half a mile out to sea, it looks peaceful enough,' remarked Thomas. 'Serene, even.'

'Would that it were. But since the latest news we have is more than six months old, who knows what we shall find?'

What they found as the ship made its way up Southampton Water early on a beautiful May morning was a bustling port with a dozen vessels anchored in the harbour, their cargoes of sugar, spices, livestock, timber and tools being loaded and unloaded in a chaotic muddle of noise, movement and smells. No visitor from a distant land would have guessed that England had been suffering from years of bloody civil war.

While they waited for their ship to manoeuvre its way to a berth, they watched screeching gulls swooping, grunting seamen lowering barrels and crates down from deck to quayside and illtempered carters cursing them for their carelessness. Their ponies stood quietly in their traces, depositing their dung where they stood and adding its stench to the rich mix of salt, fish and sweat.

Having made sure Margaret and the girls were safely ashore, Thomas supervised the offloading of their baggage, most of which had been crammed into the two chests which held the Gibbes's gold — a fortune in guineas, guilders and louis d'or. If the brutes had accumulated this much, how much more had Rush taken and what had he done with it? Thomas had known from keeping the ledgers that the estate was turning them all into Midases; what he had not known was how much gold the brutes had tucked away before he arrived. Not that it mattered; he had more than enough to do what he planned.

The chests were heaved off the ship by four struggling seamen and loaded on to one of the carriages waiting to take returning passengers home. Thomas agreed a steep fee with the coachman and the ladies were handed up to make themselves as comfortable as they could for the journey to Romsey. Before joining them, Thomas took a last look round the harbour. Among the piles of rope and mountains of barrels a small group of merchants stood waiting for their goods to be offloaded. An image of the group he had seen the day he left sprang immediately to his mind. He could not have known it then but now he was sure. Tobias Rush, black cloak around his shoulders and black hat pulled low over his face, had been one of them.

The road from Southampton to Romsey followed the river Test for most of its eight miles. While the girls, tired and cross from weeks of travelling, squabbled over the ropes they had been given by the captain for practising their knots, Margaret and Thomas watched the Hampshire countryside pass slowly by. The Test shone in the morning sun, the fields were shades of green and yellow and the oaks were in full leaf. 'There's nothing quite like it, is there?' mused Thomas. 'I missed the seasons, even the frost and the snow. One can have too much sunshine.'

'We'll see if you're still saying that in November, Thomas,' replied Margaret, knowing how much her brother hated the cold. 'I assume we're going to the bookshop?'

'Where else would we be going?'

'The shop is boarded up and it will be dark and dirty. We could spend the night in the Romsey Arms.'

'Nonsense. We'll soon put it in order and the girls would much rather stay there, wouldn't you, girls?'

'No,' replied Polly, 'we would not.'

'Not if it's dark and dirty,' agreed Lucy. 'Why can't we stay at the inn?'

The reason, thought Thomas, is that in these two chests are tens of thousands of pounds' worth of gold which I intend to keep my eye on until I can deposit it in a safe place. 'Inns are no places for young ladies,' he said sternly.

'Really, Uncle Thomas,' exclaimed Polly, 'after four years without you, weeks cooped up like chickens on ships and the strain of looking after our mother, why do you imagine a night or two in an inn would inconvenience us?'

'Thank you, Polly,' replied Margaret tartly, 'we will do as Uncle Thomas wishes.'

When the carriage reached Romsey, it turned left off the Southampton road into the street known as the Hundred, then right into Love Lane. It passed the baker's shop where Thomas often stopped on his way back from the Romsey Arms to savour the aroma of new-baked bread and drew up outside the bookshop. The town seemed quiet and Love Lane was deserted. As Margaret had told him, the shop was boarded up, with stout planks nailed across the door and windows. Thomas jumped down and stood outside his shop. He wanted to see his books, feel their weight in his hands and inhale their leathery smells. Planks or no planks, they would find a way in.

With the help of the coachman, they managed to drag the chests off the carriage. Thomas promised him another guinea and sent him off to find four strong men to lever the planks off the door, force open the lock and carry the chests inside. He had not suffered, starved and killed, only to have the gold stolen from under his nose in Love Lane. He and Lucy sat on one chest, Margaret and Polly on the other.

The coachman was back within half an hour with four drinkers from the Romsey Arms, happy to earn a shilling each for a few minutes' work. One of them, who carried an iron crowbar, looked familiar. When he saw Thomas he stopped and stared. 'God's wounds, Master 'ill,' he exclaimed, 'is that you? We all thought you was long gone.'

Thomas could not remember the man's name. 'It certainly is, my friend, alive and, I'm glad to say, home again. Now would you and your friends oblige us by opening up my shop and helping us get our baggage inside? I fear the chests are a trifle heavy.'

'Certainly we will, sir,' replied the man, 'and it's good to see you again.' He tipped his hat to Margaret. 'And you, of course, madam.'

It did not take long for the planks to come off and the door was barely open before Thomas was inside. He stood and stared. The dirt and dust he barely noticed — they were to be expected. What he had not expected were empty shelves. There was not a single book in the place. Not one. He shook his head in disbelief. Rush's final act of revenge had been to steal his books. Not that he would have expected Thomas ever to know it; he must have planned to show the empty shop to Margaret.

There was no point in staring at bare shelves. Thomas asked the men to drag the chests inside and then remove the boards from all the windows. When they had done so, he handed over four shillings and they returned happily to the Romsey Arms. Thomas and Margaret dragged the chests through the shop to the stairs which led up to their bedrooms. They opened the chests to take out the few clothes they had crammed in with the gold, then Thomas pulled back the first three steps to reveal the place where the girls had once hidden from a pair of looting soldiers of Parliament, and they pushed the chests inside. The gold would be as safe there as anywhere.

The kitchen was intact and their beds were still in the

bedrooms. There were even blankets and pillows. But the light now shining through the windows revealed a layer of dust on every surface and the house smelled damp. 'Are we really going to stay here, Uncle Thomas?' asked Lucy.

'Of course we are,' he replied. 'We'll soon have the house cleaned up. We'll light the fire in the kitchen, sweep the floors and shake out the bedding. Then you and your mother will go and buy our dinner while I guard the house and fix a bar on the door. I'll use timbers from the windows.' Catching his tone, the girls did not try arguing. Their uncle was just as stubborn now as he had been four years earlier.

After several hours of sweeping and scrubbing Margaret took the girls to the market, while Thomas found suitable timbers and fashioned an adequate bar across the door. They returned with bread, cheese, onions, a chicken and a copy of *Mercurius Politicus*, a new weekly government newsbook. Thomas sat down at his old table to read it.

Among a number of articles extolling the virtues of the 'Lord Protector' was one calling, in the name of true godliness, for a law against Ranters. The Ranters Thomas had seen were a harmless lot, if alarmingly eager to dance about naked, and he could think of a good many other people he would rather have a law against, including intolerant politicians and religious fanatics. In fact a law like the Barbados 'turkey and shoat' law which had prohibited the use of the words 'Cavalier' and 'Roundhead', but prohibiting instead the use of the words 'Puritan' and 'Catholic', might be a good idea. Perhaps he would suggest it.

There was also an article on the cowardice of Charles Stuart, presently skulking in France with his mother, Henrietta Maria. Thomas remembered 'The Generalissima' well — a formidable lady, fond of spaniels and dwarves and devoted to her late husband. And an article on the back page of the newsbook contemplated the threat of war with the Dutch, following the recent ordinance which banned foreign vessels from transporting goods from European ports to England. Thomas smiled when he read it and could not help thinking of Adam and Charles, who had joined with the other planters in ignoring all attempted restrictions to their trade and happily sold their sugar to the Dutch merchants who had helped them with finance and advice. It was another foolish law, unenforceable and short-sighted. Perhaps there should also be a law against using the words 'restriction' and 'navigation'.

Much as he would have liked to walk down to the Romsey Arms, Thomas dared not leave the girls and the gold unattended, so after they had eaten, his first evening on English soil for more than four years was spent quietly at home.

Before they went to their old beds, Margaret asked, 'Are you still set on the idea, Thomas?'

'I am,' he replied, 'and I shall go to Winchester tomorrow morning.'

The coach which carried Thomas, two armed guards and his two heavy chests to Winchester the next morning had been arranged by Margaret, who had found the coach and the guards at the Romsey Arms. They made good time to Winchester and Thomas was in the house of Jacob Rose, goldsmith, before noon.

It took Mr Rose three hours to count the coins and a little longer for them to agree values for the guilders and louis d'or. When they had done so, Thomas deposited with Mr Rose all the coins he had brought — one small bag of coins he had left under the stairs — and a letter of instruction, in exchange for a promissory note and a statement of the interest he would receive on his deposit. While the coachman and the guards refreshed themselves, Thomas went next to the office of Henry Cole, lawyer, where he handed over another letter of instruction, showed Mr Cole Lord Willoughby's letter confirming the death of Tobias Rush and made a payment in advance against Mr Cole's fee. His final visit was to a draper's shop near the cathedral, where he ordered twenty yards of silk to be delivered to Romsey. His business completed, he collected the coachman and guards and was back in Romsey before dark. 'It's done,' he told Margaret. 'Tomorrow we will make our inspection.'

The four of them left the house soon after dawn the next morning and walked together down Love Lane, through the square and past the old abbey. At the edge of the town, they stopped outside a grand house, set apart and surrounded on three sides by its own land. It was three storeys high, built of red brick, with a red-tiled roof, tall chimneys and large latticed windows. The oak door, too, was large and looked strong enough to with-stand any amount of battering. If he had not known better, Thomas would have guessed the house to belong to a successful wool merchant.

'There are fifteen rooms,' Margaret told him, 'all well proportioned. There are stables and a well at the back.'

'It looks perfect,' said Thomas, smiling. 'Quite large enough and plenty of land upon which to build. I can see why Rush bought it. It would have been a wise investment if he had lived to enjoy it.'

'Thank God he didn't. The world does not need monsters like Tobias Rush.'

'Indeed not. But let us hope that in death his money serves a useful purpose.'

'We're not going to live here, are we?' asked Lucy.

Thomas laughed and put his arm around her shoulders. 'No, my dear, we are not going to live here but we are going to buy it. Your mother and I have plans for it.'

They walked around the house, peering into the windows and trying the doors. All were locked. An internal inspection would have to wait until Mr Cole had done his work. They were about to leave when a troop of soldiers appeared from the direction of the town and marched up to the house. Polly and Lucy immediately hid behind Thomas and Margaret, who stood to face them. The captain and his six men wore the red coats of Parliamentary infantrymen, their twelve 'apostles' containing powder and ball in loops on their bandoliers, iron helmets and tall leather boots. They carried muskets and swords. Even to Thomas's untutored eye they looked better equipped and more disciplined than the men whom Rush had sent to arrest him on that cold March morning.

'We are looking for Tobias Rush,' announced the captain.

Thomas grinned. 'I fear you will not find him here, captain,' he replied.

'Is that so? And where might we find him?'

'Tobias Rush is dead and was buried on the island of Barbados. I have a letter from the governor, Lord Willoughby, to prove it.'

'And who are you, sir?'

'My name is Thomas Hill. I own a bookshop in Love Lane. My family and I have a mind to buy this house and we're inspecting it.'

The captain looked suspicious. 'Were you now? Or were you planning to break in and steal what's inside?'

'Certainly not, captain. As I have told you, Rush is dead. The house will be sold and we intend to buy it.'

The captain turned to his troop and spoke quietly to them. Thomas could not hear what was being said but he did see the glances in his direction. God in heaven, not again. If these men had orders to find Rush, they would not want to return with only the word of a stranger that he was dead. It would be more sensible for them to escort Thomas to whomever had sent them and let him tell the story himself. Even with the letter he would have to do more explaining than he would like – he had, after all, helped defend Barbados against Ayscue's Parliamentary fleet. He put his arm around Margaret and braced himself.

The captain turned back to face him. 'Master Hill, we have decided to believe you. We did not like Tobias Rush and we are not unhappy to hear that he is dead. However, if he should come to life again you will have some awkward questions to answer. In that case, you may expect a visit from us at your shop in Love Lane.'

Thomas let out a quiet sigh of relief. Rush had returned from the dead once. He would not be doing so again. 'That is understood, captain. And if you do see Tobias Rush, be sure that you will be looking at a ghost.' The captain did not reply but gave his soldiers the order to turn and off they marched.

'I did not enjoy that,' said Margaret. 'I did not think they would believe you.'

'Nor did I. Another spell in Winchester gaol looked horribly likely. Still, the war's over and a man's word may be worth something again. Let's hope so.'

*

The next six months were spent in trips to Winchester to visit Mr Rose and Mr Cole, meetings with the mayor and aldermen of Romsey, and weekly conferences with builders, carpenters and stonemasons. Thomas watched impatiently as the work progressed, until, at last, just before Christmas Day, it was finished. The house that had once belonged to Tobias Rush had been transformed and a new house, perfect for a well-to-do family of four, had been built in its grounds.

On the first day of January 1653, Thomas Hill, accompanied by his sister and nieces, all three dressed in new bonnets and new gowns made from the silk he had bought in Winchester, attended the official opening. The mayor spoke warmly of the man who had conceived the idea, paid for the work and endowed the establishment with a capital sum sufficient for its needs for many years to come. Then he announced that the new Romsey School was now open. It would start with eight pupils, all of whom had lost their fathers during the war, including Polly and Lucy Taylor. Until a schoolteacher was appointed the children would be taught mathematics, Latin and English by the benefactor himself.

After the ceremony the party repaired to the Romsey Arms. He had survived, he had prospered and he had made good use of the Gibbes's gold. The celebrations were long and merry and when eventually they were over, he set off unsteadily up Love Lane. Only when he reached the baker's shop did he remember that he no longer lived above the old bookshop. With an embarrassed grin, he retraced his steps down the lane, past the inn and the abbey, to his new house beside Romsey School.

AUTHOR'S NOTE

For an island of only 166 square miles and a population, white and black, of fewer than forty thousand, Barbados played an important role in the English Civil Wars, especially after the execution of Charles I. This was all the more extraordinary for the fact that the brothers John and Henry Powell, the first planter colonists, had only arrived there in 1627. When the Royalist and Parliamentarian forces met at Edgehill, the Barbados planter community was no more than fifteen years old.

Thomas's experience was not uncommon because the success of the sugar industry had one terrible drawback – its insatiable demand for cheap labour. This demand was met not only by slaves from Africa and South America but also by prisoners, convicts and Royalist supporters, who found themselves 'Barbadosed'. Some were well treated; many, like Thomas, were brutally exploited and abused. Very few returned home.

Among the events in *The King's Exile* which really did take place were Humphrey Walrond's coup to gain the governorship, the appointment of Lord Willoughby to replace him, the false intelligence carried by the Dutch ship, the blockade by Sir George Ayscue's fleet, the arrival of the fleet from Virginia, the battle on the ridge above Oistins that was 'rained off', the signing of the Charter of Barbados and its subsequent ratification in 'Ye Mermaid Inn'.

Having been negotiated by Sir George Ayscue on behalf of the English Parliament, the terms of the charter had the unforeseen result of giving the island, after the restoration of the monarchy, more independence than it would otherwise have enjoyed.

Sharp-eyed readers will have noticed that, for the sake of the story, I have delayed the arrival of Lord Willoughby in Barbados by about twelve months.

ACKNOWLEDGEMENTS

As always, my thanks to my long-suffering wife Susan for her moral and practical support and to my daughter Laura, son Tom and brother Michael for their encouragement and suggestions.

Emma Buckley, my editor at Transworld, has nursed me through two Thomas Hill books with skill and patience. It is a delight to work with her and her colleagues and I thank them. Without them, *The King's Exile* would have been a much poorer thing.

SELECT BIBLIOGRAPHY

Hilary Beckles, *A History of Barbados*, Cambridge University Press, 1990

Michael Braddick, *God's Fury, England's Fire*, Penguin Books, 2008

Charles Carlton, *Charles I – The Personal Monarch*, Routledge, 1983

Richard S. Dunn, *Sugar and Slaves*, University of North Carolina Press, 1972

Antonia Fraser, *Cromwell, Our Chief of Men*, Weidenfeld & Nicolson, 1973

Cynthia Herrup, *The Common Peace*, Cambridge University Press, 1987

Don Jordan and Michael Walsh, *White Cargo*, Mainstream Publishing, 2007

Richard Ligon, *A True amd Exact History of the Island of Barbadoes*, 1657

Matthew Parker, *The Sugar Barons*, Windmill Books, 2012

Carla Gardina Pestana, *The English Atlantic in the Age of Revolution*, Harvard University Press, 2004
Diane Purkiss, *The English Civil War*, Harper Perennial, 2006
Ivan Roots, *The Great Rebellion 1642– 1660*, B. T. Batsford, 1966
Ronald Tree, *A History of Barbados*, Granada Publishing, 1972

After reading Law at Cambridge University, **Andrew Swanston** held various positions in the book trade, including being a director of Waterstone & Co. and chairman of Methven's PLC, before turning to full-time writing. Inspired by a lifelong interest in seventeenth-century history, his Thomas Hill novels are set during the English Civil War and the early period of the Restoration. He lives with his wife in Surrey.